18.04

P9-CLR-954

RAPTURE

RAPTURE

John Shirley

TOR®

A Tom Doherty Associates Book
New York

Newmarket Public Library

This is a work of fiction. All of the characters, organizations, and events portrayed in this novel are either products of the author's imagination or are used fictitiously.

BIOSHOCK: RAPTURE

Copyright © 2011 by Take-Two Interactive Software, Inc.

BioShock and the BioShock logo are trademarks of
Take-Two Interactive Software, Inc.

All rights reserved.

JAN 3 1 2012

A Tor Book
Published by Tom Doherty Associates, LLC
175 Fifth Avenue
New York, NY 10010

www.tor-forge.com

Tor® is a registered trademark of Tom Doherty Associates, LLC.

ISBN 978-0-7653-2484-9 (hardcover)
ISBN 978-0-7653-2485-6 (trade paperback)

First Edition: July 2011

Printed in the United States of America

0 9 8 7 6 5 4 3 2 1

Dedicated to the fans of *BioShock* and *BioShock 2*

ACKNOWLEDGMENTS

Thanks to Eric Raab and Paula Guran.

Special thanks to Dustin Bond for additional game research.

Special thanks to everyone who put up with my bitching.

I am Andrew Ryan and I'm here to ask you a question: Is a man not entitled to the sweat of his own brow? No, says the man in Washington. It belongs to the poor. No, says the man in the Vatican. It belongs to God. No, says the man in Moscow. It belongs to everyone. I rejected those answers. Instead, I chose something different. I chose the impossible. I chose . . . Rapture. A city where the artist would not fear the censor. Where the scientist would not be bound by Petty morality. Where the great would not be constrained by the small. And with the sweat of your brow, Rapture can become your city as well.

—Andrew Ryan in **BioShock**

Imagine if you could be smarter, stronger, healthier. What if you could even have amazing powers, light fires with your mind? That's what plasmids do for a man.

—The man who calls himself Atlas in **BioShock**

PROLOGUE

Sullivan, chief of security, found the Great Man standing in front of the enormous window in his corporate office. The boss was silhouetted against city lights. The only other illumination was from a green-shaded lamp on the big glass-topped desk across the room, so that the Great Man was mostly in shadow, hands in the pockets of his crisply tailored suit jacket as he gazed broodingly out at the skyline.

It was eight o'clock, and Chief Sullivan, a tired middle-aged man in a rain-dampened suit, badly wanted to go home, kick off his shoes, and listen to the fight on the radio. But the Great Man often worked late, and he'd been waiting for these two reports. One report, in particular, Sullivan wanted to have done with—the one from Japan. It was a report that made him want a stiff drink, and fast. But he knew the Great Man wouldn't offer him one.

"The Great Man" was how Sullivan thought of his boss— one of the richest, most powerful men in the world. The term was both sarcastic and serious, and Sullivan kept it to himself—the Great Man was vain and quick to sense the slightest disrespect. Yet sometimes it seemed the tycoon was casting about for a friend he could take to heart. Sullivan was not that man. People rarely liked him much. Something about ex-cops.

"Well, Sullivan?" the Great Man asked, not turning from the window. "Do you have them?"

"I have them both, sir."

"Let's have the report on the strikes first, get it out of the way. The other one . . ." He shook his head. "That'll be like hiding from a hurricane in a cellar. We'll have to dig the cellar first, so to speak . . ."

Sullivan wondered what he meant by that cellar remark, but he let it go. "The strikes—they're still going on at the Kentucky mines and the Mississippi refinery."

The Great Man grimaced. His shoulders, angularly padded in the current style, slumped ever so slightly. "We've got to be tougher about this, Sullivan. For the country's good, as well as our own."

"Sir—I have sent in strikebreakers. I have sent Pinkerton men to get names on the strike leaders, see if we can . . . get something on them. But—these people are persistent. A hard-nosed bunch."

"Have you been out there in person? Did you *go* to Kentucky—or Mississippi, Chief? Hm? You need not await permission from me to take personal action—not on this! Unions . . . they had their own little army in Russia—they called them Workers Militias. Do you know who these strikers *are*? They are agents of the Reds, Sullivan! Soviet agents! And what is it they demand? Why, better wages and work conditions. What is that but Socialism? Leeches. I had no need of unions! I made my own way."

Sullivan knew that the Great Man had the benefit of luck—he'd struck oil, as a young man—but it was true he'd invested brilliantly.

"I'll . . . see to them myself, sir."

The Great Man reached out and touched the glass wall, remembering. "I came here from Russia as a boy—the Bolshies had just taken the place over . . . We barely got out alive. I won't see that sickness spread."

"No sir."

"And—the other report? It's true, isn't it?"

"Both cities are almost entirely destroyed. One bomb apiece."

The Great Man shook his head in wonder. "Just one bomb—for a whole city . . ."

Sullivan stepped closer, opened one of the envelopes, handed over the photographs. The Great Man held the glossy photographs to the window so he could make them out in the twinkling light of the skyline. They were fairly sharp black-and-white snaps of the devastation of Hiroshima, mostly seen from the air. The city lights were caught on their glossy surface, as if somehow the thrusting boldness of the New York skyline had itself destroyed Hiroshima.

"Our man in the State Department smuggled this out for us," Sullivan went on. "Some in the target cities were . . . atomized. Blown to bits. Hundreds of thousands dead or dying in Hiroshima and Nagasaki. A great many more dying from . . ." He read aloud from one of the reports he'd brought. "'Flash burns, radiation burns and trauma . . . It is expected that an equal amount will be dead of radiation sickness and possibly cancer in another twelve months or so.'"

"Cancer? Caused by this weapon?"

"Yes sir. It's not yet confirmed, but—based on past experiments . . . they say it's likely."

"I see. Are we indeed certain the Soviets are developing such weapons?"

"They're working on it."

The Great Man snorted ruefully. "Two gigantic empires, two great octopi struggling with one another—and equipped with monstrous weapons. Just one bomb to destroy an entire city! These bombs will only get bigger, and more powerful. What do you suppose will happen, in time, Sullivan?"

"Atomic war is what some are saying."

"I feel certain of it! They'll destroy us all! Still . . . there *is* another possibility. For some of us."

"Yes sir?"

"I despise what this civilization is becoming, Sullivan. First the Bolsheviks and then—Roosevelt. Truman, carrying on much of what Roosevelt began. Little men on the backs of great ones. It will only stop when real men stand up and say 'no more'!"

Sullivan nodded, shivering. At times the Great Man could convey the power of his inner conviction, almost like a lightning rod transmitting a mighty burst of electricity. There was an undeniable power around him . . .

After a moment the Great Man looked curiously at Sullivan, as if wondering how much he could be trusted. At last his employer said, "My mind is made up, Sullivan. I shall move ahead on a project I was toying with. It will no longer be a toy—it will be a glorious reality. It entails great risk—but it *must* be done. And you may as well know now: it will take, perhaps, *every penny I have* to make it happen . . ."

Sullivan blinked. Every penny? What extreme was his boss going to now?

The Great Man chuckled, evidently enjoying Sullivan's astonishment. "Oh yes! At first it was an experiment. Little more than a hypothesis—a game. I already have the drawings for a smaller version—but it could be bigger. Much bigger! It is the solution to a gigantic problem . . ."

"The union problem?" Sullivan asked, puzzled.

"No—well, *yes*, in the long run. Unions too! But I was thinking of a more pressing problem: the potential destruction of civilization! The problem, Sullivan, *is the inevitability of Atomic war.* That inevitability calls for a gigantic solution. I've sent out explorers—and I've picked the spot. But I wasn't sure I would ever give it the go-ahead. Not until today." He peered again at the photos of the devastation, turning them to catch the light better. "Not until this. We can escape, you and I—and certain others. We can escape from the mutual destruction of the mad little men who scuttle about the halls of government power. We are going to build a *new world* in the one place these madmen cannot touch . . ."

"Yes sir." Sullivan decided not to ask for an explanation. Better to just hope that whatever overblown scheme the Great Man was caught up in, he'd drop it, in the end, when he faced the full cost. "Anything more, sir? I mean—tonight? If I'm going to break up those strikes, I'd better leave early in the morning . . ."

"Yes, yes go and get some rest. But there'll be no rest for me tonight. I must plan . . ."

So saying, Andrew Ryan turned away from the window, crossed the room—and tossed the photos aside. The destruction of Hiroshima and Nagasaki skidded across the glass-topped desk.

~~~~~~~

Left alone in the shadowy office, Ryan slumped in the padded leather desk chair and reached for the telephone. It was time to call Simon Wales, give him the go-ahead for the next stage.

But his hand hovered over the phone—and then withdrew, trembling. He needed to calm himself before calling Wales. Something he'd said to Sullivan had sparked a painful, harshly vivid memory. *"I came here from Russia as a boy in 1918—the Bolshies had just taken the place over . . . We barely got out alive . . ."*

Andrew Ryan wasn't his name, not then. Since coming to the USA he'd Americanized his name. His real name was Andrei Rianofski . . .

~~~~~~~

Andrei and his father are standing at the windswept train station, shivering in the cold. It is early morning, and both of them are staring down the tracks. His father, heavily bearded, his lined face grim, is holding their single bag in his left hand. His large right hand is resting on young Andrei's shoulder.

The dawn sky, the colors of a deep bruise, is closed by clouds; the cutting wind is serrated by sleet. A few other travelers, huddled in long dark coats, stand in a group farther down the platform. They seem worried, though a woman with a round red face, her head in a fur wrap, is smiling, talking softly to cheer them up. Beside the door to the station, an old man in a tattered coat and fur hat tends a steaming samovar. Andrei wishes they could afford some of the old man's hot tea.

Andrei listens to the wind hiss along the concrete platform and wonders why his father stands so far from the others. But he guesses the reason. Some from their village, on the outskirts of Minsk, know that father was against the Communists, that he spoke up against the Reds. Now many who'd once been their friends were beginning to denounce all such "betrayers of the People's Revolution" . . .

His father had word from the priest the night before that the purge was to begin today. They were first in line when the station opened, Father and Andrei, purchasing a ticket to Constantinople. Father carries traveling papers, permissions to purchase Turkish rugs and other goods for import. The papers might be good enough to get them out of Russia . . .

Father fiddles with the money in his pocket he'd brought to bribe customs officials. They will probably need it all.

His father's breath steams in the air . . . the train steams as it approaches, a big dark shape hulking toward them through the grayness, a single lantern above the cowcatcher projecting a rain-scratched cone into the mist.

Andrei glances toward the other travelers—and sees

another man approaching. "Father," Andrei whispers, in Russian, turning to look at a tall lean man in a long green coat with red epaulets, a black hat, a rifle slung over his shoulder. "Is that man one of the Red Guard?"

"Andrei." His father grips his shoulder, brusquely turns him so that he looks away from the soldier. "Don't look at him."

"Pyotr? Pyotr Rianofski!"

They turn to see his father's cousin Dmetri standing with his arm around his wife, Vasilisa, a stocky, pale, blond woman in a yellow scarf, her nose red with the cold. She rubs wetness from her nose and looks at Andrei's father imploringly.

"Please, Pyotr," she whispers to Andrei's father. "We have no more money. If you pay the soldiers . . ."

Dmetri licks his lips. "They are looking for us, Pyotr. Because I spoke at the meeting yesterday. We have train tickets, but nothing more. Not a ruble left! Perhaps a bribe will make them let us go."

"Dmetri, Vasilisa—if I could help, I would. But we will need every kopek! I have to think of this boy. We have to pay our way to . . . our destination. A long journey."

The train chugs into the station, looming up rather suddenly, reeking of coal smoke, making Andrei jump a little as the engine furiously sprays steam.

"Please," Vasilisa says, wringing her hands. The militiaman is looking toward them . . . and another Red guardsman and then a third step onto the platform from the station door, all of them carrying rifles.

The train is grinding slowly past. It slows, but to Andrei it seems it will never completely stop. The militiaman is calling out to Cousin Dmetri, his voice a bark. "You! We wish to speak to you!" He takes his rifle off his shoulder.

"Dmetri," Father hisses. "Keep your peace—do not make a sound!"

The train is still shuddering as it finally stops, and Andrei feels his father's hand clamping the back of his neck—feels himself propelled up the metal stairs, onto the train. He almost falls on his face. His father clambers on after him.

They bang through a door into a smoky car, the windows greasy and steam-coated. They find a seat on the wooden benches, and, as father hands the scowling conductor their tickets, Andrei wipes the window enough to see Dmetri and Vasilisa talking to the militiamen. Vasilisa is weeping, waving her arms. Dmetri is standing stiffly, shaking his head, pushing his wife behind him.

The discussion goes on, as the armed men frown at the travel papers.

"Andrei," Father mutters. "Don't look . . ."

But Andrei cannot look away. The tall militiaman tucks Dmetri's papers away somewhere and then gestures with his rifle.

Dmetri shakes his head, waving his train tickets. The train shudders, a whistle blasts . . .

Vasilisa tries to pull him toward the train. The soldiers wave their guns. Andrei remembers Dmetri coming to the feast for his tenth birthday, smiling, bringing with him a wooden saber carved as a gift.

The train whistle screams. The guards shout. One of them jabs at Vasilisa with his rifle, knocking her to her knees. Dmetri's face goes white as he grabs at the rifle barrel—the man turns it toward him and fires.

The train lurches into motion—as Dmetri stumbles back. "Oh, Father!" Andrei cries out.

"Look away, boy!"

But Andrei can't look away. He sees Vasilisa flailing at the soldiers, weeping—and two more guns fire. She spins and goes down in a heap atop Dmetri. The two of them lie there, dying together on the platform, as the steam from the train cloaks them, and the past cloaks them too. The train, like time, moving away . . .

~~~~~~~

Andrew Ryan shook his head. "Workers Militia," he muttered bitterly now. "A revolution for the poor. To save us all . . . for a cold death on a train platform."

And that had been just the beginning. He'd seen far worse things traveling with his father.

Ryan shook his head and looked at the pictures of Hiroshima. Madness, but no worse than the devastation of Socialism.

His dream had always been to build something that would survive anything the little madmen could throw at him.

If only Father could be there to see it rise from the shadows, magnificent, unafraid, a fortress dedicated to freedom.

Rapture.

PART ONE

The First Age of Rapture

The parasite hates three things: free markets, free will, and free men.

—*Andrew Ryan*

1

Park Avenue, New York City
1946

Almost a year later . . .

Bill McDonagh was riding an elevator up to the top of the Andrew Ryan Arms—but he felt like he was sinking under the sea. He was toting a box of pipe fittings in one hand, tool kit in the other. He'd been sent so hastily by the maintenance manager he didn't even have the bloody name of his customer. But his mind was on earlier doings in another building, a small office building in lower Manhattan. He'd taken the morning off from his plumbing business to interview for an assistant engineer job. The pay would start low, but the job would take him in a more ambitious direction. They had looked at him with only the faintest interest when he'd walked into the Feeben, Leiber, and Quiffe Engineering Firm. The two interviewers were a couple of snotty wankers—one of them was Feeben Junior. They seemed bored by the time they called him in, and their faint flicker of interest evaporated completely when he started talking about his background. He had done his best to speak in American phraseology, to suppress his accent. But he knew it slipped out. They were looking for some snappy young chap out of New York University, not a cockney blighter who'd worked his way through the East London School of Engineering and Mechanical Vocation.

Bill heard them say it, through the door, after they'd dismissed him: "Another limey grease monkey . . ."

All right then. So he was a grease monkey. Just a mechanic

and, lately, a freelance plumbing contractor. *A dirty little job
screwin' pipes for the nobs.* Heading up to some rich bloke's
penthouse. There was no shame in it.

But there wasn't much money in it either, working on assignment for Chinowski's Maintenance. It'd be a long time
before he could save up enough to start a big contracting
outfit of his own. He had a couple of lads hired on, from time
to time, but not the big contracting and engineering company
he'd always envisioned. And Mary Louise had made it clear
as polished glass she was not really interested in marrying a
glorified plumber.

"I had enough of fellas that think they're the cat's meow
because they can fix the terlet," she said. A pretty girl from
the Bronx was Mary Louise Fensen and raring to go. But not
terribly bright, after all. Probably drive him barmy anyway.

The moment he'd got home the phone rang, Bud Chinowski, barking about getting his ass to an address in Manhattan, on Park Avenue. Their building maintenance was
AWOL—probably drunk somewhere—and the Bigshot at the
penthouse needed plumbers "fast as you can drag your lazy
ass over there. We've got three bathrooms to finish installing.
Get those witless wrench-jockeys of yours over there too."

He'd called Roy Phinn and Pablo Navarro to go on ahead
of him. Then he'd changed out of the ill-fitting suit, into the
gray, grease-stained coveralls. "Limey grease monkey . . ."
he'd murmured, buttoning up.

And here he was, wishing he'd taken time for a cigarette
before coming—he couldn't smoke in a posh flat like this without permission. He stepped glumly out of the elevator, into an
antechamber to the penthouse, his toolbox clanking at his side.
The little wood-paneled room was scarcely bigger than the
elevator. An artfully paneled mahogany door with a brass knob,
embossed with an eagle, was its only feature—besides a small

metal grid next to the door. He tried the knob. Locked. He shrugged, and knocked on the door. Waiting, he started to feel a little claustrophobic.

"'Ello?" he called. "Plumbin' contractor! From Chinowski's! 'Ello!" *Don't drop your Hs, you bastard,* he told himself. "*Hel*-lo!"

A crackling sound, and a low, forceful voice emanated from the grid. "That the other plumber, is it?"

"Uh . . ." He bent and spoke briskly into the grid. "It is, sir!"

"No need to shout into the intercom!"

The door clicked within itself—and to Bill's amazement it didn't swing inward but slid into the wall up to the knob. He saw there was a metal runner in the floor and, at the edge of the door, a band of steel. It was wood on the outside, steel inside. Like this man was worried someone might try to fire a bullet through it.

No one was visible on the other side of the open doorway. He saw another hallway, carpeted, with some rather fine old paintings, one of which might be by a Dutch master, if he remembered anything from his trips to the British Museum. A Tiffany lamp stood on an inlaid table, glowing like a gem.

This toff's got plenty of the ready, Bill thought.

He walked down the hall, into a large, plush sitting room: luxurious sofas, a big unlit fireplace, more choice paintings and fine lamps. A grand piano, its wood polished almost mirrorlike, stood in a corner. On an intricately carved table was an enormous display of fresh flowers in an antique Chinese jade vase. He'd never seen flowers like them before. And the decorations on the tables . . .

He was staring at a lamp that appeared to be a gold sculpture of a satyr chasing an underdressed young woman when a voice spoke sharply to his right. "The other two are already at work in the back . . . The main bathroom's through here." Bill turned and saw a gent in the archway to the next room already turning

away from him. The man wore a gray suit, his dark hair oiled
back. Must be the butler. Bill could hear the other two lads,
faintly, in the back of the place, arguing about fittings.

Bill went through the archway as the man in the suit answered a chiming gold and ivory telephone on a table in front
of a big window displaying the heroic spires of Manhattan.
Opposite the window was a mural, done in the sweeping
modern-industrial style, of burly men building a tower that rose
up out of the sea. Overseeing the workers in the mural was a
slim dark-haired man with blueprints in his hand.

Bill looked for the WC, saw a hallway with a gleaming
steel and white-tile bathroom at its end.

That's my destination, Bill thought bitterly. *The crapper. A
fine crapper it might be, one of three. My destiny is to keep their
WCs in working order.*

Then he caught himself. *No self-pity, now, Bill McDonagh.
Play the cards you're dealt, the way your Da taught you.*

Bill started toward the door to the bathroom hall, but his
attention was caught by the half-whispered urgency of the
man's voice as he growled at the telephone.

"Eisley, you will not make excuses! If you cannot deal with
these people I will find someone who has the courage! I'll find
someone brave enough to scare away this pack of hungry dogs!
They will not find my campfire undefended!"

The voice's stridency caught Bill's attention—but something
else about it stirred him too. He'd heard that distinctive voice
before. Maybe in a newsreel?

Bill paused at the door to the hall and had a quick look at the
man pressing the phone to his ear. It was the man in the mural—
the one holding the blueprint: a straight-backed man, maybe
early forties, medium height, two thin, crisply straight strokes
of mustache matched by the dark strokes of his eyebrows, a
prominent cleft chin. He even wore a suit nearly identical to
the one in the painting. And that strong, intense face—it was a

face Bill knew from the newspapers. He'd seen his name over the front door of this very edifice. It never occurred to him that Andrew Ryan might actually *live* here. The tycoon owned a significant chunk of America's coal, its second biggest railroad, and Ryan Oil. He'd always pictured a man like that whiling the days away playing golf on a country estate.

"Taxes are theft, Eisley! What? No, no need—I fired her. I've got a new secretary starting today—I'm elevating someone in reception. Elaine something. No, I don't want anyone from accounting, that's the whole problem, people like that are too interested in my money, they have no discretion! Sometimes I wonder if there's anyone I can trust. Well they'll get not a penny out of me more than absolutely necessary, and if you can't see to it I'll find a lawyer who can!"

Ryan slammed the phone down—and Bill hurried on to the bathroom.

Bill found the toilet in place but not quite hooked up: an ordinary Standard toilet, no gold seat on it. Looked like it needed proper pipe fittings, mostly. Seemed a waste of time to send three men out for this, but these posh types liked everything done yesterday.

He was aware, as he worked, that Ryan was pacing back and forth in the room outside the hall to the bathroom, occasionally muttering to himself.

Bill was kneeling to one side of the toilet, using a spanner to tighten a pipe joint, when he became aware of a looming presence. He looked up to see Andrew Ryan standing near him.

"Didn't intend to startle you." Ryan flashed his teeth in the barest smile and went on, "Just curious how you're getting along."

Bill was surprised at this familiarity from a man so above him—and by the change in tone. Ryan had been blaring angrily into the phone but minutes before. Now he seemed calm, his eyes glittering with curiosity.

"Getting on with it, sir. Soon have it done."

"Is that a brass fitting you're putting in there? I think the other two were using tin."

"Well, I'll be sure they didn't, sir," said Bill, beginning not to care what impression he made. "Don't want to be bailing out your loo once a fortnight. Tin's not reliable, like. If it's the price you're worried about, I'll pick up the cost of the brass, so not to worry, squire . . ."

"And why would you do that?"

"Well, Mr. Ryan, no man bails water out of privies built by Bill McDonagh."

Ryan looked at him with narrowed eyes, rubbing his chin. Bill shrugged and focused on the pipes, feeling strangely disconcerted. He could almost feel the heat from the intensity of Ryan's personality. He could smell his cologne, pricey and subtle.

"There you are," Bill said, tightening with the wrench one last time for good luck. "Right as the mail. These pipes, anyhow."

"Do you mean the job's done?"

"I'll see how the lads are getting on, but I'd guess it's very nearly done, sir."

He expected Ryan to wander back to his own work, but the tycoon remained, watching as Bill started the water flow, checked it for integrity, and cleaned up his tools and leftover materials. He took the receipt book from his pocket, scribbled out the cost. There'd been no time for an estimate, so he had a free hand. He wished he were the sort to pad the bill, since he gave a percentage to Chinowski and Ryan was rich, but he wasn't made that way.

"Really!" Ryan said, looking at the bill, eyebrows raised.

Bill just waited. Strange that Andrew Ryan—one of the richest, most powerful men in America—was personally in-

volved in dealing with a plumber, scrutinizing a minor bill. But
Ryan stood there, looking first at the bill, then at him.

"This is quite reasonable," Ryan said at last. "You might have
stretched your time, inflated the bill. People assume they can
take advantage of wealthy men."

Bill was mildly insulted. "I believe in being paid, sir, even
being paid well—but only for the work I do."

Again that flicker of a smile, there and gone. The keen,
searching gaze. "I can see I've struck a nerve," Ryan said, "because you're a man like me! A man of pride and capability who
knows who he is."

A long, appraising look. Then Ryan turned on his heel and
strode out.

Bill shrugged, gathered up the rest of his things, and returned to the mural room, expecting to see some Ryan under-
ling awaiting him with a check. But it was Ryan, holding the
check out to him.

"Thank you, sir." Bill took it, tucked it into a pocket, nodded to the man—was he mad, staring at him like that?—and
started hastily for the front door.

He'd just gotten to the sitting room when Ryan called to
him from the archway. "Mind if I ask you a question?"

Bill paused. Hoping it didn't turn out that Andrew Ryan
was a poof. He'd had enough of upper-class poofs trying to
pick him up.

"Where do you think a man's rights should end?" Ryan asked.

"His *rights,* sir?" A philosophical question asked of a plumbing contractor? The old toff really was mad. McDonagh hu-
mored him. "Rights are rights. That's like asking which fingers
a man should do without. I need all ten, me."

"I like that. Now—just suppose you lose one or two fingers?
What would you do? You'd think yourself unable to work, and
you'd have a right to a handout, as it were, eh?"

Bill hefted the toolbox as he considered. "No. I'd find something to do, with eight fingers. Or four. Make my own way. I'd like to be able to use my talents more—that's right enough. But I don't take handouts."

"And what talents are those? Not that I discount a gift for plumbing. But—is that what you mean?"

"No sir. Not as such. I'm by way of being an engineer. In a simple way, mind. Could be I'll start me own . . . my own . . . building operation. Not so young anymore, but still—I see things in my mind I'd like to build . . ." He broke off, embarrassed at being so personal with this man. But there was something about Ryan that made you want to open up and talk.

"You're British. Not one of the . . . the gentry types, certainly."

"Right as rain, sir." Bill wondered if he'd get the brush-off now. There was a touch of defensiveness when he added, "Grew up 'round Cheapside, like."

Ryan chuckled dryly. "You're touchy about your origins. I know the feeling. I too am an immigrant. I was very young when I came here from Russia. I have learned to control my speech—reinvented myself. A man must make of his life a ladder that he never ceases to climb—if you're not rising, you are slipping down the rungs, my friend.

"But by ascending," Ryan went on, shoving his hands in his jacket pockets and taking a pensive turn about the room, "one makes one's own class, do you see? Eh? One classes oneself!"

Bill had been about to make his excuses and walk out—but that stopped him. Ryan had articulated something he fiercely believed.

"Couldn't agree more, sir!" Bill blurted. "That's why I've come to the USA. Anyone can rise up, here. Right to the top!"

Ryan grunted skeptically. "Yes, and no. There are some who don't have the stuff. But it's not the 'class' or race or creed that they were born into that decides it. It's something inside a man. And that's something you have. You're a true mugwump, a real individual. We'll talk again, you and I . . ."

Bill nodded good-bye, not believing for a second that they'd speak again. He figured a rich bloke took it into his mind to have a natter with "the little people," patronizing a chap to prove to themselves how fair and kindly they could be.

He headed to check on Pablo and Roy before he made his way to the lobby and went about his business. This had been an interesting encounter—it'd be a story to tell in the pub, though no one would likely believe him. *Andrew Ryan? Who else did you hobnob with—Howard Hughes? Yer ol' pal William Randolph Hearst?*

~~~~~~

Bill McDonagh's head was only moderately sore the next morning, and he answered his flat's clangorous telephone readily enough, hoping for work. A good sweat always cleared his head.

"This Bill McDonagh?" said a gruff, unfamiliar voice.

"Right enough."

"My name's Sullivan. Head of Security for Andrew Ryan."

"Security? What's 'e say I've done, then? Look here, mate, I'm no crook—"

"No no, it's nothing like that—he just set me to find you. Chinowski didn't want to give up the number. Claimed he lost it. Tried taking the job himself. I had to get it from our friends at the phone company."

"*What* job?"

"Why, if you want it, Andrew Ryan's offering you a job as his new building engineer . . . Starting immediately."

2

Sullivan sometimes wished he were back working the Meat-
ball Beat in Little Italy. Ryan paid him well, sure, but having
to dodge G-men on the docks was not his idea of a good time.

It was a bracing, misty evening, supposed to be spring but
didn't feel much like it. The waves were choppy and the gulls
were huddled on the pylons with their beaks under their wings,
their feathers ruffled in the cold northeast wind. Three hulking
great ships were tied up at the beat-up old dock, all freighters.
This was not one of the fashionable wharfs, with passenger
liners and pretty girls waving hankies. Just a couple of red-
faced, sour-looking salts in pea jackets tramping by, trailing
cigarette smoke, boots crunching on old gull droppings.

Sullivan walked up to the gangplank of the *Olympian*, the
largest of the three ships in the fleet Ryan had bought for his
secretive North Atlantic project. He waved at the armed
guard, Pinelli, huddled into a big coat on the top deck. Pinelli
glanced down at him and nodded.

Ruben Greavy, head engineer for the Wales brothers, was
waiting on the lower deck at the top of the gangplank. Greavy
was a fussy, pinch-mouthed, bespectacled little man in a
rather showy cream-colored overcoat.

Sullivan hesitated, glancing back down the dock—just
making out the dark figure of the man who'd been following
him. The guy in the slouch hat and trench coat was about

seventy yards down the wharf, pretending to be interested in the ships creaking at their moorings. Sullivan had hoped he'd dodged the son of a bitch earlier, but there he was, lighting a pipe for a bit of realistic spycraft.

The pipe smoker had been tailing Sullivan since he'd gotten a cab at Grand Central and maybe before. There wasn't much the guy could learn following him here. The ship was already loaded. The feds would never get an inspection warrant before it sailed at midnight. And what would they make of the prefabricated metal parts, giant pipes, and enormous pressure-resistant sheets of transparent synthetics? It was all stuff you could legitimately call "export goods." Only it wasn't being exported across the ocean. It was being "exported" to the bottom of the ocean.

Sullivan shook his head, thinking about the whole North Atlantic project. It was a crazy idea—but when Ryan put his mind into something, it got done. And Sullivan owed the Great Man a lot. Almost ruined him, getting kicked out of the NYPD. Shouldn't have refused to grease those palms. They'd set him up to look like a crook, fired him, and taken away his pension. Left him with almost nothing.

Sullivan took to gambling—and then his wife ran off with the last of his dough. He'd been thinking about eating a bullet when he crossed paths with the Great Man, two years earlier . . .

Sullivan reached into his coat pocket for the flask—then remembered it was empty. Maybe he could get a drink from Greavy.

Sullivan waved at Greavy and climbed the gangplank. They shook hands. Greavy's grip was soft, fingers puny in Sullivan's big grasp.

"Sullivan."

"Professor."

"How many times . . . I'm not a professor, I have a doctor-
ate in . . . never mind. You know someone's shadowing you on
the dock back there?"

"Different gumshoe this time. Probably FBI or IRS." He
turned his collar up. "Kind of chilly out here."

"Come along, then, we'll have a drink."

Sullivan nodded resignedly. He knew what Greavy's idea of
a drink was. Watered brandy. Sullivan needed a double Scotch.
His father had sworn by Irish whiskey, but Sullivan was a
Scotch man. *Sure, the black betrayal of yer heritage, it is,* his
pa would say. A steady liquid diet of Irish whiskey had killed
the old rascal at fifty.

Greavy led him along a companionway to his cabin, which
was not much warmer. Most of the little oval room that wasn't
the narrow bed was taken up by a table covered with overlap-
ping blueprints, sketches, graphs, intricate designs. The Wales
brothers' design sometimes looked like Manhattan mated
with London—but with the power of a cathedral. The designs
were overly fancy for Sullivan's taste. Maybe he'd get to like it
once it was done. If it ever was . . .

Greavy took a bottle from under his pillow and poured
them two slugs in glasses, and Sullivan eased the stuff down.

"We need to be ready for any kind of raid," Greavy said,
distractedly looking past Sullivan at the blueprints, his mind
already back in the world of the Wales's design—and, very
nearly, Ryan's new world.

Sullivan shrugged. "With any luck he'll get the place finished before they can screw with us. The foundation's already
laid. Power's flowing, right? Most of the stuff's in place on the
support ships. Just a few more shipments."

Greavy snorted, surprising Sullivan by pouring himself a
second drink—and irritating Sullivan by not offering him one.
"You have no idea of the work. *The risk.* It's enormous. It's the

very soul of innovation. And I need more men! We're already behind schedule . . ."

"You'll get some more. Ryan's hired another man to supervise the—'foundational work' he calls it. Man named McDonagh. He's going to put him on the North Atlantic project once he proves he really can be trusted."

"McDonagh. Never heard of him—don't tell me, he's not another apple picked from an orange tree?"

"A what?"

"You know Ryan, he has his own notions of picking men. Sometimes they're remarkable, and well, sometimes they're—strange." He cleared his throat.

Sullivan scowled. "Like me?"

"No, no, no . . ."

Meaning yes, yes, yes. But it was true: Ryan had a way of recruiting black sheep, people who showed great potential but needed that extra chance. They all had a spirit of independence, were disillusioned with the status quo—and sometimes willing to skirt the law.

"The problem," Sullivan said, "is that the government thinks Ryan is hiding something because he's trying to keep people from finding out where these shipments are going and what they're for . . . and he *is* hiding something. But not what they think."

Greavy went to the blueprints, shuffling through them with one hand, his eyes gleaming behind his thick spectacles. "The strategic value of such a construction is significant, in a world where we're likely to go toe-to-toe with the Soviets—and Mr. Ryan doesn't want any outsiders going down there to report on what he's building. He wants to run things his way, 'specially once it's set up. Without interference. That's the whole point! Or to be more accurate—he wants to set it up to run *itself*. To let the laissez-faire principle free. He figures if governments know about it, they'll infiltrate. And then there's the union types, Communist organizers . . . suppose *they* were to worm their way in? The best way to keep people like that out is to keep it completely secret from them. Another thing—Ryan doesn't want any outsiders to know about some of the new technology . . . You'd be amazed at what he's got—new inventions he could patent and make a fortune on, but he's holding it back . . . for this project."

"Where's he getting all these new inventions?"

"Oh, he's been recruiting people for years. Who do you think designed those new dynamos of his?"

"Well, it's his call," Sullivan said, looking wistfully into his empty glass. Weak brandy or not, a drink was a drink. "You've been working for him twice as long as I have. He don't tell me much."

"He likes information to be compartmentalized on this project. Keeps a secret better."

Sullivan crossed to the porthole and peered out. Saw his shadow, out there, still clamping that pipe in his mouth. But now the G-man was pacing by the *Olympian*, looking the freighter up and down. "Son of a bitch's still out there. Doesn't seem empowered to do anything but ogle the ship."

"I've got to meet the Wales brothers. You know what they're like. Artists. All too aware of their own genius . . ." He frowned at the blueprints. Sullivan could see he was jealous of the Waleses. Greavy sniffed. "If there's nothing else—I'd better get on with it. Unless there's something else besides this new man that Ryan's taken on?"

"Who? Oh, McDonagh? No, I'm here to confirm the time you ship out. Ryan wanted me to come down personally. He's beginning to think they might be listening in on the telephones somehow. I'm thinking if you can leave earlier than midnight, it'd be better."

"As soon as the captain's back. I expect him within the hour."

"Leave soon as you can. Maybe they'll get a warrant after all. I don't think they'd find anything illegal. But if Ryan wants to keep them from knowing what he's up to, the less they see, the better."

"Very well. But who could imagine what he's up to? Jules Verne? Certainly not these drones at the IRS. But Sullivan, I assure you—Ryan is correct: if they knew what he really has in mind, they'd be quite worried. Particularly considering how little help he gave the Allies in the war."

"He took no sides at all. He didn't care for Hitler or the Japs neither."

"Still—he showed no special loyalty to the United States. And who can blame him? Look at the wreckage the ant society made of Europe—for the second time in the century. And the horror of Hiroshima and Nagasaki . . . I can't wait to leave all that behind . . ." Greavy escorted Sullivan toward the door. "Ryan has every intention of creating something that will grow—and grow! First across the seabed, and then, in time, above the surface of the sea—when they've done such damage to themselves, these so-called nations of the earth, that they can no longer pose a threat. Until then, he is right to mistrust them. Because he is creating something that will *compete* with them. A whole new society. Indeed, in time a whole new world! One which will utterly replace the vile, squirming anthill humanity has become . . ."

New York City
1946

"Merton? Get outta my bar."

Merton was gaping at Frank Gorland from behind the beer-stained desk of The Clanger's smoky little office. Harv Merton was a man with a large round head and thick lips, a skinny body, and a brown turtleneck sweater. Hell, he *looked* like a damn turtle—but a turtle in a bowler hat. "Whatta hell ya mean, *your* bar?" he asked, tamping a cigarette out in a butt-filled ashtray.

"I'm the owner, ain't I? As of tonight anyhow."

"Whatta hell ya mean you're the *owner*, Gorland?"

The man who called himself Frank Gorland smiled without humor and leaned against the frame of the closed door. "You know any expressions besides *whatta hell*? You're about to sign this bar over to me, is whatta hell." Gorland ran a hand over his bald head. Prickly, needed to shave it. He took the papers from his coat, all legal down to the last period, and dropped them on Merton's desk. "That look familiar? You signed it."

Merton stared at the papers, eyes widening. "That was you? Hudson Loans? Nobody told me that was—"

"A loan is a loan. What I seem to recall is, you were drunk when you signed it. Needed some money to pay off your gambling vig. A big fucking vig it was too, Merton!"

"You were there that night? I don't remember—"

"You remember getting *the money,* don't you?"

"It—it don't count if I was drunk!"

"Merton, if there was no business done drunk in this town, half its business wouldn't get done."

"I think you put something in my drink, that's what I think; the next day I felt—"

"Stop whining; you cashed the check, didn't you? You got the loan, couldn't pay the interest, time's up—now this place is mine! It's all there in black and white! This dump was your collateral!"

"Look, Mr. Gorland . . ." Merton licked his thick lips. "Don't think I disrespect you. I know you've hustled—uh, worked your way to a good thing, this end of town. But you can't just take a man's *bidness* . . ."

"No? My attorneys can. They'll come after you hammer and tongs, pal." He grinned. "Hammer, Tongs, and Klein, attorneys at law!"

Merton seemed to shrivel in his seat. "Okay, okay, whatta ya want from me?"

"Not what I want—what I'm *taking*. I told you, I want the bar. I own a bookkeeping operation. I own a drugstore. But—I don't have a bar! And I like The Clanger. Lots of dirt on the fights, what with the boxin' setup and all. Might be useful . . . Now you call that fat-ass bartender of yours in here, tell him he's gotta new boss . . ."

~~~~~~~

Gorland. Barris. Wiston. Moskowitz. Wang. Just some of the names he'd had the last few years. His own name, quite another Frank, seemed like it belonged to somebody else.

Keep 'em guessing, that was his way.

The Clanger wasn't just a cash cow—it was the place for Frank Gorland to hear the right conversations. It was just a short walk from the docks—but it was not just a nautical bar. There was a big boxing bell on the wall behind the bar; when they tapped a new keg, the bell was loudly clanged and the beer lovers came running, sometimes from down the street. Best German-style brew in New York City. The walls of the dusty, cavelike bar were decorated with worn-out boxing gloves, frayed ropes from rings, black-and-white photos of old-time boxers going back to John L. Sullivan. He had a bartender, an old Irish lush named Mulrooney, working down at the other end. But Gorland liked to work the bar so he could hear the talk. Good for his bookmaking action, and you never know how it might fit the next grift. *When you serve a beer— cock an ear.*

The talk at the crowded bar tonight was full of how Joe Louis, the Brown Bomber, back from the war with a pocketful of nothing and a big tax debt, was going to defend his

world heavyweight title against Billy Conn. And how the re-
tired Jack Johnson, first Negro to win the heavyweight champ
title, had died two days before in a car accident. None of
which was what Gorland needed to know. But there were a
couple of guys here who'd have the skinny on the up-and-
comer Neil Steele versus the fading boxing-circuit bum
Charlie Wriggles.

Gorland had heard a rumor that Steele might be throwing
the fight, and he had a theory about how that information
might pay off—way past the usual payoff. Only, Gorland
needed more assurance that Steele was taking the fall . . .

Gorland hated bartending because it was actual physical
work. A great grifter should never have to do real work. But
he wiped down the bar, made small talk; he served a beer,
and cocked an ear.

The jukebox was finishing a rollicking Duke Ellington
number, and in the brief interval before it switched over to
an Ernie "Bubbles" Whitman big-band cut, Gorland zeroed in
on the conversation of the two wise guys in the white ties and
pinstripes whispering over their Sambocas. He wiped at an
imaginary spill on the bar, edging closer. "But can we count
on Steele?" said the one some called Twitchy. He twitched
his pencil-thin mustache. "Thinks he's going to challenge the
Bomber next year . . ."

"So let him challenge; he can lose one fight. He needs the
payoff, needs it big," said the chunkier one of the two, "Snort"
Bianchi—with a snort. Bianchi scowled, seeing the bartender
hanging around too nearby. "Hey bartender—there's a broad
over there trying to get a drink, how's about you fuck off and
serve 'er!"

"I'm the owner here, gents," Gorland said, smiling. "You
want to come back in here, show some respect for the estab-
lishment." Wasn't good to let these greasers get the upper
hand.

Bianchi frowned but only shrugged.

Gorland leaned closer to the wise guys, adding in a murmur, "Psst. Maybe you better take a powder if these feds are looking for you . . ." He nodded toward the door where an FBI flatfoot by the name of Voss stood in his gray snap-brim and overcoat, glaring about with his piggish little eyes. He looked about as "undercover" as the Statue of Liberty.

The wise guys slipped out the back way as the federal agent made his way to the bar. He was reaching into his coat when Gorland said, "Don't bother with the badge, Voss, I remember you." He didn't want badges flashed anywhere near him if he could avoid it.

Voss shrugged and dropped his hand. He leaned across the bar so he could be heard over the noise. "Word on the street is, this here's your joint now."

"That's right," Gorland said evenly. "Lock, stock, and leaky barrels."

"What you calling yourself now? Gorland still?"

"My name's Frank Gorland, you know that."

"That's not the name you had when we tried to connect you to that interstate bookmaking operation."

"You wanta see my birth certificate?"

"Our man's already seen it. Says maybe it was forged."

"Yeah? But he's not sure? Not much of an expert, if he doesn't know for sure."

Voss snorted. "You got that right . . . You going to offer me a drink or not?"

Gorland shrugged. Decided not to make a smart remark about drinking on duty. "Bourbon?"

"Good guessin'."

Gorland poured the G-man a double. "You didn't come in here to cadge drinks."

"You got that right too." He took down a slug, grimaced appreciatively, and went on, "I figure you're gonna hear stuff in a place like this. You give me something now and then—we might lay off finding out who the hell you really are."

Gorland chuckled. But he felt a chill. He didn't want his past poked into. "If I tip you, it'll be because I'm a good citizen. No other reason. Anything special going on?"

Voss crooked a finger, leaned even farther across the bar. Gorland hesitated—then he leaned close. Voss spoke right in his ear. "You hear anything about some kind of big, secret project happening down at the docks? Maybe bankrolled by Andrew Ryan? North Atlantic project? Millions of bucks flowing out to sea . . . ?"

"Nah," Gorland said. He hadn't heard about it—but the millions of bucks and the name Andrew Ryan got his attention. "I hear anything, Voss, I'll tell you. What kinda deal's he up to?"

"That's something we don't . . . something you don't need to know."

Gorland straightened up. "You're killing my back, here, with this. Listen, I gotta make it look like . . . you know." He'd been seen talking to the fed a little too chummily.

Voss nodded, just slightly. He understood.

"Listen, flatfoot!" Gorland shouted, as the jukebox changed records. "You won't find out anything from me! Now charge me with something or buzz outta my place!"

Some of the customers laughed; some grinned and nodded. Voss shrugged. "You better watch your step, Gorland!" He turned and walked out. Playing his part.

Only he was going to find out, one of these days, that "Frank Gorland" wasn't going to play along with anything the feds wanted. He'd feed them some hooey—and find out for himself what Andrew Ryan was up to. That kind of money—must be some way to tap into it . . .

Especially as this was Frank Gorland's territory. He was owed.

He didn't hear anything about Ryan for a couple of days, but one day he heard a drunk blond chippie muttering about "Mr. Fatcat Ryan . . . goddamn him . . ." as she frantically waved her empty glass at him.

"Hey wherezmuh drinkie?" demanded the blonde.

"What'll you have, darlin'?"

"What'll I have, he sez!" the frowsy blonde slurred, flipping a big, mussed curl out of her eyes. Her eye shadow had run from crying. She was a snub-nosed little thing but might be worth a roll in the hay. Only the last time he'd banged a drunk she'd thrown up all over him. "I'll have a Scotch if I can't have my man back," she sobbed, "that's what I'll have! Dead, dead, dead, and no one from that Ryan crew is saying why."

Gorland tried out his best look of sympathy. "Lost your man, didja? That'll get you a big one on the house, sweet cakes." He poured her a double Scotch.

"Hey, spritz some goddamn soda in there, whatya think, I'm a lush 'cause I take a free drink?"

"Soda it is, darlin', there you go." He waited as she drank down half of it in one gulp. The sequins were coming off the shoulder straps of her secondhand silver-blue gown, and one of her bosoms was in danger of flopping out of the décolletage. He could see a little tissue sticking up.

"I just want my Irving back," she said, her head sagging down over the drink. Lucky the song coming on the juke was a Dorsey and Sinatra crooner, soft enough he could make her out. "Jus' wannim back." He absentmindedly poured a couple more drinks for the sailors at her side, their white caps cocked rakishly as they argued over bar dice and tossed money at him.

"What became of the unfortunate soul?" Gorland asked, pocketing the money and wiping the bar. "Lost at sea was he?"

She gawped at him. "How'd you know that, you a mind reader?"

Gorland winked. "A little fishy told me."

She put a finger to one side of her nose and gave him an elaborate wink back. "So you heard about Ryan's little fun show! My Irving shipped out with hardly a g'bye, said he had to do some kinda diving for them Ryan people. That was where he got his lettuce, see, what they call deep-sea diving. Learned it in the navy salvage. They said it'd be pennies from heaven, just a month at sea doing some kinda underwater buildin', and—"

"Underwater building? You mean like pylons for a dock?"

"I dunno. But I tell ya, he came back the first time real spooked, wouldn't talk about it. Said it was much as his life was worth to talk, see? But he tol' me *one* thing—" She wagged a finger at him and closed one eye. "Them ships down at dock 17—they're hidin' something from the feds, and he was plenty scared about it! What if he was in on somethin' criminal, not even knowin', and he took the fall? And then I get a telegram . . . a little piece of paper . . . saying he ain't comin' back, accident on the job, buried at sea . . ." Her head wobbled on her neck; her voice was interrupted by hic-cupping. ". . . And that's the end of my Irving! I'm supposed to jus' swallow that? Well, I went over to the place that hired him, Seaworthy Construction they was called—and they threw me out! Treated me like I was some kinda tramp! All I wanted was what was comin' to me . . . I came out of South Jersey, and let me tell you, we get what we're owed 'cause . . ."

She went on in that vein for a while, losing the Ryan thread. Then a zoot-suiter put a bebop number on the juke and started whooping it up; the noise drowned her out, and pretty soon she was cradling her head on the bar, snoring.

Gorland had one of those intuitions . . . that this was the door to something big.

His lush bartender came weaving in, and Gorland turned

the place over, tossing over his apron, vowing inwardly to fire the bastard first chance. He had a grift to set up . . .

~~~~~~

First thing Gorland noticed, coming into the sweat-reeking prep room for the fight, was that hangdog look on Steele's face. *Good.*

Sitting on the rubdown table getting his gloves laced on by a black trainer, the scarred, barrel-chested boxer looked like his best friend had died and his old lady too. Gorland tucked a fiver into the Negro's hand and tilted his head toward the door. "I'll tie his gloves on for 'im, bud . . ."

The guy took the hint and beat it. Steele was looking Gorland up and down, his expression hinting he'd like to practice his punching right here. Only he didn't know this was Frank Gorland, what with the disguise. Right now, the man the east side knew as "Frank Gorland" was going by . . .

"My name's Lucio Fabrici," Gorland said, tying Steele's gloves nice and tight. "Bianchi sent me."

"Bianchi? What for? I told him not an hour ago it was a done deal." Steele showed no sign of doubting that he was talking to "Lucio Fabrici," a mobster working with Bianchi.

"Fabrici" had gone to great lengths for this disguise. The pinstripe suit, the toothpick stuck in the corner of his mouth, the spats, the toupee, the thin mustache—a high quality theatrical mustache carefully stuck on with spirit gum. But mostly it was his voice, just the right Little Italy intonation, and that carefully tuned facial expression that said, *We're pals, you and I, unless I have to kill you.*

Not hard for him to pull off the character, or almost any character. Running off from the orphanage, he'd taken a job as a stage boy in a vaudeville theater—stuck it out for three years though they paid him in pennies and sausages. He'd slept on a pile of ropes backstage. But it had been worth it.

He'd watched the actors, the comics—even a famous Shake-spearean type who played half a dozen parts in his one-man show. Young Frank had sucked it all up like a sponge. Makeup, costumes—the works. But what most impressed him was the fact that the people in the audience *believed*. For a few minutes they believed this laudanum-addicted Welsh actor was Hamlet. That kind of power impressed young Frank. He'd set himself to learn it . . .

Judging from Steele's reaction, he'd learned it good. "Look here, Fabrici, if Bianchi's gonna welsh on my cut . . . I won't take it! This is hard enough for me!"

"You ever hear of a triple cross, kid? Bianchi's changed his mind!" Gorland lowered his voice, glanced to make sure the door was closed. "Bianchi doesn't want you to throw the fight . . . we've let it out you're throwing the fight so we can bet the other way! See? You'll get your cut off the proceeds, and double!"

Steele's mouth hung open. He jumped to his feet, clapped his gloved hands together. "You mean it? Say, that's swell! I'll knock that lug's socks off!" Someone was pounding on the door. The audience was chanting Steele's name . . .

"You do that, Steele—I hear 'em calling you . . . Get out there and nail him early, first chance! Make it a knockout in the first round!"

Steele was delighted. "Tell Bianchi, I'll deliver—and how! A KO, first round! Ha!"

Half an hour later Gorland was at his bookie operation in the basement of the drugstore. Gorland and Garcia, his chief bookie, were in the room behind the betting counters, talking quietly, as Morry took bets at the window. Two or three freight-ship deckhands, judging by their watch caps and tattoos, stood in line to place their bets, passing a flask and yammering.

"I dunno, boss," Garcia said, scratching his head. Garcia was a chubby second-generation Cuban in a cheap three-piece suit, chomping a cigar that had never been anywhere near Cuba. "I get how knowing about Steele throwing the fight'll get us paid off if we place our own bets through our guys," Garcia was saying. "But, boss, I don't see how you're going to get the kinda money out of it you're talking about . . ."

"'Cause he *isn't* going to throw the fight. All the smart mob money'll be on him losing—and we'll bet on him winning. And we'll take 'em big-time when he surprises 'em!"

Garcia blinked. "They'll take it outta Steele's hide, boss."

"And how's that my worry? Just you make sure the mob's up to their neck betting against Steele. They're gonna be sad little monkeys when they lose. But they won't trace it to us. If you see Harley, tell him to keep an eye on that poker game up at the hotel, got some real big money suckers comin' in . . ."

He walked over to Morry, to have a gander at the take, and heard a couple of the dockworkers talking over their flask. "Sure, Ryan's hiring big down there. It's a hot ticket, pal, big paydays. But problem is—real QT stuff. Can't talk about the job. And it's dangerous too. Somewhere out in the North Atlantic, Iceland way . . ."

Gorland's ears pricked up at that.

He slipped outside by the side door and set himself to wait. Less than a minute later a couple of the deckhands came out, weather-beaten guys in watch caps and pea jackets, headed for the docks. The deck rats didn't notice him following. They were too busy whistling at a group of girls having a smoke across the street.

He shadowed the sailors close to dockside, then hung back in the shadows of a doorway, sussing the scene out. The deckhands went aboard one of the ships—but it was another one that caught Gorland's eye—a new freighter with a lot of activity on its decks, getting ready to cast loose. The name on the bow was *The Olympian*. That was one of Ryan's ships. There was a guy in the lee of a stack of crates near the loading dock, smoking a pipe. Something about him said G-man. It wasn't Voss—probably one of his men, if Gorland was any judge of cop flesh.

If Andrew Ryan was attracting G-men, he must be up to something of "questionable legal status." Which meant, at the very least, he could be blackmailed—if Gorland could find out exactly what to blackmail him for.

Seemed like the agent was watching the two guys arguing at the gangplank of Ryan's freighter—but he wasn't close enough to listen in without them noticing.

Gorland tilted his hat so the G-man wouldn't see his face and strolled over, hands in his pockets, weaving a bit, making like he was drunk.

"Maybe I can get me some work on one of these ships," Gorland said, slurring his words. "Mebbe, mebbe . . . Back bustin' work, they got . . . Don't care for it . . . mebbe they need a social director . . ." He did a good drunk—and all three men discounted him immediately as he approached.

Gorland paused near the gangplank, muttering to himself as he pretended to struggle with lighting a cigarette. All the while, he listened to the argument between the man standing on the roped gangplank, and a mustachioed man on the dock who looked like he might be a deckhand.

"I just ain't shipping out to that place again, and that's all there is to it," snarled the deckhand in the black peacoat. He wore a knit cap on his head and a handlebar mustache on his upper lip. A swarthy type, eyebrows merged in a single black bar. But getting old, maybe—skin leathery, hair salt and pepper, hand trembling as he jabbed a finger at the ship's officer. "You ain't going to make me go out there! Too goddamned risky!"

"Why, percentagewise, they're losing less people than building the Brooklyn Bridge," said the officer. "I have Mr. Greavy's word on that. Stop being such a coward!"

"I don't mind being on the ship—but in that hell down below, not me!"

"There's no use trying to say you'll only take the job if you stay on the ship—it's what Greavy says that goes! If he says you go down, you go down!"

"Then you go down in my place—and *you* wrestle with the devil! It's unholy, what he's tryin' to do down there!"

"If you leave here now, matey, you don't get paid a penny more! Get aboard this instant—we sail in ten minutes—or you can say good-bye to your contract!"

"Two weeks salary for my life? Pah!"

"You won't die down there. We had one run of bad luck is all—"

"I say it again: Pah! Good-bye to you, Mr. Forester!"

The deckhand stalked off—and Gorland realized the ship's officer was glaring at him with unconcealed suspicion. "You—what are you doing hanging 'round here?"

Gorland flicked his cigarette butt into the sea. He grinned drunkenly. "Just having a smoke, matey."

He set off to follow the deckhand, wondering what he'd stumbled onto. It was like a trail of coins gleaming on a moonlit path. If he kept following the shiny little clues he'd find the moneybag they were leaking from.

Gorland knew this trail could lead him to trouble, maybe jail. But he was a restless man, unhappy if he wasn't out on an edge. He either stayed busy working the game or lost himself in a woman's arms. Otherwise he started thinking too much. Like about his old man dumping him in that orphanage when he was a boy.

The deckhand turned the corner of one of the loading docks to go up the access road. It was a foggy night, and there was no one else on the short side road to the avenue. No one to see . . .

Frank Gorland had two approaches to getting what he wanted from life. Long-term planning—and creative improvisation. He saw a possibility—a foot-long piece of one-inch-diameter metal pipe, fallen off some truck. It was just lying in the gutter, calling to him. He scooped up the piece of pipe and hurried to catch up with the slouching shape of the deckhand.

He stepped up behind the man, grabbed his collar, jerked him slightly off balance without knocking him over.

"Hey!" the man yelped.

Gorland held the deckhand firmly in place and pressed the end of the cold metal pipe to the back of his neck. "Freeze!" Gorland growled, altering his voice. He put steel and officiousness into it. "You turn around, mister, you try to run, and I'll pull the trigger and separate your backbones with a bullet!"

The man froze. "Don't—don't shoot! What do you want? I don't have but a dollar on me!"

"You think I'm some crooked dock rat? I'm a federal agent! Now don't even twitch!"

Gorland let go of the deckhand's collar, reached into his own coat pocket, took out his wallet, flipped it open, flashed the worthless special-officer badge he used when he needed bogus authority. He flicked it in front of the guy's face, not letting him have a real look at it.

"You see that?" Gorland demanded.

"Yes sir!"

He put the wallet away and went on, "Now hear this, sailor: you're in deep shit, for working on that crooked project of Ryan's!"

"They—they told me it was legal! All legal!"

"They told you it was *a secret* too, right? You think it's legal to keep secrets from Uncle Sam?"

"No—I guess not. I mean—Well I don't know nothing about it. Just that they're building something out there. And it's a dangerous job, down them tunnels under the sea."

"Tunnels? Under the sea? For what?"

"For the construction. The foundations! I don't know why he's doing it. None of the men do—he tells 'em only what they need to know. Only, I heard Greavy talking to one of them scientist types! All I can tell you is what I heard . . ."

"And that was—?"

"That Ryan is building a city under the sea down there!"

"A what!"

"Like, a colony under the goddamn ocean! And they're laying out all kindsa stuff down there! It don't seem possible, but he's doing it! I heard he's spending hunnerds of millions, might be getting into *billions*! He's spending more money than any man ever spent buildin' anything!"

Gorland's mouth went dry as he contemplated it, and his heart thumped.

"Where is this thing?"

"Out in the North Atlantic—they keep us belowdecks when we go, so we don't see where exactly. I ain't even sure! Cold as death out there, it is! But he's got the devil's own heat coming up—steam comes up someways, and sulfur fumes, and the like! Some took sick from them fumes! Men have died down there, buildin' that thing!"

"How do you know how much he's spending?"

"I was carryin' bags into Mr. Greavy's office, on the platform ship, and I was curious, like. I hears 'em talkin' . . ."

"The *what* kind of ship?"

"That's what they call it. Platform ship! A platform to launch their slinkers! The *Olympian* there, it supplies the platform ships!"

"Slinkers, that what you said?"

"Bathyspheres, they is!"

"Bathyspheres! If you're lying to me . . ."

"No officer, I swear it!"

"Then get out of here! Run! And tell no one you spoke to me—or you go right to jail!"

The man went scurrying away, and Gorland was left in a state of mute amazement.

Ryan is building a city under the sea.

3

Ten A.M. and Bill McDonagh wanted a cigarette. He had a pack of smokes calling to him from his jacket pocket, but he held off. He was right bloody nervous about this meeting with Andrew Ryan. He was sitting literally on the edge of the padded velvet waiting-room chair outside the door of Ryan's office trying to relax, his report on the tunnel in a big brown envelope on his lap.

Bill glanced at Elaine working diligently at her desk: a sturdy brunette in a gray-blue dress suit. She was about twenty-nine, a self-contained woman with snappy blue eyes— and that upturned nose that reminded him of his mum. But the jiggle when she shifted in her seat—that sure wasn't like his bony old mum. He'd watched Elaine walking about the office whenever he could do it discreetly. She had slightly wide shoulders and hips, long legs. One of those leggy American women like Mary Louise, but smarter, judging from the brief contact he'd had with her. Bet she liked to dance. Maybe this time he'd get up his nerve and ask her . . .

Bill made himself sit back in the seat, suddenly feeling weary—he was still knackered from staying up past midnight supervising the night crew in the tunnel. But he was glad for the work—he was making far more money than he'd ever made before. He'd moved up to a nicer flat on the west side of Manhattan after his first month working for Ryan, and he was thinking of buying a car. The work was sometimes like plumbing writ large. But the gigantic pipes in the tunnel project weighed tons.

Maybe he should talk to Elaine. Ryan didn't respect a man without enterprise. Didn't matter what the enterprise was in.

Bill cleared his throat. "Slow day, innit, Elaine?"

"Hm?" She looked up as if surprised he was there. "Oh—yes, it has been a bit slow." She looked at him, blushed again, bit her lip, and looked back at her paperwork.

He was encouraged. If a woman blushed looking at you that was a good sign. "Things are slow, got to make 'em brisker, I always say. And what's brisker than the jitterbug?"

She looked at him innocently. "Jitterbug?"

"Yeah. Fancy a jitterbug sometime?"

"You mean—you'd like to go dancing . . . ?" She glanced at the door to Ryan's inner office, and lowered her voice. "Well, I *might* . . . I mean, if Mr. Ryan doesn't . . . I'm not sure how he feels about employees who . . ."

"Employees who cut a rug?" Bill grinned. "All quite 'armless . . ." He cleared his throat again. "*Harm*less."

"Ah Bill, you're here—!"Andrew Ryan was at the door to the inner office. He seemed cheerful, almost ebullient.

"Right you are, sir," Bill mumbled. He got up, trying to catch Elaine's eye as he went. She was studiously back at work.

"I expect you've brought the report," Ryan said, looking at Bill's manila envelope. "Good man. But I already know how it's going. Tell you what: let's skip the office meeting. You and I, Bill, if you are up for it, are going on a trip. Couple of stops. One in town, and one—far beyond town . . . we'll talk about it on the way . . ."

~~~~~~

It was Bill's first ride in a limousine. A smooth, quiet ride, a world away from the traffic outside. But Bill felt out of his social depth.

He'd only had a few meetings with Ryan since being hired. He'd been working mostly with contractors, and sometimes with Greavy when the engineer was back from the North Atlantic. Only it had seemed to Bill like Greavy came out to the site mostly to watch him. Like the boffin was trying to guess his weight. One time Greavy had brought a couple of bearded, scowling Irishmen in fancy suits to look him over— brothers by the name of Daniel and Simon Wales. Greavy never did bother to explain what that was about.

"When you get a chance to take a dekko at the figures, sir," Bill said, "you'll see we're caught up on the schedule and just about done—"

Ryan held up a hand to stop him. But he was smiling— faintly. "I'm not surprised that you're almost finished, Bill. In fact the crew can finish without you, at this point. That's why I hired you—I knew that you'd do a good job. Greavy was testing you on this tunnel assignment. But I had you figured right all along. There's something else I need to know. Something far more important, Bill."

"Yes sir?" Bill waited, fascinated by the electric charge of sheer *certainty* that seemed to shimmer around Andrew Ryan.

Ryan looked at him seriously. "I need to know if you're ready to meet the greatest challenge of your life."

"I . . ." Bill swallowed. Whatever Ryan had in mind, he had to be equal to it. "Anything you want to throw at me, sir—I'll take it on."

"Bill—" Ryan leaned forward, glancing at the chauffeur to make sure the window to the front seat was closed, and spoke in a low, urgent voice. "Have you heard of something called the North Atlantic project?"

Bill couldn't suppress a chuckle. "Heard those four words and not a word more. They're all like monks with a vow of silence when I ask what it is."

"Yes. Yes, and for several good reasons. Reasons like the

United States government—the OSS. British intelligence, Soviet intelligence."

"OSS—that's American spies, yeah? When I was with the RAF we'd get a report from those blokes from time to time . . ."

"Right. Office of Strategic Services." He snorted. "We run rings around them *and* the FBI, I can tell you." The bonhomie faded from his eyes, replaced by a hard glitter as he looked sharply at Bill. "You fought in the war—tell me a little about it."

It wasn't something Bill liked to talk about any more than he had to. "Not so much the fighting end. More like support. Onboard radioman for the RAF. Never had to kill a man personally. Eleven bombing missions over Germany—after I was wounded, they found me a place in the Royal Engineers. Liked that better. Got my schooling."

"Did you feel a great loyalty to the government you fought for?"

Bill sensed this was a key question. "Wouldn't put it that way, sir. Wasn't loyal to the government. Never liked 'em. It wasn't who I was *for*—it was who I was against. I was *against* the bloody Nazis—the bastards bunging flyin' bombs at London."

Ryan nodded gravely. He made eye contact—and Bill felt the voltage of it.

"My feelings about loyalty," Ryan said carefully, "are very . . . particularized. I believe a man must be loyal to himself first. But I also look for men who believe what *I* believe—men who believe it enough that they know that being loyal to me *is* being loyal to themselves! Men like you, I hope."

Bill was moved. This man, one of the world's most powerful, was opening yet another door to him—and at the same time acknowledging him as an individual. "Yes sir—I believe I understand."

"Do you? Of course I run a corporation, and I ask for cooperation from people under me. But self-interest is at the root of cooperation, Bill. I intend to prove that self-interest oils the wheels of business—and that freedom from the . . . the *tentacles* of government, from the usual social shackles on science and technology and growth, will produce unstinting prosperity. I have envisioned a great social experiment. But Bill, ask yourself, where can a social experiment on a large scale take place? Where in this world is there a place for men like us? My father and I fled the Bolsheviks—and where did we end up? This isn't the 'land of the free' it pretends to be. It's the land of the taxed. And it was his reluctance to pay taxes that put my father in jail. Every society is the same on the face of the earth these days. But Bill—suppose it were possible . . . ," his voice pitched low, breathless, ". . . to *leave* the face of the earth? Just for a time. Just for a century or two. Until the fools have destroyed themselves with their Hiroshima bombs."

Bill was flummoxed. "*Leave* it sir?"

Ryan chuckled. "Don't look so astonished. I don't mean we're going to the moon. We're not going *up*. We're going down! Bill—I have something to show you. Will you take a trip with me . . . to Iceland?"

"Iceland!"

"Just the first leg. A plane to Iceland—then, immediately, a boat to the North Atlantic. To see the foundation, the beginning, of the North Atlantic project. I'm going to have to trust you—and you're going to have to trust me . . ."

"Sir . . ." Bill swallowed. He was not usually so open with people. But he was moved by Ryan's passion—and his trust. "You trusted me, guv'nor. Right out of the Christmas cracker. And I'll trust you."

"Good—but you'll be giving me your point of view, Bill.

Because I feel you're trustworthy. Ah—we've reached our first stop. We'll have a few words with one of our resident artists here, and then we're taking a very late plane to see the North Atlantic project. I'm going to show you a marvel taking shape southwest of Iceland. And I promise that you will be . . . enraptured."

~~~~~~

Driving a delivery truck later that night, Gorland spotted the small, discreet sign on the warehouse front: SEAWORTHY CONSTRUCTION. He drove around the corner and pulled up near the loading dock. Even this time of night the place was a hive of activity. One shift clocking out, another one clocking in.

Gorland turned off the engine and adjusted his stomach padding. Hiring a delivery truck was easy. Coming up with a new disguise had used up another hour. He got the delivery service coveralls, stuffed a pillow in them for a big belly, gave himself a scar, and rearranged the toupee. Most of all he rearranged his facial expression—made it the expression of a bored wiseacre.

"Hey how ya doin'," Gorland said to himself, in the rearview mirror. He made the voice a little higher. He didn't want anyone recognizing "Frank Gorland." He was now Bill Foster, delivery driver—because *Bill Foster* happened to be the name sewn onto the overalls.

He looked over the clipboard that the driver of his borrowed truck had left on the dash. *Heinz canned goods,* it said. That'd work. The truck was empty—the stuff had already been delivered somewhere—but the warehouse didn't need to know that.

Gorland climbed down from the truck and stalked over to the loading dock, acting like he was in a hurry to get a delivery over with. He went up the steps like he owned the place. Big steel doors into the warehouse were wide open, and inside a whole separate crew bustled and grunted about crates and palettes supporting intricate steel equipment, the likes of which he'd never seen before.

A sign over the doors, bigger than the business sign out front, read AUTHORIZED PERSONNEL ONLY.

A grumpy-looking man in a long coat, horn-rimmed glasses, and a patch of a mustache was supervising a crew of eight men offloading a truck backed to the loading dock—maybe the biggest truck Gorland had ever seen. Gorland watched for a minute as a hefty wooden crate was swung with a block and tackle, several men wrestling it into place on a wheeled pallet. Some of the other crates in the back of the truck looked big enough to hold a small car. Stenciled on one of the crates was DESIGN FACING BLDG FOUR.

"You!" barked the man in the horn-rims. He scowled, not seeming happy to find Gorland staring into the back of the big truck. "What do you want here?"

Gorland meditatively chewed a wooden match and considered the question. Then he hooked a thumb at the truck he'd driven here in. "Got a delivery for a Ryan." He flashed the clipboard he'd brought along. "Canned goods."

The man turned to shout, "Careful with that!" at two burly workmen, then turned back to Gorland. "Canned goods? They'll be glad to hear that out at the site. Second we get this truck unloaded, you back yours up here . . ."

"Hold on now!" Gorland said, furiously chewing his toothpick. "This here delivery is for a man named Ryan! You him?"

The man snorted in contempt. "Don't be a fool. Mr. Ryan doesn't come here in person! I'm Harry Brown; I sign for everything!"

Gorland shrugged and turned away. "Says here Mr. Ryan. I don't have no other instructions."

"Now wait a minute, hold on!" Brown stopped him with a hand on his shoulder. "They go through food out there like there's no tomorrow! We got the word from Rizzo yesterday that we had to step up on the canned goods!"

"Fine," Gorland said, chewing his match. "Then get Mr. . . ." He paused to squint at his clipboard as if it was written on there. "Mr. Andrew Ryan out here to sign for it."

"Look—" Brown seemed to be working hard to hold onto his temper. "You know who Andrew Ryan *is*?"

"I heard of him. Some big muckety-muck. I don't care if he's Harry Truman; my instructions say he's got to sign or no delivery. Hell, I'll come back tomorrow, it's just a truckload of canned food."

"We've got a ship coming in tonight—and they need those goods! They've got an army of men out there to feed!"

"So why don't they buy 'em something to eat local, wherever that is, till we get this straightened out?" Gorland asked, as if innocently amused. "They don't have a corner grocery there?"

"No, you tubby fool—it's off the coast of Iceland! And if he buys in Iceland . . ." He broke off, frowning.

Gorland scratched his head, as if trying to puzzle it out. "Well, maybe I can let you have this one truckload. How many men's he got out there—one truckload going to be enough? Maybe you want us to send out another?"

"Hell, we could probably use three more!"

"Cost more to get it out here that quick. He give you guys enough budget for that?"

"Enough budget!" Brown snorted and crossed his arms over his chest. "If you only knew what we spent on the air pumps already . . . Money's . . . what they call it . . . no object. You get it? Now back that truck up here!"

"I dunno. This whole thing—how do I know it's on the up-and-up if the guy who ordered ain't here to sign? Who's in charge at Seaworthy if it isn't Ryan?"

"Ryan's the owner, you damned . . ." He took a deep breath,

removed his glasses, polished them with a handkerchief. That seemed to calm him. "Ryan's the *owner*. Man named Rizzo, over at the administration office, he's in charge."

Brown turned to sign a manifest held up for him by a thickset black man in overalls. Gorland leaned over, trying to make out what was on it. All he could gather was *Air purification system bldg 32, 33*. And the cost of that system added up to well over a million dollars . . .

Brown saw Gorland trying to see the manifest and stepped to block his view. "Mister, you sure are a nosy sort . . ."

Gorland shrugged. "Just as curious as anybody else. Well, I can't let you sign for this stuff. Where's this Rizzo's office at? Maybe I better talk to him . . ."

Brown hesitated, looking at him suspiciously. Then he shrugged and told him, and Gorland wrote it down on the clipboard. He turned to peer inside the warehouse. "Hey— that one of those bathysphere things?"

Brown stared at him. "What delivery company you say you were with?"

"Me? Acme. Name's Foster."

"Yeah? Let me have another look at that clipboard of yours . . ."

"Now who's the nosy one? See you when I get the signature, pal." Gorland turned and hurried down the stairs. He felt the men on the loading dock staring at him. He glanced back and saw one big fist-faced palooka take a sap out of his pocket, and slap it in his palm.

He hurried to the truck, forcing himself not to run, and got out of there as fast as he could. Smiling to himself as he drove away. Maybe this wasn't going to be a blackmail operation. Maybe it'd be something much bigger . . .

Yeah. If he figured out where to stand, it'd be raining money—and all he needed was a bucket.

~~~~~~~

"It's not generally known that I sometimes back Broadway musicals," said Andrew Ryan, as the limousine pulled up in front of the theater. "I prefer to do it quietly. I have a rather old-fashioned taste in music, they tell me—George M. Cohan or Jolson, they're more my style. Or Rudy Vallee. I don't care much for this jitterbug business. Don't understand it." He waved a hand at the marquee. "You know the work of Sander Cohen? Some say he is getting a bit long in the tooth, but I think he's every bit the musical genius he ever was . . . a Renaissance man of the arts, really."

Bill read the marquee: SANDER COHEN IN "YOUNG DANDIES."

"Cor!" he burst out. "Me ma took a liking to Sander Cohen, a few years back. Fair wore out his 'Kissing the Tulip' on her old Victrola!"

"Ah yes. I was a fan of his 'No One Understands Me.' You shall meet him tonight, my boy! We're just in time to catch his final number—I've seen the show many times of course—and we'll have a word backstage. Karlosky—this is fine here!"

The chauffeur, Ivan Karlosky, was a pale-haired man, scarred and impassive, with a distinctively Russian bone structure. He gave a small salute with his gloved hand and nodded. Bill had heard that Karlosky was not only one of the finest auto mechanics around but also pretty much invincible. No one messed with Karlosky.

Bill got out of the limo, instinctively holding the door for Ryan and closing it behind him. A group of swells spilled out of the theater, laughing—though the music of the show could be heard through the open theater door. The show was still going on. A bored-looking man in spats and tuxedo was escorting a platinum-haired girl in a white mink; two other young men followed with elaborately coifed girls on their arms, all of them tipsy from intermission cocktails.

Bill hesitated as Ryan paused, glowering at the swells, seeming to disapprove of them leaving the theater early.

"Say," laughed one in a top hat, "that Sander Cohen is a funny old character!"

"I heard some young men go into his dressing room never come out again!" said a sleepy-eyed swell in a bowler hat more seriously, voice low.

"Well, you won't get me to one of his shows again," said the top hat, as they strolled wobblingly off. "Mincing about like that! Constantly in the spotlight! All that makeup! Looked like a clown!"

Ryan growled audibly to himself as he glared after them. "Drunks!" He shook his head, stalking toward the alley between the theaters that led to the stage door. Bill followed, feeling a bit squiffy himself though he hadn't had a drop today. He felt socially out of his depth with Ryan—but the whole experience exhilarated him too.

"This way, Bill," Ryan muttered. ". . . Those decadent young poltroons . . . but it's ever that way. Inconsequential people know only mockery—only the great understand the great . . ."

He rapped on the stage door, which was opened by a cigar-chewing bulldog of a man. "Well? Who is it now?"—and then his cigar dropped from his slack mouth. "Oh! Sorry, Mr. Ryan, I didn't realize it was you, please come in sir, right this way sir, nice night ain't it?"

What an arse kisser, Bill thought, as the man, practically curtseying, let them in. An echoing passage, and then they were backstage, standing in the wings, watching Sander Cohen. He was just finishing off his climactic number, "Hop Away to Heaven."

Strange to see a stage show from this angle, everything looking oddly overlit, the clack of heels on the wooden stage audible, the extreme angle not showing the dancers to best effect. They seemed almost to lumber around.

And Sander Cohen was stranger still. The fading Broadway star was wearing a silvery jacket that might have seemed more natural on a Busby Berkeley dancing girl. He had matching silvery trousers with a red stripe down the side; his boots, with heels like a flamenco dancer's, glittered too. He had a rather bulbous head, with thinning hair emphasized by a great pale swath of forehead not much helped by a spit curl, and a puckish little mustache, upturned at the ends. He did wear a surprising amount of pancake—and what seemed to be eyeliner.

Cohen was sashaying rhythmically about, singing in a jaunty tenor, spinning a silvery walking stick in his fingers. Two rows of very handsome young men and pretty girls danced in chorus patterns behind him. Cohen sang:

"If you want to hop hop hop with me
We'll multiply like crazy
Like a couple of bunnies
Oh hop to Heaven, just hop to Heaven—with meeeeeeee!"

"Admittedly, a trivial number," said Ryan, leaning over to whisper behind his hand to Bill, "but the public needs that sort of thing, you know, something light from time to time. Sander would like to be more serious. Artists should have their chance to work without interference. So long as it's profitable, of course . . ."

Bill nodded, hoping that this blighter did have some better numbers than this rubbish. He wouldn't have pictured Ryan listening to this prancing chap—would have thought him more the Wagner type, or maybe Tchaikovsky. But then, you never knew what kind of music a man might relax with. He'd once known a bare-fisted bruiser of a longshoreman who thought nothing of taking on three men in a bar fight—but burst into sentimental tears when he saw Shirley Temple singing "The Good Ship Lollipop." Wiping his eyes, sniffing, "Ain't she a pip?"

The curtain rang down to a rather puny spatter of applause and went back up almost immediately so that Cohen could take several bows that no one was asking for. The dancers hurried offstage.

A gesture from Ryan, and one of the dancers lingered: a corn-fed chorus girl in a bathing suit trimmed in white fur; a great flowing spill of blond hair fell over her pink shoulders; golden bangs stuck to her forehead in a light sheen of perspiration. She was a big girl, in an Amazonian, voluptuous way, and seemed several inches taller than Ryan—but almost shrank in his presence, while her china-blue eyes grew large.

"Mr. Ryan!" Her voice was not melodious. It was rather squeakily grating, to Bill—he hoped she was a good dancer.

Ryan gazed at her benevolently—but with a hungry light in his hard eyes. Then the hunger was somehow folded away, and he seemed almost paternal—carefully reserved. "You positively glowed with talent tonight, Jasmine," Ryan said. "Ah—allow me to present my business associate, Mr. Bill McDonagh."

She barely glanced at Bill. "Did you really think I was good, Mr. Ryan? You could see me out there?"

"Of course, my dear. I've watched you dance many times. You're always stimulating."

"Enough for a lead? I can't seem to get anywhere in this business, Mr. Ryan. I mean—I got *here*, but I can't get any farther than the chorus. I've tried to talk to Sander, but he doesn't seem interested in me. He's so involved with his, what does he call them, his protégés . . ."

"A big talent like yours will pop out in good time, Jasmine, don't you worry," Ryan said as the curtain closed on another uncalled-for bow by Sander Cohen.

"Do you really think so, Mr. Ryan? I mean, if you wanted to—"

"In fact—" Ryan interrupted—with such authority that her voice cut off in midsqueak. "I'm going to help you—I'm going to pay for you to take elocution lessons. Your only weakness as an artist is . . . shall we call it vocal presentation. I took such lessons myself, once. You'll sound differently—and people will look at you differently."

"El-o-quew-shun! Sure, I know what that is!" She seemed a bit frustrated, though. Seemed improving her elocution wasn't what she'd had in mind.

"I am founding . . . a new community," he said, glancing about them. "In another place, some distance away. You might call it a resort—in a sense. It will take a while to complete. But, given the right dedication, you could work there—in show business. It would definitely be a new start."

"Where will it be exactly?"

"Oh—foreign places. You know."

"Like Bermuda?"

"Well—um, more or less. Ah, Sander!"

"Ooh, a resort, that'd be swell!" she said, walking away but looking at him as she went—so that she almost collided with Sander Cohen.

"Do excuse me, my dear," Cohen muttered, with a forced smile. Cohen brightened when he saw Ryan, putting on a completely different aspect, beaming, one eyebrow arched. "Andrew! My dear fellow! You caught the show after all!"

"We have been standing here entranced. Allow me to introduce you to Bill McDonagh."

"Bill, eh?" Cohen scrutinized him with sleepy eyes. "Mm—earthy!"

"Right you are," Bill said. "Keep the ol' feet on the ground, me."

"And British! How charming. You know, just the other day

I was saying to Noël Coward . . ." He went into a lengthy an-
ecdote, much of which was lost in the buzz of the backstage
bustle, but it seemed to be something about Coward's rather
embarrassing admiration for Cohen. ". . . one wishes he
wouldn't fawn so."

Bill noticed that Cohen's left eyebrow seemed permanently
cocked, stuck higher than the other, never going down—as if
he'd been paralyzed in a condition of irony.

"You're a real artist, not just a cocktail wit like Noël
Coward," Ryan said, "it's only natural the man should be
overwhelmed."

"You are too good, Andrew!"

It bothered Bill, hearing this man call Mr. Ryan by his first
name. Didn't seem right, somehow. He took a step back, feeling that Cohen was standing rather too near him.

"Andrew—can I expect you at my little opening in the
Village?"

Ryan frowned. "Opening?"

"Did you not receive the invitation? I shall have to positively flay my personal assistant alive! Ha ha! I have a bit of a
gallery show, at the Verlaine Club. My new obsession. An art
form almost unknown in America." Looking sleepy eyed
again, he turned to explain to Bill. "It's a *tableau vivant* show."

"Ah yes," Ryan said to Bill. "*Tableau vivant*. It's a French
artistic tradition—they pose people on a stage, in different
ways, to represent scenes from history or drama. They stand
there in costume . . . almost like sculptures."

"Precisely!" Cohen crowed, clapping his hands together
with delight. "Living sculptures, in a way—in this case they
are representing scenes from the life of the Roman emperor
Caligula."

"Sounds fascinating," Ryan said, frowning slightly. "Caligula. Well, well, well."

"My protégés, such artistic courage—they stand there

posed in a state of near undress in a cold room, minute after minute, as if frozen in place!" He tossed his head like a stallion and whispered, "They're in fierce competition to please me! Oh how hard they work at it—but art calls for an agony of self-sacrifice, for submission, an inverted immolation upon its altar!"

"That's what I admire about you, Sander," Ryan said. "Your complete devotion to your art. No matter what anyone thinks! You are yourself completely. That's essential to art, it seems to me. Expressing one's true self . . ."

But it seemed to Bill that whatever Sander Cohen really was, it was all hidden away, even as he presented another side of himself to the world with great verve. It was like there was a scared little animal looking out of his sleepy eyes. And yet he spoke with flourishes, moved with striking dynamism. Queer sort of duck.

"I may be out of the country for your opening, I'm afraid," Ryan was saying. "But I was just telling Jasmine—"

"Oh—Jasmine." Cohen shrugged dismissively. "She does have her charms. Believe me, I understand. But Andrew—I'm told that this show may close rather sooner than we expected. *Dandies* was to be my re-emergence, my metamorphosis! And the cocoon, I find, is rather constricting and may squeeze me out too soon—" He hugged himself tight, seemed to writhe in his own hug as he said it. "I feel positively squeezed!"

"Artists chafe at constraint," Ryan said, nodding sympathetically. "Don't worry about the show—Broadway will soon be old hat. We'll create our own venue for genius, Sander!"

"Really! And with what sort of . . . scope? A large audience?"

"You'll see. As for scope—well, there will be plenty of people to appreciate you there. Almost a captive audience in a way."

"Ooh, nothing I'd like better than a captive audience! But I must away! I see Jimmy signaling desperately to me from the dressing room. Do keep me informed as to this . . . this new project, Andrew!"

"You will be among the first to know when it's ready, Sander. It will take some courage on your part"—Ryan smiled crookedly—"but if you take the leap, you'll find yourself immersed in something beautiful."

They watched Sander Cohen strutting off toward the dressing rooms. It seemed to Bill that Cohen was off his trolley, but Ryan was right—genius was eccentric. As if guessing his thoughts, Ryan said, "Yes, Bill, he can be . . . outrageous. Exasperating. But all the great ones hurt the eyes and burn the ears a bit. He calls himself the Napoleon of Mime sometimes—and so he is, when he's miming. Come along, Bill. We're off to the airport. If you're quite ready to go. Or are you having second thoughts?"

Bill grinned. "Not me, sir. I'm in, A to Zed. I'm diving in at the deep end, Mr. Ryan . . ."

4

"Look, Mr. Gorland—I don't know that much about it." Merton was sitting in the backroom of The Clanger, across from what used to be his own seat. Now Gorland was behind the desk, with Garcia standing to one side, eyeing Merton and tapping a blackjack in his palm, while on the other side was Reggie, a bruiser from the Bronx, wearing the doorman's uniform that went with his day job.

Gorland knew Reggie from the old days—he was one of the only people alive who knew Frank's real last name—and he sometimes hired him as extra muscle. Tonight, Gorland had to put the fear of God into Merton. Harv Merton needed to have more fear for Frank Gorland than for the powerful Andrew Ryan.

"I mean, if I *knew* anything else," Merton went on, wringing his hands, "I'd *tell* ya."

"Hey, you got any hot advice on the horses, Merton?" Garcia, asked, grinning.

Gorland signaled for Garcia to be quiet. The bookie shrugged, put away his sap, and took out a cigar instead. In the lull, the sound of the bar seeped through the closed door. A girl squealed with laughter; a man hooted, *"Aw you don't know nothin' about Dempsey!"*

"Let's all just think this through, Merton," Gorland said, pouring Merton a drink from the bourbon bottle. "You're telling me you got a job with Seaworthy, on the North Atlantic project, from this guy Rizzo—you were working as a steward on one of their ships. Right? And they take your ass out to the North Atlantic and keep it there for *a month and a half*—and you didn't see a *thing* out there?"

Gorland shoved the shot glass across the desk, and Merton snatched it up. "Thanks. Uh—that's about the size of it. I mean . . . some stuff was taken down, you know, under the water. But . . ." He laughed nervously. "I didn't go down with it! They were all hush-hush about what was going on down there. Much as your life was worth to talk about it, one fella said, after he come up. I don't know what they're up to."

"You see, I know what they're up to—in a general kind of way," Gorland said, pouring himself a drink. "Building something big. But I don't know what Ryan's angle is. Where the money is. You seen 'em bring up any . . . *ore*? You know, mining goodies? Gold, silver, oil?"

"No, nothin' like that. Just a lotta ships. Never saw Mr. Ryan. Heard his name sometimes, that's all. I was busy the whole time. Seasick too. I was glad to get back here and look for another job . . ."

"Yeah, you'll live to look for another job too," Reggie said helpfully, his voice mild. "If you tell Mr. Gorland exactly what he needs to know."

"I swear—I didn't find out anything else! I hardly left the galley on that big ol' ship! Now, Frank Fontaine—*he* might know something. He's got boats going out there to supply 'em with fish! And they get to talk more. You know, to the guys in the construction . . ."

Gorland frowned thoughtfully. "Frank Fontaine. Fontaine's Fisheries? He used to smuggle stuff from Cuba up here in those fishing boats of his. Now he's delivering . . . fish? You kiddin' me?"

"I saw him on the dock—that's what he told me! I used to buy some of the rum he smuggled up here for my . . . for your place." Merton swallowed. "Fontaine says there's more money selling fish to Ryan for that crew out there than there is selling rum to New York! They got a cryin' need for food out there—got an army of workers to feed . . ."

Gorland grunted thoughtfully to himself. That did dovetail with what he'd heard at the loading dock. The one sure way to get close to that operation . . . was to supply it.

A crazy thought came to him. Bringing with it some interesting possibilities . . .

But if he did go that far—and *far* was the word, all right— he'd be way out of his own stomping ground. He'd be splashing around in the North Atlantic.

There was something about this secret project of Ryan's that fascinated him, that drew him the way rumors of buried pirate gold drew a treasure hunter. Millions of dollars were being sunk into the North Atlantic. He ought to be able to scoop some of it up.

Years ago, when "Frank Gorland" was dodging the law, he'd hopped a freight train. Riding the boxcar he'd read an old newspaper about the newly minted industrialist Andrew Ryan. There was a picture of him standing in front of a fancy building with his name on it. That picture had stirred something in him. The picture of Andrew Ryan standing there in front of the skyline of Manhattan, like he owned it, had made Frank think:

Whatever he's got—I want it. I'm going to take it from him . . .

Could be now was his chance. But first he had to figure out what Ryan's angle was. What he was up to—or down to—out there with a city down in the cold guts of that dark ocean . . .

Somewhere over the Atlantic
1946

"It's a converted Liberator, really." Andrew Ryan led Bill Mc-Donagh through a big, humming aircraft cabin, toward the tail. "A stratocruiser now—United Airlines has ordered eleven of them for luxury flights. But this is the prototype. Of course, this is a prop plane, but the next generation will be jets . . ."

"Saw a fighter jet in the war, my last trip out," Bill said. "ME-262 it was. German prototype. Didn't even engage us—I reckon they were test flying . . ."

"Yes," Ryan said distractedly. "Fast and efficient, the jet engine. Haven't bothered developing them—not as aircraft—because after the North Atlantic project we hope to need no aircraft. We'll have a great many submersibles—and in time we'll hardly need those. We hope to be entirely self-sufficient . . ."

Submersibles? Bill must have misheard him.

Bill had mixed feelings about being on this plane. The drone of its engines was just close enough to the sound of the bombers he'd flown on in the war. He'd taken a ship to get to the USA, after. He'd had enough of planes. Seen his best friend turned to red marmalade that last time out.

Inside, though, this plane wasn't much like a bomber. Except for the sound, the vibrations through the floor, the curved "inner skin," it could easily be a luxury suite at a hotel. The Victorian-style chairs and sofas were bolted down, but they were luxurious, their silken red cushions trimmed in gold. Lace curtains were elegantly swept back from the windows with silk cords. The cabin was quietly served by three liveried servants and a chef. Behind a stainless-steel bar, an Asian servant in a red and black jacket, with gold braid, looked up attentively as they passed.

But Ryan wasn't after drinks yet. They passed through a red velvet curtain into an after cabin, smaller, with a metal table bolted to the center of the floor. On the table was a fairly large object, rising like a ghost under a white muslin covering. The room contained almost nothing else—except taped to one interior wall, to the left, was a full-color drawing of a crowded, highly stylized city. It reminded Bill, at first glance, of the Emerald City of Oz. Only the city in the colorful drawing appeared to be underwater—a school of colorfully sketched fish swam past its windows. Was it Atlantis, the day after it went down?

Ryan strode dramatically up to the table and whipped off the cover. "Et voila!" he said, smiling. He had revealed a scale model of the city. It was all one structure formed of many lesser structures, all in the industrial-arts style, as if the designer of the Chrysler Building had made an entire small city to go with it. The model was about three feet high, a construction of linked towers, sheaths of green glass and chrome, transparent tubular passageways, statues, very little open space between buildings. The structure seemed quite sealed off, and indeed Bill made out what appeared to be air locks near the bases of several towers resembling artfully turned lighthouses. Outside the air lock sat the mock-up of a small submarine. Through one of the miniature city's transparent panels he saw what looked like a tiny bathysphere, partway risen up through a vertical shaft.

"This," said Andrew Ryan, breathing hard as he said it, the muslin sheet dangling at his side, "is *Rapture!*"

A surge of turbulence hit the plane at exactly that moment, making the model city quiver dangerously on its table.

Bill stared at it, careful in the turbulence. "Right. Lovely, innit? Rapturous, like."

"No Bill—*Rapture* is the name of this city. What you see here is just the core, the downtown you might say. Its foundations are already under construction—a habitat for thousands of people beneath the waters of the North Atlantic."

Bill gaped at him. "You're taking the piss!"

Ryan flashed one of his pensive smiles. "But it's true! It's being constructed in secret—in a part of the sea rarely plied by anyone. The architecture is glorious, isn't it? The Wales brothers designed it. Greavy's been implementing their vision—and now so will you, Bill."

Bill shook his head in wonder. "It's—being built right now?" The turbulence died down, to Bill's relief. It brought ghostly memories of being in a plane hit by flak. "How big's Rapture to be, then?"

"It will be a small city, hidden away under the ocean . . . Miles to a side . . . lots of open space inside it. We don't want claustrophobia . . ."

The model's shape reminded Bill of the densest parts of Manhattan in some ways, all those buildings packed together. But in this case the buildings were crowded even closer, and even more interconnected.

"Do you see what's in there, through that little window?" Ryan pointed. "That is going to be park land . . . a park under the sea! I call it Arcadia. We have a system for bringing reflected sunlight down, as well as electrical light. Arcadia will help provide oxygen as well as being a place for relaxation. Now here you see—"

He broke off at a sudden rough turbulence and the boom of thunder, somewhere close at hand. Both men looked nervously at the window opposite the drawing.

Bill put one hand to the edge of the table and ducked to see through the port—black and gray storm clouds billowed angrily outside, flickering with lighting. "Dodgy ride coming."

Another boom, another quiver, and Bill closed his eyes, trying to will away the pictures rising in his mind. *The boom of a flak shell, the clatter and whine of many small, vicious*

*impacts. Another shell exploding just outside, a section of the
bomber hull suddenly gone, blown out by the Jerries. Wind
roaring in through the ragged gap like a mad house invader, as
Bill McDonagh, radioman, sees the curly-headed Welsh lad, a
green little blighter just a week out of training, being sucked
backward against a five-foot breach in the curved metal wall,
pulled hard by the sudden drop in air pressure, the boy's face
contorting in terror. Bill shouts to the pilots, "Reduce altitude!"
as he rushes to the young flyer, gripping a stanchion with his
right hand so he can try pulling the Welsh lad back with his
left—knowing full well it was no good. The boy screams as the
suction around the breach jerks him harder into the jagged
edge, the sharp metal ripping through his left shoulder; his blood
precedes him, streaming out through the gap—and then he follows it, just gone like a magic act, vanished into the roaring sky.
All that remains are scraps of torn clothes and skin flapping on
the ragged edges of the bulkhead. The boy is falling somewhere,
out in the gray mist. Bill clings to the stanchion as the bomber
angles sharply down to equalize air pressure . . .*

"Bill? You all right?"

Bill managed a sickly grin. "There's a reason I took a ship
to America 'stead of a plane, guv. Sorry. I'm all right."

"I think we both need a drink . . ."

"Right you are, Mr. Ryan. That's the very medicine . . ."

"Let's have a seat in the main cabin and ride out this storm.
We should be at the airport in another hour or so—winds are
behind us. Then it's to the ship. Come on, I'll have Quee pour
you the best single malt you ever tasted, and I'll tell you about
the Great Chain . . ."

～～～～～

The bar in Staten Island was almost deserted tonight. But
Captain Fontaine was there, as arranged, sitting in a booth in
the dim corner, frowning at his beer. Just waiting for Frank
Gorland.

Captain Fontaine did look a lot like the man who called himself Frank Gorland—but he was more weather beaten, a little older. He wore a red watch cap and a long green corduroy double-breasted coat. His calloused red hands showed the life he'd led at sea—first as a smuggler, now as the head of a small fishing fleet.

Gorland ordered a bottled beer from the stout barmaid, who seemed to be flirting with a drunken marine, and carried it over to Captain Fontaine's table.

Fontaine didn't look up from brooding on his beer as Gorland sat across from him. "Gorland, seems to me that every time I run into you, something goes wrong."

"How's that? What about all that cash you made from what I did for you on your last cargo?"

"Your cut was near as big as mine, and all you did for it was run your mouth."

"Well, running my mouth is how I live, friend. Now look, Fontaine. You want the information I have or not? I'm offering it for free. I'm hoping we can work together again, and we can't do it if you're in jail. So you'd better cock one of those shell-like ears—I've got word they're going to wait till you head out— and raid you on the way back."

Fontaine slurped at his brew. "They . . . *who?*"

"Why the . . ." Gorland leaned over the table and lowered his voice. "Just the Federal Bureau of Investigation, that's who. Agent Voss is chewing at your rump!"

Fontaine sat up straight. Gorland looked at him calmly, believing it himself, almost, as he said, "I got it from my sister's best friend—she's a secretary for them. Keeps an eye on things for me." That was the secret to being a good liar—believing it when you said it. "So she's typing up some kind of warrant, and there you are. Captain Frank Fontaine. Smuggling, it says. *Drugs,* it says."

"Keep your voice down. Anyhow it don't signify—I gave up

smuggling that stuff. Company I work for now is bringing me crazy money to bring my catch over by Iceland . . . long ways, but it's big money. Safe and legal!"

"You mean your deal with Andrew Ryan's operation out there?"

Fontaine shrugged. "Nothin' you need to know about."

So he took the fish out there himself. Interesting. The exact whereabouts of the North Atlantic project would be on the charts in one of those boats.

Gorland sighed and shook his head. "You don't get it. Voss is out to get you. He's going to look down in your hold, first time you set to sea, and plant the dope down there! You gave him the slip one too many times."

"I . . . I don't believe it!"

"They're raiding you all right. And suppose they don't set you up—they know that Ryan's trying to hide something out there. So they'll take you in for questioning. How'll Ryan feel about that? You want to go to jail for standing in the way of an investigation?"

"What proof is there a raid's coming, Gorland?"

"Proof? Just a carbon from the raiding order." Gorland passed it over. Every good con man knows a good forger. "You can sell your boats to me and slip off to Cuba . . ."

Fontaine looked at the order—and his shoulders slumped. "Hmmf . . . maybe. It's true I'm sick of being on those boats. Like to retire to Cuba. But I want a good price."

"Sure, I'll give you top money."

Fontaine looked at him narrowly. "And why would you be so goddamn *helpful*, Gorland? It don't add up."

"It's you they're looking for, not me—I'll play fisherman till things cool off. Make some money from Ryan. And have the trawlers for when it's safe to smuggle again."

Fontaine expelled a long, slow breath. Gorland knew that meant he was giving in. He felt the physical thrill, an almost sexually delicious inward shiver, that always came when a mark surrendered.

~~~~~~

Two nights later, Frank Gorland was waiting in the pilot-house of a fishing trawler, trying to get used to the smell of old codfish, and drinking coffee. The trawler was called *Happydrift*. Christ, but it was chilly on this old tub.

He heard a hail from the dock and smiled. Captain Fontaine was here for his money.

Gorland nodded to his grizzled gray-haired helmsman and said, "When I give you the signal, head due East."

"You got it, boss."

"Call me captain. I'm about to be one . . ."

"Aye aye, cap'n."

Gorland went down the ladder to the main deck, where he found Fontaine stalking back and forth, scowling.

"Gorland—I hear you fired my crew! You're up to something! This whole thing is starting to stink."

"Surprised you can smell a stink at this point. But come on down to the galley and I'll explain—I've got a parcel of money for you."

Gorland turned and went belowdecks, humming to himself. Fontaine hesitated—then followed.

There was no crew staying warm in *Happydrift*'s little galley. Gorland planned to pick up the rest of the crew later.

On a small foldout table near the stove was a small brown suitcase. "There you are, Fontaine—open it up and count it."

Fontaine looked at him—and he looked at the suitcase. Then he licked his lips, went to the suitcase, opened it—and stared. It was filled with dead fish. Red snapper.

"I'm thinking," Gorland said, taking a blackjack from his coat pocket, "of changing the name of this boat to *Happygrift*. What do you think?"

Captain Fontaine turned angrily to Gorland—who hit him

hard with the blackjack, *crack,* right on the forehead. Fontaine went down like a sack of bricks.

Gorland put the blackjack away and went to the ladder, climbed to the deck, turned, and waved up at the pilothouse, where the helmsman, Bergman, was watching for his signal. The helmsman pointed at the dock—and Gorland remembered he had to cast off. That much he knew how to do. He cast the ropes off, and the boat roared to life, swinging out from the dock toward the open sea.

Humming "My Wild Irish Rose," Gorland descended to the galley. Captain Fontaine, facedown, was still out cold. Gorland went through the man's pockets, removing his identification, money, personal effects. Might need them.

He considered Captain Fontaine, now stirring slightly on the deck—and then he muttered to himself, "Do it. Go all the way, Frank."

He took a deep breath—then pulled off his shirt and pants. He dragged Fontaine's outer clothing off him, then switched clothes with him, wincing at the smell of Fontaine's unwashed trousers. Just a little too large. Had to tighten the belt.

Then he used his old clothing to tie Fontaine's hands behind him. "Whuh yuh doing?" Fontaine asked, starting to come to. "Lemme go . . ."

"I will let you go, right now, Captain," Gorland said. "But you got to climb that ladder. I'll help you."

"I need clothes, it's freezing out here."

"You'll be all taken care of. Up the ladder . . ."

He got the bleary Fontaine up, at last, and out on the tilting deck. Fog streamed by and wreathed the sea. He glanced at the pilothouse. Bergman was facing out to sea. Not that he would probably have cared. The man had done five years in prison not so long ago. He was being well paid—he'd go along with whatever his new boss wanted.

Fontaine was swaying on deck, goggling blearily about him. "We're . . . we're out tuh sea . . . why are . . . we . . ."

"I'll show you why," Gorland said, escorting him to the side. "You ever notice how much you and I look alike . . . Frank? We even have the same first name! Possibilities, Frank—possibilities! I've got a whole new concept here—I call it, 'Identity theft.' What do you think?" Then he bent, grabbed the vessel's former captain by the ankles, and tilted him over the side, headfirst down into the cold sea. A yell, a splash or two—and Captain Fontaine went down . . . He didn't come up.

Captain Fontaine was dead. Long live . . . Captain Frank Fontaine.

5

The *Andrew Ryan* was pitching at sea-anchor that gray morning, and Bill was queasy. The cigarette helped a little.

He tried to ignore the steward throwing up over the starboard rail. Gazing into the sea, he watched the frothing bathysphere bob to the surface . . .

"These are no ordinary bathyspheres," Ryan said proudly, joining him at the taffrail, his hair so slicked down the considerable wind didn't budge it. "Some of the men call them slinkers because they get around with such agility."

"Never seen the like. Almost elegant, it is."

Ryan looked at him closely. "Feeling seasick? I have a pill . . ."

"No," said Bill, stepping back from a burst of spray. The spray put his cigarette out, and he flicked the butt overboard. "I'll take this rust bucket over your bucketing palace in the sky any day, guv'nor." He grabbed the rail as the deck pitched under him.

"Now then, Bill—" Ryan took a good grip on the rail himself and looked at Bill closely. "Are you ready to go down? I'm informed that the wind's dropping; in an hour the sea will be just calm enough for the launching."

Bill swallowed. He looked out to sea at the other two platform ships and the retreating shape of the *Olympian* as it headed back to New York for supplies. The platform ships were modified barges, linked by chains and buoys, marking out a square half mile of sea. It was an enormous enterprise. He had to do his part and accept going down in the bathysphere. He had been expecting this, but he wasn't eager. "Ready, Mr. Ryan. Always ready, me."

He expected to change into a diving suit or something aquatic, but an hour later they went as they were, both of them in overcoats—Ryan's cut of the best material, precisely tailored. The bathysphere was hoisted onto the deck, steadied by the stoic crewmen in their rubber slickers and sou'westers as Ryan and Bill got in. It was roomy enough for two inside, with a window in the hatch and small ports on the sides. The smell was a bit like a locker room, but it was comfortably padded and equipped with handholds. Between them was a bank of controls and gauges. Ryan didn't seem concerned with them as the bathysphere was hoisted up, lowered over the side, and released.

A light switched on inside as the sea closed over them . . .

Bill, licking his lips, waited for Ryan to somehow pilot the vessel. But he didn't. He simply sat back, smiling mischievously, seeming amused by Bill's transparent attempt at appearing unworried. They sank deeper and deeper.

Then the bathysphere stopped with a slight jolt and began to move horizontally of its own accord.

"It's radio controlled," Ryan explained, at last, "we don't have to do a thing. It follows an underwater radio signal to the entrance shaft, uses turbine props. You will experience no discomfort from increased air pressure—there isn't any increased air pressure needed. The same will hold true in Rapture itself. There is no danger of the bends. We have a new method for constantly equalizing air pressure at any depth with no special gasses. It will be almost always exactly the same as on the surface, with only minor variations."

Bill looked at him skeptically. "Air pressure always the same—at any depth?"

Ryan gave him a mysterious smile, leveraging the opportunity to brag a bit. "We have gone to great lengths to keep our discoveries to ourselves. I have found some of the most unusual, extraordinarily talented scientists in the world, Bill—and in some very difficult spots." He peered through a porthole, smiling absently. "The hardest one to get at was this quite peculiar but brilliant fellow, name of Suchong—he was stuck in Korea during the Japanese occupation. The Japs had accused him of selling their men opium to pay for his experiments. Imperialists have such a narrow view of things. Ah, speaking of marvels, you can just see the foundations of Rapture there, before we go into the dome shaft . . . And let us have some appropriate music . . ."

Bill bent and peered through the port. Below them, electric lights glowed through the blue gloom along the rocky bottom of the sea—lines of lights like landing markers for a plane on a foggy night. He saw the rugged outlines of what might be a decayed volcanic crater, like a miniature mountain range, around a mysterious electrical glow. The music kicked in: Gershwin's *Rhapsody in Blue,* the Grofé arrangement for piano and symphony flowing from hidden speakers in the bathysphere. As the rhapsodic music swelled, Bill made out structures looming through the dark blue water beyond the stony natural ramparts: the frameworks of elegant buildings, the panels of unfinished walls, the silhouette of what might be a statue, tilting as it waited to be craned into place.

"The genius of the Wales brothers," Ryan said, as more mighty, soaring structures came into view. "Simon and Daniel. Ironic, really, their starting with cathedrals and coming to build Rapture. But Simon says that Rapture *will* be a great cathedral—but not to God. To man's will!"

"How'd you get the foundations done?" Bill asked, peering through the viewport. "That had to be a great challenge."

"We retrofitted my steamer the *Olympian,* fixed it up to take cargo—and we brought the sinker out here and put it together. It's a big submersible platform. We'd lower it to the bottom with the deep-sea team and everything they needed. It's there permanently—absorbs vibration, offers insulation, for the biggest central section of Rapture . . . Brought in the platform ships for the next stages . . ."

A small submarine equipped with mechanical arms glided by the construction site . . .

"You can see the remains of a very ancient volcanic cone," Ryan went on, pointing. "That's a clue about Rapture's energy source. You see that dark spot there, to one side—that's the opening of a deep crevice, a real abyss—but the city's foundations rest on solid rock. It's quite secure."

And then the panorama vanished, swallowed up in shadow. The music continued as they dipped into the dark, vertical entrance shaft leading down to the dome. It was as if they were going down a chimney. The descent was sickeningly fast and smooth until they bumped against the concrete and steel sides of the water-filled shaft with an alarming clang. A metallic squeal came as a hatch in the shaft shut above them. A shivering *clunk*—and they came to a complete halt. They were in an air lock, Bill reckoned, as the water drained away. A mechanical grating sound and another metallic screech— and the hatch of the bathysphere opened.

"Come along, Bill!" Ryan switched off the music and climbed out through the hatch.

Bill followed and found himself in a short metal-ribbed passage of rough concrete. Electric lights burned overhead. The smell of the sea mingled with the smell of new cement.

Two strides along the short passage, then a metal door swung open for them and there was Dr. Greavy, in a long work coat and metal construction helmet. Greavy's mouth trembled as he gazed at Ryan. He backed away, to let Ryan enter the sizable hemispherical room, like a courtier backing away from a sovereign.

"This is an honor, sir," Greavy sputtered, "but really, it's a bit too risky—"

"Risky!" Ryan said, looking around. "Nonsense! Bill, he's trying to keep me out of here!" But Ryan was chuckling as he looked around at the equipment in the dome.

"Only until we have more safety structures in place—McDonagh understands."

"I'm here now, Greavy," Ryan said, "and I mean to have a look around. I am sinking my life into this project, and I need to see it flourishing. Is Simon here?"

"Not here, sir, he's in sub three."

"Let him do his work. You can show us around." The dome was about two hundred feet in diameter, about thirty-five feet to the ceiling in the center, which was supported by a grid of metal girders. To Bill the girders looked like steel, but he knew if they were only steel they'd all be buried under a mountain of saltwater. He supposed they must be made of some special alloy.

Bill recognized some of the big, wheeled machines crowded into the room: routers as big as small cars, mining drills, scoops and cranes, many of them still dripping water; some, adapted for deep-sea use, looked strange to him. One machine was about twenty feet long, with enormous pincers at the ends of the jointed arms, like the ones on the submarine.

"What's that thing do?" Bill asked, pointing to it.

"The mechanical gripper?" Greavy said. "That's one of our basic workhorses. Remote controlled. It's a concept that came out of weapons development in the war."

"Right—like the teletanks the Russians use. Didn't work out so well, them things."

"Our remote control is reliable—like the bathysphere you

came in. Remote-controlled machines speed up construction. Very difficult to set up the foundations of Rapture in this deep cold water otherwise. We have a good deal of the Hephaestus level set up already—and indeed geological energy is already flowing into the finished units . . ."

Greavy glanced at Ryan for approval before continuing. Ryan nodded, and Greavy went on: "It's heat-driven electrical energy drawn from volcanic sources under the sea floor— hot springs and fumaroles, sulfur chimneys, and the like. 'Geothermal' some call it. A virtually endless source of power. Wonderful, isn't it? No coal needed, no oil!" Greavy said, rubbing his hands together gleefully. "Once the supply line is set up, the energy flow goes on as long as the earth retains its heat!"

"We have twelve domes like this one arrayed around the site," Ryan added proudly. "We sank them, pumped them out. Pipe in clean air. The domes are all connected by tunnels we've built right on top of the seabed."

"Not sure I believe it, guv," Bill said, staring at the big gripper, "and here I am looking at it!"

Ryan chuckled. "Then you shall see it up close! Greavy— ask Wallace to take us in for a closer look!"

~~~~~~~~

Roland Wallace was a bearded, dour man of about forty with deep-set eyes and a furrowed brow. Ryan introduced him. "This is a man you can count on to get things done in tough conditions."

Wallace led them to a large steel door, one of three placed symmetrically around the dome. He checked a couple of dials on a panel beside the door, nodded to himself, and spun the wheel. He grunted as it swung open into a tunnel made of some amalgam pocked by vents and ribbed in metal. "Now if you gentlemen will wait to the side here . . ."

They pressed against the wall to the right, Ryan with an

expression of proprietary pride. After a minute, the battery-powered gripper drove slowly through the doorway, whirring to itself. Affixed to its rear was a small cockpit, where Wallace drove, the gripper's jointed, black-metal arms retracted; behind him came a little radio-slaved tram, reminding Bill of a small funicular without the cable. It seemed to be driving itself—and it stopped in front of Ryan and Bill when the gripper stopped.

"Step in," Ryan said, and they climbed into the leather-mesh seats of the shuttle, side by side. The gripper moved off, and the little shuttle followed.

They passed under the electric lights of the tunnel for what seemed a quarter mile when suddenly a killer whale flashed overhead, its toothy mouth agape. Bill recoiled. "Oi!"

Ryan laughed dryly. "Look closer!"

Bill leaned out of the tram and saw that the walls here were transparent—they were a heavy, polished glass of some kind banded with metal. Light shone upward from electric lamps on the seabed outside the transparent section. He could see the tunnel, mostly cement, occasionally glass, wending out across the seabed toward the framework of Rapture. The foundations of Rapture stood out in shades of dark green and indigo.

"It's hard to reckon where the water stops and the glass starts—it's like we're in the water with 'em!" Bill muttered. A diffuse shimmer from the surface far above answered the glow from the seabed lamps. Schools of fish emerged from billowing forests of green kelp and purple sea fans: tuna, cod, and fish he couldn't identify, gleaming with iridescence, threading in and out of light and shadow. A squid pulsed by and then another great black-and-white orca swept by. Bill was awestruck. "Look at that bloody thing! Fast as a swallow but big enough to swallow a man! It's flyin' right over us!"

"Wonderful, isn't it?" Ryan mused, gazing through the curving, transparent pane as they rolled along. "Fairly obvious, looking out at a glorious prospect like this one, why I'm calling the city *Rapture*! Of course, I've always had a fascination with the deep sea. It's another world—a *free* world! For years I read of giant squid netted from the depths, the adventures of explorers in diving bells and bathyspheres, strange things sighted by submariners. The thrilling potential of it all! I detest the warmongering of the 'Great Powers'—but world wars did generate workable submarines . . ."

"Nothing but glass, holding out all that water?" Bill marveled. "We're down fair deep! All that bloody great pressure . . . !"

"I'm not ready to share all my secrets with you yet, Bill, but that is in fact a perfect merging of glass—and metal. Something new called submolecular bonding. Astonishingly pressure resistant. Expensive, but worth every cent."

The two vehicles paused under the curving transparent pane of the tunnel, and Bill gazed into the shaded blue distances of the sea. He glimpsed great shadowy shapes swimming along out there, murk-veiled outlines not quite definable—appearing and vanishing. An object on the seabed about five hundred yards away gave off a faint red glow.

"What's that—glowing, over there?"

"That's our geothermal energy valve," said Ryan. "We lost three men setting it up," he added casually. "But now it seems quite secure . . ."

"Three men lost?" Bill looked at him, suddenly feeling what a deep, cold place this was. "How many have died working out here?"

"Oh, not so many. Why, when they built the Panama Canal, Bill—how many do you think died there?"

Bill thought back to his reading as he watched the silhouette of a bathysphere drifting by overhead. "If I recall, the French lost about fifteen thousand men. When the Americans finished the job, another five thousand died."

Ryan nodded briskly. "Risk, Bill—nothing is built without risk. Build an ordinary house and lay the foundations a few inches wrong, the whole thing might collapse on you. Men died for the canal. Men died in the building of great bridges, died attempting to scale the highest mountains. Pioneers died crossing deserts. But we don't take *pointless* risks. We are observing safety precautions—we don't wish to lose skilled workers. Ah"—Ryan pointed— "look there."

Bill saw something like a giant lobster flying over, fifty feet long. Then it passed from a patch of dimness into the glow around the edges of Rapture, and he saw it was one of the smaller, specialized submarines he'd glimpsed earlier. Beams of light projected from headlights like shining eyes; its jointed, pincered mechanical arms were extended to grasp a big ornate segment of metal wall lowering on a cable.

Bill watched a gripper move up opposite it, mechanical arms poised to help ease the big metal section into place on a wall. The wall sections appeared to be sculpted, prefabricated metal pieces. Bill thought of the way the Statue of Liberty had been constructed, with the separate pieces made in Europe, then shipped to America and fitted precisely together to form the gargantuan figure.

He noticed there was no one in the small cockpit at the rear of the gripper—he could just make out the connective control cable trailing behind it.

"How does anyone see enough to control it?" he asked. "The controller watches through a window?"

Ryan smiled. "He's watching on a screen. We use a television camera on that one."

"Television! Me second cousin in the Bronx had one. Got a headache, me, when I tried to watch one of those boxes, not a week ago. Fellas caperin' about in dresses, dancing packs of cigarettes . . ."

"The technology can be used for more than entertainment," Ryan said. He pointed across the site. "One of our supply submarines . . ."

Bill saw it gliding along on the far side of Rapture's foundations: a larger submarine, without mechanical arms, that could almost have belonged to the British Navy—except that it was pulling a massive oblong shape behind it on a doubled chain. "It's towing freight in some kind of container," he remarked.

"There is a little air in the cargo bag, for buoyancy," Wallace said. "Mostly it contains some dry goods and medical supplies. All netted together."

"Costly process," Ryan said. "Off we go, Wallace . . ."

Wallace returned to the gripper, and they drove on, through tunnel after tunnel, passing through domes crowded with tool racks, machinery, tables. Here and there a lighted window looked out into the deep. Just outside a dome window a crowd of translucent pink jellyfish billowed, trailing long, delicate-looking stingers. A strong smell of sweat and old laundry was a physical presence in the domes; some were partly screened off, and Bill glimpsed men sleeping in cots back there.

"The construction goes on twenty-four hours a day, seven days a week," Ryan said. "The men work in shifts, ten hours on, fourteen off. We have a recreation dome where beer is sold, music is played, movies are shown. They showed the latest Cagney film there last week . . ."

"Fan of 'opalong Cassidy meself," Bill murmured, as they passed into another covered tunnel. A transparent panel gave a glimpse of workers in deep-sea diving suits wrestling a culvert-sized copper pipe into place.

"We'll be sure to get you some Hopalong Cassidy films to watch when you're down here," Ryan said.

"Will I be working down here a great deal, then?"

"You'll be with me in New York much of the time. And in Reykjavík. I need the perspective of someone I can trust. But we'll be down here too—I intend to supervise the next stage closely. Rapture will be my legacy. I fully expect to spend the rest of my life down here, once the city is built."

Bill tried to conceal his shock. "The *rest of your life,* guv'nor? *All* of it? Down here?"

"Oh yes. The ant society up above is not for us. And radiation from the atomic wars, when they come, will last for many years above the surface of the sea. We'll be safe down here."

That's when Bill noticed the hissing sound of wheels through water—he looked over the lower window frame of the little transport and saw two inches of water accumulated on the floor of the tunnel.

"What's that! Wallace—pull us over! Look at the floor!" The two vehicles jarred to a stop and Bill climbed out. He knew that Ryan wasn't pleased to have him suddenly giving orders, but he also instinctively knew this could be a matter of life and death. "Look there!" Bill pointed to the thin coating of water over the amalgam floor.

Wallace was getting out, flashing an electric hand torch. "What the devil! We haven't had any leaks in this section!" His eyes had grown big; his hands trembled, making the light jiggle on the wet floor.

"Didn't you say the water pressure wasn't a problem . . . ?" Bill asked, examining the curved walls of the tunnel more closely.

"Well, these tunnels aren't entirely made of the new alloy—it's tremendously expensive to make. We keep most of that back for Rapture itself. Only the support ribs . . . But they should be enough, when you consider the steel mesh in the concrete, the doubling of—"

"What's this about?" Ryan asked nervously. "Wallace—is there something I should know?"

"Need to get you back to Dome One, sir!" But Wallace, eyes flicking about, looked more scared for himself than for Ryan.

"Let's identify the problem first!" Ryan snapped.

"There!" Bill said, pointing. "You see—the support ribs, they're about a foot and a half farther apart in that spot—someone's been sloppy! The weakened support's yielding to pressure, stressing the concrete. You see? It's trickling through at the bottom . . ."

"I swear to you this flooding wasn't here two hours ago!" Wallace said, looking around desperately. "I . . . I passed through this very section! There was no leak!"

"That's bad," Bill said. "Means it's happening fast! And it's going to accelerate! We've got to get Mr. Ryan back right bloody now before it—"

A resounding, high-pitched *crick!*—and water began to sheet powerfully down from the edge of a metal rib supporting the tunnel, about forty feet down. A crack spread visibly through the ceiling, like a slithering, living thing; there was a squeal, an extended creaking sound of metal buckling.

A sizzling sound, then, followed by sparks spitting down—and several of the lights went out near the spraying, hissing leak.

Wallace backed away from it—bumping into the little funicular where Ryan was staring down the tunnel.

Bill grabbed Wallace's arm, squeezed it hard to snap him out of his panic. "Wallace, listen—this thing I came here in, can it go back without the gripper?"

"Yes, yes, there's a switch, I can reverse it—but there's not room for three men, and I doubt it could carry so much weight, it's not meant for—"

"Quiet and listen! Get in it, take Mr. Ryan back to the next dome! Soon as you get there, communicate with the other domes—there must be some kind of public address system—"

"Yes, yes—there is—" Wallace was staring aghast at the sheets of water shooshing down, spraying hard on the tunnel floor, driving water to surge against their ankles.

"Tell them to seal off the domes connected to this tunnel!"

"What about you?" Ryan asked.

"Someone can watch for me—and if there's time they can let me through! I'm going to work up a temporary support to slow this down! *Go!*"

"Right! Right, I . . ." Wallace jumped into the little transport beside Ryan and flicked a switch.

Bill just had a glimpse of Ryan's appalled face looking back at him as the transport lurched off down the tunnel the way they'd come.

He turned and ran splashing through deepening water, up to his shins now, to the idling gripper. He climbed into the cockpit, aware of the strengthening smell of brine and a kind of fog thickening in the tunnel. Mist rose from the swirling, swishing flood. In the wan light of the gripper cockpit he found a series of switches, levers, a small steering wheel, a gearshift, an accelerator pedal . . .

Bill flicked the toggle on a switch labeled Grip, and the mechanical arms extended and opened their pincers in front of him, like a lobster warning off a rival. Two levers jutting beside the steering wheel seemed to control the arms . . .

The rising water was already seeping into the cockpit when he worked out how to manipulate the mechanical arms. Bill leaned out of the cockpit, peering upward in the muted light, and made out the spot he was looking for before another two overhead lights sparked, sizzled, and went out. He shifted gears and drove the gripper forward a few yards, leaving a wake in the water behind him as cold brine gathered around his ankles.

God send the gripper mechanism didn't short-circuit before he could do the job.

The sounds of metal creaking were becoming ominously loud . . .

Bill took a deep breath and then manipulated the arms so that they bent at the nearest joints, angling sharply upward. He forced them hard against the ceiling, just where the water was spraying through. And the leak slackened. It was still coming, but not so fast.

He noted a switch marked Hold and flicked it. The gripper's arms went rigid, holding in place, but already he could see the mechanical arms shivering, starting to buckle . . .

Heart thudding, he clambered quickly out, knocking his head against the metal cockpit in his hurry. "Bloody buggerin' *fuck!*" Bill grabbed a spanner from a toolbox at the back of the gripper and hurried down the tunnel, splashing through shadow toward the lights, the saltwater above his knees now.

Another squealing sound from behind . . . the sea was going to crash through and flood the tunnel—damn quick too. But he might have the leak slowed down just enough to see to it Mr. Ryan got to safety. He wasn't optimistic about his own chances.

Then he was in a lighted area of the tunnel, sloshing as fast as he could around a curve—and seeing a steel doorway up ahead in the recessed arch of a dome entrance. He splashed up to it, almost falling again. No window in this door, no intercom grid. The door was equipped with a wheel that could be used to open it—but he didn't dare unless they judged it safe. They'd have water-pressure gauges. They'd know better than he would. He couldn't risk all those lives for his own. He'd brought the spanner to let them know he was here—and used it to bang hard on the door. He heard faint voices on the other side, but couldn't make out exactly what they were saying. It sounded like an argument.

He looked over his shoulder and saw a wave rushing toward him along the tunnel. That was it, then. He was done for. He'd be toes-up in no time.

But then the door grated within itself and swung open. Water rushed past his knees into the dome. "No!" he shouted. "Close it! No time! Don't let the water in!"

But strong arms were circling him, Ryan dragging him into the bright lights and human smells of the dome. Bill turned and, with Ryan and Wallace, took hold of the handle on the door, and pulled. The water flow was with them, helping them slam the big metal door shut. They got it closed only a moment before the big wave rushing down the tunnel struck it with a dull booming . . .

"Good lord but that was close," Wallace said, panting, as the water receded about their ankles. "Thank God you're safe, Mr. Ryan!"

Ryan turned to Bill—and then they spontaneously shook hands, grinning at each other. "Don't thank God, Wallace," Ryan said. "Thank a *man*. Thank Bill McDonagh."

The Lighthouse, Rapture
1947

It was a chilly, breezy early evening as Andrew Ryan stepped off the launch. Ryan gestured for his bodyguards and coxswain to wait in the boat, then turned and climbed the steps of the great lighthouse structure. It was modeled on ancient descriptions of the lighthouse of Alexandria, and it radiated that classical majesty. He paused partway up to take it all in, entranced by the tower, the surface entrance to Rapture.

He had ordained this . . . This was the manifestation of *his will* . . .

WELCOME TO RAPTURE, read the metal letters over the great, round copper-plated Securis door. To either side of the art deco entrance rose streamlined chromium figures of men, statues built into the walls, looking as if they were supporting the building, their elongated, upraised arms straining for the heights.

The door opened as he approached, and Chief Sullivan, smiling, emerged to shake his hand; along with a beaming Greavy; a wryly glum, bearded Simon Wales—and Bill McDonagh, looking a bit stunned. Ryan was glad Bill was here to see this. He had sensed doubts in Bill sometimes—now Bill would see, they'd all see, that the "impossible" was possible.

Wales nodded to Ryan, barely managing a smile. "I think you'll be pleased, Andrew." He had a mild Dublin accent. "Sure, we're nearly there . . ." The architect wore a pea jacket, a black turtleneck sweater, and black trousers, his round, balding head shiny with perspiration, his bruised-looking eyes gleaming.

They entered the high-ceilinged, hexagonal chamber, like the interior of a particularly grand observatory, their footsteps echoing on the marble floors. Intricately trimmed, picked out in precious metals, the entryway to Rapture had the spacious marble-and-gold gravitas of a capitol building's rotunda—exactly as planned. Ryan felt a certain awe, gazing up at himself—at the giant gold bust of Andrew Ryan looking gravely down at whoever entered this place. The expression was stern but not angry. It expressed authority but also objectivity. It gave notice: *Rapture would tolerate only the worthy.*

The statue seemed oddly mute, however. He would add a banner to let people entering here know that they were on the brink of a new society where men were not cramped by superstition or big government:

NO GODS OR KINGS. ONLY MAN.

He made a mental note of it. He would not forget. And why not have welcoming music playing for those entering the lighthouse? Perhaps an instrumental of "La Mer," a whimsically pertinent song.

Wales was talking about veneers and trim—"certain endemic leakage issues that have Daniel quite concerned"—but Ryan scarcely heard him. Wales was caught up in a designer's fixation on details, superficialities. It was the big picture that was thrilling, and, gazing about himself now, Ryan was almost speechless with its power.

Sullivan led the way to the bathysphere that would take them down the shaft of water, a kind of specialized elevator, into Rapture herself . . .

"After you, sir," Sullivan said.

Mouth dry with excitement, hands gently trembling, Ryan climbed into the bathysphere, the first transport in the Rapture Metro. The others followed and took their places in the small craft, knees nearly touching. It was a bit crowded, but it didn't matter. The air crackled with anticipation.

Too bad the bathysphere's television screen was blank at the moment; in time it would show a short film, "Welcome to Rapture," for those permitted secret immigration to the new undersea colony.

Down they went, bubbles in the water-filled shaft streaming past them. The bathysphere's cable creaked, but the ride was comfortable. "Runs smooth as silk, this," Bill chuckled.

Then they'd arrived at the first vantage, the lounge from which they'd view the city of Rapture. The bathysphere opened almost soundlessly.

They climbed out of the bathysphere, and Ryan clapped Bill on the shoulder. "Bill—you've been down here a lot more than I have. You'd know the best view. Lead the way!"

Simon Wales didn't seem pleased at that—but Bill had a great deal to do with the internal structure of Rapture. "Got 'er guts 'n' garters in me hands," he'd said once. And Ryan simply liked Bill McDonagh better than Wales. Though his genius was undeniable, there was something subtly unstable about the glum, spade-bearded man—as if Simon Wales were always a heartbeat from a shout that never quite burst free.

Bill grinned and made a sweeping "right this way" gesture. They struck off toward the big picture window to one side, where blue-and-green tinted light rippled across the floor . . .

Ryan stepped up to the window and gazed out at Rapture. The marvel rose up before them, seeming almost a natural outgrowth of this aquatic world, as much a part of the planet as the Himalayas. Electrically illuminated canyons of steel and glass gleamed; art deco towers soared; sunken buildings stood sturdily, dry inside; watertight skyscrapers reared without a sky in sight to scrape. The lines of Rapture's magnificent architecture seemed to rocket toward the reticulating surface of the sea, some distance above, where light and shadow played tag. A school of golden-tailed fish swam by the window like a flock of birds, glittering as they passed. A raft of sea lions gamboled by up above, silhouettes near the surface.

Base lights streamed colored rays up the sides of the building—subtle reds and greens and purples attiring the towering edifices in a royal splendor. It was as impressive as the Grand Canyon or the Swiss Alps—but it was the work of man. It took Ryan's breath away to look on it.

"Of course, it's not quite finished—but you see what man's *will* can do," Ryan said, his voice catching with emotion. In the distance, down the "street" crisscrossed with glass tunnels, an electric sign rippled with the gay life of an undersea Times Square: RYAN ENTERPRISES. The first of many electric signs that would shine within the cold, dark sea. Billboards, neon signs, all the trappings of a truly free market would be found here, both inside and outside, a shining declaration of liberty and unrestrained enterprise.

"It's a wonder, is Rapture," Bill said, huskily. "One of the wonders of the world!" Adding with a touch of regret: "Pity most of the world won't know . . ."

"Oh, in time, they will," Ryan assured him. "All who survive the destruction of the upper world—they will know Rapture! One day it will be the capital city of all civilization."

"You've done it, sir!" Greavy declared, his voice trembling with an emotion he rarely showed.

Wales glanced at Greavy. "We've done it, all of us," he said, irritated.

"Oh, it's not quite fully realized, Greavy—but it is alive," Ryan said glowingly. "A new world—where men and women will stand up on their own two feet in the glory of competition. They will empower themselves with struggle!"

Bill said, "But what about populating this miracle? Got to fill up all those buildings, guv . . ." So far, only a relatively few people lived in Rapture, mostly maintenance workers, engineers, some security.

Ryan nodded and took a folded paper from his coat pocket. "I've brought something along I wanted to share with you." He unfolded the paper and read aloud to them. "*Letter of recruitment.*" He cleared his throat and went on,

"Tired of taxes? Tired of bullying governments, business regulations, unions, people expecting a handout from you? Want a new start? Do you have a skill, an ambition to be a pioneer? If you're receiving this notice, you've already been considered and selected to fill out an application for a life in Rapture. This amazing new enterprise will require emigration. But it will cost you nothing except sweat and determination to come and take part in a new world. If our vetting team has done its job, you are

*not a trade unionist; you are a believer in free enterprise,
competition, and carving your own path through the wilderness of the world. There is room for up to twenty thousand pioneers to thrive in this new society. We ask that
you show this letter to no one, whatever your decision. If
you're interested . . ."*

Ryan shrugged and folded the letter. "Just one of our recruiting tools, discreetly distributed. An early draft . . . Of
course, Rapture's not quite ready for the bulk of its population."

"Has Prentice Mill made any progress on his Express?"
Ryan asked, turning to Wales.

Wales grunted. "Oh, that he has. Two stations completed,
a good deal of rail laid down. He's down in Sinclair Deluxe,
supervising construction." He sniffed and drew a pipe from
his coat and then stuck it in his teeth but didn't light it.
"Complains he needs more workers, of course. They all do."

"The Express is its own business," Ryan pointed out. "Let
him get busy and hire more workers himself. Those who are
finished working on the outer shell can start on the rail."

He turned to gaze out the window at Rapture again. Who
knew how long it would take to grow—this almighty expression of his will that could continue proliferating in steel and
glass and copper and Ryanium, long after Andrew Ryan himself had passed away . . .

PART TWO

The Second Age of Rapture

I believe in no God, no invisible man in the sky. But there is something more powerful than each of us, a combination of our efforts, a Great Chain of industry that unites us. But it is only when we struggle in our own interest that the chain pulls society in the right direction. The chain is too powerful and too mysterious for any government to guide. Any man who tells you different either has his hand in your pocket, or a pistol to your neck.

—*Andrew Ryan*

6

Standing on the stage with Ryan, Bill McDonagh exulted in Ryan's speech as it boomed through Apollo Square. Rapture rose in sturdy magnificence around them.

"To build a city at the bottom of the sea! Insanity! But look around you, my friends!" Andrew Ryan's voice boomed, with only a little feedback squeal. Wearing a caramel-colored double-breasted suit, his freshly barbered hair slicked back, Ryan seemed to emanate personality from the podium. Bill could *feel* Ryan there, to his left—and the almost frighteningly deep conviction in his tone kept his listeners riveted. The crowd of more than two thousand seemed a bit stunned by their surroundings when they'd first come. Now Bill could see them nodding, the pride shining from their faces, as Ryan told them they were a unique people in a unique place—each one of them with a chance to make their own destiny within the walls of Rapture. Those at the front were mostly the moneyed patricians, eccentrics, and pioneering professionals Ryan had recruited. The determined blue-collar types milled at the back of the crowd.

Hands clasped in front of him, Bill stood to Ryan's right and as close to Elaine as propriety allowed. Beside Bill and Elaine stood Greavy, Sullivan, Simon and Daniel Wales, Prentice Mill, Sander Cohen, and Ryan's new "personal assistant," the statuesque beauty Diane McClintock. She looked like she fancied herself a queen. Bill had heard she was originally some cigarette girl Ryan had picked up—and now she was putting on airs.

Under the bunting-swathed stage overlooking the square, a tape recorder took down Ryan's speech. He planned to record all his speeches and put edited sections of them out as "inspirational talks" on public address throughout Rapture.

"But where else," Ryan demanded, "could we be free from the clutching hands of parasites?" His deep voice resonated in the gleaming windows looking out to the shadowy, light-shafted depths of the sea. Bill nudged Elaine and nodded toward the windows as a school of large fish swam up to the glass. The fish seemed to be taking in the speech, ogling Ryan as if awestruck. She hid a smile behind her hand. Bill wanted to take that hand and kiss it, draw his new fiancée away from this pensive crowd, up to the privacy of his apartment in Olympus Heights—celebrate the culmination of so much hard work with another sort of climax. But he had to be satisfied with winking at her, as Ryan went portentously on: "Where else could we build an economy that they would not try to control, a society that they would not try to destroy? It was not impossible to build Rapture at the bottom of the sea! It was impossible to build it anywhere else!"

"Hear hear!" Greavy said, leading a patter of applause.

"The *ant society* misunderstands the nature of true cooperation!" Ryan boomed. "True cooperation is enlightened self-interest, not grubbing parasitism! True cooperation is not based on the bloodsucking that the parasites call 'taxation'! True cooperation is people working together—each for their own profit! A man's self-interest is at the root of all that he accomplishes! But there is something more powerful than each of us: a combination of our efforts, *a Great Chain of industry* that unites us. It is only when we struggle in our own interest that the chain pulls society in the right direction.

The chain is too powerful and too mysterious for any government to guide. The Great Chain may sound mystical . . ." Ryan shook his head contemptuously. "It is not! Some would imagine the hand of their so-called God behind every mystery! The best of human nature, the laws of natural selection—such is the power behind the Great Chain, not God! We need no gods or kings in Rapture! Only man! Here, man and woman will be rewarded with the sweat of their brows. Here, without interference, we will prove that society can order itself with unfettered competition, with unfettered free enterprise—with unfettered research! I have scientists in Rapture working on new discoveries that will astound you—and the persecution of the small-minded is all that kept those discoveries from happening till now. Science will advance without the oversight of pompous tyrants who would impose their personal view of 'morality' on us." He cleared his throat and smiled, his tone becoming friendly, fatherly. "And now, in celebration of the opening day of Rapture—a song performed by Sander Cohen, written by Miss Anna Culpepper . . ." Anna Culpepper was an unfinished English major, a naïve but ambitious young woman whom Ryan had recruited out of her third year in college and who fancied herself a lyricist.

Wearing a tux, the impish performer stepped up to the microphone. Bill winced. Cohen got on his nerves.

From somewhere canned music played, and Cohen sang along.

"The paradox of our city
is the freedom of the chain,
the chain that holds youuuu
to meeeee,
a chain that oh so strangely, so very strangely,
Sets me at lib-er-tyyyy—
As the blue world scintillates

outside our gates,
and the fish gyrate and the lovely, lovely ocean awaits . . ."

It was a sluggish number, taking a long time to reach its chorus, and Bill lost interest, letting his attention wander to the majesty of Apollo Square, Rapture's "Grand Central Station" . . .

Rapture's architecture and design was a fusion of the style of the World's Fair of 1934—an event that had a great impact on Andrew Ryan—and the industrial grandiosity of "The Art of the Great Chain." To either side of the stage, heroic statues of electroplated bronze, forty feet high—the elongated forms of sleek, muscular, idealized men—stretched their arms toward the heights as if straining for godhood. To Bill they looked a bit like giant hood ornaments, but he'd never say as much to Ryan, who loved that sort of art. Bill had been a trifle taken aback the first time he'd seen a towering statue of Ryan, like the one at the other end of the big room—there were many about Rapture, the figures looming magisterially, seeming to embody an iron determination. In Apollo Square, relief images of lines of men—cheerfully pulling chains—decorated the walls. Everywhere was *art decoratif* trimming, often shaped like rays of light emanating from glistening knobs, intricate borders evoking both the industrial scale of the modern world and the temples of Babylon and Egypt.

As the song droned on, Bill felt suddenly giddy, riding an inner rush of amazement at what he'd helped build. The Waleses had created the look and feel of Rapture, but he and Greavy had built its flesh, its bones, its inner workings—and Ryan was its animating "soul." They'd done it with the help of all those men who'd labored in the tunnels, under the sea— who'd risked their lives in the completed, watertight sections of Rapture, levels built from Hephaestus to Olympus Heights.

Rapture was a reality: a small city, three miles to a side so far, rising from the depths to tower over the deep seabed.

Rapture. *They'd really done it!* Oh, there weren't enough maintenance workers, there were still more heating ducts to be put in, still pipe to be laid in some levels. So far, only three of the five geothermal turbines were running in Hephaestus. Slow seepage was a problem in some areas. But Rapture was real: a man had conceived it, funded it at gigantic cost— spending the kind of money that small countries spent every year—and saw it through to completion. It was breathtaking.

He looked over at Sullivan, who always seemed gloomy, worried. Rumors were still rampant about G-men sniffing around in New York, wondering if Ryan was dodging taxation on some new project.

Some of the faces in the crowd seemed pinched with a vague anxiety of their own, were staring restlessly around at their strange new habitat. A lot of Rapture's people were high-tone types, moneyed or formerly moneyed nobs who'd become disaffected with society. They'd come here looking for a new start and liking the fact that a wealthy man like Ryan had offered them one.

Bill hoped it was all worth it. So much was sacrificed down here. Like the time he'd seen three men boiled alive setting up the geothermal central heating. The volcanically heated water in the feed pipes had been released at too high a pressure—something he'd tried to warn Wallace about— and the pressure burst a pipe joint. Superheated water gushed to fill a room in seconds. Barely got out in time himself. Wallace should have known better after that close call the first day in the domes. Bill had felt those deaths hard—he'd watched the men die through a port, and the sight had given him nightmares for a week.

That first accident, though, in the dome tunnel, had cemented Bill's relationship with Ryan. He had saved Andrew Ryan's life—and Ryan had rewarded him with a nice raise, for one thing.

But he wondered if money really meant the same thing down here. Initially most of the inhabitants of Rapture were required to change their money for Rapture dollars, some percentage kept by Ryan to pay for maintenance services. And what would happen to a man when his Rapture dollars ran out? People couldn't wire out for money—or even send letters out of Rapture. Did they really understand how sealed off from the outside world they were?

The song ended, and Elaine reached over, giving Bill's hand a discreet squeeze. Long as Elaine was there, Bill was happy. It didn't matter where they were.

He had helped build something glorious, something unprecedented. Sure, Rapture was untried, was a glaringly new idea. A gigantic experiment. But they'd planned Rapture down to the last detail. How badly could it go wrong?

The North Atlantic
1948

A raw morning on the North Atlantic. Broken light slanted fitfully through silver-gray clouds. Wind snapped the tops off waves, smacking packets of saltwater into the men manning the decks of the six Fontaine's Fisheries trawlers. The man who now called himself Fontaine had invested some of his own cash, and somewhat to his surprise he'd made a success of Fontaine's Fisheries, selling tons of fish to Ryan's project—and to Reykjavík. Cold comfort, so to speak.

Frank Fontaine—formerly Frank Gorland—could see the peculiar little tower rising tantalizingly from the waves, a quarter mile off. Beyond it were two ships, one of them the platform ship with its winches and hoists. Slabs of ice still floated about the trawler, brightly white against the green-blue water.

The object was to get from up here—to *down there*—to get safely into the city marked by that anomalous lighthouse. The first time Rapture's buyers had come to his trawlers to purchase fish, he'd given them a letter to take down to Ryan.

To the Overseer of the Undersea Colony: The commerce between us has made me aware of your enterprise, & I have inferred something of its heroic scope. I have always yearned to be a frontiersman, & an appreciation for the mysteries of the deep draws me to offer you my services. I have a plan for harvesting fish underwater using modified submarines. Up above, this idea is dismissed as "crackpot." I hope that you, clearly a forward thinker, will be more open-minded to this innovation in enterprise. Accordingly, I request your permission to relocate to your colony and develop my subaquatic fishery.

Yours Sincerely, Frank Fontaine.

In fact, he'd sent variations of the same letter with three different deliveries to Rapture.

Standing at the prow of the pitching deck of the trawler, unscrewing the top of his flask, Frank Fontaine asked himself: *Am I after fish—or a wild goose?* Sure, he always dreamed about a big-paying long con, but this one was threatening to go on indefinitely—and though it was afternoon and supposedly summer, it was cold as a son of a bitch out here. Made a witch's tit seem like a hot toddy. Was it worth giving up Gorland—becoming Fontaine?

A city under the sea. It was becoming an obsession.

Fontaine looked up at the streaming charcoal-colored

clouds, wondered if it was going to storm again. Just being on this damn tub was too much like work.

Talking to the men who picked up the fish for Rapture's food supply, Fontaine had confirmed that Ryan had indeed built some gigantic underwater habitat, a kind of free-market utopia—and Fontaine knew what happened with utopias. Look at the Soviets—all those fine words about the proletariat had turned into gulags and breadlines. But a "utopia" was pure opportunity for a man like him. When this undersea utopia fell apart, he'd be there, with a whole society to feast on. Long as he didn't step too hard on Ryan's toes, he could build up an organization, get away with a pile of loot.

But he had to get down to Rapture first . . .

The trawler lurched, and so did Fontaine's stomach.

A small craft was being lowered over the side of the platform ship—a thirty-foot gig. Men descended the ladder and clambered aboard it. When it started motoring toward the trawlers, almost a quarter mile away, it was bristling with men, rifles glinting in their hands.

But he hadn't come this far to run. He waited as his crew lined up behind him. Peach Wilkins, his first mate, came to the rail. "Doesn't look good, boss," Wilkins said as the launch came steadily closer. "What they need all those guns for?"

"Don't worry about it," Fontaine said, trying to sound more confident than he felt.

The launch cut through the tossing waves and then came about to ease up against the trawler's starboard side. A man in early middle age, wearing a top coat, rubber boots and leather gloves, climbed the ladder and swung aboard, followed by two burly, watchful younger men in watch caps and slickers, rifles on straps over their shoulders.

Looking chilly and gray-faced, the older man braced himself on the bucking deck and looked Fontaine up and down.

"Name's Sullivan, chief of security for Ryan Industries. You're Frank Fontaine. Am I right?"

Fontaine nodded. "That's me. Owner and operator, Fontaine's Fisheries."

"Mr. Ryan's been watching your operation out here. Seen you build it up, edge out the competition—make a success of it. And you've done a good job supplying us. But you're nosy. You've been asking questions about what's down below—" He hooked a thumb at the sea and grinned unpleasantly. "You even bribed some of our platform workers with booze . . ."

"I just want to be part of what you're building down there. I sent several letters—"

"Sure, we got the letters. Mr. Ryan's read 'em." Sullivan looked the trawler over. "You got anything left to drink on this boat, besides water?"

Fontaine took out the flask, passed it over. "Help yourself . . ."

Sullivan opened the flask, drank deeply. He passed it back empty.

"Listen," Fontaine said. "I'll do what I have to—anything it takes to make my way . . . in Rapture."

Sullivan pursed his lips. "You know—once you go where Mr. Ryan is, you ain't coming back. You live there; you work there. Maybe you do real good there. But you *don't leave there*. There ain't a whole lot of rules. But that's one of them. And that takes commitment, Fontaine. You ready for that?"

Fontaine looked out to sea, as if he were thinking, puzzling out some great truth. Then he nodded to himself. There'd been a kid at the orphanage—whenever the nuns asked him if he wanted to please God, the kid had looked at them, all mistylike. The kid had ended up a priest. Fontaine put that simple, misty-eyed *belief* on his own face. And he said, "All the way, Chief."

Sullivan gave him a long, close look—and then grunted.

"Well—Mr. Ryan liked your letters. And he's inclined to offer you a place in Rapture. Says you've earned it, sticking at your vigil out here. I guess we're taking a chance on you. Same offer goes for your men."

"So—when do we go? Down to Rapture, I mean . . ."

Sullivan chuckled and turned to look at the sea, then nodded to himself. "Right now."

And at exactly that moment, the crew of the trawler gasped and pointed—seeing a submarine suddenly rise to the surface in a roaring wash of froth just forty yards off the port bow.

7

"So what's your problem with this Tenenbaum woman?" Chief Sullivan asked. He shifted in the stiff little straight-backed chair across from Sinclair's desk. Glaringly visible through the big round window behind the desk, a SINCLAIR SOLUTIONS sign glowed in red-gold neon outside, against the indigo backdrop of the sea.

Augustus Sinclair rubbed his clean-shaven chin at that, as if he wasn't sure of the answer himself. The pharmaceuticals investor was a trim, darkly handsome half-Panamanian in his thirties, with a faint line of mustache. You had to look close to see the mustache wasn't just penciled in. "Well—she's been working for us, development, see. Me, I don't understand exactly what she's working on—something to do with heredity I gather—but I'm a big booster of science. That's one reason Andrew asked me down here, I guess. That's where the money is—new inventions, new drugs. Why, if a man can . . ."

"We were talking about Brigid Tenenbaum," Sullivan reminded him. Sinclair had a tendency to rattle on. And it was almost five o'clock. Ryan's security chief was looking forward to a half bottle of what passed for Scotch in Rapture, which he had stashed in his apartment.

"This Tenenbaum," Sinclair said, running a finger along the negligible line of his mustache, "she's a damn peculiar woman and . . . I just want to make sure that if she's working for us, she's not breaking any rules around here. She had her own lab, for a while, financed by a couple of interests around Rapture, and those guys dropped her like a hot potato. See, word got out she used to do experiments on people for this doctor of Hitler's. Vivisections and—I don't even want to think about it. Now, we do some human experiments at Sinclair—you got to—but we don't kill people off. We don't force 'em. We pay 'em good. If a man's hair turns orange and he starts acting like a monkey for a week or two, why it doesn't do him no harm in the long run . . ."

Sullivan started to laugh—then realized that Sinclair wasn't joking.

"But Tenenbaum," Sinclair went on, "she's taking blood from people by the bucket—and more'n one of them collapsed."

"You afraid you're doing something . . . unethical?" This was a word that didn't get too much use in Rapture.

Sinclair blinked. "Hm? Unethical? Hell, Chief, I've been on the same page as Andrew about altruism, all that stuff, for years. Why do you think I was brought in so early? Worrying about ethics—I don't do it. I came here to strike it rich; you won't catch me blowing my last bubble for any other personage—" He jabbed a finger at Sullivan to emphasize the words: " —plural or singular. I read every issue of *Popular Science and Mechanics* front to back—I'm a hard charger behind the Rapture science philosophy. But . . ."

"Yes?"

"Well, there's *some* rules here, ain't there? I just feel like people might get up in arms if we go too far. I'm not sure this Tenenbaum isn't likely to do that. Or that other fellow, Suchong . . ."

"We got detention for troublemakers—but they've got to be, say, outright murderers. Thieves. Rape. Major smuggling. Stuff like that. We're strict about watertight integrity—and about leaving Rapture. But apart from that . . ." Sullivan shrugged. "Not much in the way of laws. Fella opened a shop called Rapture Grown Coca the other day. Grows his own coca bushes under some kinda red lights. I'm hearing he makes cocaine from the leaves. Or claims he does. Might be anything in those syringes. Gave me a bit of a turn, seeing the people come out of there—looked like they might get up to any goddamn thing. But Ryan's all right with it. So I guess taking a bit of extra blood . . . long as it's voluntary . . ." He shrugged. "Isn't a problem."

"Yeah. Well I hope it isn't." Sinclair shook his head. "My old man was sure we got to do things for the greater good—and what happened? I don't hold with worrying about anything but number one. Still—I don't want to get the public up in arms neither. You hear any rumblings like that? People talking . . . unions? That kind of thing?"

Sullivan had been thinking about his Scotch, but this stopped him. "You heard something, I take it? Mr. Ryan worries constantly about Communist infiltrators."

"Some rumors from our maintenance guys. Heard 'em talking about that place the workers have made up for themselves, down below. Not much more than a shacktown. Who knows what goes on down there?"

Sullivan pulled a paper and pencil from his coat. "Got any names for me?"

Sinclair opened a desk drawer, took out a pint bottle. "A few. Care for a drink, Chief? It's that time of day. This is from my own Sinclair Spirits distillery. Very good, if I do say so myself . . ."

"Augustus, you're a man after my own heart. You pour; I'll write . . ."

Lower Wharf, Neptune's Bounty
1949

Andrew Ryan had an odd feeling as he looked up at the sign that read, FONTAINE'S FISHERIES. He and Chief Sullivan watched two burly workmen on stepladders hanging it from the ceiling of the lower wharf area. Ryan didn't believe in omens, in anything supernatural. But there was something about that fisheries sign that bothered him. Frank Fontaine had installed an office, a conveyor belt for fish, big freezers for long-term storage down below. Nothing unexpected.

But the feeling of vague dread returned every time Ryan looked at the neon sign—and it seemed to increase, becoming an inner shudder, as the neon sign was switched on. A nice-looking sign, really, with *FONTAINE'S* in electric-blue neon, *FISHERIES* in glowing yellow, under a neon fish shining against the wooden backdrop.

"Seen enough of Neptune's Bounty, boss?" Sullivan asked, glancing at his pocket watch. It was cold in here—they could see their breath—and they'd been inspecting new businesses for hours, trying to get a sense of what was taking root in Rapture.

Ryan heard a splash of water on the pylons nearby and glanced over to see a small tugboat-style vessel pulling up at the wharf, the smoke from its engine sucking into vents on the low ceiling. The lower wharf was an interior space designed to look exterior, with shallow water around the jutting wooden dock and the occasional boat from neighboring chambers where fish and other goods were off-loaded. Another peculiarity of Rapture—a boat that wasn't a submarine, putting around deep under the surface of the sea.

"Mr. Ryan, how are you sir?"

Ryan turned back to Fontaine's Fisheries to see Frank Fontaine standing at the open door, hands in pockets, dressed in a yellow overcoat and three-piece tailored suit, black shoes decked out in spats, bald head shining in the blue light from his sign—Fontaine's own name glowing over his head. Stepping out beside him, smoking a cigarette and squinting past the smoke, was the thuggish bodyguard Fontaine had brought in recently—Reggie something. Reggie was looking at Sullivan with a kind of smirking contempt.

Ryan nodded politely. "Fontaine. You seem to be settling in, all right. I like the fisheries' sign. Neon brightens Rapture up."

Fontaine nodded, glancing up at the sign. "Sure. Just like the forty-deuce. I help you, Mr. Ryan? I was just about to check on my fishing sub . . ."

"Ah, yes. The fishing subs—I like to keep tabs on them myself."

"That right? Got you worried?" Fontaine's tone was cool, a little mockery behind the respect.

"Rapture leaks enough," Ryan said, wryly. "We don't want too much coming in—or too much slipping out. Nobody comes or goes without our authorization."

"For a place that likes to keep the rules down, Rapture's sure got a lot of 'em," Reggie muttered.

"We've got only as many rules as we need," Ryan said. "No robbery. And nobody leaves Rapture—or brings in stuff we don't want here. No outside product or religion—no Bibles, 'holy' books of any kind. Luxury goods—we're going to make our own, soon's we can. No letters, no correspondence with the outside world. Secrecy is our protection."

"I couldn't miss the contraband rules." Fontaine chuckled. "Being as you posted them in my office, in big black letters. Or your man there did."

Sullivan grunted to himself.

"I think you understand me," Ryan said, carefully keeping his tone civil. "The fisheries could be a weak link . . ." Ryan hesitated, choosing his words carefully. Fontaine was a forceful entrepreneur, and Ryan liked that. He'd even outbid Ryan Enterprises for some shop space. All in the spirit of Rapture.

But Ryan needed to let Fontaine know where the boundaries were. "The only thing a fisherman should bring to Rapture is fish."

Fontaine winked—flashing a smile. "We have no trouble identifying what's fish and what isn't, Mr. Ryan. There's the smell. The scales."

Reggie laughed softly.

Ryan cleared his throat. "We're all individuals here, Fontaine. But we're also part of the Great Chain of industry . . . The Great Chain unites us when we struggle in our own interest. If anyone breaks that chain by bringing in contraband, that's a weak link. Even ideas can be contraband . . ."

Fontaine smiled. "The most dangerous kind, Mr. Ryan."

"I do wish you luck, and a prosperous business," Ryan said.

"Might feel more like I'm part of things if you invited me to join the Rapture Council," Fontaine said mildly, lighting a cigar with a gold lighter. "Care for a smoke?"

"No. Thank you." Ryan examined the cigar. "I presume that is a Rapture-made cigar?"

"Naturally." Fontaine raised the cigar for Ryan to see.

Ryan smiled noncommittally. "You perhaps have the impression the council is some grand, powerful organization. It's a very loose commission to oversee enterprise, keep a bit of an eye on things without interfering. Time consuming, to be honest." Ryan wasn't enthusiastic about bringing the glib, forceful Fontaine into the Rapture Council. He liked competition, but not breathing down his neck. "But ah—I'll take your request under advisement."

"Then we're in good shape!" Fontaine said, blowing blue cigar smoke in the air.

The man seemed relaxed, certain of himself, unworried. And maybe there was something in his eyes that Ryan recognized. A hint, a flicker that suggested Fontaine's willingness to do whatever he had to do . . . to get what he wanted.

<u>*Olympus Heights*</u>
1949

"Mr. Ryan likes to talk about choices," Elaine was saying. "And I keep wondering if we made the right one, coming to Rapture in the first place."

"We did, love," Bill said, glancing around the comfortable flat with some satisfaction. He patted her pregnant tummy absently with his left hand, his right around her shoulders. They sat gazing out at the sea from their viewing alcove.

Before opening day, Ryan had purchased a great many furnishings wholesale and warehoused them in the undersea city, selling them at a profit to Rapture entrepreneurs. He'd brought in raw materials too, and a modest manufacturing base had sprung up.

Elaine's tastes didn't run to the rococo excess found in so much of Rapture. She had chosen simple lines, craftsman-style furnishings: curving dark wood, polished redwood tables, silver-framed mirrors. A smiling portrait of Bill—his mustache curling up, his russet hair starting to recede— hung over their shark-leather living room sofa. Materials found in the undersea environs around Rapture were being increasingly used in furnishings—locally mined metals, many-hued corals for tabletops and counters, glass from deep-sea sands, even beams and brass from sunken ships.

The curving window of the viewing alcove, the glass arching over them sectioned by frames of Ryanium alloy, looked out on a deep channel between towering buildings. An uneven dull-blue light prevailed through the watery space; the new, glowing sign across the way, seeming to ripple in the funhouse lens of the water, read:

FUN IN FORT FROLIC!
Always a Grand Floor Show at Fleet Hall!

"I don't mind the smell of Rapture," Elaine said. "It's kind of like the laundry room of the building I grew up in. Kind of homey. Some of it."

"We're working on that smell, love," Bill put in. "The sulfur smell too."

"And I don't mind so much not seeing my family. But Bill—when I think of raising a child here . . ." She put her hand over his, on her swollen belly. "That's when I worry. What will the schools be like? And living without churches, without God . . . And what will the child learn of the world up above? Just the hateful things Ryan says about it? And—will she . . . if it's a she . . . will she really never get to see the sky?"

"Oh in time she will, love—in time. Someday, when Mr. Ryan thinks it's safe, the city will be built higher up, above the waves. And we'll come and go freely, Bob's your uncle. But that's a generation off, at least. It's a dangerous world out there. Bloody atom bombs, innit?"

"I don't know, Bill. When we went to dinner in Athena's Glory, with him and his friends—Well, Mr. Ryan ranted a good deal, don't you think? On and on about the world above and how we have to accept our choice and rejoice in it. And to be stuck in Rapture with . . . well some of the people here, like that Steinman. He kept touching my face, talking about how it was 'so close, so close and yet'! What did he mean?"

Bill chuckled and tightened his arm around her shoulders. "Steinman's a prat, all right. But don't worry. We'll all be just fine. I'm going to protect you, darlin'. You can trust me to do that. It'll all come right in the end . . ."

Atlantis Express, Adonis Station
1949

Stanley Poole had never been this nervous on a reporting assignment. Maybe it was being this close to larger-than-life personalities like Andrew Ryan, Prentice Mill, and Carlson Fiddle—them being all casual-like, almost acting like he was one of them.

The four men were sitting together at the front of the first train car. Poole couldn't quite make out what Ryan and Mill were saying over the rumble of the Atlantic Express. A pensive, pinch-faced man, Mill seemed worried about something . . .

They were all on their way to the Adonis Luxury Resort, though it was far from finished—only the Roman-style public baths were ready, steaming for bathers. Ryan wanted *The Rapture Tribune* to report some progress. To Poole's right were Mill and Ryan; to his left sat Carlson Fiddle, a bespectacled, nattily dressed, soft-faced man, gently wringing his hands in his lap. Fiddle looked put-upon and preoccupied—and prissily startled as the train lurched into motion. The kind of fussy little man who made you think of an old lady. It was like he'd spent too much time with his mother. They'd just come from the future site of what was to be Ryan Amusements, and now, as the train started for Adonis, Poole sensed that there was a story in Carlson Fiddle's pensiveness.

"Well, Carlson—" Poole began. "May I call you Carlson?"

"No," Fiddle said, frowning at the floor.

Poole winced as he took out his pen and notebook. He knew he wasn't a person who easily commanded respect. As the train passed through a tunnel he could see his reflection in the dark window, beyond Fiddle—the reflection was sickly, the dark glass making him look even more hollow eyed than normal. But, at best, how did anyone take him seriously, with those jutting ears, that skinny neck, and protruding Adam's apple? The gauntness was worse lately—he had trouble keeping his food down. Maybe it was the binges on booze and drugs he'd gotten into since arriving in Rapture.

Poole cleared his throat and tried again: "Quite a job you've got, Mr. Fiddle—designing Ryan Amusements, I mean. Amusement park for the kids, that the ticket?" He smiled encouragingly, hoping Fiddle would get the joke. But not a flicker of amusement came from the guy.

Fiddle adjusted his glasses. "Yes, yes, we'll have animatronics, some interesting, ah, exhibits planned. I'm a bit baffled about what Mr. Ryan wants exactly." He glanced sharply at Poole. "Don't quote that in the paper. About me being baffled."

Poole winked at Fiddle. "Oh, Mr. Ryan was clear . . ." He lowered his voice. ". . . this is going to be a puff piece all the way. All about the swell new constructions coming, the new branch line, the spa. So—what's this animatronics thing?"

Tired of adjusting his glasses, Fiddle adjusted his tie. "Oh, not everyone calls it that. But—there was that Westinghouse exhibit, in '39, with Electro the robot and his little pal Sparko. That kind of thing. Animated mannequins, some say. They'll talk to visitors."

"Animated mannequins! Do tell!"

Fiddle went back to gently wringing his hands in his lap. "It'll be about the history of Rapture. I'd *like* to put in some fairy-tale material too, to keep the kids coming back. Maybe something like the Walt Disney cartoons. But he . . . well, never mind. Just print that I—that I think it's *a wonderful project,* and I'm looking forward to making it a reality."

"Sure thing!"

The train jolted as it took a turn, rising up to pass into a transparent tunnel through the sea. Coldly magnificent, like some sunken fairyland, Rapture rose about them. A school of big fish zigzagged by, glinting silver. A private bathysphere whipped along below them as they entered another building.

Poole glanced over at Ryan and Mill, when Mill raised his voice. "He does keep implying, Andrew, that I . . . that eventually—"

"Come, come," Ryan said equably. "You worry too much, Prentice! Augustus is not some predator of the sea."

Mill snorted bitterly. "Then what does Sinclair mean when he says, 'Enjoy the Atlantic Express while you have it'?"

"Oh, that's just one businessman using a bit of psychology on another! He probably plans to make you an offer and wants you to worry about a takeover. Keep you off-balance. Perfectly normal business tactic."

"But it's not a public company . . ."

"Perhaps it should be! You need not sell out to Sinclair. You could pump up your liquidity by selling shares freely about Rapture. Rapture is still growing! It's a bubble that will never burst. You will want the capital for investment, Prentice . . . Ah—here's our new luxury resort . . ."

The train slowed as they came into the station near Adonis. Poole, scribbling on his notebook, was somehow aware of Ryan's scrutiny.

He looked up to see Andrew Ryan frowning at him. Ryan raised an inquiring eyebrow. "You do remember our talk? Nothing unauthorized, Poole."

Poole swallowed, tempted to point out that Ryan's heavy hand on Rapture's newspaper was counter to his talk of freedom. But then Ryan was the major shareholder in the *Tribune,* and Stanley Poole had never heard of a newspaper that expressed an opinion its owners didn't like.

"You *betcha,* Mr. Ryan," Poole said cheerfully, winking.

He rubbed his nose but quickly stopped, knowing it was an irritating mannerism. *Man,* he'd like to get out from under that hawkish gaze of Ryan's, get a bottle from Sinclair Spirits and a little sniff-sniff from Le Marquis D'Epoque, that new liquor-and-drug shop over in Fort Frolic. "This branch line, Mr. Ryan—mighty impressive. Quite a view."

Ryan nodded, his expression becoming neutral. But he kept staring, a look that could be felt like a finger prodding at Poole's forehead. "I do think I may have some special assignments for you, in time, Poole, if you prove to be discreet. I'll need someone . . . very discreet indeed."

The doors of the train slid open, and Ryan forgot about Poole, turning to clap Prentice on the shoulder, smiling. "The doors were a tad slow to open once we arrived, don't you think, Prentice? Let's make them brisker. Let's keep Rapture moving ahead!"

Medical Pavilion
1949

"Bill, do we have to do this?" Elaine whispered as she lay back on the examining table, awaiting Dr. Suchong. "Why do I have to see these two? I don't think that Tenenbaum woman is even a doctor. And Suchong—he's some kind of brain surgeon or something . . . what does he know about obstetrics?" She smoothed out the hospital gown so it covered a bit more of her pregnancy-swollen belly.

Bill patted her tummy. "The regular doctor was booked up, love. I mentioned to Ryan you were having some unusual cramps, and he insisted that someone here would see to you. Tenenbaum and Suchong were working with Gil Alexander, who's doing a bit of work for Ryan." He shrugged.

Elaine licked her lips and said nervously: "I heard someone say she's got a reputation of being kinda crazy with her experiments . . ."

"Haven't heard that. She's just another genius type that Ryan took an interest in. Sure she's odd—they all are. Can't make people understand what she wants half the time . . ."

"Ahh," Dr. Suchong said, bustling in, his glasses catching the shine in the overhead lamp. His thin Asian face had a faint gloss of sweat. "Here is soon-mother!"

Brigid Tenenbaum came drifting in after him—a very young woman, superficially pretty but with bruised-looking eyes, a shapeless bob of brown hair, a distant expression on her face. Both of them wore lab coats, Tenenbaum with the skirt of a shabby brown dress showing under her white coat.

"Third trimester, yes?" she said. "Interesting." Her accent, mixing German and Eastern European, was almost as pronounced as Suchong's. "Well fed, yes? Circulation—good."

Elaine scowled—Bill could see she felt like a lab animal. Tenenbaum hadn't even said hello. But it was true—she wasn't what you'd call a physician. She just happened to be available today. It was all a bit slapdash for Bill's liking.

"Yes she is, what is expression, 'well along,'" Suchong remarked, prodding at Elaine's belly. "Yes . . . I can feel the . . . offspring moving. Almost ready for emergence. The creature wishes to come out and feed."

Tenenbaum had turned to a nearby table of instruments, moving them minutely, squaring them up so that they were at precise right angles and equidistant.

"Mrs. McDonagh," Suchong said, examining Elaine's thighs, "does fetus make the reflex movements with extremities?"

Elaine rolled her eyes. "Do you mean does the little one kick, Doctor? The child does; yes."

"Excellent sign. Long since I have examined a fetus. Difficult to obtain them in healthy state."

He stepped around to her feet, reached out, and pulled her legs apart with a sharp, decisive movement of his hands like a butcher preparing to gut a chicken. Elaine made a squeak of surprise.

"'Ere, Doc, easy on my girl!" Bill said.

Suchong was lifting up the hospital gown—and he and Tenenbaum were both leaning over the exam table, frowning at Elaine's private parts. Suchong grunted, pointing. "Interesting distention, there and there—you see? Part of peculiar metamorphosis of pregnant woman."

"Yes, I see," Tenenbaum said. "I have dissected many in this stage . . ."

"Enviable. Perhaps you have specimens?"

"No, no, all my specimens were taken when the Americans came, but—"

"Bill!" Elaine squeaked, snapping her legs shut and pressing the gown down over her crotch.

"Right! See any problems, you two?" Bill said.

"Hm?" Suchong looked at him in puzzlement. "Ah! No, no, she will do very well. It would be interesting to probe a bit—"

"Won't be necessary, Doc! We're off." Bill helped Elaine down from the table. "Come on, love. Back in here, there's your clothes, time to get dressed."

He heard Andrew Ryan's voice from the lab next door. "There you are, Dr. Suchong—is all well?"

Suchong said, "Yes, yes, nothing abnormal. I am glad you are here, Mr. Ryan—please to look at experiment thirty-seven . . ."

Bill stepped to the door of the lab, with half a mind to tell Ryan how coarsely Elaine had been treated. But he stopped, staring.

Andrew Ryan, Suchong, Gil Alexander—a researcher who worked for Ryan most of the time—and Brigid Tenenbaum were gathered around a big motley figure in a sort of glass coffin filled with water; the case was hooked up to a tangle of translucent tubes. Bill had only met Gil Alexander a few times—a serious-eyed man with a thick mustache. He was quite professorial and intelligent, but, it seemed to Bill, cold-blooded.

Stretched out in the glass coffin was a man whose body seemed a patchwork of flesh and, in some places, steel. Corpse-pale, the man lay motionless in the bubbling water—Bill thought it could have been a drowning victim.

Gil Alexander was adjusting a tube sinking into the supine man's left leg. "A little inflammation. Not bad. We have good induction . . ."

Bill found himself staring at the exposed left leg—it looked as if flesh and metal were fused at the thigh. It was all puckered, and Bill thought he saw the skin quiver, as if reacting to a perfusion of bubbles. He wanted to speak up or leave, but there was something that held him, something weirdly fascinating in the scene . . .

"You see, Mr. Ryan," Tenenbaum said, "fusion is incomplete, but I feel if we were to perhaps try viral gene transfer, we make body more capable of unifying with . . ."

"Bah!" Suchong said, glancing at her in annoyance. "You always think genes the way. Viral transfer of genes is entirely theoretical! Not needed! Body can be conditioned so that cells bond with metal! We have no way to control genes without breeding program!"

"Ach—forgive me, Doctor," she said, her voice faintly contemptuous, as she needlessly straightened tools on a nearby table, "but you are mistaken. The way will reveal itself to us. When we consider Gregor Mendel . . ."

Alexander seemed amused by the simmering between Suchong and Tenenbaum. He smiled, Bill noticed, but said nothing.

Ryan made a dismissive gesture as he frowned over the figure in the transparent, liquid-filled coffin. "I'm more interested in the practical uses—I need a process that makes our men capable of longer hours out there—"

"Cor!" Bill burst out—as the legs of the supine man contracted, an armored knee striking the top of the glass case, cracking it. Water spurted up through the crack . . .

Ryan and Suchong turned to stare at Bill—Tenenbaum and Alexander seemed more caught up in changing the flow of a chemical through the tubes that communicated with the glass coffin.

"Bill," Ryan said softly, coming over to him. "I thought you'd gone."

"Just leaving," Bill said. "That fellow in there all right?"

"Him? Oh he's a volunteer—helping us with an experiment." Ryan took his arm. "Come—let's leave them to it, shall we? How's Elaine . . . ?"

And he escorted Bill from the lab.

Fort Frolic
1949

Bing Crosby crooned "Wrap Your Troubles in Dreams" from flower-shaped speakers, and Bill hummed along as he escorted Elaine along the upper atrium. There was just time for a stroll before the musical at Fleet Hall. Bill had brought Elaine for a Christmas-season outing. Their friend Mariska Lutz was looking after the baby.

"It's funny about this place," Elaine murmured, as she and Bill strolled along the balcony walk of Poseidon Plaza, in the neon-bright upper atrium of Fort Frolic. Elaine wore a shiny pink satin dress and Bill wore a white linen suit. Other couples hurried by, dressed up, hair coiffed, faces glowing with laughter. *Almost like New York,* Bill thought.

"What's funny about it, love?" he asked. They were passing the entrance to the Sir Prize Games of Chance Casino, with its big knight's helmet projecting between *Sir* and *Prize*. The neon signs seemed to radiate sheer insistence in an enclosed space. There was no sky to put them in perspective.

"Well, I mean—I thought it'd be really different from the surface world. It is, of course, in some ways—but—" She glanced through the windows at the people working the slot machines. "The idea was to bring just the best of the world down with us—but maybe we brought some of the worst too."

Bill chuckled, tucking her hand under his arm. "That happens when a place is settled with *people,* love. They bring the worst and best with 'em wherever they go. People've got to have some place to let their 'air . . . their *hair* down. Got to have their Fort Frolic."

They went down the stairs to the lower atrium, past Robertson's Tobaccoria, and she sighed as they passed Eve's Garden. She looked at it askance. "A strip club was *necessary,* was it?"

Bill shrugged. "Especially necessary, some would say—with all the men we've got here. Men building, working maintenance. Now me, I don't need any such diversion. I've got the best-looking bird in Rapture to admire."

"Well, don't expect a strip show." She batted her eyes at him like a flapper in a movie. "Until we get home I mean."

"That's my girl!"

She laughed. "Oh I don't mean to sound like a bluenose—Let's get some wine in Sinclair Spirits . . . or maybe something in the Ryan Club. You'd probably rather have ale . . ."

"It's wine for milady! But we've got tickets for the show at Fleet Hall, love. Thought we'd have our drinks after."

"Oh, Fleet Hall! I've been wanting to see it. That Footlight Theater place is kind of cramped."

"Fleet's big. Mr. Ryan planned for big all through Rapture."

She glanced quizzically up at him. "You really admire Mr. Ryan, don't you, Bill?"

"What, me? You know I do! Gave me everything I've got, he has. I was installing toilets, love—and he made me a builder of a new world!"

They passed the liquor and drug emporium Le Marquis D'Epoque—which was quite thronged, mostly with young men. He saw someone he knew inside, the rat-faced Stanley Poole, shifting from foot to foot, nervously buying a vial of some narcotic. Bill hurried on, not wanting to talk about the place with his wife—and not wanting to make small talk with the execrable Poole.

The piped music had become Fats Waller jazzily banging out the Jitterbug Waltz. Happy voices echoed from the high spaces of the atrium. People looked a bit ghostly in the reflected light from the neon, but they were happy ghosts, smiling, teasing one another. A young red-haired woman squealed as a young man pinched her. She remembered to slap him, but not very hard.

Bill saw one of Sullivan's constables, big Pat Cavendish, looking like a hotel dick in his cheap suit and badge, swaggering about, hands in his pockets and gun on his hip, leering at a parcel of young girls.

Elaine brightened when they came to the Sophia Salon, and Bill resigned himself to standing about with his hands in his pockets as Elaine poked through the finery in the "high fashion" boutique. He bought her a nightgown and a new coat to be delivered to their flat, and then it was time to go back upstairs to Fleet Hall.

They hurried out of the boutique and up the stairs, where Bill spotted the architect Daniel Wales talking to Augustus Sinclair. But the younger Wales was in close conversation with the mercurial businessman and didn't even look up.

Bill peered up at the ceiling, thinking about watertight integrity, and was pleased to see no sign of leakage. Some parts of Rapture were more scrupulously maintained than others. This one was pampered like a baby's bottom.

It seemed to Bill that Rapture was thriving: the Atlantic Express rumbled efficiently from one building to another. Shops bustled with business. Rapture's galleries and atriums glowed with light; its art deco fixtures gleamed with gold leaf. Crews of workmen kept the carpets clean, picked up trash, and repaired cracks in bulkheads. Looking down at the lower atrium, the increasing crowd, and the shining signs, Rapture seemed fully alive, thrumming with economic brio. And just maybe Mr. Ryan, the Wales brothers, Greavy—just maybe they couldn't have done it without Bill McDonagh.

Bill and Elaine reached Fleet Hall, pausing to admire the grand blue-and-white sign. The archway was tricked out with radiant lines of white neon. A buzz of mingled conversations came from inside. Bill pressed Elaine's arm to him and bent and kissed her cheek, and they went in.

The big, ornate concert hall was thronged, and they had seats in the orchestra section. The lights went down, the band struck up, and the musical *Patrick and Moira* commenced. It was a Sander Cohen production, thankfully without Cohen in it, and Elaine was enthralled. Bill found it all rather sentimental and a tad morbid—the play was about a ghostly couple who found each other in the afterlife—but he was happy to be there with Elaine, pleased she was having a good time. She seemed lost here on occasion. Now—he felt like they'd really found their place in the world . . . deep under the sea.

Heat Loss Monitoring, Hephaestus
1950

Bill almost had the heat monitor adjusted. Temperature control was just one of Rapture's numerous points of vulnerability, one of many maintenance linchpins that had to be constantly adjusted to keep the city from breaking down. The city under the sea had been settled for just two years—a little less—but there was a great deal of repair to be done already.

Caught between fire and ice, me, Bill thought.

A certain amount of the cold water outside Rapture was drawn in through sea vents to modify the heat from the volcanic gases used to drive the turbines—water in one was cold enough to kill a man from hypothermia in under a minute; the water in the other hot enough to boil him. Bill had witnessed both tragedies.

Bill turned wheels to balance the mix of frigid coolant and volcanically heated water. He glanced out the window into the sea, where a complex of transparent pipes glowed dull red, conveying mineral-rich heated water from geothermal sources. Bill could faintly smell sulfur, though they tried hard to filter it all out. Still and all, the air in Rapture was usually cleaner than it was in New York City. Clean air was provided by gardens like Arcadia and the intake vents in the lighthouse structures.

The heat meters were bobbing just right now. He had the balance. Pablo Navarro was working at the other end of the apparatus-crowded room with Roland Wallace and Stanley Kyburz.

"That Navarro is always looking for a leg up," Wallace grumbled, coming over. "Wants to be head engineer of the section, don't you know."

"That's Greavy's call, mate. But I don't know as Pablo keeps at the job hard enough to deserve that title. How's Kyburz working out?"

"Getting his work done. Good technical know-how. But those Aussies—they're odd. And he's the sullen sort, don't you know."

"Every Australian I ever knew was a sullen ol' sod," Bill said absently, eyeing the meters. "Holding steady so far."

"Anyhow, there was an intercom buzz for you. Mr. Ryan wants you in Central Control."

"Should've told me before! Right, I'm off."

Bill checked the meters once more and then hurried out, hoping Elaine would be working in Ryan's office.

He found Ryan pacing in front of his desk. No sign of Elaine. "Ah, Bill. I sent Elaine home early."

Bill felt a sudden inner coldness. "Is she all right?"

"Yes, yes," Ryan said distractedly. "Seemed fine. Wanted to look in on the nanny. Perhaps she came back to work too soon after the baby was born. How is the child?"

"The little one's right as rain. Smiling and waving 'er arms about like she's conducting a band . . ."

"Splendid, splendid . . ."

Bill hoped Elaine was all right. But she had insisted on getting a sitter and going back to work. She seemed to get cabin fever in the flat. Not easy to take the baby in a stroller through the park in Rapture—a bit of a journey to the small park areas.

"Bill, would you come with me? I have to have a chat with Julie Langford. I'd like your opinion on the new tea garden in Arcadia. And some other things. Plenty to talk about along the way . . ."

They traversed several passages and then entered a transparent corridor between buildings, sauntering untouched through the sea itself—heat vectored through the floor, protecting them from the North Atlantic's frigidity. "I'm hearing rumblings in Rapture I don't like, Bill," Ryan muttered, pausing to watch a school of bright fish swim frantically by, pursued by an orca. "Out there, it's all as it should be. The big fish eats the smaller fish. Some fish elude predators and thrive. But here . . . there are those who disturb the balance."

Bill stepped up beside Ryan, the two of them gazing through the glass like two people chatting at an aquarium. "Rumblings, guv'nor? Which sort? The pipe sort or the people sort?"

"It's the people—if you want to call them that." Ryan shook his head and added, "Parasites!," his mouth twisting sharply with the word. "I thought we could weed them all out. But people are *tainted,* Bill—there are rumors of union organizers here in Rapture! Unions! In my city! Someone is encouraging them. I'd like to know who . . . and why."

"Haven't heard anything quite like that myself," Bill remarked.

"Stanley Poole caught some union talk in the tavern. There's a pamphlet being passed around complaining about 'unfairness to the workingman of Rapture' . . ."

"People being tense—they naturally need to blow off steam, guv. Toss around their ideas, freelike. Even some ideas you . . . we . . . don't like, Mr. Ryan. Unions and whatnot. Now, I won't defend 'em—" he added hastily, "—but there's a kind of marketplace of ideas too, yeah? People need to be able to trade in ideas . . ."

"Hm. Marketplace of ideas. Maybe. I *try* to be tolerant. But unions—we saw where that leads . . ."

Bill decided not to argue that one. They both silently watched a blue whale swim majestically overhead. Bubbles streamed up from the seabed; lights blinked on in the buildings of Rapture, rising spectrally through the blue-green water. The Wales brothers' designs mixed sweeping lines with a certain artful intricacy. The architecture seemed calculated to project boldness, even bravado.

A neon sign across the watery way, running vertically down a building that could almost have been from mid Manhattan, read FLEET HALL. Another neon sign glowed in grape-purple to advertise WORLEY'S WINERY, the letters rippling with intervening sea currents. Most of the apartment buildings had square windows, not portholes—for the most part they looked like apartment buildings on dry land. The effect, at times, was more like a sunken Atlantis than a metropolis deliberately built beneath the sea—as if the polar ice caps had melted, flooding Manhattan, its steel and stone canyons immersed in a deep, mysterious watery world without a clear horizon.

"It could be," Ryan went on at last, "that we were too hasty in some of our recruiting for Rapture. I may have picked some people who were not as likeminded as I'd hoped."

"Most of our people believe in the Rapture way, Mr. Ryan—there's plenty of free enterprise in Rapture." Bill smiled as a stream of bubbles rose a few inches beyond the glass. "It's bubblin' with it!"

"You hearten me, Bill. I hope everyone stays busy—competing, carving out their place in our new world. Everyone should branch out, create new businesses! Do you still plan to open a tavern?"

"Right enough I do. Fighting McDonagh's it'll be called. After me old man; he was a boxer in his youth."

"We'll have a grand-opening party for you!" Ryan looked up, toward the heights of the towers mounting through the sea—hard to see the tops of many of them from here. He took a deep breath, looking pleased, seeming to buoy into a better mood. "Look at it, rising like an orchestral climax! Rapture is a miracle, Bill—the only kind of miracle that matters! The kind a real man creates with his own two hands. And it should be celebrated every day."

"Miracles need a lot of maintenance, Mr. Ryan! Thing is, we're short on people to deal with the sewage, the cleaning, and the landscaping in Arcadia. We got posh types who never suffered worse than a paper cut—but precious few who can dig a ditch or plumb a pipe."

"Ah. We'll have to lure men who have the skills we need, then. Find ways to house them. We'll bring them in, don't you worry about it. The light attracts the enlightened, Bill!"

Bill wondered how that would work out—bringing ever more blue-collar workers, men who might not take to a place where the guv'nor despised unions. Could be trouble down the road.

"Ah," Ryan said, with satisfaction. "A supplies sub is coming in . . ."

They watched the submarine ghost by overhead, its lights glowing against the indigo depths. From here, its lines muted by the depths, the sub looked like a giant creature of the sea itself, another kind of whale. It would be heading to Neptune's Bounty. Bill watched the sub angle downward for the hangar-sized intake airlock that led up to the wharf and Fontaine's Fisheries.

"Dunno," Bill said, "who might be encouraging unions—but I can tell you one person I don't much trust is that Frank Fontaine."

Ryan shrugged. "He's quite the productive one. He's got a lot of enterprise rolling. He keeps me thinking; I like the competition . . . ," adding, as if thinking aloud, "within reason."

Fontaine had worked with Peach Wilkins to develop a way to do Rapture's fishing more discreetly—underwater. A few simple adaptations to the smaller subs, refitting them to drag nets, and they had purely subaquatic fishing.

But the fishery gave Fontaine a potential access to something that Bill knew made Ryan nervous—the outside world. His subs left Rapture on business of their own—and they might be contacting anyone out there. Every year Ryan cut more ties with the surface world, liquidating his properties, selling factories and railroads.

"You think maybe Fontaine's using the subs to bring in contraband, guv?" he asked suddenly.

"I'm monitoring that possibility. I warned him—and it seemed to me he took the warning seriously."

"Some smuggling's going on, Mr. Ryan," Bill pointed out. "A Bible turned up in the workers' quarters."

"Bibles . . ." Ryan said the word with loathing. "Yes—Sullivan told me. The man says he bought it from 'a fellow I didn't know over to Apollo Square.'"

Bill had no love for religion himself. But privately he thought some people probably needed it as a safety valve. "All I can tell you, Mr. Ryan, is that I've never trusted that bugger Fontaine. He talks all silky, like—but none of it feels like real silk."

"We can't *assume* anything, you know. Come along . . ."

Bill sighed. Sometimes he got tired of being 'Come Along Bill.'

An electric eye triggered the semicircular Securis door to slide open. They strode along corridors decorated with posters extolling the glories of Rapture's commerce, down a curving stairway, to a bathysphere station where a banner declared COMMERCE, INDEPENDENCE, CREATIVITY. Ryan remained silent, brooding as they went.

Bill expected to take the Atlantic Express, but Ryan ignored the train station and continued to the Rapture Metro. They passed a party of maintenance workers who tipped their hats at Ryan. He paused and shook hands all around. "How's it going, boys? Patching up the ceiling? Good, good . . . don't forget to invest some part of your paychecks in one of Rapture's new businesses! Keep it growing, fellas! You working for Bill here? If he isn't treating you right—don't tell me about it!" They laughed all around at that. "Start a competing plumbing business, give ol' Bill here a run for his money, eh! How do you like that new park of ours, by the way. Seen it yet? Fine place to take the ladies . . ."

When he was in the mood, Ryan could be quite convivial, even chummy, with the workingman. He seemed almost to be performing for Bill today.

Ryan put his hands in his pockets and rocked on his heels as he reflected, "When I was a young boy, my father took me to a park in . . . well, it was in a foreign capital . . . the czar was still alive then, but my father's business was faltering, and that park lifted his spirits! 'This is where I met your mother!' he said. So boys—if you want to meet the right young miss, we've got just the place! Plenty of privacy for sparking the ladies, eh?"

The workmen laughed; he clapped two of them on the shoulders, wished them a profitable day's work, and sent them on their way. The men went away beaming—they'd be able to boast of chatting with the great Andrew Ryan.

Ryan led Bill into the waiting bathysphere. When its hatch lowered into place, Ryan tapped the selector for their destination and hit the GO lever. The bathysphere dropped neatly into its passageway and then set out horizontally with a bubbling *whoosh*.

The two men sat back, riding in companionable quiet till they were halfway to the nearest air lock for Arcadia, when Ryan said, "Bill—have you heard residents whining about not being permitted to leave Rapture?"

"Here and there," Bill admitted reluctantly. He didn't want to snitch on anyone.

"You know we cannot trust anyone outside Rapture, Bill. We'd have American intelligence agents down here, or the jackals from the KGB, fast as . . ." He snapped his fingers.

"It can be hard for some down here, sir. There's some as wonder if they made the right choice immigrating to Rapture . . ."

"I have no respect for quitters! You don't *visit* Rapture—it's a way of life!" He shook his head bitterly. "They are spineless! They were told, before they came, that there were certain inviolable rules. No one leaves! There is no place for men like us on the surface."

Bill was in awe of Ryan; he knew it, and Ryan knew it. But maybe it was time to give Ryan some guff about this lockdown. Because he was afraid that if Ryan stuck to this policy, it could be explosive. "It's human nature, guv'nor, to want freedom to come and go. People get stir-crazy, like, when you pen them up. You believe a man should make a choice—but how can the poor sod *choose* to stay in Rapture? We took that choice away!"

"A man has thousands of choices in Rapture. But *that* one he gave up when he came to this world—a world that *I* created. I built it with money and resources earned with *my sweat*! It's all a lot of absurd whining! In time we will expand Rapture across the seabed and there will be far more room to move about." He flicked his hand in a gesture of contemptuous impatience. "They entered into a contract coming here! In the end, our choices make us what we are. A man *chooses*, Bill! They chose—and they must accept the responsibility."

Bill cleared his throat. "Natural enough for some blokes to want to change their minds . . ."

The bathysphere reached its destination, clunking into place, and the hatch creaked open—but Ryan made no move to get out. He remained in his seat, looking at Bill with a new solemnity. "Have you changed *your* mind, Bill?"

Bill was taken by surprise. "No! This is my home, Mr. Ryan. I built this place with my bare hands." He shrugged. "You asked what I've heard . . ."

Ryan looked at him for a long moment, as if peering into Bill's soul. Finally, he nodded. "Very well, Bill. But I'll tell you something. The residents of Rapture *will* be purged of the habits of ant society! They must learn to stand up beside us, like men—and build! I plan to start a new program of civic education. Banners, a great many more of them—educational announcements on televisions and public address, and billboards! I'm bringing in someone to help us train them to see that the world outside Rapture is the real prison . . . and Rapture is the real freedom." Ryan climbed out of the bathysphere. "Come along, Bill. Come along . . ."

8

"Miss Lamb," Diane announced. "Dr. Sofia Lamb . . ." There was a certain coolness in her voice as she said it, Andrew Ryan noted. Had she already taken a dislike to the woman? Dr. Lamb had been a kind of missionary, both physician and psychiatrist, working in Hiroshima before and after the bomb—maybe Diane was intimidated. Diane was sensitive about her working-class background.

"Escort her in. Have the guards wait outside."

Diane sniffed but went back into the outer room and held the door for Sofia Lamb.

"He'll see you now, Dr. Lamb," Diane said, as if wondering why he was seeing her.

"Splendid. It's been a long journey . . . I'm curious to find the final chamber of this great nautilus shell of a city . . ."

Ryan stood politely as she strode in. Dr. Lamb carried herself like the educated, well-heeled elite professional she was. He knew protocol would matter with her.

She was tall, almost cruelly slim, her blond hair coifed into large curls atop her head. She had a long neck, a narrow face with stark bone structure, icy blue eyes behind stylish horn-rimmed glasses, lips darkly rouged. She wore a navy-blue dress suit with sharp white collars and dark blue pumps.

"Welcome to Rapture, Miss Lamb. Won't you have a seat? I hope your journey wasn't too exhausting. It's a pleasure to have you join us in our brave new world."

She sat in the chair across from him, crossing her long pale legs. "Brave new world—a reader of Shakespeare! *The Tempest,* was it not?" Her long slender fingers expertly extracted a platinum cigarette case from her small handbag as she went on, looking blandly at him, "O brave new world that has such creatures in it . . ."

"Are you surprised, Miss Lamb, that I'm familiar with Shakespeare?" Ryan asked, coming around the desk to light her cigarette with a gold lighter.

She blew smoke at the ceiling and shrugged. "No. You're—a wealthy man. You can afford to educate yourself."

It was not an obvious criticism—yet somehow, it was condescending. But she smiled—and he saw a glint of charisma. "I must say," she went on, glancing around, "this place is remarkable. Quite astonishing. And yet no one seems to know about it."

"As few as we can manage. We work hard at keeping it secret. And we shall require you to keep it secret too, Miss Lamb. Or should I call you Doctor Lamb . . . ?"

He waited for her to say, *Oh, call me Sofia.* But she didn't. She merely nodded, just faintly.

Ryan cleared his throat. "You are well aware of the driving forces behind Rapture—its philosophy, its plan. The Great Chain . . ."

"Yes, but I can't claim to completely understand your . . . operative philosophy. I am of course attracted by the possibilities of a new society that has no . . . no interference from the outside world. A self-sustaining colony that might rediscover human possibilities—the possibility of a society free from the warmongering of the upper world . . ."

"I understand you were in Hiroshima when . . ."

"I was in a sheltered, outlying place. But yes. People I sometimes worked with were burnt to shadows on the walls of their homes." Her eyes held a flat horror at the memory. "If the modern world were a patient in my care . . ." She shook her head. "I would diagnose it suicidal."

"Yes. Hiroshima, Nagasaki—they were a large part of the reason we built Rapture. I suspected you might understand our imperative, after seeing what happened there, firsthand. I'm certain the surface world *will* commit nuclear suicide in time, Dr. Lamb. One generation, two, three—it will happen— and when it does, Rapture will be safe, here below. Self-sufficient and thriving. Rapture is deliverance."

She tapped her cigarette ash into the brass floor ashtray beside her chair, nodding eagerly now. "That is the great appeal for me. Deliverance. A new chance to . . . to remake society into something innately good! Everyone has a duty to the world, Mr. Ryan—and we've lost all that, up above, in all the grubbing chaos of that perverse civilization . . ."

Ryan frowned, not exactly understanding her. But before he could ask her to elucidate, she went on:

"And I was gratified to hear that everyone has equal opportunity here! Including women, presumably?" She glanced at him questioningly. "In ordinary society the male hierarchy crushes our dreams. They see a woman with a spark"—she crushed her cigarette out angrily in the ashtray—"and they crush it out! 'Lady doctors,' as they call them, are sometimes tolerated. But . . . real advancement for a woman in the field? No."

"Oh yes, I see . . ." Ryan thoughtfully stroked his mustache with the ball of his thumb. Theoretically everyone in Rapture started on an equal footing—and anyone could rise to the top with hard work, enterprise, talent, ruthless dedication to the simple, liberating power of free enterprise. Even women.

He'd invited Sofia Lamb to Rapture because she'd graduated at the top of her class. She was said to have written brilliant theses—which Ryan hadn't had time to read—and to have shown a fearlessness in psychiatric experimentation. Scientific fearlessness was axiomatic to Rapture.

"You can compete with the rest of us here," Ryan said firmly, as much to convince himself as her. "But of course your initial work would be to evaluate Rapture, help us develop a means of preparing the public for the future. More pressingly, some residents may be developing psychological problems—little, ah, *personal difficulties* that bubble up from isolation down here. Your first task will be to diagnose those problems and suggest a solution."

"Oh, of course, that is quite understood. But later—if I want to develop my own . . . institute, here in Rapture?"

"Ah yes. That would be splendid. Why shouldn't people have a psychiatric doctor to consult with? A whole institute for self-exploration."

"Or perhaps for redefining the self," she murmured. She stood. "If you'll excuse me, I'd like to be shown my quarters. The trip here has been—a lot to absorb. I need to change, rest a bit—and I'll need a full tour of Rapture. I'll start my diagnosis right away—this evening."

"Good! I'll have Chief Sullivan send over his files about . . . problem people. The little malcontents cropping up—the complainers, and so on. You can start with those."

Neptune's Bounty, Rapture
1950

Brigid Tenenbaum was walking down the chilly dock toward the water, thinking that perhaps she might get some fresh fish for dissection. If they were iced, she could extract their genetic material with some hope it might be intact. She didn't have a definite contract with Sinclair Solutions anymore, but she could still use their lab after-hours, since she had the door combination. The tale of her attempt to extract semen from one of the submariners with a large syringe had gotten her dropped, unreasonably she felt, from Sinclair's research labs. Certainly, she'd used bad judgment in implying she wanted something else from the man's evil-smelling genitals. Perhaps she'd thrust the needle into his gonad rather too vigorously. But for him to run screaming from the lab, naked from the waist down, with a syringe dangling from his groin, trailing blood and shrieking, "The crazy bitch put a spike in my goddamn nuts!" seemed like an overreaction.

Since then she'd scarcely seen Rapture's founder. Nor had she been able to get an appointment with the man. There was always an excuse from that snippy Diane McClintock.

Sometimes she wished she were back in the camp, working with her mentor. At least they had real creative freedom.

Brigid sighed and tugged her coat closer around her shoulders. It was always nippy down here, in the strange, underwater docks. A kind of artificial cavern, really, within Rapture, filled with water, where the delivery boats pulled up, loaded with fish and other approved goods brought from the submarine bays. The docks were wooden, the walls and ceiling were metal—the water lapped at the pylons with a strange hollow, echoing whisper.

A constable and a black man who seemed to be a deputy were walking past, both of them looking at her curiously.

She saw a couple of dockworkers in heavy pea jackets, standing on the pier below her, waiting for a small tugboatlike vessel to pull up so they could offload it. They were amusing themselves as they waited, tossing a ball back and forth. She recognized both of the men—she'd seen them under Dr. Suchong's hands. He'd tried to cure one of them, Stiffy, of a partial paralysis—and the other one . . .

The other one saw her first. He was a stubby-nosed man with a windburned face—but his red face went white when he saw Tenenbaum. He dropped the ball and clapped both hands to his genitals. "No you don't, lady, you ain't getting near 'em!"

He backed away from her, shaking his head. "Uh *uh*, lady!"

"Don't be such a fool!" she called out wearily, searching for the right English words. "I am not here for you. I want fresh fish."

"You're calling them fish now, are you?" the man demanded, backing away—and falling off the dock into the water. He got up, sputtering, spitting water—it was only four feet deep here.

"Ha, ha, Archie!" the other fisherman called gleefully to him, going to pick up the ball. "You finally got that bath you been avoidin'!"

"Screw you, Stiffy!" Archie called, splashing off toward the approaching boat. "Ahoy there, give me a hand; I'm comin' aboard!"

"Ah, whatya scared of a skinny little dame for!" Stiffy yelled, laughing.

She approached Stiffy, putting on a professorial, officious manner so that he wouldn't try to become too familiar.

"You throw the ball—it is very . . . unusual for you, no?" she asked, staring at his hands. She'd stood by and observed when Suchong had examined him. "Your hands—one paralyzed, the other only half working, this I remember. You carry some things on shoulders, not do so much work with hands."

"Sure—that's why they called me Stiffy. I got another kinda Stiffy, lady, if you—"

She gave him her severest frown. "Do not trifle with me! I wish only to know—how you can catch ball now. With fingers that were paralyzed. Dr. Suchong repaired your hands, yes?"

"Suchong? Hell no! Made a lotta excuses. Funniest thing. We had a net fulla fish, see. I was scoopin' 'em out of the net, sortin' 'em out—that much I could do, anyhow—and there was some kinda sea slug mixed in with 'em, floppin' around. Weirdest lookin' little slug you ever saw! Little bastard bit me on the hand!" Stiffy chortled. He didn't seem angry about it at all. "I didn't even know they could bite! Well, my hands got kinda swole—but when the swelling went down"—he looked at his hands in renewed wonder—"they started to come to life!" He tossed the ball in the air and deftly caught it. "You see that? Before the little bastard bit me, I couldn't do that, no way, no how!"

"You think it was sea slug that release paralysis?"

"Something in that bite—I could feel it spreading out, like, in my hand!"

"Ach! Indeed!" She peered at his hands. Saw the curious bite marks. "If only I had this creature . . . You can find another such sea slug?"

"I still got the same one! Chucked it in a bucket of seawater! It was such a crazy-lookin' little thing I actually thought I could maybe sell it to one of you scientist types. You wanta buy it?"

"Well—perhaps I do."

Sofia Lamb's Office
1950

"I guess . . . I guess I shouldn't have brought my kids to Rapture. But they told me we had to come together, the whole family, or nothin' . . . They said they needed skills with a boiler, I'd be taken care of and make a pile of dough . . ."

Dr. Sofia Lamb was watching the middle-aged man in the workman's overalls pacing back and forth in her office, wringing his hands. "Wouldn't you like to relax on the couch as we work on this, Mr. Glidden?"

"No, no I can't, Doc," Glidden muttered. He sniffled, as if trying not to cry. His eyes were bruised looking from fatigue; his thin lips quivered. His big hands were reddened from his work in the geothermal plant. "I need to get back home. Ya see, my wife, my kids, they're alone in the new apartment . . . if you can call it an apartment. A dump is what it is. Lotta shifty characters around there. I feel like the kids ain't safe in

that place . . . We're havin' to share it with another family—
there ain't enough housing in this crazy town. Nothing I can
afford, I mean. They said there'd be more housing here . . .
and better pay. I thought it was a road-to-riches thing, like
the Comstock Mine . . . They talked like . . ." He bit his lip.

She nodded, shifted in her chair, and made a note. She'd
heard a similar story from a number of workers she'd inter-
viewed as part of her project for Ryan. "You feel you were . . .
misled about what would happen here?"

"Yeah, I—" Glidden broke off, stopping in the center of the
room, staring at her suspiciously. "You . . . you work for Ryan,
right?"

"Well, in a manner of speaking—"

"So *no,* no I wasn't, what'd you say, *misled.*" He licked his
lips. "They were straight with me."

"It's all right; you can say what you really think," Sofia said
reassuringly. "It's true that these therapeutic sessions will be
summed up in a report—but I'm not naming specific people
in my report. It'll be about the trends . . ."

"Yeah? How come this 'therapy' thing here is free? I
wouldn't-a come except my wife says I'm all tense and like
that . . . but . . . *free?* Nothing's free in Rapture!"

"Really—you can trust me, Mr. Glidden."

"So you say. But supposin' I get fired because of this?
Maybe they blackball me! So I got no work! And then what?
You can't leave Rapture! You . . . can't leave! Not even you,
Doc! You think he'll let you leave if you want to? Naw."

"Oh, well I . . ." Her voice trailed off. She hadn't given
much thought to leaving Rapture. There seemed so many
possibilities here. But what if she *did* try to leave? What
would Ryan do? She was afraid to find out. "I'm . . . in the
same boat, so to speak, with you, Mr. Glidden." She smiled.
"Or *under* the same boats."

He crossed his arms in front of him and shook his head. He wasn't going to say anything else.

She wrote, *Subjects are typical in mistrust of Ryan and feeling of alienation. Social claustrophobia at boiling point for some. Financial status a key factor. Higher incomes show less anxiety . . .* She underlined *higher incomes* and then said, "You can go, Mr. Glidden. Thanks for coming in."

She watched Glidden rush from the room, and then she went to her desk, unlocked a drawer, and took out her journal. She usually preferred it to the audio diaries. She sat down and wrote,

> *If the Rapture experiment fails—as I suspect it will— another social experiment could be carried out in this strange, undersea hothouse. The very conditions that make Rapture explosive—its sequestering from the outside world, its inequities—could be the source for a radical social transformation. It's something to consider . . . the danger of even contemplating such a social experiment is enormous, however . . . I must not let this journal fall into Sullivan's hands . . .*

Sofia put the pen down and wondered if what she was contemplating was too risky. Politics. Power . . . An idea that was becoming an idée fixe. Possibly it was sheer madness . . .

But madness or not—it had been growing like a child within her all the time she'd been in Rapture. She'd been quietly gestating the notion that what Rapture could destroy—men like Glidden—it could also save, if it were guided by a new leader.

She could turn Rapture sharply to the left—from within.

Dangerous thinking. But the idea would not go away. It had a life of its own . . .

Pumping Station 5
1950

Bill McDonagh was switching on drainage pump 71, to pump out the insulation and ventilation spaces in the walls of the Mermaid Lounge, when Andrew Ryan walked into station 5. Rapture's visionary genius was smiling but seemed a bit distant, distracted.

"Bill! How about taking a quick inspection walk with me, as we're both near Little Eden. Or are you handling an emergency?"

"No emergency, Mr. Ryan. Just a bit of an adjustment. There, that's done it."

Soon they were strolling along the concourse of Little Eden Plaza, walking past the gracious façade of the Pearl Hotel. People ambled by, couples arm in arm, shoppers with bags. Ryan seemed pleased by this evidence of thriving commerce. Some of the shoppers nodded shyly to Mr. Ryan. One rather matronly woman asked for his autograph, which he patiently provided before he and Bill hurried on.

"Anything you're particularly concerned with, 'round here, Mr. Ryan?" Bill asked as they walked past the Plaza Hedone apartments.

"There's talk of chemical leakage, and we had some kind of complaints at a shop in the area, so I thought I'd look into both at once. I don't care much for complaints, but I like to know what's going on and had some free time . . ."

They came to a corner that was covered with what appeared to be a thick green-black chemical leaking from a seam in a bulkhead. It smelled of petroleum and solvents. "There it is, Bill—were you aware of it?"

"I am, sir. That's why I was adjusting the valves in station five. Trying to cut back on flushing so I could reduce this 'ere toxic overflow. There's a factory upstream, you might say, or anyway upstairs from 'ere, turns out new signs and the like. Augustus Sinclair owns the place, what I remember. They use a lot of chemicals, dump them in the outpipes—but they corrode the pipes, and the solvents work their way out to the sidewalk. What might be worse, the rest of it gets dumped outta Rapture, Mr. Ryan—I checked on it. These chemicals, they go out into the ocean and down current—could be they'll get all mixed up with the fish down there. We could end up eatin' these chemicals when we eat those fish."

Ryan was looking at him with arched eyebrows. "Really, Bill—how ridiculously alarmist! Why, the ocean is vast. We couldn't possibly pollute it! It would all be diluted."

"Right enough, sir, but some of it accumulates, what with currents and eddies, and if we create enough of a mess—"

"Bill—forget it. We've got sufficient concerns right here inside Rapture. We'll have to replace those pipes with something stronger, and we'll charge Augustus for it . . ."

Bill gave it one more try. "Just thought it'd be better if he'd use chemicals that wasn't so corrosive, guv. Could be done, I reckon, if—"

Ryan laughed softly. "Bill! Listen to yourself! You'll ask me to *regulate* industrial waste, next! Why, old Will Clark, up in Montana, created a wasteland around his mines and refineries, and did anyone suffer?" He cleared his throat, seeming to recollect something. "Well—perhaps some did, yes. But the world of commerce is restless; it's like a hungry child that keeps growing and never quite grows up—it becomes a giant, Bill, and people must get out of its way or be stepped on by its ten-league boots! Oh, I'll look into stronger drainage pipes outside factories, to prevent a mess on the sidewalk. Ryan Industries will bill Rapture, and Rapture will bill the factories. Come along, Bill, this way—ah! Here's the other problem . . ."

They'd come to a shop in Little Eden Plaza called Gravenstein's Green Groceries. Across the "street"—more of a wide passageway—and a little ways down was another, larger business called Shep's ShopMart.

Reeking garbage of all sorts was piled up high in the gutter around Gravenstein's. Bill shook his head, seeing every kind of garbage imaginable, most of it decaying. The fish heads were especially pungent. Shep's, by contrast, looked immaculate. A small man in a grocer's apron rushed out of Gravenstein's as they approached; he had a hatchet face and flaplike ears, intense brown eyes, curly brown hair. "Mr. Ryan!" he shouted, wringing his hands as he ran up to them. "You came! I must've sent a hundred requests, and here you are at last!"

Ryan frowned. He didn't respond well to implied criticism. "Well? Why have you let all this trash pile up here? That's hardly in the spirit of the Great Chain . . ."

"Me letting it pile up? I didn't! *He* did! Shep did it! I will pay any reasonable price for trash pickup but he—!" Gravenstein pointed across the street at the big man stepping out of Shep's. Gordon Shep wore a big blue suit, his swag belly straining out of the jacket; he had a jowly face, an unpleasant gold-toothed grin, and an enormous cigar in his hand. Seeing Gravenstein pointing at him accusingly, Shep crossed the street, shaking his head disparagingly, and managing a good deal of swagger despite the obesity.

He pointed at Gravenstein with his cigar as he walked up. "What's this little liar here yellin' about, Mr. Ryan?"

Ryan ignored Shep. "Why should this man be responsible for your trash, Gravenstein?"

Bill could guess why. He remembered that Shep here had diversified . . .

"First of all," the smaller man said, shaking, clearly trying not to shout at Ryan, "it's not all mine!"

"Feh!" Shep said, chuckling. "Prove it!"

"Some of it's mine—but some of it's his, Mr. Ryan! And as for what's mine—he runs the only trash-collection service around here! He bought it two months ago, and he's using it to run me out of business! He's charging me ten times what he charges everyone else for trash collection!"

Bill was startled. "Ten times?"

Shep chuckled and tapped cigar ash onto the pile of garbage. "That's the marketplace. We have no restraints here, right, Mr. Ryan? No price controls! Anyone can own anything they can buy and run it how they like!"

"The market won't bear that kind of pricing," Bill pointed out.

"He only charges *me* that price!" Gravenstein insisted. "He's my grocery competitor! He's got more business than I do, but it's not enough; he wants to corner the grocery business around here, and he knows if garbage piles up because I can't afford to pay him to take it away, nobody'll come to shop at my place! And nobody does!"

"Looks like you'll have to move it out yourself," Ryan said, shrugging.

"Who'll look after my shop while I do that? It's a long ways to the dump chute! And I shouldn't have to do that, Mr. Ryan; he shouldn't be gouging me, trying to run me out of business!"

"Shouldn't he?" Ryan mused. "It's not really a business practice I admire. But the great marketplace is like a thriving jungle, where some survive and become king of their territory—and some don't. It's the way of nature! Survival of the fittest weans out the weaklings, Gravenstein! I advise you to find some means of competing—or move out."

"Mr. Ryan—please—shouldn't we have a *public* trash-collection service?"

Ryan raised his eyebrows. "Public! That sounds like Roosevelt—or Stalin! Go to one of Shep's competitors!"

"They won't come clear over here, Mr. Ryan! This man controls trash pickup in this whole area! He's out to get me!

Why, he's threatening to buy the building and have me evicted, Mr. Ryan! Now I believe in competition and hard work, but—"

"No more whining, Gravenstein! We do not fix prices here! We do not regulate! We do not say who can buy what!"

"Hear that, Gravenstein?" Shep sneered. "Welcome to the real world of business!"

"Please, Mr. Ryan," Gravenstein said, hands balling into fists at his sides. "When I came down here, I was told I'd have an opportunity to expand, to grow, to live in a place without taxes—I gave up everything to come here! Where am I to go, if he drives me out? Where can I go? *Where can I go!*"

A muscle in Ryan's face twitched. He looked at Gravenstein with narrowed eyes. His voice became chilled steel. "Deal with it as a man should, Gravenstein—do not whine like a child!"

Gravenstein stood there, shaking helplessly, pale with rage—then he ran back into his store. Bill's heart went out to him. But Ryan was right, wasn't he? The market had to be unregulated. Still, there were other problems cropping up in Rapture from predatory types . . .

"Say there, Ryan," Shep said, "how about coming in the office for a drink, eh?"

"I think not, Shep," Ryan growled, walking away. "Come along, Bill." They strode onward, and Ryan sighed. "That man Shep is an odious sort. He's little better than a mafioso. But the marketplace must be free, and if some eggs are broken to make that omelet, well . . ."

There was a shout from behind. And a yell of fear.

Bill and Ryan turned to see Gravenstein, hands trembling, pointing a pistol at Shep in the midst of the passageway. Gravenstein shouted, "I'll deal with it like a man, all right!"

"No!" Shep shouted, stumbling back, the cigar flopping from his mouth.

Gravenstein fired—twice. Shep shrieked, clutching himself, staggering with each shot—and then fell like a great sack of dropped groceries onto the passageway floor.

"Dammit!" Ryan grunted. "That, now, *is* against the rules! I'll have a constable on the man!"

But that would not be necessary. As Bill watched, Gravenstein put the gun to his own head and pulled the trigger.

Sofia Lamb's Office
1950

Sofia Lamb balanced her notebook on her knee, poised her pen, and said, "Tell me about this feeling of being trapped, Margie . . ."

"There's one way I can get out of this burg, Doc," Margie said in a flat voice. "If I kill myself." She sat up on the therapy couch and chewed a knuckle. She was a slender, long-legged, brown-haired woman in a simple blue dress, worn-out white flats, a small, shabby blue velvet hat. The paint on her fingernails hadn't been renewed for a long time; they were patchy red. Margie had a sweet, lightly freckled face with large brown eyes, her face going a bit round, and her belly pooching out—she was a couple of months pregnant. "But maybe not. Maybe killing yourself doesn't get you out either." Her large brown eyes seemed to get larger as she added in a whisper, "I've heard there's ghosts in Rapture . . ."

Sofia leaned back in her chair and shook her head. "Ghosts are in people's minds—so is the idea that you have to escape. That's just . . . just a notion that's haunting you. And . . . after what you've been through . . ."

"What I been through—maybe I got only myself to blame." She wiped tears away and took a deep breath. "They said I'd have a career as an entertainer here. I shoulda known better, Doc. My ma always said, you don't get a free ride in this world, and she was right. Ma died when I was sixteen, my pop was long gone, so I was on my own, working as a taxi dancer when I got recruited for Rapture. I come here, fulla hopes and dreams, end up in that strip joint in Fort Frolic. Eve's Garden, what a joke! All the big shots come there, grinnin' like apes at the girls. I've seen Mr. Ryan there even. When he got interested in Jasmine Jolene—what airs *she* put on, I can tell ya! The manager of that place, I wouldn't have sex with him. So he fired me! It's not supposed to be part of my job . . ."

"Naturally not . . ." Sofia wrote, *Consistent pattern of disappointed expectations in patients.*

"So I tried to get work some other place in Rapture—waitressing, ya know? Nope, no work. Sold most of my clothes. Ran out of money, ran outta food. Living on stuff cadged outta trashcans. Asked to be taken back to the surface. No way, sister, they tell me. Never thought I'd ever end up a whore. A little dancing for money, sure, but *this*—selling my 'assets' to those fishermen down at Neptune's Bounty! All the damn day in the bar—or on my back in the rooms they got out behind. And Fontaine—he said I had to give him a percentage. My ma always said so: I get stubborn—and I told him to go to hell on a sled. He tells that Reggie to knock me around."

Sofia clucked her tongue sympathetically, and wrote, *No recourse for those stricken by bad luck. No WPA here. Nothing to catch those who fall. Enormous potential for social ferment.*

"You're in my care now," Sofia said soothingly. Her heart was wrenched at Margie's story. "I can even offer you a job."

"What kinda work?"

"Gardening, assisting. I intend to start a new program I'm calling Dionysus Park. Nothing you'll have to be ashamed of. But I will need something from you. I need your *trust*. Your complete trust."

Margie sniffled, and her eyes welled with tears. "Gee, if

you'll help me—gosh, you got it, Doc! I'll trust you from here to the stars!"

"Good!" Sofia smiled.

If you could get people to trust you, really trust you—you would get their loyalty too.

And she would need loyalty, unthinking loyalty, for what she had in mind. A gradual revolution, first in mind and then in fact—transforming Rapture from within . . .

Between Neptune's Bounty and Olympus Heights
1951

Frank Fontaine felt like a fat kid with the keys to a candy store.

Gliding through the sea in his private, radio-controlled bathysphere, from Neptune's Bounty to the station for Olympus Heights and Mercury Suites—past neon signs for several shops, including one of his own—Fontaine reflected on what a feast Rapture was for a man like him. Ryan kept business regulations to the absolute minimum. If you had enough Rapture dollars to hire a space from Ryan Industries, you could open pretty much any business you wanted. Fontaine had even cultivated one of Ryan's bookkeepers, Marjorie Dustin. As long as he diddled Marjorie every so often and kicked her some cash, she cheerfully added forty percent, on paper, to his fresh fish take—Ryan Industries was paying for forty percent more fish than they received.

He knew Ryan had men keeping an eye on him. That very morning Fontaine had spotted that Russian thug Karlosky following him through the Lower Concourse. Ryan was setting up security cameras around Rapture. Not a lot of them yet, but more were coming—and Ryan controlled them. Hard to keep a secret for long from those cameras.

Fontaine watched an enormous fish with a gigantic mouth swim past. He had no idea what kind it was—it swiveled an eye to look through his bathysphere port, seeming intrigued. Fontaine shook his head, amused at how much he'd grown accustomed to living in a giant aquarium. Maybe someday, when he'd gotten control of Rapture, he could use the undersea city as his base for forays onto dry land. He'd always have a place to escape to, where the cops would never find him . . .

Fontaine caught a glimpse of one of his own subs sliding by below, heading toward the underwater wharf entrance, dragging a net full of glistening silvery fish. Silver—like silver dollars. Cash just swam along in the sea, and all you had to do was find some sucker to scoop it up for you. Sometimes he thought he was the only guy in the world who wasn't a sucker.

People in Rapture were getting sick of eating fish. Fontaine had started smuggling in beef, which was all but impossible to get in Rapture otherwise. Shortage was opportunity. A lot of these saps were even feeling short on religion, so Fontaine brought in Bibles. Which was sure to make Ryan angry. Ryan hated religion—whereas Fontaine simply laughed at it.

The bathysphere arrived at the station, locked into place, and Fontaine emerged. He hurried past a group of snazzy partiers heading through the Metro for one of the nightclubs. The overhead lights were dimming, as they were designed to do in the evening, to give people in Rapture a more normal sense of night and day.

Fontaine took a tram up to Olympus Heights, and then the elevator to his place in Mercury Suites. He arrived just in time to grab a quick bite before his meeting. He walked through the marble-lined rooms, past small bronze statues of dancing women and the comforting paintings of New York City scenes. He did miss New York.

He sat at a marble-topped, gold-legged table by the big window looking out on the blue, lamplit sea, where glowing purple jellyfish wafted by like skirts on invisible dancing girls.

His cook Antoine made him beef bourguignon with sea-weed and a few lonely leafs of lettuce on the side. He drank a glass of a pretty dull Worley wine, and then the doorbell rang. Reggie let them in.

"Da boss's in here," Reggie said.

Reggie ushered Dr. Suchong and Brigid Tenenbaum into the sitting room. "Keep an eye on the door, Reggie," Fontaine said. "We don't wanna be interrupted . . ."

"Sure thing, boss."

Dr. Yi Suchong was still wearing a long white lab coat over a shabby suit peppered with rusty spots that looked like bloodstains. Brigid Tenenbaum wore a calf-length blue dress. She walked somewhat awkwardly in red pumps, clearly un-used to them. She was a young woman—the wunderkind they'd called her. Her face, however, its angularity reflecting Belorussia, was marked by experience. There was a cold dis-tance in it. Fontaine understood that distance. He didn't let anyone close to him either. But there was something almost robotic in her movements. And she never met his eyes, though sometimes he felt her watching him.

She obviously dressed up for the meeting, with a touch of lipstick, awkwardly applied. She wasn't so bad, despite her tobacco-stained teeth and chewed-down fingernails.

As they sat on ornate sofas across from each other, Fon-taine ran a hand over his bald head, wondering if he should grow out his hair—but women seemed to like him bald. "May I smoke, please?" she asked.

"Sure you can. Have one of mine." He passed her the or-nate silver cigarette box he kept on the coral and glass coffee table.

She took a cigarette with trembling fingers, inserting it into an ivory holder she produced from a small pocket in her dress. Fontaine lit it with a silver lighter shaped cunningly like a seahorse. She glanced at him as she blew smoke toward the ceiling—then looked quickly away.

Both of the scientists, sitting widely apart, seemed quite stiff and formal. Seemed like they didn't trust him. They'd get over it when he started shoveling mounds of money over them. Something nice and cozy about a blanket of cash.

Suchong was a lean Korean, wearing wire-rim glasses. He must've been twice Tenenbaum's age. She didn't at all seem in awe of him, though he had a string of degrees.

"How about some wine?" Fontaine asked.

She said yes and Suchong said no at precisely the same instant. Suchong laughed nervously. Tenenbaum just stared fixedly at the end of her cigarette.

Fontaine got wine for himself and her and said, "Dr. Suchong—I understand you've been working for Ryan Industries."

Suchong sighed. "Suchong works for himself. There is the Suchong Institute and Laboratories. But—contracts with Ryan and Sinclair, yes . . ."

"And Miss Tenenbaum—you're working . . . as a free agent?"

"Yes. This is a good description." She looked past him, over his shoulder, as if she were trying to give the impression of looking at him without quite being able to.

"This is where I say, You're all wondering why I called you here," Fontaine said, putting down his wineglass. "I asked you two here because I'm thinking there's bigger opportunities in this science stuff than I ever thought of. I've got people who work for Ryan giving me the inside skinny. What I hear, you two are feeling somewhat frustrated."

Tenenbaum bobbed her head, her eyes flickering at everything but Fontaine. "This is true, what you say. Ryan says work on anything—but research costs money. Financial support is, what is the word—inconsistent." She flicked her eyes at Suchong. "Dr. Suchong does not wish to make Mr. Ryan angry—but we both need . . . more!"

Suchong frowned. "Woman, do not speak for me." But he didn't deny it was true.

They were ripe and ready to pluck. "Well now," Fontaine said, "given the right situation, the three of us could start our own little research team. Suchong, I understand you're working on a new kind of tobacco?"

"Not precisely." Suchong's accent was heavy—it took Fontaine a moment to translate *plee-cise-lee* into *precisely.* "Suchong alters genetics of another plant to make nicotine. Make nicotine in sugarcane! We will extract and make 'Nicotreats.' Nicotine candy!"

"Clever!" Fontaine said, grinning. "Yeah, I've been reading up on this whole genetics business. You could make all kinds of things by switching genes around, seems to me. Maybe miniature cattle we could keep down here somewhere for fresh beef, yeah? And from what I hear, you could switch a person's genes around. You could make changes in people, right?"

Her frown deepened into a scowl, which she directed at the floor. "What do you know of that?"

"Just rumors. That you're paying for some kind of special sea slug. I hear you've bought ten of them . . ."

She nodded once, briskly. "I would buy more if I could. No ordinary sea slug. This species is a living miracle! I asked Ryan to help fund these experiments. He was not listening." She sniffed, taking her cigarette butt from the holder and dropping it vaguely toward the ashtray. It fell onto the table and smoldered there. She gnawed at a nail, her eyes unfocused, seeming halfway in another world, oblivious as Fontaine reflexively put the cigarette out in the ashtray.

Making a sudden awkward pushing gesture with her hand,

she went on, "Ryan, he put me off! 'Maybe later,' all this sort of thing."

"You on the point of a breakthrough?"

"Perhaps." She glanced at Suchong. He shrugged.

Fontaine smiled. "Then it's something I want to invest in. I'll pay well for a stake—and Ryan doesn't have to know about it. When you're ready, you can come and work for me completely. Both of you! I figure this genetics dodge could be the wave of the future—and I've got a few things in mind. The two of you could work on it—Suchong could bring you into his lab, and I could pay your salary, for now . . . Maybe get this guy Alexander involved. Only I don't want Ryan to know about any of this. I want it on the QT, see. He'll move in and take anything we come up with otherwise—and he'll find some excuse to keep all the rights to himself."

Tenenbaum smiled crookedly. "Meanwhile, Ryan pays for Suchong's expensive lab, yes?"

"Why *not* let him pay for the big stuff?" Fontaine said, toying with his wineglass. "I'm doing good here—but Ryan controls more resources in Rapture. He's got deeper pockets. For now."

"Suchong needs more research money, yes!" said the Korean abruptly. "But also need something else." He put his hands on his knees, leaned stiffly forward, his eyes washing out behind his glasses as they caught the sea lights from the window. "Yes. We both think of altering human genes. Difficult to do without *humans*! What Suchong really needs is—*young humans*! Their cells have very much more possibility. But—everyone crazy about children! Overprotect them!" He made a face. "Vile creatures, children—"

"Don't much like kids, eh?"

"Suchong grow up in a household where my father is very poor servant, only children there the brats of rich man. They treat me like dog! Children are cruel. Must be trained like animals!"

"Children—all are lost creatures," Brigid Tenenbaum said softly, her voice almost inaudible.

"You were pretty young when you started working as a scientist, Miss Tenenbaum," Fontaine prompted. Understand what makes 'em tick, and you can wind up their clock. Set 'em for whatever time you want. "How'd that happen?"

She took a sip of wine, lit another cigarette, and seemed to gaze into another time. "I was at German prison camp, only sixteen years old. Important German doctor; he makes experiment. Sometime, he makes scientific error. I tell him of this error, and this makes him angry. But then he asks, 'How can a child know such a thing?' I tell him, 'Sometimes, I just know.' He screams at me, 'Then why tell me?'" She smiled stiffly. "'Well,' I said, 'if you're going to do such things, at least you should do them properly!'" She took a drag on her cigarette and made a ghostly little smile—and a ghost of cigarette smoke rose from her parted lips as she let the smoke drift slowly out of her lungs.

Suchong rolled his eyes. "She tells that story many times."

Fontaine cleared his throat. "I don't know as I can get you the kind of experimental subjects you're talking about right *away*, Doc," Fontaine said. "Might draw too much attention. But what I can get you is some grown-up guys who've run afoul of the rules around here. Couple of guys disappear from Detention, who's going to care? We'll give out they escaped and got drowned trying to get out of the city."

Suchong made a single brisk nod. "That can be useful."

"So—supposing you could find a way to control genes," Fontaine said, toying with his wineglass. "Is it true what I heard—that genes control how we age?"

Again Suchong said no and Tenenbaum said yes at the same moment.

Suchong grunted in irritation. "This is Tenenbaum theory. Genes only one factor!"

"Genes, they are almost everything," Tenenbaum said, sniffing.

"But I mean—you could help a man stay young," Fontaine persisted. "Maybe change his body in some way. Give him more hair, stronger arms, a longer . . . you know. If we could sell that . . . and give a guy, I don't know, more talents . . . more . . . abilities."

"Yes," Tenenbaum said. "This is something my mentor talked about. To enhance a man's powers—make him *der Übermensch*—the superman. A super man—or woman! Many risks in this. But yes. With time—and much experimentation."

"When Suchong get money and experimental subjects, Mr. Fontaine?" Suchong asked.

Fontaine shrugged. "I'll get you the first research payment tomorrow. We'll work out a contract, just between us . . ."

Fontaine paused, reflecting that if he had to give them shares in the business, it might cost him a lot of money in the long run. But once he had the basic products started, the technology going, he could hire other researchers cheaper. And then he could get rid of Suchong and Tenenbaum. One way or another.

He smiled his best, most convincing, most openhearted smile at them. Never failed to lure the suckers in. "I'll get you the contract and the money fast—but we've got to do it carefully. 'Free' enterprise or not—Ryan watches everything . . ."

9

Chief Sullivan didn't like being out on the lower wharf when the lights had been dimmed this much. He could still see to get around, but the shadows around the pylons multiplied and seemed to squirm at the edge of his vision. This wasn't a safe place even in broad "daylight." A couple of guys had disappeared on this wharf over the past week. One of them had been found, or what was left of him, his body carved up pretty good. Seemed to Sullivan, when he'd examined the body, that those nice straight cuts had been made by scalpels . . .

Sullivan's boots creaked on the planks as he walked to the end of the wharf. The cold came off the water. The smell of fish was strong—the reek of decay. Three wooden crates were lined up together on the wharf with a curious palm-print logo on them—but he figured breaking into them wasn't likely to provide him proof of the contraband smuggling he knew was going on. They were marked "Rotten—for discard" and smelled like it. He figured Fontaine was too smart to have his contraband right here on the wharf.

The lower wharf resembled a wooden pier. It slanted down toward water released into the big chamber that enclosed part of the fisheries. The shallow water around the wooden projections was mostly just to give a feeling of a real wharf, to break up the claustrophobia—part of the psychology of Rapture design. A big electric sign, hanging from the ceiling, switched off, read **FONTAINE'S FISHERIES**. The walls here were mostly corrugated metal; above the lower wharf area was the upper wharf, with cafés and taverns like Fighting McDonagh's—the tavern owned by Bill McDonagh, though he had little time to run it in person.

The wharf area felt, to Sullivan, like a kind of man-made cavern. Wood and sand and a pool of water below, the looming walls, the ceiling overhead—it was like an undersea cave. Only the walls and ceiling were metal.

The actual docking area for the fishing submarines, complete with cold storage vaults, was hidden down in the back, in a fish-reeking labyrinth of passages, conveyor belts for seafood processing, and offices—like the wharf master's office. The wharf master was Peach Wilkins—Fontaine's man. So far, Wilkins had stonewalled Sullivan when it came to the smugglers.

Reaching into the pocket of his trench coat to feel the reassuring grip of his revolver, Sullivan descended the switchback ramp to get closer to the water. The briny water lay quiet as a sheet of glass. But something splashed off in the shadows close to the wall.

He drew the pistol but kept it low, thumb ready to cock the hammer back. He bent down, glanced under the pier, thinking he saw a dark shape moving back there in the dimness.

Sullivan squatted a little more, trying to peer into the darkness under the pier, but saw nothing but the glimmer of water. Nothing moved. Whatever he thought he'd seen was gone. But then he saw it, bobbing back there, close to the corrugated metal walls. Someone had been pushing a floating crate along. He wished he had a flashlight.

A distinct splashing sound came from back near the crate. He raised the revolver and shouted, "Come out of there, you!"

He was distantly aware of a creaking noise on the ramp

behind him. But his attention was fixed on the darkness under the pier, where that splashing had come from . . .

"You in there! I'm going to start opening fire if you don't—"

He broke off, hearing the creaking more distinctly behind
him, and turned—in time to see the silhouette of a man
against the dim light of the ceiling, leaping down at him from
the higher wharf ramp—a monkey wrench in the stranger's
hand poised to bash Sullivan's skull.

Sullivan just had time to twist himself to the right so that
the monkey wrench came whistling down past his left ear,
thumping painfully into his shoulder—then the man tackled
him.

Sullivan was slammed backward, hand convulsively firing
the pistol. He heard the man grunt as they both splashed into
the shallow seawater. Sullivan twisted as he fell, coming
down on his left side. Salty water roared in his ears and
choked him, big rough hands closed around his throat, a
great weight bore him downward. He struck out with the gun
butt, felt it connect with the back of the man's head. The two
of them thrashed; then Sullivan got his feet under him and
managed to stand, thigh deep, water streaming off him. The
other man was getting up, staggering, blood dripping from a
head wound. A big square-jawed, ham-fisted man in a pea
jacket glared at him with one little brown eye through black
hair pasted down by water. He'd lost the monkey wrench in
the water.

The man swung a bunched fist hard at Sullivan—Sullivan
jerked back so that the blow missed, but he was sent off-
balance. He tried to fire the gun, but water had gotten in, and
it misfired. Sullivan was staggering back to try to stay upright.
The man grinned, showing crooked teeth, and sloshed toward him, big hands outstretched.

A flash from up on the wharf—a gunshot—and Sullivan's

brawny assailant grunted, gritted his teeth, took one more step, then fell on his face in the water. He thrashed for a couple of moments—then went limp, floating facedown.

Sullivan steadied himself and looked up to see Karlosky smiling coldly down at him from the wharf ramp, pocketing a smoking pistol. The air smelled of gunsmoke.

"Nice shot," Sullivan said as blood welled from the hole in the left side of the stranger's head. "Assuming, that is, you weren't aiming for me!"

"If I shoot at you," Karlosky said in his Russian accent, "you already die."

Sullivan pocketed his own pistol, grabbed the dead man by the collar, and dragged him to the lower ramp, laboring in his water-heavy clothing. Pulling the thug onto the ramp, he bent over—aware of the pain from a deep bruise in his left shoulder—and turned the corpse over. There was just enough light to make out the face. He still didn't recognize him. Or did he? He reached out and wiped wet hair away from the dead man's face. He'd seen that face in a photo, in the Rapture admissions records. A maintenance worker. "The guy tried to brain me with a wrench," he said as Ivan Karlosky joined him.

"I heard you shoot," Karlosky said. "But you miss."

"Didn't have time to aim. You see anybody else on the other side of the wharf?"

"Da! Running away! Could not see who!"

"I've seen this one's file. Don't remember his name."

"Mickael Lasko. Ukrainian! All sons of bitches, Ukrainians! Lasko, he work maintenance, then do something for Peach Wilkins. I heard in a bar, maybe he knows about smuggling—so I follow him this morning. The bastard lose me down in the docking maze. Some hidden passages down there . . ."

"Seemed like this particular Ukrainian son of a bitch

wanting to do me in . . ." Shivering with the chill from the water soaking his clothing, Sullivan went through the dead man's coat pockets—and came up with an envelope full of Rapture dollars and, in another pocket, a small notebook. He opened the notebook. It contained a list, blurred from the water. He read it aloud:

"Bibles—7 sold
Cocaine 2 g sold
Liquor 6 fifths
Letters out, 3 at 70 RD each."

"Looks like he's smuggling," Karlosky said.

Sullivan shook his head. "Looks like Fontaine or Wilkins don't have much respect for me. Like I'm supposed to believe this guy is behind it all. He's not going to keep a notebook listing cocaine and Bibles. I doubt he knew how to spell 'em. The envelope with the cash in it was payment to this knucklehead to try to take me down. They were okay with it if he got killed. Make it look like the smuggler was all done for, take the heat off them . . ."

He tossed Karlosky the envelope. "You can have that—for saving my life. Come on, I'll send someone down to pick up this patsy." They started back up the ramp, hurrying into better lighting. "Shit, I hate walking with salt water in my pants. It's rasping my ball sack, goddammit . . . let's get a drink. I'll buy you a vodka."

"Vodka is good to get smell of rotting fish out! And smell of dead Ukrainian—even worse!"

A Locked Laboratory, Rapture
1953

"Absurd, Tenenbaum!" Dr. Suchong jeered as he walked ahead of Frank Fontaine and Brigid Tenenbaum.

"This discovery is very great," Tenenbaum retorted confidently. She seemed to simmer with subdued excitement. "Mr. Fontaine, you will see!"

Frank Fontaine's deal with Dr. Suchong and Brigid Tenenbaum hadn't quite paid off yet. Maybe, he figured, as he followed her and Suchong into the laboratory, today was the day that particular roll of the dice was going to come up lucky sevens. Tenenbaum's excitement—which she almost never showed—seemed to hint she'd stumbled across something explosive.

Tenenbaum led the way to a sedated man in a hospital gown lying on a padded gurney in the most secretive inner chamber of the laboratory complex. She looked the unconscious man over with analytical coolness as she spoke. "Germans, all they can talk about is blue eyes and shape of forehead. All I care about is why is this one born strong, and that one weak—this one smart, that one stupid? All the killing, you think the Germans could have been interested in something useful? Today—I think we have found something very much useful . . ."

The sleeping man on the gurney was bound to it with leather restraints. He was quite an ordinary-looking man of medium height, brown hair, blotchy skin. Fontaine had seen him playing poker in Fighting McDonagh's—Willy Brougham. On the white metal table beside Brougham was an enormous syringe with a thick red liquid in it. Occupying most of a shelf beyond the table was a five-gallon aquarium tank bubbling with seawater. Immersed in the tank, pulsing repugnantly on a bed of sand, was one of Tenenbaum's sluglike wonders. It was about eight inches long, with a primitive armor fringing its edges. It had striated, grainy skin; faintly incandescent blue panels on its humped back. Teeth gnashed at one end on its elongated body; a small tapered tail twitched at the other.

"This Tenenbaum, she believes genes answer to everything.

Suchong think genes important—but the control of subject's mind, conditioning of synapses, these things are more important! Who controls such, controls all!"

"I like that," Fontaine said. "Conditioning is something real interesting to me. Read about it in some magazine. The Nazis were experimenting with it . . ."

Tenenbaum cleared her throat and said, "Now this man, Brougham, he is wounded—I will show you injury . . ." She lifted up the gown of the man on the gurney, and Fontaine winced to see a nasty, puckered, ragged tear in the man's flesh, about seven inches long, haphazardly taped shut just above the groin. "He tries to use fishing hook to steal fish from fishery tanks! Ryan's men catch him, slice him with his own hook. Now—we have extracted special material from slugs. Purified it. This material is made of special stem cells. Unstable. Highly adaptable. Please observe."

She picked up the syringe and jammed it in the flesh just above the man's groin. Brougham's back arched, his body reacting—but he didn't wake. Fontaine winced at the sight of the three-inch needle piercing deeply into the man's gut.

"Now," she said, "observe the wound."

Fontaine did. And nothing happened.

"Ha!" Dr. Suchong said. "Maybe it not work this time. And your great theory—poof, Tenenbaum!"

Then the skin around the wound twitched, reddened, and the serrated flesh inside the wound seemed to writhe about . . . and seal shut. In a minute, only a faint scar remained of the ragged gash. It had healed before their eyes.

"I'll be damned!" Fontaine said.

"I call it ADAM," said Brigid Tenenbaum. "Because from Adam in the myth came life for mankind. This too brings life—it destroys damaged cells, replaces them with new ones—transferred by plasmids, unstable genetic material.

Now, stem cells can be manipulated—their genes changed! We can make them this, make them that. If it can do this, heal instantly—what else can it do? Transform a man, a woman? Into what? Many things! Endless possibility!"

Suchong chewed at a thumbnail, staring at the experimental subject. Then he pointed. "You see there? On his head—some lesions!"

She shrugged. "Hardly visible. A few minor side effects . . ."

"Some may have much more! Your man with the miracle hands—that one behaves a little strangely now. And there are some curious marks on his arms. Like cancer! Uncontrolled cell growth!"

"So that's the key," Fontaine mused. "These stem-cell things and this . . . this ADAM? You can use it to change things up in a man—give him special abilities, like we discussed?"

"Precisely!" she said proudly.

Fontaine could tell she was speaking to him, though she never looked at him. She would turn her head his way, but her eyes were always fixed on some point over his left shoulder, as if she were talking to an invisible person behind him. "Growing hair, growing a bigger pecker, bigger muscles, bigger breasts for the ladies, bigger brains for the highbrows . . ."

"It is all possible with ADAM!"

"Hmf," Suchong said. "You do not tell him how ADAM must be constantly re-energized!"

"Not a concern, Dr. Suchong!" Tenenbaum said, listening to Brougham's heart with a stethoscope. "I have design for energizer—we will call it EVE!" She frowned. "But—the sea slug can only make so much ADAM and EVE. These sea slugs—we believe they are also parasites. We find on sharks, other creatures. Maybe they can be attached to human beings. A person could become a . . . a factory for ADAM. Then we have more ADAM for experiments." She scratched thoughtfully in her unwashed hair. "Working with my men-tor, all he thought of was how to find greater power in men! To breed them, to change them! Working at his side, I was thinking of another researcher. A greater one! Ha, ha!"

That was the first time Fontaine had ever heard her laugh—a brittle, almost inhuman sound.

"So this ADAM thing," Fontaine went on, looking at the healed skin on the sedated man. "If you could get enough sea slugs, maybe some people to work with as . . . what would you call them, hosts . . . you could mass-produce this stuff?"

She nodded to the imaginary person behind Fontaine. "In time—yes."

"But . . ." Dr. Suchong shook his head. "Suchong believe—ADAM could be addictive! My study of human beings shows me anything that make easy change in people, the people quickly become addicted! A man feels bad, takes drink of alcohol, very quick feels a little better—he becomes addicted to alcohol! Same with opium! Maybe same with ADAM—quick fix in man: addictive! Organism develops need for it. Suchong observe agitation in this man Tenenbaum found on dock. Sometimes he is . . . what is it you people say? He is 'high'!"

Addictive? Even better. Fontaine thought of the time, risk, and expense of bringing in poppy from Kandahar.

Yeah. He could feel it. His cultivation of Suchong and Tenenbaum was paying off.

"Keep on this," Fontaine told them eagerly. "I'll make it worth your while—worth all our whiles!"

Medical Pavilion
1953

Sitting pensively behind his inner-office desk in the medical pavilion, Dr. J. S. Steinman was bored, and tired of fighting his own impulses. And only just now beginning to understand why he'd come to Rapture.

Steinman took a cigarette from the box on the coral desk, lit it with a silver lighter shaped like a human nose, and got up to open the curtains on his office port hole so he could gaze out at the sea—at kelp and sea fans waving in the current. Restful, that view. Nothing like New York. Always hectic in the Big Apple. People interfering with a man.

It was the implied condemnation he resented, the small-minded judgment of his greatness. How to explain what it was like to reach out for the planet Venus, in hopes of making it his pocket watch? How could he explain that he was sometimes visited by the goddess Aphrodite? He had heard the goddess's voice so clearly . . .

"My darling Doctor Steinman," said Aphrodite. *"To create like the gods is to be a god. Can only a god fashion a face? You have done it again and again—you have taken what was lumpen and made it exquisite; you have taken the mediocre and made it the marvelous. But in every man and woman's face a secret is hidden. The lost perfection—masked. Under the face of a woman whom low, vulgar people regard as 'beautiful' is another face, the perfect face, the Platonic ideal—hidden under the surface beauty. If you can liberate the perfect face from the almost perfect, you become a god. What is more important than beauty? It was I, Aphrodite herself, who inspired the poet Keats. Truth is beauty; beauty is truth! The hidden symmetry underlying the ugly irregularity of surface reality. And here is the paradox: only by passing through the dark gate of chaos, through the shadowy valley of so-called 'ugliness,' is the quest at last completed and the hidden perfection found!"*

Oh, how the goddess had thrilled him! Yes, it was true that he'd heard her voice while taking ether—cocaine and ether by turns, in fact—but it had been no mere hallucination. He was sure of that.

So when Ryan had approached him, saying that innovative surgeons would be needed in Rapture, he'd heard Aphrodite whispering to him again: *"Here it is! Here is the chance, here is the opportunity, here is the secret realm you've dreamed of, where you can at last unearth perfection! A refuge where the small-minded scorners cannot find you!"*

Steinman blew a plume of blue smoke toward the ceiling vent and turned to look at himself in the office mirror. He knew very well he was a "handsome" man. The elegant chin, the striking ears, the dark eyes, that understated, perfectly clipped mustache like an accent mark over a bon mot when he uttered a witticism . . .

And yet there was another face under that one waiting to come out. Did he dare to find his *own* perfect face? Could he do surgery on his own face—perhaps using a mirror? Could he—

"Doctor? Miss Pleasance is waking up . . ."

He glanced up at the doorway, where his assistant waited for him: Miss Chavez, a small, pretty Puerto Rican woman in a white uniform, white shoes, nurse's cap. She didn't seem surprised to find him gazing into the mirror.

Chavez was a petite little creature with a heart-shaped face, Cupid's-bow lips. Could he find that *perfect* face underneath Miss Chavez's features? Suppose he were to reduce the pterygoideus muscles by half, then doubly tighten the temporalis muscle, and he might just bisect the eyelids . . .

All in good time. "Ah—yes, go ahead and begin unwrapping her face, Miss Chavez; I'll be right there . . ."

Miss Sylvia Pleasance was engaged to Ronald Greavy, son of the Ruben Greavy who worked closely with Ryan. They were an influential family in Rapture.

He stubbed his cigarette out on the seashell ashtray on his desk and walked down the hall. Stretched out in the recovery room, Miss Pleasance was wearing a nightgown and socks.

She had a sheet draped modestly over her. Look at those fat little arms. Too bad he couldn't cut into those fat little arms and reduce them. Perhaps down to the bone. Even expose the bone in places. Like ivory jewelry . . .

Nurse Chavez had cranked the upper part of the patient's bed to a forty-five-degree angle and was beginning to unwind the bandages. Miss Pleasance's large green eyes were gazing out at him from the gaps in the mummylike facial wrap with a mixture of fear and anticipation. Her red hair spilled almost stylishly over one side of the bandage. He thought, once more, that there might be a certain appeal to leaving the bandages on—forever. One would see only the hair and eyes— and mystery. Like a mummy . . .

Sylvia Pleasance's face was slowly revealed . . . Nurse Chavez gasped . . .

And clapped her hands together. "Isn't she lovely, Doctor! You've done a wonderful job!"

He sighed resignedly: it was true. All quite lovely. He hadn't done anything experimental with this woman. He was trying not to do anything unusual in his new practice. Just give them what they wanted. But it was hard. The temptation had been strong . . .

She had a conventionally attractive, delicately sculpted face now, with dimples on her pale cheeks, a matching dimple in her chin. It was a sweetly rounded visage but with all the unpleasant chunkiness gone. Her fiancé would probably be pleased. She looked rather like an adult Shirley Temple. How tiresome. But the Pleasance woman cooed over her reflection when Nurse Chavez gave her the hand mirror.

"Oh, Doctor! It's perfect! God bless you!"

"Yes, yes," he muttered, approaching, taking her chin in his hands, turning her head from side to side, looking at it under the light from the gooseneck lamp. "Yes, only . . . I cannot escape the feeling that there is more, far more, to be done . . . some hidden perfection lurking underneath this pretty little mask!"

"What?" Miss Pleasance seemed startled. She swallowed and drew back from him. "I . . ." She frowned and looked at herself again in the hand mirror. Turned her head this way and that. "No! This *is* what I wanted! Exactly! I'm amazed at how you got it! I wouldn't alter it a jot, Doctor!"

He shrugged. "Just as you like. I simply think . . ." Thinking to himself: *If I could just cut a quarter inch off the nose . . . and then . . . perhaps narrow the forehead, entirely remove the orbicularis oculi . . .*

But aloud he said, "I'm so glad you're pleased with the results. Go ahead and let her get dressed, Nurse, release her to her fiancé, and I'll, uh . . ." He turned vaguely and walked, as if through a dream, back to his office.

Surgical knives are so limited. If only there were some way to transform people on the cellular level. If one could only sculpt people genetically; if only a surgical artist could reach into the very essence of a person, transform the subject from within—just the way God would.

The way Aphrodite would want him to . . .

Fontaine's Fisheries
1953

It was late. Fontaine's office was closed, the shades drawn. Reggie was somewhere outside, keeping watch. Fontaine and Tenenbaum were alone in the fisheries' office on a comfortable sofa. Brigid Tenenbaum was stretched out, wearing a negligee and red pumps. Fontaine was half-sitting on the edge, leaning over her, her hands clasped in his. Beside them on the floor was an empty Worley wine bottle and their glasses. Fontaine wore only his boxers and a T-shirt. His clothes were folded neatly on a chair at his desk across the room.

She seemed frightened, and yet he could see anticipation in her eyes too when she glanced at him and—as always—looked quickly away.

"You look kinda scared," he said. "You sure about this?"

"I . . . do not like to be touched," she said. "But . . . I need it, when the feelings of desire come. What I dream of is a man who . . . who simply *takes* me. I will make some token resistance. But it will not be real. I must fight a little. I can only do it that way . . ."

"Well, kid," he said, using his 'voice of reassurance,' "you came to the right shop." She'd cleaned up rather nicely and put on some perfume, even seemed to have brushed the cigarette stains off her teeth. "So this is something you haven't done exactly—but you . . . imagined?" he asked.

"Yes. I am afraid to touch. But I *must* be touched . . ."

"What they call a contradiction in terms. That's you, eh?"

"Perhaps. Now . . . please . . . put the blindfold on me."

"Oh yeah." He took the black blindfold from his pocket and tied it over her eyes. "There. You can't see me now."

"No . . . now that I cannot see you . . . you can touch me—if you hold my arms down . . ."

He pressed her arms back by her wrists to either side of her head and stretched out on her, pressing his hips to hers. She tried to twist away—but she wasn't trying hard.

"Just remember," Fontaine said as he did his duty, enjoying it more than he'd thought he would, "you want it done your way—you do your work my way. You work exclusively for me . . ."

Ryan Amusements
1953

Bill McDonagh felt a bit foolish taking the Journey to the Surface ride alone. It was made for Rapture's children, really, to "satisfy their curiosity" about the surface world. Supposedly. In a few years his child would want to go on a ride in

Rapture's only amusement park. Bill wanted to know, in advance, if what he'd heard about the ride was true. If it was, the ride would probably upset Elaine . . .

He'd been here before to do some maintenance work, but he hadn't taken the tour. He'd bought a ticket and everything.

Now he climbed into the ride car—shaped like an open bathysphere—and settled back. It lurched into motion and then creaked along its track into the tunnel.

The car rumbled slowly past an animatronic mannequin of Andrew Ryan sitting at his desk, looking almost fatherly. The mannequin moved and gestured, in a herky-jerky way, and "talked": *"Why, hello there. My name is Andrew Ryan, and I built the city of Rapture for children just like you, because the world above's become unfit for us. But here, beneath the ocean, it is natural to wonder if the danger has passed . . ."*

"Crikey," Bill muttered. The Ryan robot gave him the willies.

Then the car moved on to the mechanical tableau that warned about taxation on the surface world. Up on his left was a farmhouse, where a farmer tilled his field and his happy wife and child stood behind him . . . but then a giant hand—truly gigantic—moved clutchingly into the tableau, reaching down from above. It had suit sleeves on it—like the suit worn by a bureaucrat. It grabbed the roof of the house and tore it off . . . The tax man taking away all that the man had worked for . . . The animatronic farmer slumped in despair . . .

"On the surface," said the deep voice of Andrew Ryan booming from hidden speakers, *"the farmer tills the soil, trading the strength of his arm for a land of his own. But the parasites say, 'No! What is yours is ours! We are the state; we are God; we demand our share!'"*

"Oh lord," Bill said, staring at the hand. It was terrifying, that giant hand . . . And the hand—as if from some cruel

bureaucratic jehovah—came inexorably down in other tableaus as the ride trundled slowly onward. An animatronic
scientist made a glorious discovery in his laboratory, rose up
on a pedestal in triumph—and then was crushed back down
by that giant hand from above. *"On the surface, the scientist
invests the power of his mind in a single miraculous idea and
naturally begins to rise above his fellows. But the parasites say,
'No! Discovery must be regulated! It must be controlled and
finally surrendered.'"*

That one ought to make Suchong and his like happy, Bill
supposed.

The next tableau showed an artist painting away in rapturous inspiration—before a giant hand came down and suppressed his freedom again . . .

The final tableau was the most frightening of all. A child
was happily watching TV with his family. Then Ryan's God-
like voice warned, *"On the surface, your parents sought a private life; using their great talents to provide for you, they learned
to twist the lies of church and government, believing themselves
masters of the system, but the parasites say, 'No! The child has a
duty! He'll go to war and die for the nation.'"*

And the giant hand came down, pushed through the
wall—and dragged the child away—into the darkness . . .
into death.

Bill shook his head. This was all about scaring children it
seemed to him. He'd heard that Sofia Lamb, when she'd first
come, had given Ryan the idea—an "amusement ride" that
was a kind of aversion therapy, a way of imprinting children
with a revulsion for the surface world—and a consequent
commitment to the only alternative: Rapture . . .

Between the big tableaus, animatronic Ryans appeared,
lecturing, hectoring—warning the child about the horrors of
the surface world.

As the ride ended he heard Cohen's song, "Rise, Rapture, Rise," playing . . .

Oh rise, Rapture, rise!
We turn our hopes up to the skies!
Oh rise, Rapture, rise!
Upon your wings our dreams will fly.
A city in the ocean's deep
A promise that we'll always keep
To boldly turn our eyes upon the prize!
So rise, rise, rise!
Oh rise, Rapture, rise!
We merrily sing this reprise.
Oh rise, Rapture, rise!
To help us crush parasites despised . . .

Bill sighed. He was going to do whatever he could to keep Elaine away from here. She wouldn't understand. She already had her doubts about Rapture, and this would only deepen them. Whatever happened, they were committed to Rapture and Andrew Ryan. Weren't they?

Dionysus Park, Rapture
1954

"How can a house divided stand, Simon?" Sofia Lamb asked gently as they sat in the sculpture garden of Dionysus Park. Simon Wales sat beside her on the carved coral bench, smoking a pipe, seeming troubled; Margie and several of Sofia's other followers were scattering fish-gut fertilizer around the plants at the other end of the park's gallery of sculptures. Across from them was an example of "unconscious art," a sculpture by one of her followers showing a squirming octopus—but the creature had a human face that was oddly like Andrew Ryan's. "Rapture is designed for conflict, for competition—but can this marvel of a community survive that division, bottled up down here? We need unity to make Rapture thrive! And that means a *communal* concept, not a competitive one . . ."

Simon glanced around nervously. "Really, you shouldn't use those kinds of . . . well, Ryan would regard that as red propaganda . . . Could be dangerous. They're building a new detention center, and I have a feeling Ryan might want it for, ah, people who talk about undermining his master vision . . ."

Sofia shrugged. "If I must go to prison—so be it. The people need me! More are coming every day, Simon! The vision of wholeness is taking hold! Rapture must be a single society—not some schizophrenic social organism forever wrestling with itself. Look at what's been happening—people forced into prostitution, living on top of one another. How is that better than the surface world?"

"If he suspects what you're up to . . ."

She chuckled. "He's convinced I'm on his team. I advised him on how to set up that little child-training amusement park . . . it's absurd, really; I doubt if it does anything but frighten children, but he believes it'll train them to accept Rapture. I gave him an edited report on all my . . ." She glanced at him. "I *can* trust you, can't I, Simon?"

He looked at her with a stunned expression and swallowed hard. "But—of *course*! How could you doubt it? You know how I feel . . ."

"Mommy, look!" Eleanor said pipingly. Sofia glanced over to see her small daughter, just three years old, in her pink pinafore, dragging one of the audiodiaries behind her. "I'm going to play with the Mr. Diary you gave me!"

Sofia nodded. "Wonderful, my love!"

His voice lowered, Simon asked, "Don't you think it's time she had some contact with other children, Doctor?"

"Hm? No. No, they're under the influence of the poisonous

paradigm of Andrew Ryan. I will keep her right here, train her in safe isolation—make her a paragon of the society to come . . ."

"And—" He cleared his throat. "What happened to her father?"

"Ah, as to that—it's a private matter."

Eleanor was sitting in the grass, talking to the tape recorder as if it were a friend; she clutched a small screwdriver in her hand. "Hello, Mr. Diary. Want to play?" She mimicked its voice: "'Actually, I'm quite busy right now, Miss Eleanor. Maybe later.' Well, all right! But do you mind if I take you apart while I wait? I promise I'll put you back together! 'Wait! You can't do thaaaat . . . noooo . . . waaaaiiiit, wait Eleaaa-noooorrrr . . .'"

And to Sofia's surprise, Eleanor commenced stabbing at the tape recorder, breaking it apart with the screwdriver . . .

10

"Some plasmid effects proved to be more difficult than we expected," Brigid Tenenbaum said, leading Fontaine down the hallway.

Suchong was leaning out an open door, gesturing for them to come. "Suchong is ready now for demonstration!"

Feeling a bit sick inside but determined to see this through, Fontaine followed Tenenbaum to the lab's experimentation room.

As they entered, Fontaine saw it was the same experimental subject as last time, the fellow Brougham. But now he was awake—though not entirely awake. His eyes were open and flicking about.

They were in lab 3 of Fontaine Futuristics—an almost bare room but for a cabinet, a brushed-steel table of instruments, and an examination bed fitted with restraints. Steel walls were textured with rust and rivets; the room smelled of antiseptics and seawater leakage. He heard it dripping between the walls. A single naked electric lightbulb glowed in the middle of the ceiling. The floor was covered with what looked to Fontaine like a thin carpet of black rubber.

"You guys don't go in for extras, do you," Fontaine observed. "Maybe a little decoration . . ."

"We will add more equipment later," Dr. Suchong said, bending over the table. "Decorations are superfluous." He selected a syringe and set about drawing a glowing blue fluid from a beaker. The man on the table looked at the syringe with frightened eyes; he writhed and made a mewing sound.

"In time, Suchong will add computers, such other devices."

"Computers?" Fontaine asked. "What's a computer?"

"Like . . . adding machine," Suchong said, putting alcohol on Brougham's shoulder. "But faster, smarter. Mr. Ryan has designs. We can take to Fontaine Futuristics . . . Now— injecting the solution we call EVE. It will activate the ADAM we have already incorporated into him . . ."

He injected Brougham's shoulder with EVE. The man strapped to the table groaned and tried to pull away. Suchong relentlessly drove the syringe plunger home.

"We are ready," Suchong said. "Please back away from subject . . ."

All three of them backed away from the man on the exam table, all the way to the door. "The subject" was muttering to himself. Visibly quivering in the leather restraints. Shuddering. Shaking. Till shaking became convulsing. He shrieked, and his back arched, bones audibly creaking. Fontaine was afraid the guy was going to snap his own spine.

"It's coming out of me it's coming out of me it's coming out of meeeeee!" Brougham shrieked.

Then there was a sizzling sound—the smell of ozone and burning flesh—and blue electricity arced up, passing from the man's restrained hands to his head, the arc crackling for a moment—and then it snapped up at the electric light—which burst and went out.

The room went dark. Black as the pit of hell.

"What the devil—!" Fontaine said.

As if the devil in question were responding to Fontaine, a reddish-blue glow surged up again, much brighter now, illuminating the room. The exam room strobed in and out of visibility, Brougham's hands hissing great fat sparks that blackened the walls. The only light source was the eerie glow generated by the man on the table. A hissing sound filled the room. The glow in the man's eyes began to pulse.

Fontaine shook his head, not at all certain of what he had gotten himself into. He realized he should have brought Reggie, maybe Lance too.

"Doctor!" Tenenbaum shouted. "The tranquilizer!"

Fontaine saw for the first time that Suchong had something ready in his hand—it looked like a gun, but when he fired it at the man on the exam table it made a soft spitting sound, and there was no muzzle flash. The man yelped, and Fontaine saw that a dart of some kind had shot into the man's hip, where it waggled with his movements.

Those movements calmed . . . and the light diminished as the electrical glow ebbed away.

"You see," Suchong said, "when mind shuts down, his power too shut down . . ."

"We should have insulated that lightbulb," Tenenbaum said, reaching back to open the door, as the last of the electrical shine vanished.

The light from the hall indirectly illuminated the chamber, and the three of them approached Brougham, who once more seemed semiconscious, moving his head gently from side to side.

The experimental subject seemed relatively unhurt, to Fontaine's surprise, though the man's hospital gown was reduced to charred threads. "He should have gotten burned, shouldn't he, with all that electricity shooting around in him? Maybe he's all burned inside himself?"

Tenenbaum shook her head as she examined the experimental subject, taking his pulse. "No. He is not burned. This is part of plasmid phenomenon. He emanates the electricity but is not harmed by it. Not exactly . . . harmed."

"So—what's the practical use of this stuff?" Fontaine demanded. "How're we going to make money on it?"

Tenenbaum shrugged. "Can be used to start engines, galvanize equipment that is missing power, yes?"

Looking closer, Fontaine saw there *was* a mark on Brougham—around his eyes. Not exactly scar tissue, but more like a thickening of the skin—a cancerlike growth across his face. Radiating outward from his eyes was a fanciful mask of thickened red tissue.

"You notice the extraneous tissue," Dr. Suchong said, nodding. "Does not seem . . . lethal. But it is curious. Some subjects have more than others . . ."

"Some of them? How many of these guys do you have?"

"A few still alive. Come—this way." He led the way from the chamber.

Fontaine was glad to get out of there. He might've gotten fried during that demonstration. "So—what did we just see? That was a plasmid, right?" He added wonderingly, "Lightning coming out of a man!"

Dr. Suchong paused in the barren metal corridor under a naked yellow light and rubbed his hands together.

Fontaine and Tenenbaum lingered with him in the hall, all of them a little shaken up. Fontaine glanced through an open door into a small, cluttered lab where one of the nondescript sea slugs squirmed in a bubbling aquarium on a table seething with fluid-filled tubes. "Suchong is most impressed by plasmid possibilities! Powerful electrical charge, drawn from atmosphere, can be used to activate machines—or to attack enemies! Maybe for self-defense against sharks when our men work in sea! That Brougham—he cannot control it. But soon Suchong will improve stem-cell communication with the nervous system! Soon a man can *control* this power! And other powers!"

Fontaine found that his pulse was racing with a mounting excitement. "What other powers?"

"We have found special genes, can be changed with stem

alteration, using ADAM—so a man has power to project cold, as Brougham project lightning! Power to project fire! To project rage! To make things move—with power of mind alone!"

Fontaine looked at him. Was he in earnest—or was this a sell job? Was Suchong trying to con him? But he'd just seen a sample of plasmid power. "If that's true, ADAM is the ultimate score. ADAM—and EVE. It's fuckin' amazing."

Tenenbaum nodded, looking through the door at the sea slug in the aquarium. "Yes. The little sea slug has come along and glued together all the crazy ideas I've had since the war. It can resurrect cells, bend the double helix—so that black can be reborn white, tall can be short. Weak can become strong! But we are just beginning . . . there is more we need, Frank. Much more . . ."

Fontaine grinned—and winked at her. "You'll get whatever you need! Fontaine Futuristics will *transform* Rapture! I feel it in my bones."

Tenenbaum looked curiously at Fontaine—right at him. But he suspected she could look right at him only because she was thinking of him as a *specimen*. "Really? You feel that in bones?"

"Nah, that's just an expression—what I'm saying is, this is going to go big. And it's got to be *presented* big. I'm going to buy space from Ryan Industries . . . and we're going to move Fontaine Futuristics out of this dump, into the best-designed location in Rapture! It'll look like the inside of a mansion, with lots of décor and sculpture so that people'll sense the power behind those doors!" He broke off, shaking his head. Thinking that he was starting to sound like . . . a *businessman*.

Won't have to do it long, he told himself. *The bunko possibilities in this one are all about selling something to people they only think they want—until they've got it. And once they've got it—it's got them. Meaning I'll have 'em in my hip pocket.*

Suchong glanced at the sea slug—and licked his lips. Something was troubling him. "But Mr. Fontaine—there *is* danger." He looked gravely at Fontaine. "Danger in using ADAM—and in developing plasmids. You should know before proceeding. Come this way. You shall see . . ."

They went down a metal-walled corridor, feet clumping on wooden planks. The air at this end smelled like raw chemicals and curdled human sweat. They came to a steel door stenciled

SPECIAL STUDIES: KEEP OUT.

Suchong put his hand on the knob . . .

"Perhaps we should not go in!" Brigid Tenenbaum said suddenly, not looking at either of them but holding the door shut with the flat of her hand. She stared at the closed door.

"Why?" Fontaine asked, wondering if they were planning to lock him up in there. It occurred to him that maybe he should be careful around scientists who strap random people to tables and inject them with things . . .

"It is dangerous inside—perhaps diseased . . ."

Fontaine swallowed. But he made up his mind. "There can't be any part of this I don't know about. It's all my business." He wanted plasmids—bad. But he needed to know what the risks were. If this was something that exposed him too much . . .

She nodded once and stepped back. Suchong opened the door. Immediately, a disturbing, unnatural smell emanated from the room. It was a scent Fontaine would expect from exposed human brains when the top of the skull was sawed away . . .

His stomach lurched. But he followed Suchong one step, just one, into the room. "We try to mix some genes from sea creatures with human," Suchong was saying. "Give man powers of certain animals. But . . ." The musty, ill-lit rectangular chamber was about thirty-five feet by thirty, but it seemed smaller because of the shifting heap of the thing that dominated it. Clinging to the walls opposite Fontaine was something that might've once been human. It was as if someone had taken human flesh and made it as malleable as clay—bones and flesh made pliable—and plastered it onto the wall. Beaded with sweat, the mass of human flesh seemed to simply cling there, spread over two walls and a corner. A bloated face muttered to itself, at the center of the creature, near the ceiling; several human organs were exposed, including a heart and kidneys, damp and quivering, dangling like meat in a butchery from crust-edged gaps in its body, the creature's big limbs . . .

"What the hell!" Fontaine blurted.

The thing's beak clicked and muttered in response.

Fontaine turned and dashed from the room. He went five paces down the hall and, feeling dizzy, gagging, came to a stumbling stop, leaning against Rapture's cold metal bulkhead.

He felt a surge of relief when he heard the door of the Special Studies room clang shut. Tenenbaum and Suchong strolled up beside him, Suchong with his hands casually in his coat pockets, looking faintly amused. Tenenbaum seemed almost humanly concerned for him.

"So . . ." Fontaine swallowed bile. "You got this process under control or not?"

"We do now," Tenenbaum said, looking thoughtfully at the yellow overhead light. "Yes. We will not be producing more of . . . those."

"Then—I want you to do something for me. *Kill* that thing in there. Incinerate it. No traces left—I want no bad publicity. I want more plasmids like the one that makes lightning. But more variety. More controllable . . . easy to package . . . Stuff that makes a man smarter, stronger. The stuff that makes us money. You understand? *Money!*"

Ryan Amusements, Rapture Memorial Museum
1954

Stanley Poole stood at the outer edge of the small crowd waiting for Dr. Lamb to begin. Discreetly passed-out flyers in
maintenance station 17 and Apollo Square advertised "A Free
Public Lecture by the Eminent Psychiatrist, Dr. Sofia Lamb,
on a New Hope for the Working Man."

The lanky, swan-necked blonde in the modish horn-rims
stepped up in front of the museum's *Rapture Grows* tableau,
with its stylized images of Rapture's founding workers. She
gazed at the little crowd like a prophetess, her benevolent expression condescending but motherly, her smile infinitely
knowing. She pressed the button to start the museum tableau's recording. A friendly male voice intoned, *"After the
platform is secured, work progresses at an astounding rate. Designed to be the foundation of Rapture, workers toil around the
clock to create the metropolis you see today."*

"Do you hear that?" She clasped her hands behind her
back and chuckled ironically, making eye contact with the
small crowd—mostly low-level workers, all listening raptly,
though Poole realized that Simon Wales was there too. "That
recording," Sofia Lamb went on, "is a compact little insight
into Rapture! 'Workers toil around the clock to create the
metropolis'! And in the *Laying the Foundation* exhibit, right
over there—what does the recording say?" Her voice was
mockingly arch as she recited: "'Engineers work to overcome
obstacles, such as diamond-hard rock, obstinate sea life and
unexpected casualties!' Think about it, my friends—how
much needless suffering have we taken for granted?" She
shook her head sadly. "Unexpected casualties? Oh, Andrew
Ryan fully expected them! He just didn't care! A great many
lives were lost in building Rapture—those lives were sacri-
fices to the 'god' that is the human ego! Ryan's ego! The com-

mon man and woman in Rapture is overworked and underpaid; they're left exhausted. They toiled around the clock to create this city—but how much of what they created do they really share in? What did Andrew Ryan really offer—but *paper*? A little something called Rapture dollars . . . mere documents, paper money! Paper for paupers! And precious little of that! Who, I ask you, really owns Rapture? The people who built it? or the plutocrats who control it? The many—or the few? You know the answer!"

A good many in the crowd were nodding. Some frowned, unsure—but most seemed convinced. They'd been thinking something of the sort themselves, Poole supposed. Here was someone who said it right out loud . . . Dr. Sofia Lamb. A psychiatrist—using her psychology on the common man.

"This woman Lamb is becoming troublesome, Poole," Ryan had said. *"See what she's up to. Stay discreet . . ."*

If Ryan could hear this, Poole thought, he'd blow his carefully barbered top.

Sofia Lamb paused thoughtfully, then pointed at the ornate walls. "Rapture looks like a great big palace at times, doesn't it? It abounds in luxury—but where's housing for those who maintain it? You're crowded into places like Maintenance Seventeen! But that's *traditional* in a palace, isn't it? There are the luxury quarters for the elite—and then there's the little cubbyholes under the stairs where the servants live! Palace servants have always outnumbered kings and queens! Yet we blindly continue to serve them! My vision of a new, united Rapture is revolutionary—yes, *revolutionary*! I say it proudly! And yet all I'm bringing is a new spirit of cooperation, my friends. A new shape for love! Cooperation, in a place like Ryan's Rapture, is transformative, and the word I'm bringing is a sacrament, the beginning of a new church of cooperation. I have had an inspiration that seems to come from some cosmic place of certainty—and it is telling me that Rapture's foundation on competition is cracking! Competition is division, my friends. *A house divided cannot stand!*" As she spoke, Poole noticed, she became more intense; her nostrils flared, her eyes flashed, her hands fisted. She radiated charisma—just as Ryan did. But her magnetism was somehow powerfully maternal. Poole glanced at Simon Wales and noticed he seemed totally captivated by Lamb. She went on, declaring loudly, "We must evolve to *heal* Rapture—and we will heal it by redesigning it from within! We will create a true utopia—and utopians fit to live in utopia! We will build a unity that will thrive, even as the surface world fails! But the new Rapture will not be based on greed—it will be a collective based on sharing! What is the collective? *It is the body of Rapture!* Therein will lie its truth! An end to the burden of mindless competition—a turning to cooperation, altruism, community—and communality!"

Holy cow, Poole thought. Ryan was going to flip. The boss was caught between a rock and a hard place. Ryan was officially against censorship—so how could he censor this woman? But from what Poole had heard about the secret structures being expanded in the Persephone Project, Ryan had a plan for taking care of Red organizers . . .

As the speech ended he turned away—and spotted someone at the back of the crowd he hadn't noticed here before—a man with dark glasses and a hat covering his bald head.

Poole knew him, despite the man's attempt at going incognito. It was Frank Fontaine. And Fontaine had a mighty thoughtful look on his face . . .

~~~~~~~~~

Frank Fontaine wasn't aware of Poole watching him. He was mesmerized by Sofia Lamb.

The woman's amazing, Fontaine thought. *What a con artist.* She was a grifter with two or three college degrees—he had to admire her. "What is the collective?" she'd said. "*It is the body of Rapture!"* Good stuff. You could plug almost any feeling you wanted into that. Conning one guy at a time wasn't much challenge.

But a whole crowd—conning a whole population. Man, that was a thing of beauty.

This Lamb woman knew how you got "the people" on your side. Figure out what was bothering them and use it as a kind of harness, and pretty soon they're pulling your wagon for you. Smart. *"But that's traditional in a palace, isn't it? There are the luxury quarters for the elite—and then there's the little cubbyholes under the stairs where the servants live! Palace servants have always outnumbered kings and queens!"*

Smart—give 'em something to repeat to one another. *"We're like the palace servants, living under the stairs, see?"*

This Dr. Lamb was going to be too much competition, of course. In time he'd have to see to it that Ryan got the info he needed to arrest her. Meantime, she was inspiring him, along with the crowd. Only, not the same way . . .

He'd do it all his way, of course. She was kind of the female version. His own version of radical leadership would be very different.

Maybe it was too early to really get going on it. But he could start to plant the seeds. Get it growing. And in time—harvest.

Andrew Ryan's Office
1954

Bill found Andrew Ryan at his desk. "Mr. Ryan—I have that maintenance report."

Ryan glanced up. "Oh, Bill, have a seat . . ." He looked back at the folder in his hands as Bill sat down across from him. The folder was marked *CONFIDENTIAL.* "I just want to have another look at the end of this one . . . I had Stanley Poole look into some things . . . this Lamb woman is a problem . . ." He flipped a page. "Bringing that woman in was bad judgment . . ." He grunted to himself, closed the folder, pushed it aside, and opened another. "Yes. Poole's also found out something about Fontaine's new venture he's calling Futuristics . . . Seems quite . . . pregnant with possibility . . . Take a load off while I sort through this . . ."

Ryan made notes, nodded to himself. Then he looked up at Bill, smiling. "I get so caught up in the day-to-day business—I forget to really take a good look at the people around me. You look a bit careworn, Bill. That's natural. How's Elaine?"

Bill smiled, relaxing a little. He liked to see this side of Ryan. "Grand, Mr. Ryan. Knows how to make a man happy, that one."

"Good, good. I too will settle down when the time comes. I dream of having a son one day, you know. Someone to take what I've built in his hands and keep it thriving—build on it! An investment in the future. What a wonderful place to grow up, Rapture is, too. A wonderland for kids, I should think . . ."

Bill wasn't so sure of that. Not at all. But he only smiled musingly and nodded.

Sullivan came bustling in. He nodded to Bill and stood beside the desk with the tense air of a man who was fitting this stop into a tight schedule. "You called me, sir?"

"Ah—Chief. There you are! Yes . . ." He pushed the folder toward Sullivan. "I need you to jump with both feet into this. Have you heard something about a . . . a new development called plasmids?"

"Plasmids? No sir. What the blazes are they?"

"Some kind of product. Look at this . . ." He reached into a desk drawer, drew out a folded copy of *The Rapture Tribune,* and laid it out on the desk for Bill and Sullivan to see. It was opened to the back page, on which an advertisement proclaimed,

EVERYTHING YOU ALWAYS WANTED TO BE
YOU **CAN** BE
WITH PLASMIDS! THE WAVE OF THE FUTURE
FROM **FONTAINE FUTURISTICS**
Free Samples of **HairGro**
BrainBoost
SportBoost
Electro Bolt
BruteMore Muscle Enhancer
And watch for **Incinerate!**

Ryan shrugged. "Fontaine is putting them out. Grows new hair, new teeth, makes you prettier, stronger, younger, even faster. Already selling big to the maintenance workers. A genetic breakthrough, according to Poole. Our restless young rival is at it again. I want you to find out what you can about these 'plasmids,' Sullivan, and everything about Fontaine Futuristics. Apparently he's hired Dr. Suchong and Brigid Tenenbaum to develop these products. That woman seemed unstable to me—but she's a whiz."

Bill looked at the advertisement and shook his head. "Too good to be true, innit? I mean—got to be side effects. They test these things first?"

Ryan waved a hand dismissively. "I'm not really concerned with weighing down progress with a lot of testing. People want to try it, they can take their chances. Well Sullivan—can you take this on? Poole's got his hands full watching that Lamb woman . . ."

Sullivan rubbed his jaw. "Working on that smuggling thing pretty hard right now, sir. Fontaine's changed his MO."

"We'll take care of their smuggling later. Unless you have solid proof it's Fontaine?"

"No sir. Not *arresting* proof. Of course, the constables would probably arrest anybody you told them to . . ."

Ryan leaned back in his desk chair, seemed to consider it. Then he shook his head. "No. If I did that, we'd be no better than the Reds. No, we'll get evidence. But first I want to know what this plasmid thing is all about. My instinct tells me it's something that could change Rapture's marketplace."

Sullivan nodded, ran a hand through his hair, licking his lips as if he were thinking of bringing up another issue. Then he shrugged. "I'm on it, sir."

He headed out the door, a man on a mission.

"How are those leakage problems I've been hearing about, Bill?" Ryan asked, though the glazed look in his eyes suggested his thoughts were roving elsewhere.

"Constant maintenance, guv. The bloody sea doesn't just sit quiet out there—we push it out of our way, and it pushes right back. Always throwin' its weight around—sheer water pressure, currents, changing temperature, ice formation, sea creatures a-scrapin' and squeezin'. Barnacles and starfish and seaworms. Had to send scraping crews out twice the last month."

"Yes. Some of the men spend so much time in deep-sea diving suits they're beginning to feel like part of them." Ryan smiled to himself.

Bill remembered the experimental subject he'd seen in the labs. Not something he wanted to think about.

Ryan tossed the pencil on the desk, tented his fingers, and scowled broodingly. "Fontaine is shaping up to be my great rival here. He can only sharpen me. It is like fuel for the fire of my talent. But I cannot let him come to *fully* dominate the marketplace in Rapture. No. I may have to take action. We may have to get tough with Mr. Fontaine . . ."

Maintenance Station 17
Early 1955

It was right depressing, visiting the old maintenance workers' colony. Bill McDonagh didn't like coming here. It made him

feel obscurely guilty as he walked along from the Metro passage to the back of the pawnshop at the corner, picking his
way past moraines of trash. Bill felt responsible for Rapture—
he sure hadn't planned on any slums.

Someone had written "Welcome to Pauper's Drop" in red
across one wall in dripping paint. Below it, a long, tatty row of
sullen indigents squatted against the metal bulkhead, shivering, some of them in carapaces of cardboard. The heating
duct for this area was blocked, and the few merchants down
here were reluctant to pay the Ryan Industries service fee for
getting them unblocked. Bill had come down to do it in his
spare time. Not that he would tell Ryan that. If Ryan knew he
was doing charity work . . .

Bill had gotten Roland Wallace to help—each swearing
the other to secrecy—and Wallace promised he'd bring an
electrician along. But neither Wallace nor his wire jockey was
here now.

Bill was beginning to feel nervous about being here alone.
The surly unemployed along the wall watched his every step.
He heard them muttering as he went along. One of them
said, "She's watching him too . . ."

He was relieved to see Roland Wallace at the corner. With
Wallace was a bearded man in overalls, carrying a toolbox—a
tall, gaunt man with an aquiline profile.

"Oi!" Bill called, his breath steaming in the chill. "Wallace!" Wallace saw him and waved. Bill hurried to him. "I'm
bloody well glad to see you, mate," Bill said, keeping his voice
low. "These ragamuffins over 'ere've been giving me the gim-
let eye. Half-expecting a knock in the head."

Wallace nodded, looking past him at the ill-kempt men and
women along the wall, many with bottles in hand. "Drinking
too, a lot of them. No rules against making your own in
Rapture—someone's been selling cheap absinthe to this bunch,
I hear. Three people died from bad hooch, and two went

blind." He cleared his throat. "Well, come on—the best way into the duct is in the back of the pawnshop. Glad to get the heat working here—it's damn cold . . ."

The electrician said nothing, though it seemed to Bill that the man was muttering to himself under his breath, his hawkish, deep-set eyes darting this way and that. Bill noticed thick red blotches on the man's forehead.

They stepped over small piles of trash and went around a quite large one to get to the back of the pawnshop. "There's no trash pickup here either?" Bill asked.

"We can't afford it."

"You live down here too?"

"Why you think I'm doing this job free?" the electrician said, clipping the words. His tone dripped venom. "Need the heat. Can't get into the ducts without you Ryan Industries types along. Not if I don't want the constables after me."

Bill nodded and thumped on the back door of the pawnshop.

"Who is it?" called a gruff voice from inside.

"Bill McDonagh! Looking for Arno Deukmajian! You got my Jet Postal?"

"Yeah, yeah, come on in." The man who opened the brass-sheathed door looked as gruff as his voice sounded. He was a squat-faced man in a rumpled suit with a scar through his lower lip. His arms were too long for his suit jacket. His hair was bristly short. "Yeah, I'm Arno Deukmajian. This here's my shop. Come in, come in . . . if you have to."

The three men entered the dusty, dimly lit back room where there was barely room to move about. Piled floor to ceiling were appliances, radios, lady's shoes, gowns, boxes of guns, boxes of watches, silver picture frames, anything that could be hocked. "I've cleared off the trapdoor," Deukmajian said. "This place was built right over it."

Building over the trapdoor might've been a violation of

some building regulation up on the surface, Bill figured, but in Rapture there were almost no building regulations.

Wallace had the key. He knelt on the metal floor and opened the trapdoor, as the electrician held an electric torch for him. The light slanted down to reveal a grimy iron shaft and a rusty ladder.

A sickening smell rose up from the shaft. "Must be something dead down there," Bill said. He climbed down as the electrician held the light. It got a little colder each step he descended. The other two joined him at the bottom, and they ducked to enter a tunnel, the electrician going first to light the way. The reek of death was growing stronger. They had to move along hunched over—the tunnel was about eight inches too low to stand up in. "If they're going to make it big enough for a short man, why can't they make it big enough for a tall man," the electrician grumbled. "It ain't that much more."

Just thirty echoing steps in, where the tunnel narrowed to a large pipe, they found the source of the smell—and the cause of the obstruction. A body was jammed in the heating duct. It appeared to be the partly mummified body of a boy— perhaps twelve or thirteen—lying facedown in the vent pipe. He wore ragged clothing, and his black hair was matted with old dried blood. A large fan blade, pitted with rust, had sliced partway through his neck . . .

"Oh Jesus fookin' Christ," Bill muttered. "Poor little blighter."

Wallace was gagging. It took him a few moments to get his composure. Bill had seen enough death in the war—and in the building of Rapture—and he was almost inured to it. Almost. Still, he felt a deep queasiness looking at the shriveled hands of the child, clutching at the tunnel wall—as if frozen in a last attempt at reaching out to life.

"I reckon," Bill said, his voice a bit hoarse, "the kid was

exploring . . . and the fan's not on all the time. It was off, and he tried to crawl past—and that's when it came on."

The electrician nodded. "Yeah. But he wasn't exploring. Didn't have any place to live. One of the orphans. Nobody took him in, so . . . he came down into the tunnels to sleep, where he'd be safe. Maybe got lost."

"The orphans?" Bill asked. "Quite a few, are there?"

"There's some, hereabout. People come here, work, then they finish a project and the bosses lay 'em off. No more work. But they're not allowed to leave Rapture either. So they start to fighting over food and such—kill one another. And now with these plasmids . . . some people don't know how to handle 'em. Got to know how. Surely do. If you don't—you might get a little carried away. Leaves some orphans . . ."

"There ought to be an orphanage," Wallace said.

The electrician chuckled grimly. "Think Ryan can figure out how to run one for profit?"

"Someone'll start one, we get enough orphans," Bill said. "Well, let's move him and see if we can get this thing started . . ."

Glad to leave the impromptu metal tomb, Wallace volunteered to get the necessary items. He hurried back to the ladder, returning a few minutes later with a large burlap sack and extra gloves. "Kid's kinda shriveled; I suppose we can get him in this . . ."

Grimacing, they worked the child's body free of the jam, carefully blocking the blades with a hammer from the toolbox in case they should decide to start running.

But after they'd gotten the dried-out husk of a child removed and stuffed the desiccated body into the burlap sack and removed the hammer, the vent blades were still motionless.

The electrician opened a panel near the fan and made some adjustments inside with a tool. He squirted lubricant in and used a small device to test for current. "It's live over there but . . . I'm going to have to give it a jolt to get it going. Some parts sat too long—rusted inside. Stand back . . ."

He stretched his left hand out toward the panel—seemed to concentrate for a moment—his eyes glowed faintly—and a small lightning bolt shot blue-white from his hand and crackled into the open panel.

Startled, Bill straightened suddenly—and banged his head on the ceiling. "Bloody buggerin' hell!"

"Electro Bolt plasmid," Wallace muttered.

"Holy . . ." Bill said, rubbing his head. "They just fookin' . . ." Then he realized that the fan was whirring, blowing warm air into his face.

"That'll do it," the electrician said. "When this one stopped, the other ones stopped too. Should all be working now . . ."

He turned and glared at Bill—and there was still a bit of glow in his eyes, so that he looked like a feral animal in the tunnel dimness.

"You just got to know how to handle 'em, see?" he said. "The plasmids." Then he picked up his tools and started back to the ladder.

11

"You don't mean you spent it *all*, Rupert?" demanded Rupert Mudge's wife—just as he'd figured she would—with that disgusted look on her face that he was getting so *very* sick of seeing.

She was a hip-heavy, short-legged bottle blonde with permanent frown lines in the corners of her mouth that made her face look like a wooden puppet. She wore a tattered red-and-yellow flower-print dress and the work boots she used in her housecleaning job.

I'm outgrowing that woman, Mudge thought as he ran a hand through his luxuriant hair. He'd gone from partly bald to this glorious brown mane thanks to Fontaine's plasmids. He shook his head—harder than he needed to, so he could make all that hair fly about—and then he reached for his new ADAM. He already had a good charge of EVE going to activate it.

"You take that plasmid stuff back to Fontaine's!" Sally grated between grinding teeth. "I worked hard for that money!"

"Oh Christ, Sally," said Mudge, injecting the plasmid, "a man's gotta put on a good appearance out there in the world. I need . . ." His teeth started chattering as the stimulant effect of SportBoost hit him. The room was swirling slowly around him, pulsing with energy. It was like he was the center of the universe. It scared him and exhilarated him both. It almost made the shabby little studio apartment they rented in the so-called Sinclair Deluxe seem like something worth living in—if it weren't for the cracks in the walls, the naked lightbulb, the leaks in the corners, the smell of rotting fish. "Sal . . . Sal . . . Sally . . . I need . . . I needa . . . needa . . . needa show people I'm fast and strong, I'm gonna get one that makes you smart . . ."

"Ha! I wish you'd taken the smart one first! Then you'd've been smart enough not to blow our little stash of moolah on any of this! You don't need that fancy hair; you don't need those muscles—"

"These muscles are gonna get me a new job on the Atlantic Express! They're gonna put up a new line!"

"What I heard, more people are taking the trams and the bathyspheres—the Express might be, what you call it, obsolete. They aren't gonna rehire you nohow after you went flippy on the foreman!"

"Aww, that big lug flew off the handle for nothin'!"

"You were on one of those crazy plasmid things, and you went nutso on him! You threw a wrench at his head!"

"Plasmids—you gotta get used to 'em, is all! I wasn't used to it yet! All the fellas are usin' 'em!"

"Sure—and most of 'em are going broke from it! They sit around jabbering, high on the damn things! Not a single one as doesn't have side effects! What's them marks on your face, there?"

"What, you never got a pimple?"

"That ain't no pimple; it's like skin growing where there oughtn't to be any!"

"Woman—shut your trap and bring me some dinner!"

"Shut my trap! I've been working all day scrubbing floors in Olympus Heights for the high muckety-mucks, and I gotta come back to a dump and hear 'bring me some dinner'! Why don'tcha try *earning* your dinner! How about them apples— the apples we ain't got! How'm I going to pay for the food if you spent all the money on plasmids! You know Ryan doesn't allow no soup lines around here!"

"I heard that Fontaine's starting up some kinda soup kitchen . . ."

"I wouldn't go near that man, if I was you. Mazy says he's a crook!"

"Aw, what does that loopy bimbo know? Fontaine's okay. I thought maybe I could get some work over there . . . I'm strong now! Look at that!" He flexed his bicep—and his shirt ripped with the expanding muscle. "That's from BruteMore! Plasmids are the future, see!"

She sat down on the sagging sofabed across from him. "That's what worries me—the future." Her voice was soft now. And that had a way of upsetting him even more than when she yelled. "I wish we could afford a place with a window. Not that there's much to see but fish. A person gets sick of looking at fish."

His knee bouncing with nervous energy, Mudge looked around the small, dingy apartment for something to sell at the pawnshop. He wanted another SportBoost. Just to make sure. He didn't like to run short on plasmids. All he had was another BruteMore in the icebox. The radio maybe—could he sell that? She kind of prized that radio. Only luxury they had left . . .

"Funny, Mr. Sinclair calling this flophouse 'deluxe,'" Sally said. "Must be his sense of humor. But we won't have even this if you don't get off your tuckus and work. What I make can't keep us in a home—'specially with you jabbing yourself with those crazy goddamn potions!"

"Oh, stop running your yapper . . ." Maybe he'd take his last hit of BruteMore—see how it did with the SportBoost real fresh in his system. He wondered if he could get Sally to take some BreastGro . . .

He got up, went to the icebox—he'd hidden the Brute-More behind an open, half-empty can of beans.

He injected it standing right there, with his back to Sally. A glowing red energy suffused him. He could feel it move through his body—it was like individual cells growing from inside.

Sally kept rattling on. "This area wasn't supposed to be no permanent place to live! Supposed to be temporary housing for train maintenance! Not much better than one of those shacktowns we had in the Depression, when I was a kid, out in Chicago!

"You know what they're starting to call this parta Rapture under the train station? Pauper's Drop! Can you beat that? Pauper's Drop, Rupert! That's where you've taken me! I shoulda listened to my old man. He warned me about you. What're you doing over there? Look at you! You look like you're getting all swollen up . . . it ain't natural!"

He spun to face her—and look at the expression on her face! Sally knew she should've kept her mouth shut. Her scrambling away like that—that was a clue. She was trying to get to the door.

"Should've kept your mouth shut, woman!" he roared. The metal walls seemed to vibrate with the sound. "Your old man warned you, did he? I'll show you somethin' that old fool never thought of!"

She was tugging at the door handle. Rupert Mudge turned, seized the icebox, lifted it up, spun around—and threw it at her.

Funny how light it seemed in his hands . . .

And funny too, how fragile she turned out to be. She had seemed like a real terror, sometimes. A little ball of fury. But now, just a big wet red splash all over the rusty metal door. And the wall. And the floor. And the ceiling. And a head all by itself, facing into the corner . . .

Uh-oh. Sally was paying the bills around here. And now she was dead.

He'd better get out of here. Get over to Fontaine.

Mudge stormed out the door, headed for the passage to the Metro. Yeah—Fontaine's. Find work there. Any work at all. No matter what they asked him to do. Because he had needs. That's what Sally hadn't understood. He had powerful needs—and a need to be powerful.

Arcadia, Rapture
1955

"You know what's missing, here?" Elaine said, looking around at the enclosed parkland. "The sounds of birds. There're no birds in Rapture." A soft, golden, artificial light suffused the air. Pushed by hidden fan blades Bill himself had installed, the breeze blew the perfume of daffodils and roses to them.

Bill and Elaine were sitting on a bench holding hands. They'd decided to spend most of his day off together. They'd had lunch and then gone for a long walk. It was getting near dinnertime, but it was a delight being in the park. Smelling flowers, looking at the greenery. Hearing a stream chuckling and murmuring. He found himself wishing they'd brought their little girl, Sophie.

Not quite four years old, Sophie liked to scamper to the miniature wooden bridge and toss blades of grass into the creek of filtered water, watch them float downstream to vanish into the walls. She would play happily among the ferns, the artfully random boulders, the small trees.

Still, he reckoned Sophie was having a good time back in the flat, playing that Sea Treasure board game with Mascha, the little daughter of Máriska Lutz. Mariska was an Eastern European woman Elaine had hired out of Artemis Suites as a part-time nanny. Funny to think Sophie and Mascha had never known a world beyond Rapture. Ryan suppressed most images of the surface world in Rapture's classrooms. That troubled Bill as much as *The Journey to the Surface*. But there were things that troubled him more. Like Mr. Gravenstein putting a gun to his head in front of his ruined grocery store. The memory still haunted Bill.

"No birds here, love, that's right enough," Bill said at last. "But there are bees. From the Silverwing Apiary. There goes one of the little buggers now . . ."

They watched the bee zip by: pretty much the only wildlife inside Rapture, unless you counted certain people. The bees were necessary to pollinate the plants, and the plants created oxygen for Rapture.

"Ah, there's your pal Julie," Elaine said. Her lips compressed as she watched Julie Langford walk up.

Bill glanced at Elaine. Did she really think he had some kind of hanky-panky going on with Julie Langford?

The ecological scientist was a compact woman of about forty, her pragmatic haircut held by barrettes. She wore transparent-framed glasses and olive-colored coveralls for her work in the tree farm and the other green zones of Rapture. Bill liked talking to her—liked her quickness, her independent way of thinking.

Julie Langford had worked for the Allies devising a defoliant in the Pacific, he knew, exposing Japanese jungle bases. He'd also heard that when Andrew Ryan talked her into coming to Rapture, the U.S. government had gotten peeved after she'd abandoned her federal job. She'd vanished, in fact, from North America. They'd been combing the world looking for her ever since.

"Hello, Bill, Elaine," Julie said distractedly, glancing around at the plants. "Still not quite enough natural light getting through down here. Need to add more sunlight mirrors in the lighthouses. Those junipers are going brown around the edges." She put her hands on her hips and turned politely to Elaine. "How's your darling little girl?"

Elaine smiled distantly. "Oh Sophie's good, she's just learning to—"

"Good, good." Julie turned impatiently back to Bill. "Bill, I'm glad I ran into you. I need to talk to you about the boss—just for a minute. Alone, if you don't mind."

Bill turned to his wife, wondering how she'd feel about it. "You mind, Elaine?"

"Go on, I'm fine. Do as you like."

"Back in a mo', love." Clearly she wasn't fine with him strolling off with Julie, but Elaine was a cheerful girl most of the time. It wouldn't do her any harm to feel a little jealousy now and then, keep her from taking him for granted. He kissed Elaine on the cheek and walked off toward the little bridge with Julie, hands in his pockets, trying to look as unromantic as possible.

"Don't mean to drag you away from the little lady," Julie said in a way Bill thought was a bit condescending toward Elaine. "But I need an ally, and I know you love this park."

"Right. What's afoot, Julie?"

"I tell you, Bill—here I am, a batty plant woman working for years to expose the Japs in the jungle, melting away plant life, and now I'm down here trying to do the complete opposite. 'We'll create a second Eden down there,' Ryan says. All that, and now he wants to turn this place into a paying tourist attraction—for residents of Rapture, I mean."

"What? But I thought this was a public park."

"So it was to be. But he doesn't really believe in *public* ownership of anything. And he's trying to keep up with Fontaine. So he's raising capital. Which means charging for everything you can imagine. Hires me to build a forest at the bottom of the ocean—then turns a walk in the woods into a luxury. Something you have to pay for! You know how he is. 'Should a farmer not be able to sell his food? Is a potter not entitled to a profit from his pots?' But what am I going to do? He's my boss, but he listens to you, Bill. Maybe you can talk him out of this. We need some kind of free public space in

Rapture. A commons. People just need it—they need the breathing room."

Bill nodded, glancing at his wife, pleased to see Anya Anyersdotter had stopped to talk to her. Elaine was smiling. She liked Anya, a smartly dressed little woman in a pageboy haircut, prone to freethinking. Anya designed shoes and clothes and had her own boutique—one of Rapture's success stories.

Bill turned back to Julie. "But here, what am I to do, Julie? You know about his own private forest fire?"

"What? No!"

"Oh yeah. Tells me: 'I once bought a forest. Then they,' says he, 'claimed the land belonged to God—demanded I establish a public park there. A public park, where the rabble can stand about gawping, pretending they've earned that natural beauty! Land that I *owned*! Congress under that bastard FDR tried to nationalize my forest—so I burnt it to the ground.'"

"Not truly . . ."

"Oh yes. Truly. You think he could be talked into making *anything* into public property?"

She made a soft little grunting sound and shook her head. "Maybe not." She gestured at the gemlike parkland around them. "Once he told me, 'God did not plant the seeds in Arcadia. I did.' But I designed all this—with a little help from Daniel Wales . . ."

"I think we ought to trust Mr. Ryan. He's known what he's been about so far . . ."

"Yeah well—it doesn't end there. He's even talking about *a surcharge for oxygen*! He says the air in Rapture is only there to breathe because Ryan Industries provided it!"

"Oh *Jay*-sus." Bill lowered his voice. "Here comes that bloody prat Sander Cohen . . ."

Sander Cohen approached over the little bridge, arm in arm with two bored-looking young men wearing hunting outfits, though they carried nothing to hunt with. Cohen wore Tyrolean lederhosen, suspenders, and a mountain climber's hat with a purple feather. The leather shorts exposed his knobby knees. He looked peculiarly pale—but that was largely because Cohen had whiteface makeup on, almost like a mime, though he was a long ways from a stage. His wiry, up-curling mustache seemed to quiver at the ends when he saw Bill. "Ah! Monsieur William McDonagh! Madame Langford!" Pronouncing the names, for no apparent reason, as if they were French.

"Cohen," Langford said, with a curt nod.

"Sander," Bill said. "You gents out for a stroll, yeah?"

"We are, in fact!" Cohen said. "These young rogues drank a bit too much. Taken a little too much SportBoost too! Talked me into a walk in the park. Though the Muse knows, I don't like parks, you know. Revile them, actually. Reminds me of *animals*." He squeezed the arm of the man on his left. "Not this sort of animal. *This* very sophisticated animal is Silas Cobb, Bill. You must have been to his darling little shop, Rapture Records! I suppose you might say it's mine too—I'm an investor."

Cobb was a skinny fellow with a shock of brown hair and a dreamy expression. He snorted and said, "Yeah. He pays the rent for my 'darling little shop.' Which just happens to have everything Mr. Cohen here ever recorded." He brightened as he added, "And some other people too—Sinatra, Billie Holiday." Cobb was still drunk, swaying in place.

"And *this* great megalith of a man," said Cohen, tilting his head rakishly at the big guy on his right, "is Mister Martin Finnegan." Finnegan was a mustached, surly-looking man, his height accentuated by the hair piled on top of his head. He seemed both grimly masculine and vaguely effeminate at once. "Martin worked backstage at the theater on Broadway where I performed my *Young Dandies* . . . if you needed a

stout heart to pull a curtain rope, he was your man. Has quite
a grip. But he's an actor himself. The next Errol Flynn, eh
Martin?"

"And why the hell not?" Finnegan growled. "I can act as
well as that bastard from . . . Where the hell is Flynn from—
he's no Irishman, is he?"

Cohen waved dismissively. "Errol's from Australia or Tas-
mania, some such place. Oh, few successful actors can act.
They're simply lit well and have nice muscle tone. A lovely
profile. Oh! What was that!" Cohen ducked his head as a bee
flew by. "Was that *an insect*? An insect here in Rapture! I
thought I was free of insects here!"

"Just a harmless little bee," Julie said. "Need 'em for the
flowers."

"Shuddersome things. Vile. Might walk on me. Might sting
me. I detest nature. It won't obey! It cannot be . . . organized.
Can one stage nature? No! Nature should be conquered,
forced to submit! How ruggedly handsome you look today,
Bill. Won't you come to the Kashmir with us, split a few bottles of wine, eh?"

"Bill! Bill!"

Bill turned to see Roland Wallace trotting up, face red, all
out of breath.

"What's afoot, Roland? Twice today I had a chance to say
that. Love to say it."

Wallace came to a stop, bent over, hands on his knees,
puffing. "Bill—emergency! In Hephaestus—flooding! Looks
like it might've been sabotage. Someone did this on purpose,
Bill. Someone's trying to kill us all . . ."

Kashmir Restaurant, Rapture
1955

Ryan held court over the dinner table. Joining him this evening were Diane McClintock; the engineer Anton Kinkaide;

Anna Culpepper, thinking herself arty in a blue beret; Garris
Fisher—a top executive working for Fontaine Futuristics—
and Sullivan. Karlosky was about thirty paces away, keeping
security watch in the restaurant's anteroom. Karlosky was
fed, as part of the job—but no vodka, not here. The Russian
could sometimes be trigger happy, especially after a vodka or
three. Once in New York, Karlosky had shot a cab driver
who'd had the temerity to scrape the limousine's shiny fender.
Ryan had to pay a pretty bribe to keep Karlosky out of jail.

Picking at the remains of his sea bass with the elegant
sterling fork, Andrew Ryan reminded himself to keep smiling. He didn't much feel like it, but he was hosting this meal
at the Kashmir and felt an obligation to keep up appearances.
He sat quietly with his talkative guests, Anna rambling about
a new song she'd written; Diane about a painting she was
engaged in, having just recently gotten the notion she might
be an artist. Kinkaide was making feeble efforts at witti-
cisms. All quite tedious to Ryan. He sensed that everyone
was trying to think of some way to talk about anything but
their feelings about Rapture. Which made him wonder what
people said about life here behind his back: Of course the
grumbling was becoming louder. The treacherous Sofia Lamb
was stoking that smoldering fire . . .

He watched his guests put on their little acts, striving to
seem cheerfully amused, happily involved in Rapture, but
starting to fray around the edges in the confinement—like so
many of the weaklings he'd allowed into the city. They had
every manner of comfort: even now they sat in the most luxurious corner booth of the restaurant, by the tiered, gurgling
marble fountain, under a big window that looked out on an
undersea garden where purple and red flabelliform plants
waved in shafts of blue light. Chopin played softly from hidden speakers. Life here for the moneyed should be enchant-
ing. But it never seemed to be enough.

Ryan noticed Anton Kinkaide staring goofily at Diane.
Kinkaide was a man with little social sophistication but a
brilliant engineering mind. His ratty sweater, crooked bowtie, and nervous nursing from a beer glass contrasted with
Fisher's easy champagne sophistication. Ryan wondered if
Diane would like Anton Kinkaide. The engineer could be
impressive—he had designed the Rapture Metro—and he
was a man who loved ideas. Diane pretended to be an intel-
lectual at times, though really she was quite a naïf.

The only other diners in the restaurant, at a table across
the big room, were the smirking Pierre Gobbi and Marianne
Dellahunt. The young Frenchman, a winemaker, was visibly
bored as he listened to the superficial Marianne, whose taut
features seemed empty of character and age. She'd made one
too many visits to Dr. Steinman.

Ryan wished Bill and Elaine had come to dinner. Bill Mc-
Donagh was damn good company. Levelheaded too.

Sullivan was finishing a third glass of Worley's best wine.
Sullivan was a bit of a stiff at any gathering; he was either
stone-faced or got drunk and started leering at the women.
After the leering phase he'd slip into the inevitable drinker's
glumness, glowering at the windows as if angry with the endless blue depths. Ryan could almost read his mind: *Taking
this nutty job and moving down here, I musta been crazy.*

But sober, Sullivan did what needed to be done. Ryan
knew he could trust his security chief. That was worth putting up with a great deal.

He wasn't sure he trusted Garris Fisher as much. The ur-
bane middle-aged Fisher, both a biochemist and an entrepreneur, had helped promote Fontaine's plasmids.

"Any interesting new developments at Fontaine Futuristics, Garris?" Ryan asked carelessly.

Fisher smiled mysteriously, as Ryan had known he would.
"Oh—" He tapped the champagne flute with his fingernail to

make it ring. "Naturally. But nothing you need worry about, Andrew . . ."

"Your BruteMore is selling rather well, I understand. Others aren't quite . . . panning out."

Fisher shrugged. "These little potholes crop up in the road of commerce, do they not? We bump right through them, change the tires, and move on. Our SkinGlow is popular with the ladies . . . And Fontaine's new one, Incinerate—quite flashy."

"Ah, yes." Ryan chuckled. "I watched the cook in the kitchen start the gas fire with it. Pointed his finger and *whoof!* A bit startling at first."

"Startling is itself an advertisement, you know. Grabs attention."

Ryan nodded. There was something to that—he'd been impressed, seeing the man shooting fire from his hand. A true sign of Rapture science at work. And according to Sullivan, Fontaine was raking in huge profits—overtaking Ryan's own. Ryan Industries truly needed to find a way into plasmids . . .

Kinkaide was gawping at Diane again. Ryan found himself wondering if he could indeed fob Diane off on Anton. Of course, he could always simply tell her to go away. But somehow she'd wormed her way into his emotional life so that he knew just dismissing her would be painful, which was partly why he wanted to get rid of her. He didn't want the distraction of a serious relationship. She'd been hinting of marriage lately. Detestable thought. Never again. But he would prefer Diane left him on her own, without having to be . . . propelled.

He felt her touch his arm, turned to see her smiling back at him with just a mild reproach. "Darling, my glass has been empty for ever so long."

Ryan sighed inwardly. The former cigarette girl, at least publicly, was always putting on that stilted chic diction she'd picked up from the movies. Thought she was Myrna Loy.

"Yes, my dear, we do need another bottle of champagne." He didn't want to suggest any more wine for Sullivan. "Brenda!"

The woman who was ostensibly the owner of Kashmir— Ryan's partner, really—came hurrying over, trotting around the heroic statue of powerful men lifting the world, beaming at Ryan. Brenda's high forehead gleamed in the light from the window; her tight, low-cut silvery gown—rather much, Ryan thought, for a woman past thirty—forcing her to take small Geisha-like steps across the carpet. "Andrew!" she gasped, in an absurdly girlish voice. "What *else* can I get for you?"

"A bottle of our best champagne, if you please."

"And," Sullivan said, "bring a, uh . . ." He noticed Ryan watching him and sighed: ". . . a glass of water."

"I'll see to it personally," Brenda fluted. "Personally *per*-son-ally! And then perhaps—the dessert cart!"

"Yes," Ryan said. "That'll be splendid; thank you, Brenda . . ."

He glanced around at the others. The smiles they'd put on for Brenda faded as she walked away—except, as always, Fisher, who seemed in his element in Rapture, still smiling confidently.

Maybe, Ryan thought, *I'm imagining all this discontent.*

But his reports from Sullivan, and other security sources, suggested that there was discontent at all levels of society— especially in Artemis Suites and "Pauper's Drop," both of which were growing dangerously crowded. He'd underestimated how many people were needed for basic maintenance work and hadn't built enough housing for them. Rapture would soon exceed eighteen thousand souls. Not all of them came equipped with investment funds. He had hoped many of the mainte- nance and construction workers would earn their way out of their slummy squalor. Find a way to branch out, take a second job, invest—the way *he* would in their position. The rumors that Frank Fontaine and Sofia Lamb's followers had been encouraging notions Andrew Ryan regarded as absolutely taboo—such as unions—were getting louder. Fontaine was slippery, however. Finding proof against him for Communist organizing was as hard as finding strong proof he was smuggling.

But Sofia Lamb—he had a plan for her. He'd get her to debate him in public. When Rapture's better element heard her Marxist sophistry flagrantly blared on the radio, no one would object if she simply . . . disappeared.

"I was thinking," Diane said, "that we might have some public performances, me and Sander and a few of them others—" She remembered her new grammar. Cleared her throat. "And a *few others,* in the park and in the atriums, get people out more. You've made all these large, lovely, high-ceilinged spaces for people—but what do they do? They huddle like little gophers in their warrens!"

Ryan found himself yearning for the simpler, less affected company of Jasmine Jolene. Perhaps he could slip away to see her tonight . . .

"Mr. Ryan?" Karlosky's thick accent broke in on his thoughts. Smelling of tobacco and too much men's cologne, Karlosky was standing at his elbow.

Ryan turned briskly to him, hoping this was an excuse to slip away early. "Yes?"

"There is problem in Hephaestus. Sabotage, they say!"

"Sabotage!" Strange that he should be almost pleased to hear of this. But it was just the excuse he needed. He stood. "Do not discommode yourselves," he told the others. "I'd better go look into this."

"I'll come too," Kinkaide said.

"Not your area of engineering, Anton. I'll see to it. Ah— perhaps you can escort Diane home for me, after?"

"Oh yes, yes, delighted, surely, I . . . yes . . ."

Ryan hurried away with Karlosky, guessing that Bill Mc-
Donagh was already dealing with the emergency . . .

~~~~~~

Bill McDonagh was up to his waist in icy water, wondering
how he was going to deal with this emergency. He had sloshed
across the valve-control room and found the right wheels to
turn, but his numb fingers were losing strength. He only had
two out of four shut down. He managed the third and fumbled
at the fourth. He should have closed the hatch to the valve
room. But if he did, he risked drowning in here. He'd switched
on the bailing pumps and hoped the machine could keep up
with the inflow till he could get this broken pipe plugged.

Roland Wallace was also wading in through the water,
wearing rubber waders up to his armpits and gloves. Wallace
pressed close at Bill's side, reached into the cold water, and
helped turn the last two valves. The valve wheels turned grat-
ingly, and it seemed to take forever—but at last the flow was
blocked.

The water stopped rushing into the room, and they found
their way to the pumps, activated them, waiting for the room
to drain—both with chattering teeth.

"You see the tool marks where they tore the pipes out?"
Wallace asked, pointing. His voice was raised to be heard
over the grinding and sucking sounds of the pumps.

Bill nodded, rubbing the feeling back into his hands. The
broken coolant pipe was jutting out, the metal ragged at the
ends, the harsh angle and the marks on the wall suggesting
strong force. "You got no argument from me, mate. Sabotage!"

The floodwater had almost pumped out when Bill saw the
package taped to the ceiling vent.

"What the hell is that, Roland!"

"What—oh! I don't know! But it's got some kind of clock
on it . . ."

"*Jay*-sus! It's a bomb! Get out!"

Wallace threw the bolt, opened the metal door—and they stepped through not a split second before a *whoomf* sound came from behind them, with a flash and a sharp smell of gunpowder.

"Fuck!" Bill sputtered. He peered through the smoky air, back through the open door, and saw a blackened mark on the vent where the bomb had gone off but no other appreciable damage. Instead, the room was littered with what looked like large pieces of confetti, which were starting to stick to the wet floor and walls.

Coughing from the acrid smoke, he stepped in, scooped up some of the confetti, and hurried back out.

There were words on the strips of paper. Printed in large black letters on one was

RAPTURE OPPRESSORS

And on another was

BE WARNED

They were all like that, one phrase or the other. "Be warned, Rapture oppressors," he said, looking over the slips of paper.

"A bomb with nothing but paper in it?" Wallace said, puzzled, scratching his head.

Bill remembered hearing as a kid about the old anarchist bombers active from the late nineteenth century. Mad bombers they'd called them. But confetti wasn't their style. "Just a way to get our attention," he suggested. "A little sabotage, yeah? A bit of a bomb, but not enough to make people go all out to find the bombers. Like it says—a *warning*, innit?"

"But the implication is that a bigger bomb will come," Wallace pointed out. "Otherwise, why a bomb at all?"

"God's truth, that. Think they're oppressed, do they? That supposed to tell us what they want? Bloody vague, I call it."

"What's vague?" Ryan asked, hurrying in. "What's happened?"

"Here, Mr. Ryan—you oughtn't to be here!" Bill said. "There could be another bomb!"

"A bomb!"

Wallace shrugged. "More like a firecracker, sir. Spreading confetti—with some kind of political warning on it. Not much damage."

Bill handed him the slips of paper. And watched Ryan's face go red, his hands trembling.

"So it's begun!" Ryan sputtered. "Communist organizers! Probably that Lamb woman's followers . . ."

"Could be," Bill said. "Or mebbe someone who wants us to think that's what's going on here . . ."

Ryan looked at him sharply, crumpling the paper up in his fist. "Meaning what, exactly, Bill?"

"Dunno, guv. But . . ." He hesitated, knowing Ryan's mixed feelings about Frank Fontaine. Ryan seemed to like Fontaine. Didn't seem to want to bring him down. "Someone like Fontaine might use this political muck to shift power around in Rapture . . ."

Ryan looked doubtful. "Someone, yes—but Fontaine?"

Wallace cleared his throat. "Rapture *does* have its vulnerabilities, Mr. Ryan. Doctors can be kind of expensive here. Fontaine could point that out. Sanitation, even oxygen—all charged for here."

Ryan looked at him with narrowed eyes. "What of it? I built this place. Ryan Industries owns most of it. People have to purchase property, *compete* their way to comfort, here!"

Wallace gulped but went bravely on. "Sure, Mr. Ryan, but—people working for most merchants here aren't getting paid much. There's no minimum wage so it's kind of hard to earn enough to save and, uh . . ."

"The resourceful will earn! We have possibilities here others don't have—no restriction on science, no interference from the superstitious control systems people call religion! These malcontents have no case! And I must say, Wallace, I'm surprised to hear these Communist ideas from you . . ."

Wallace looked genuinely alarmed at that. Bill hastily put in, "I think all he's saying, guv, is that the appearance of unfairness gives these Commie blokes a chance to get their snouts in. So we've got to be on the watch for 'em."

"That's it!" Wallace said quickly. "Just—on the . . . on the watch."

Ryan gave Wallace a long, slow, silent appraisal. Then he looked back at the remnants of the message bomb. "We'll *watch* all right. I'll put Sullivan on this. With all speed. Right now—let us find a safer place for a convocation . . ."

"For a—right, guv. For one of those. Out this way, sir . . ."

Bill had told himself, for his family's sake, that everything was going to work out. But he could no longer ignore the stunningly obvious:

Rapture was cracking at the seams.

12

"I was working in the lighthouse today," Sam said glumly. Sam Lutz was tired. His back ached as he sat beside his wife and watched their daughter play beside the family bunk beds.

Sam and Mariska Lutz were sitting on their bottom bunk in the crowded number 6 of Artemis Suites—a "suite" intended for a few people, but which the Lutzes shared with nine other families. They ignored the argument and bustle and jostling from the rest of the apartment and watched Mascha playing on the floor by the bunk with two stiff little dolls Sam had made for her from scrap wood. One of the dolls was a boy, one a girl, and little Mascha—a pale black-haired child, with flashing black eyes like her mother—was making them dance together. "La, la-la *la*, the rapture of Rapture, your heart it will capture, oh la, la-la *la-a-a!*" she sang, her reedy voice providing the music for the dance. Some song she'd heard piped over the public address in one of the atriums.

"It was good you could get the work, Sam," Mariska said as she watched Mascha. Her diction was good—she'd taught English in Prague—but her accent was thick. They'd met when Sam was stationed in Eastern Europe after World War Two. Circumstances had made it almost impossible for her to marry him and go back to the States—but in '48 they were approached by a recruiter from Rapture looking for Atlantic Express laborers. It was a way out of the wreckage that was left after the war. A way out of the U.S. Army.

Only Rapture wasn't an *out*. He felt trapped here. The work had finished up, and Sam got laid off. And he'd been summarily informed he wasn't allowed to leave the underwater colony. There was beauty in Rapture, sure—but people like Sam didn't have much chance to appreciate it. It was like Sofia Lamb said: most people here were like the backstairs servants in a palace.

"Yeah, I needed the work, sure," Sam admitted. "But it was just two days' worth. Not enough to get us out of here. Need enough to get our own place in Sinclair Deluxe, at least."

"There are some rooms they don't use behind Fighting McDonagh's—Elaine told me about them. Maybe they would let us have them cheap! The McDonaghs are nice."

He grunted. "Maybe, but . . . not sure I'd want the girl there. McDonagh's night manager hires out those rooms to women from Pauper's Drop . . . desperate women, if you know what I mean . . ."

"And is it so much better here?"

"No." Then realizing that gloom could be catching, he smiled and patted her hand, leaning close to whisper, "Some day I'll take you home to Colorado. You'd like Colorado . . ."

"Maybe someday." She twined her fingers with his, looking nervously around. "Best not to speak of such, here. We have food and shelter now . . ."

Sam snorted. He looked at the other people shuffling back and forth in the close, malodorous suite. And all the other rooms and suites in the Artemis building were just as crowded, just as prone to tension.

Little Toby Griggs appeared to be arguing with big, chunky Babcock again. Something odd about those two. It was as if in a moment they'd transform into two cats arching their backs and hissing. Then Babcock turned and walked away between the bunk beds. Griggs followed . . .

There were two rows of bunk beds in what should have

been the living room. Seven more against the two long walls in the bedroom. Junk piled in the corner. Not enough storage. He hoped the toilet wasn't plugged up again. Smelled like it might be.

And someone had been putting graffiti on the walls. *Ryan doesn't own us!* it said. *Become the body of the Lamb!* That would have to come down before the constables saw it.

"Oh, if you were up in the lighthouse," Mariska said suddenly, "you saw the sky! That must have been nice!" Her eyes were wide at the thought of seeing the sky again.

"Yes. I only had a few seconds to look at it. They had us busy fixing the entry bathysphere. We had to bowse up three hundred yards of steel spool and set it in place. Not easy with just three of us and only a hand-cranked winch. And it was cold up in that lighthouse shaft. It's winter on the surface. I remember crossing this ocean in a troopship this time of year—cold as hell and the waves higher than the ship, all of us seasick." He made a mental effort to force memories of the war out of his mind. It was helped by Toby Griggs and Babcock arguing loudly on the other side of the bunks. He tried to ignore them—you had to screen most people out, in these conditions, if you wanted to stay sane.

"Did you hear anything up there in the lighthouse?" she asked. "I mean—maybe ships passing or gulls or . . ."

"You know what I heard up there? Icebergs! We heard one of them banging on the lighthouse—boom! Big ol' clangin', echoing sound! What a noise!"

"I'd like to go up and look sometime," she said wistfully. "If they allowed it . . ."

"Oh Jesus. I'm sorry I brought you down here. They made it sound so good . . ."

She kissed him on the cheek. Her lips seemed deliciously soft to him, after dealing with cold, hard metal all day. *"Miluji tě!"* she whispered. Czech for "I love you."

"Me too, kid!" he said, putting an arm around her shoulders. She was a small woman, nestling easily against him.

Around the crowded bunk room, people muttered and argued and bitched in three, maybe four different languages: the singsong of Chinese, the bubbling flow of Spanish, and especially the sarcastic brassiness of Brooklyn English.

"Whadya doin' with ya boots under my bunk over heah? I look like I got room for your shit under my bunk fa cryin' out loud?"

"Someone fucking stole the last of my scented fucking soap! You know how hard it is to get that shit? It's probably you, Morry . . ."

"The fuck it was!"

"Somebody got into my lockbox! I had my last EVE hypo in there and it's gone!"

"Whatya talkin' about, you're the one stole my plasmids! I had a New Skills I was gonna inject for the job tomorrow!"

Frightened by the shouting, Mascha came to sit with her back against her dad's legs. She made the little dolls clack together, singing loudly to drown out the sound of all those heated voices. "La, la-la la, the rapture of Rapture, your heart it will capture, oh la, la-la la-a-a!"

Someone in the far corner shouted, but Sam couldn't make out what they said. He caught a flash, heard a crackle, smelled ozone—a shout of pain and a flare of blue light.

A ball of fire sizzled across the room, between the bunks, and charred the wall on the left.

"Mama! Daddy!" Mascha whimpered, climbing up on the bed behind them to peek over her mother's shoulder. "What is it?"

"Someone's messing with those plasmids!" Mariska whispered, her voice choked with fear. "They're way over there, little one, on the other side of the room—we'll be safe here."

"Stay at the bunk," Sam told her firmly. Mariska tried to

hold him back, but he pulled away. He had to know what was going on. If they were throwing fireballs, the whole place could catch—plenty of flammables in Artemis. They were a ways from the doors to the suite and could surely burn alive before they got out. A mighty peculiar way to die considering they were deep underwater. But he'd heard of men burning alive in submarines in the war.

He moved carefully to steal a look around the corner of the Ming family's double bunk and saw the two men quarrelling in the far corner of the room near the row of circular blue-lit ports looking out into the sea.

"Just get outta my face or the next one'll toast you, Griggs!" Babcock shouted, jabbing an angry finger at the smaller man. Babcock was a tall man with fat cheeks and patchy hair, greasy coveralls. He had one of the odd skin reactions people got from plasmid use, this one on his scalp, making an ugly mesh of red welts. Part of his hair had fallen out around it.

Toby Griggs was squared off with him—a puny, fox-faced fellow, hair slicked back; he had a tart way of talking and a lively sense of humor. Sam had always kind of liked Toby for his spunk. Toby worked as a salesman in one of the shops off Fort Frolic and still had his wrinkly green-and-black-checked suit on.

"Back off or I'll electrocute you, Babcock!" Toby crowed as energy crackled between the fingers of his raised right hand. "I'll strap you in the electric chair standin' up!"

Sam wasn't surprised that Toby had spent his paycheck on a plasmid from Fontaine Futuristics—Toby had been talking about how a good plasmid could be an equalizer. He was a little guy and didn't like to be bullied.

But Babcock had always seemed levelheaded—and he had two small girls to think of—plump little twins. Yet there was Babcock, using *Incinerate!*, making a ball of fire appear in his hands.

Toby Griggs had a look in his eyes that made Sam think of a rooster back home on the ranch about to jab a rival with its beak—that mean glitter in its little eyeballs. As for Babcock, it looked to Sam like the mesh of red welts on his head was pulsing in rhythm with his angry panting. A wavery column of hot air rose from the fire flickering over Babcock's hands. Strange that the flames emanating from his fingers didn't burn them—but plasmids were like that. It seemed to Sam that heavy plasmid use made people into something like rattlesnakes, not hurt by their own venom.

Toby and Babcock danced around each other, teeth bared, wild-eyed, drool running from the corners of their mouths, energies simmering in their raised hands. To Sam their threats sounded like babbling; like they were barely aware of what they were saying.

"Threatening me, Babcock?" Toby howled. "Is that right? *Is it?* I'm tired of you big slobs pushing me around! Why do you think I paid good money for this plasmid? I may not eat for a week, but I have power to keep plug uglies like you from throwing your weight around! I'm a new man! I can feel it! I'm no one to screw with now, Babcock! Back off or *die!*"

"Die? *Me?* I can burn you to a cinder! I swore I'd defend my family against anyone who threatened them, and I'll do it!"

"No one's threatening your family! You've been getting nutty from the moment you got that plasmid!" Toby snarled. "You can't handle it! Maybe you took too much EVE and not enough ADAM—ya don't know what you're doing! You're nuts, Babcock! Batty, crackers, crazy! Back off or I'll put a charge in you that'll turn your head into a thousand-watt lightbulb!"

"How are you gonna do that when you're a burned-up cinder, Griggs, huh? Answer me that!"

Fire whirled restlessly, roaring in Babcock's hands, as if it were eager to destroy.

Toby Griggs growled to himself and took the offensive. He twisted his shoulders about, grimacing with insane concentration. Electricity writhed from his fingers, crackling through the air at Babcock, just as Babcock's wife—a pudgy, mousy-haired woman in slippers and a loose blue frock—came rushing up to him on her short legs, throwing her stubby arms around him. "*Noooo,* Harold!" she yelled. "Don't do that! You'll get us killed!"

Then she let out a pealing shriek as the Electro Bolt struck her and Babcock at once . . . an extra-big bolt of blue-white lightning—everything Toby Griggs could summon up.

Onlookers screamed as Babcock and his wife went rigid. The two of them were doing an absurd little dance together, locked in a fatal embrace as the current raged through them, sparking blue from their bared teeth. Mrs. Babcock's hair stood on end; her dress caught fire . . .

Their eyes smoked and then boiled out of their heads. Their faces contorted.

The charge burst and sparks flew into the walls and floor as Mr. and Mrs. Babcock, flesh fused in a grotesque mock of marriage, fell in a limp, smoldering heap.

"Oh my God," Sam muttered, staring at them. "They're dead! Toby Griggs, what have you done!"

"You—you all saw it!" Toby said shrilly, backing away from the gathering crowd between the bunks. "He threw a fireball at my head! He was raving, completely out of his gourd! He was on a plasmid high! He can't handle his plasmids, and he just . . . he tried to . . . tried to kill me! He . . ."

Then Toby bolted, dodging past grasping hands, out the front door of the suites.

Two little girls, the five-year-old Babcock twins, came tiptoeing up together, clutching each other in life as their parents clutched each other in death.

"Mommy?" quavered one little girl.

"Daddy?" quavered the other.

Two little girls. All alone now. Orphans. Two little sisters . . .

Fontaine Futuristics, Rapture
1955

"We have too few sea slugs," said Brigid Tenenbaum, squint-ing into a microscope at a dead gastropod, as Frank Fontaine entered lab 23. These new research digs were bigger, roomier, with ports and windows, levels, and a balcony-walk looking down on the central concourse of Fontaine Futuristics. Tenenbaum turned, frowning thoughtfully to Fontaine. "Only special gastropod works for ADAM mutagen and base for EVE . . . and these, all gone."

"We'll have to cut back plasmid production," Fontaine said gloomily, looking at the remaining sea slugs squirming in the aquarium. *Ugly little fuckers.* "Couldn't we breed the little bastards? Create more sea slugs with, what do you call it, animal husbandry?"

"Perhaps in time. But very slow process, much experimen-tation, maybe years. Better is to increase individual sea-slug production of mutagen—of ADAM. This can be done more quickly—if we use host."

"A *host?* Oh . . . Maybe we can hijack a ship, send you down the sailors."

"We try adults already. Two subjects. They sickened and died. Screaming—very noisy. Irritating. One of them reached to me . . ." She looked in wonder at her hand. "Tried to hold on to my hand. Begging, take it out, take it out of me . . . But children! Ah—it likes to be in children. The sea slug is happy there."

"It's happy . . . in children? Well—how's it work exactly?"

"We implant sea slug in lining of child's stomach. The sea slug bonds with cells, becomes symbiotic with human host.

After host feeds, we induce regurgitation, and then we have twenty, thirty times more yield of usable ADAM."

"And how do you know it works so good on kids?"

Dr. Suchong answered him as he pushed a gurney into the room. "Suchong and Tenenbaum experiment on this child!" Stretched out on the gurney was what appeared to be a sleeping child, a rather ordinary little white girl in a dressing gown, strapped to the wheeled hospital bed. She was perhaps six years old. Her eyes opened—she looked up at him sleepily, gave him a distant, fuzzy smile. Drugged.

"Where in hell you get that kid?"

"Child was sick," Tenenbaum said. "Brain tumor. We tell parents maybe we heal. We implant sea slug in her abdomen, inside. It cures her tumor! We keep her tranquilized—she talks in her mind to sea slug . . ."

As if in response, the little girl lifted a hand—and touched her own belly caressingly.

Tenenbaum gave a little satisfied grunt. "Yes. She will be productive."

"You intend to use this child to create a new plasmid base . . ." Fontaine shook his head. "One child? Will it be enough? The market for it is exploding! People are going wild for the stuff! I was going to start major marketing, stores, maybe even vending machines . . ."

"This is tester child," Suchong said. "We need more, many more. Implant, feed, induce regurgitation—much mutagen produced, much ADAM. Better if not tranquilized. We must prepare hosts for this. Condition them!"

"How come it . . . it likes children?" Fontaine asked. He could almost feel a sea slug squirming in his own belly. Sheer imagination, but the thought nauseated him.

Tenenbaum shrugged. "Child stem cells are more malleable. More . . . responsive. They bond with the sea slug. We need children, Frank—many children!"

Fontaine snorted. "And where are we supposed to get those? From a mail-order catalogue?"

Dr. Suchong frowned and shook his head. "Suchong has not seen such catalogue. Not needed. Two children available already. Orphan girls. Babcock twins. They stay with people in Artemis Suites—their parents dead. Both parents killed by plasmid attack. And they are girls, the right age—perfect! We pay to bring them here."

"Okay; they've got to be kids—but why girls?" Fontaine asked. "People are even more protective about little girls."

Tenenbaum winced and turned back to the microscope, muttering, "For some reason girls take sea-slug implant better than boys."

Fontaine wondered what little boy they'd experimented on to determine that and what had become of him. But he didn't really care. He *didn't*.

And in fact—there was one place that could supply children for all sorts of things. "So—just girls, eh? That's okay; that'll just be fewer bunks in the orphanage."

"Orphanage?" Tenenbaum blinked in puzzlement. "There is an orphanage in Rapture?"

Fontaine grinned. "No, but there will be. You just gave me the idea, with this thing about the Babcock orphans. I'll donate the money for the orphanage! Yeah! 'The Little Sisters Orphanage.' We'll get our adorable little plasmid farms . . . and we'll train 'em up right. We got to do this soon! I've got more orders for plasmids than I can fill in a year!" Something about the idea energized him. He felt a kind of shudder, almost a release go through him as he thought about it. *Orphanages.* Like where he'd grown up. Orphanages leading to money. And money . . . leading to power. "Money and power, Brigid. Money and power! It's all right there, low-hanging fruit for the plucking . . . in a gatherer's garden."

He heard the door open and turned to see his bodyguard come in, grimacing. He'd left Reggie standing at the door outside Fontaine Futuristics—now his hand was clasping his right biceps, blood streaming from his fingers. "Say, anybody got any bandages here?"

"Reggie!" Fontaine stepped to the door, looked down the concourse. Saw no one. "What happened? You hurt bad?"

Suchong was already methodically sponging off the wound on Reggie's arm.

"Ouch! Oh, I'm not hurt bad. But I'll tell you what—somebody shot at me. Kind of at random, seemed like. The prick. I shot back, but I think I missed him. He took off."

"Shot at you . . . you mean a constable?" Fontaine asked.

"Don't think so. I wasn't doing anything to make a constable shoot at me. And he didn't have a badge. Loopy-looking plasmid-head with a pistol. Spots all over his face. It's been like this lately—random shooting. Ryan's started putting in those security turrets, to keep these guys in check. You'll want to get one of those babies for this place. Camera with a machine gun that picks out targets. I dunno how it . . . ouch, Doc, shit!"

"Suchong is so sorry," Dr. Suchong said, not sounding sorry as he wound a bandage tightly around the wound.

"Like I was saying, I dunno how the turret thing keeps from killing the wrong people. All I know is—on and off all day there's been gunfire. Plasmids . . . that's the reason I don't use that stuff. I don't like firing my gun without a goddamn reason." He winced again. "Waste of good bullets."

Andrew Ryan's Office
1955

Andrew Ryan was standing at the window, looking broodingly out at the lights of Rapture shimmering through the sea, thinking: *Steps will have to be taken . . . I have tolerated too much . . .*

"You wanted to see Poole?" Sullivan asked, coming in with the ratlike little reporter.

Ryan nodded and sat at his desk. Stanley Poole and Sullivan sat across from him. "Well, Poole? What's your report about this Topside character? People are talking about him as if he's a hero—but he's an outsider, as I understand it . . ."

Sullivan frowned. "I could've got you the dirt on him, Mr. Ryan."

"I know, Chief. But your men are sometimes too . . . obvious. Poole here has a strange gift for being ignored. Well, Poole?"

Stanley Poole licked his lips nervously. "Yes sir, well, near as I can find out, this guy they're calling Johnny Topside— he's a deep-sea diver. There was some snoopers out here, you remember; our subs made sure they stopped snooping. When they went missing, why, he came out to see what was going on. Went down at the main lighthouse and found a way in. One of the air locks, I guess. People are pretty impressed with him, making his way here. Acts like he's on his own, just wants to help. He's asking about missing girls, seems like . . ."

"Is he? What is his real name?"

"I'm sorry—he's being cagey about that. Seems like he prefers an alias. Changes 'em around. Sounds like a secret-agent type to me. G-man is what I figure—hell, how'd he get all the info on boats missing in this area, all that stuff, if he didn't have connections?"

Ryan pinched the bridge of his nose. He was having small, annoying headaches, more and more often. Hearing that there might be a government agent in Rapture made his head redouble its throbbing. "You got anything on him, Chief?"

Sullivan shook his head. "Same impression. I haven't found

out his name either. Easy enough to do. I can take him over to the new facility . . ."

Ryan snapped his fingers. "Precisely what I had in mind. He's an outsider. Who knows who he's affiliated with. We cannot let a random outsider wander about in here, asking questions . . . Arrest him immediately, Sullivan. And while you're at it bring in that wretched Lamb woman. Poole here reports she may be connected to our confetti bomber. I've had enough of her Marxist babbling. She's turned half the maintenance workers against me."

"You want her charged with something?" Sullivan asked.

"No. I want her to simply . . . disappear. Into Persephone. Let her followers feel abandoned."

Sullivan nodded. "You got it, Mr. Ryan."

"Lamb's got a daughter," Poole pointed out. "Girl named Eleanor."

"Does she? Well, find a home for the girl, Sullivan."

Poole shrugged. "That colored woman, Grace Holloway, looks after her sometimes. She'll take the kid . . ."

"Fine, fine," Ryan said, with a dismissive wave, "let her take the kid. For now. The child may be of use later . . ."

Apollo Square
1955

"Spider Splicers, that's what they are," Greavy said.

"Spider *what*?" Bill asked.

"Splicers, Bill," Ruben Greavy repeated. "Splicers. That's the common term for real plasmid addicts."

Fascinated, Bill watched the two splicers, a man and a woman, moving on all fours along the sides of a tramcar. They were crawling on the wall like bugs, defying gravity. "Seen my share o' plasmid users," Bill allowed. "But this . . . sticking to things like bloody bugs . . . Going too far, maybe."

"Going too far is the splicer way," Greavy said dryly. "They all go rogue in time. They've gotten obsessed, this bunch. They're all about their plasmid splicing. Injecting Fontaine's mutagens, looking for EVE to activate it . . ."

Bill McDonagh and Ruben Greavy were standing by the tram tracks in Apollo Square, watching the tram go by. Adhering like geckos to the metal sides of the slowly moving trams, the spider-splicer couple was ordinarily dressed, but their heads and cheeks were knobbed with ugly reddish welts, growths from abusing ADAM and EVE.

Shifting his heavy toolbox from his left hand to his right, Bill reflected on how tempting plasmids were. He could *use* that wall-climbing power for getting at difficult-to-fix places in Rapture. He could use the new telekinesis plasmid to move objects about, adding an extra pair of invisible hands to a job. One man could do the work it would normally take three to do.

But Bill knew better. Some could take them and stay more or less sane for a while. But keep taking them—and you eventually went barking mad.

He watched as the male spider splicer grinned clownishly into the tramcar from its roof, head dipping to stare upside down in a window, leering at the passengers cringing back from him. "You lovey snuggle ducks!" he yelled hoarsely. "You little chocolates in this chocolate box of steel!" He cackled something more that Bill couldn't hear as the tram trundled away from him and Greavy. But he could see the giggling woman reaching in through a window, clutching for someone's arm . . .

A gunshot cracked from inside the tram, and smoke drifted out the open window as the female spider splicer jerked her arm back. She screeched in pain and fury, and her splicer partner fired his own gun into the window while clinging upside down. Then the tramcar slipped from sight beyond the kiosks.

Bill sighed and shook his head. "Out of their ever-lovin' bloody minds, they are!"

"Yes, I suppose so," Greavy said thoughtfully. "But I think of it as part of a Darwinian process. This madness, these side effects—they'll die of it, eventually, fighting each other, perhaps. A possibly necessary winnowing in Rapture. Ryan and I knew something of the sort would come—some vector of purging. Eventually plasmids will be developed with fewer side effects. These early users are like guinea pigs . . ."

Bill glanced at Greavy. He'd never liked the man much, and that sort of comment was one of the reasons. "We'd best get to that inspection You think we should call the constables about that gunfight?"

Greavy shrugged. "There are so many gunfights now, so much antagonism—the constables can't deal with most of it. Ryan's attitude is that if two consenting adults want to duel, let them."

Troubled, Bill led the way across the tracks and down a short stairway. Workers hoisted a big sign into place at the entrance to a new institution built into a leased space. The sign, with silvery metal lettering, read:

FONTAINE'S
CENTER
For the Poor

Framing the lettering was a relief sculpture, one on each side, of hands reaching down, to pull other hands upward . . .

"Never thought I'd see that in Rapture," Bill muttered, as they paused to watch. "A charity!"

"Shouldn't be here at all," Greavy said, frowning. "Just makes things worse. Charity trains people to be dependent. It's in the natural order of things for people to strive and fail—for a good number of them to fall by the wayside,

and . . . you know. Just die. Fontaine's Center for the Poor!"
He snorted skeptically. "What's that a front for?"

"Anybody else, I'd give 'em the benefit of the doubt," Bill
said. "With Fontaine—I've got to wonder what the bastard is
up to . . ."

"Politics," Greavy murmured. "Political allies. Maybe his
own little army—the army of the poor . . ."

"He'll have no shortage of poor to draw on," Bill said as
they moved off. "Artemis Suites and Pauper's Drop are stuffed
with blokes out of work—and if they work, they still feel
crowded and underpaid. Not everyone can start their own
business. And if they do, who'll clean the toilets?"

"You know where Fontaine gets the money for that charity?" asked Greavy with rhetorical pompousness. "From selling
ADAM! And why are a lot of the poor impoverished? Because
they're addicted to ADAM! They're spending all their money
on it! The irony is naturally lost on the hoi polloi . . ."

They walked to the nearest wall, not far from the entrance
to an apartment complex—and almost immediately Bill felt
cold water dripping on his head.

He looked up, saw the discoloration high on the wall where
it met the big, heavily framed windows arching over the room,
several stories up. He admired the Wales brothers' vision,
building big public spaces like this one. The high glass ceiling
eased the sense of confinement, gave people access to something like sky. Infused by light filtering green-blue from the
surface, the sea was directly overhead. The windows curved
down to meet the walls, and through the glass near the ceiling
was a rippling vista of other Rapture buildings, light streaming
up their towering façades, neon signs blinking.

Another drop of water fell from the ceiling and splashed his
shoulder. "Pressure crack," Bill guessed. "From the look of the
puddle it's been here awhile. Wish I could climb walls like

those spider-splicer bastards, get a closer look. Well, I think we'll have a team go out in the diving suits, apply some sealant, then we'll see if—" He broke off, staring, as a wrench floated up from his tool kit, as if weightless, and bobbed in the air in front of him. "What the bloody hell is that?"

The floating wrench suddenly darted at his head, and only good reflexes and a quick duck saved Bill from being struck down. The tool flashed by him, and he turned to see it spinning along, stopping in midair, turning to swish viciously at him again.

"What the blue blazes!" Bill grabbed the wrench with his left hand, bruising his palm. It seemed to jump about in his hand like a live but rigid metal fish before it simply stopped. "Who's chucking tools at me?"

"There's your tool chucker," Greavy said, grimly amused, pointing at a woman about ten yards away, standing by the doorway into Artemis Suites. She was a petite, smirking, waiflike woman in black pedal pushers and a ragged, blood-spattered blouse, the left sleeve ripped entirely away, her left arm scratched and bloody. She wore kohl smeared around her eyes, so they looked like a panda's, and her bleached hair was teased up over her head, almost writhing around like Medusa's snakes. Bill supposed a side effect of the telekinetic plasmid she was using was affecting her hair. One side of her face was striped with red welts. Her eyes had the demented glimmer of the hard-core plasmid user. She was crazily stoned.

She raised a grimy hand and pointed it at his tool kit—which jerked from his hand and spun away from him, scattering its contents across the room. People dodged out of the way of flying tools, now under the control of her telekinetic powers.

"Hey you, stop throwing your tools!" shouted a glaring, bald-headed constable in a checked suit, stalking toward Bill. A star-shaped badge was pinned on his chest.

"Isn't me!" he yelled back. "It's 'er, Constable, the splicer over at Artemis!"

The constable turned to look, reaching into his coat pocket for a gun. But as soon as he did his badge tore itself off his coat, spun around his head, and then buried itself between his eyes.

The constable screamed in agony and fell to his knees, clutching at his blood-spurting forehead.

"That'll show you pricks!" the little female splicer screeched, pointing a finger at Bill and Greavy. "I saw you, poking around here, you official types! Ryan's little puppets! Well, we don't want you 'round Artemis! Or your bald-headed cops neither!"

She made a sudden gesture, and his tools, scattered across the intervening floor, leapt into the air and came spinning at him. Bill threw himself flat as they flashed over him. Greavy shrieked, and Bill turned to see a screwdriver driven through Greavy's chest—the screwdriver blade dripping crimson. Greavy wobbled . . .

"*Jay*-sus, Greavy!"

Bill got to his feet just in time to catch Greavy as he fell, lowering the man's quivering body to the floor. Greavy was sputtering, dribbling blood, his eyes glazing. Dying.

Maybe if they could get some ADAM to him in time they could heal him . . .

But there was no time. In moments, Greavy was dead.

Bill looked in shock over at Artemis Suites—but the telekinetic splicer was gone. He heard someone cackling from the shadowy corners of the ceiling.

And then an announcement echoed from the public-address system—Diane McClintock's recorded voice: *"Remember that here in Rapture, we're all individuals—but we're also a part of the Great Chain! Welded together by the free market, we are becoming one happy family . . ."*

Andrew Ryan's Office
1955

"Mr. Ryan? Something I've got to ask about . . ."

Bill McDonagh was nervous, demanding an explanation from Andrew Ryan. He had countless other things to do, but he was too troubled to work until he cleared this up. Worry, burning like an acid stomach, had been building up in him.

"Yes, Bill?" Ryan said, looking up from a small box of audio tapes, seeming only vaguely curious about Bill's errand. He was at his desk, sorting through labeled recordings of his speeches and debates. An Acu-Vox recorder was set up beside the box.

Ryan was wearing a caramel-colored, double-breasted suit and a blue tie. Bill wondered how he could function in a buttoned-up suit all day long. "Mr. Ryan—I've got to keep the heat evenly circulating in Rapture; I've got to keep the pipes from freezing; I've got to be able to control water pressure. Part of the engineering of this place. I can't do it when there's a big drain, a sudden drop in heat and pressure—and it comes unpredictable-like and no one'll let me inspect the source of it—"

Ryan set the box aside. "Come to the point. What does this enigmatic monologue refer to?"

"There's a whole section of Rapture I'm not even allowed in now! Sinclair's got his own people running it. Place he is calling Persephone. I knew they were building something, but I thought it was a hotel. Only it's too secretive for that. I can't be responsible for hydraulic engineering when a whole section of the city is sealed off from me! Seems like it's been functional for a long time. More than a year . . . And it's no hotel."

Ryan made a small growl of grim amusement in his throat.

"Depends on what you mean by hotel! Persephone. Yes . . . I've been meaning to talk to you about that . . ." Ryan leaned back in his chair, looking at the ceiling as if something were written up there. "Bill . . . have you heard my debates with Sofia Lamb?"

"Only caught a minute or two. Kind of surprised me, when you debated 'er . . ."

Ryan smiled ruefully at him. "I took a risk, elevating that malcontent in that way. My instinct was simply to have her arrested as a . . . a social saboteur. But—I advocate freedom; I don't wish to be a hypocrite—and I didn't wish to make her a martyr. So I thought I'd let the people hear the sort of nonsense she spouts when I'm there to refute it! Listen . . ." He pressed a button on the tape recorder.

Bill heard Ryan's voice: *"Religious rights, Doctor? You are free to kneel before whatever tribal fetish you favor in the comfort of your own home. But in Rapture, liberty is our only law. A man's only duty is to himself. To imply otherwise, therefore, is criminal."*

Lamb replied, *"Ask yourself, Andrew—what is your 'Great Chain of progress' but a faith? The chain is a symbol for an irrational force, guiding us toward ascension—no less mystic than the crucifixes you seize and burn . . ."*

Bill nodded. It bothered him too, when Ryan seized religious artifacts. He wasn't religious. But a man ought to be able to believe in whatever he liked . . .

Ryan hit Fast Forward and then Play. Lamb's voice again: *". . . Dream, delusion, or the pain of a phantom limb—to one man, they are as real as rain. Reality is consensus, and the people are losing faith. Take a walk, Andrew. It is raining in Rapture, and you have simply chosen to not notice . . ."*

Ryan stopped the tape and snorted. "Quite the little extemporaneous speaker, isn't she? If you parse it, it makes no sense. But its real message can be decoded, Bill—'reality is consensus . . . the people are losing faith.' What is that but a Marxist notion? And this business of claiming I ignore the suffering in Rapture . . ." He shook his head grimly. "I don't ignore it—but I must accept it as part of the long, weary march of evolution! The surface world is still with us here—to die to the habit of parasitism comes hard, Bill. And some fall by the wayside in that long, lonely march. I know that full well! But what does *she* do? She makes me sound like Louis the Fourteenth! Next she'll imply Diane is Marie Antoinette, and she'll call for the guillotine! Do you expect me to stand by while that happens?"

"What's all that got to do with this Persephone, guv?" Bill asked. He suspected he knew—he'd heard rumors—but he wanted it spelled out.

Ryan looked Bill in the eye—the look was almost one of defiance, though Ryan was boss here. "That's where Sofia Lamb was taken, not long ago, Bill! And incarcerated."

"Incarcerated!"

"Yes. You must have noticed her absence from the scene. That glib, sanctimonious woman can make all the speeches she likes to the walls of her cell."

"But—won't that make her a martyr?"

"As far as her followers know, she's simply disappeared. Deserted them!"

Bill shook his head sadly. "Ought to be another way, Mr. Ryan . . ."

"I cannot allow this social sabotage to go on!" Ryan aimed an index finger at Bill. "Do you know who planted that charming little confetti bomb, with its warnings? Oh, I found out, Bill." He slapped the top of his desk. "It was done by an agent of Sofia Lamb! Stanley Poole's infiltrated her little circle. He's heard that it was one of our own people who planted the thing . . . quite likely, Simon Wales!"

"Wales!"

"Oh yes! At Lamb's behest."

"Well—why not prosecute her for that? A bomb's a bomb. It was vandalism at least! But this just *disappearing* people . . ."

"Her public prosecution would become a cause célèbre! Anyway, we haven't got solid proof. Just hearsay. But think about it—how like a psychiatrist to create a bomb that blows nothing up . . . except our sense of security! Not long after she got here, she started her little game, pulling the pins out from under us one by one. Do you know what she did with the bonus money I paid her? She took that—and a great many 'donations' from her followers—and built that smarmy Dionysus Park. Named in some bizarre effort at mockery . . ."

"Dionysus Park?" Bill scratched his head. He'd only been there once, to check the drainage. "Thought it was some kind of 'retreat.' Therapeutic art, something like that."

"Oh yes." Ryan's voice dripped with cynicism as he went on. "A retreat—her sheeplike followers closeted with Sofia Lamb in her precious garden and her own cinema. Just the setting for Marxist propaganda disguised as therapy and art! Rapture is a powder keg, Bill—I knew that when Ruben Greavy died. Plasmids made Rapture unstable. We can't remove plasmids, not now—but we can remove some of the instability. Lamb, people like her—they have to be stopped."

Bill wondered exactly what happened to the "incarcerated" in Persephone. Wasn't Persephone a name from a myth—about hell?

Ryan went on, gesturing at the Acu-Vox, "I recorded a note to you about all this—but I may as well talk it straight out with you instead. You remember when you spoke of a 'marketplace of ideas'? That was you. I liked the phrase. So—I let Lamb enter the marketplace, tried to defang her in debates. But she is too dangerous to be allowed to roam freely . . . You know the place they're calling Pauper's Drop—you've been to the Limbo Room?"

"Not me. Too much a 'ole in the wall."

"Good. Because Grace Holloway was singing protest songs there—perfectly harmless colored lady was Grace, till Lamb got hold of her! And between their protest screeches, these . . . these Oblomovs hand out Lamb's manifesto! Lamb adorns every wall there! Saint Lamb! You made her, McDonagh—"

"Me!"

"You with your marketplace-of-ideas talk! You persuaded me to allow her sort! Now—I want you to talk to the council about this. They must accept that people like this are to be silenced . . ."

"I can't do that, Mr. Ryan, it's not my place . . ."

"I need to know how you really feel, Bill. That'll show me where you stand."

"But—incarceration? This place Persephone . . . What exactly is it?"

Ryan sighed. "I should have let you in on it. Quite a while back I did a deal with Augustus Sinclair to build it—it's out on the edge of Rapture. Right over that . . . big crevice—just in case. It's . . . a facility for isolation and interrogation. Something between a mental hospital and a penal institution. For political enemies of Rapture." He was busying himself with the tapes—seeming embarrassed. "Some of this woman's followers are free—and some aren't. We'll find them, in time, and they'll have their own little cells. There are various shades of malcontents in Persephone . . ." He seemed to realize he was fussing mindlessly with the tapes and put the box aside. "As for water-pressure issues—I'll have Sinclair speak to you, give you reports on all that. He has a maintenance crew to deal with any . . . internal problems of that kind."

He doesn't want me to go there, Bill realized. *He doesn't want me to see what it's like . . .*

Something else occurred to Bill, then. There was a chance, after all, he *could* see the inside of Persephone—as a prisoner. It could happen if he said the wrong thing. That's what it was coming to, in Rapture. And he couldn't risk getting put away—not with Elaine and his little girl needing him . . .

Bill let out a long, slow breath to calm himself. When things cooled down, maybe he could persuade Ryan to close Persephone.

"Okay, Mr. Ryan," he said, keeping his voice as steady as he could. "I reckon you know best."

Persephone Penal Colony
1955

Simon Wales felt a powerful mingling of superstitious awe and pride as the guard let him into Sofia Lamb's cell.

She was waiting for him on her neatly made bunk, sitting up straight, hands folded in her lap, her blond hair back in a bun. She looked thin, hollow-eyed. But the transcendent spark was there.

"So you did come," she said softly. "How'd you arrange it?"

Wales had to take a breath to calm himself before he replied. He viewed this woman as a sending from the Locus of Universal Love. It was like being with the radiant Joan of Arc as she waited for the stake. "I . . . I have some terms of friendship with Sinclair, since Daniel and I were the chief architects of Rapture. I convinced him to let me inspect the structure here, to see if it was putting strain on the rest of Rapture—all a blind, of course. He allowed it—and then it was simply a matter of bribing the guards . . ."

"Good. You must see to it that the guards will let you in whenever you come—pay them whatever you must. They fear Sullivan and Ryan—they cannot be induced to simply let me go. But they can be persuaded to let me talk freely with the other inmates." She frowned. He could see emotional pain flicker across her face, quickly suppressed. "What about . . . Eleanor? Any word?"

"*They* have her in some kind of . . . conditioning."

She grimaced. "Well. They will think she is one thing . . . but I have buried her true mission deeply inside her. Eleanor will survive! And she will surprise them. She will surprise everyone here. I have faith in that." She glanced at the door. "I'm developing a therapeutic relationship with Nigel Weir . . ."

Wales looked at her in surprise. "Weir? The warden of Persephone? He let you . . ."

She smiled. "He's a sad, disturbed little man. Under pretense of interrogating me—he asked me about himself. Indirectly, you see. I turned the interrogation back on him—we even looked at his files together. I think I've persuaded him to let me do some experimenting—and therapy on the prisoners in Persephone. He'll convince Sinclair it's all for the benefit of Ryan's little fiefdom. But in time, I plan to organize a rebellion here. One which they will never expect. They're foolish, putting so many political prisoners in one facility—it plays into our hands . . ."

Gazing at her, Wales felt dizzy. He suddenly—uncontrollably—went to his knees. "Ma'am . . . oh, Sofia! How is it that I was ever loyal to Andrew Ryan? That I let him blind me?"

She smiled. "It's all right, Simon. The ego is powerful. The will to love is weak, at first. It must be strengthened with sacrifice to the collective. It takes time! But you were one of the first to see the light. You are beloved to me, Simon Wales . . . And in good time, Ryan will fall. And I . . . we . . . will be waiting to take his place. Rapture will be ours. Tell them—tell everyone—I will be watching! I will know who is a slave to ego—and who ascends to the body with the blessed . . ."

"Yes, Sofia! I'll see that your flock knows!"

Sofia Lamb put a hand on his head, in benediction. Wales felt an orgasmic shudder go through him at her touch, and he lowered his head and wept with joy . . .

13

Sullivan was worried about Head Constable Harker. The HC was breathing through his mouth like a man who'd just finished a two-mile run, but Sullivan knew damn well he'd been sitting at that desk at least half an hour. One of Harker's cigars, still smoking, was just a butt in the seashell ashtray. Harker sat there, panting, staring into space, drumming his freckled fingers on the desk. The head constable was a short, thick, jowly man with receding red hair, a shabby black suit. Looked like he hadn't shaved in a couple of days.

"You asked me to come over, Harker, remember?" Sullivan said, sitting across from him. "You okay? You look kinda worse for wear."

"Sure, I'm . . . I'm okay." Harker reached up, unconsciously fingering the constable's badge on his lapel. "I just sometimes wonder"—he glanced at the door to make sure it was closed—"if I made a mistake coming to Rapture."

Sullivan chuckled. "Don't feel like the Lone Ranger on that one. Don't know many who don't feel that way sometimes."

Harker nodded, too rapidly. "But there's still some true believers, Chief. Like Rizzo. Wallace. Ryan, of course. That crackpot, Sander Cohen. Maybe McDonagh. 'Course, we lost some too—like Greavy . . ." Harker sighed.

"Yeah, shame about Greavy—too confident, strutting around like he owned the place. They nearly got Bill McDonagh too."

"I dunno, I don't have a good feeling about it, Chief. I'm

grateful you got me this post. But I shoulda stuck around in the States and, I don't know, gone into something else . . ."

"Me and you, we're badges, pal. Too old to change." He could see Harker was scared, plenty scared. "What is it? I mean—there's something that's got you off-balance here. Something in particular. Why'd you call me over here?"

Harker rubbed a thumbnail raspily over his two-days' growth of beard and reached into the desk drawer. He took out a pistol, stood up, stuck the pistol in his coat pocket, and said, "I'll show you. Come on."

They went into the corridor. Karlosky was waiting out there, a pump shotgun in his hands. Sullivan kept the Russian close when the Great Man didn't need him. Yesterday that pump shotgun had cut a spider slicer nearly in half—and saved Sullivan's neck.

Karlosky nodded at Harker, who just grunted and brushed past him, stumping down the hall on his short, thick legs, one hand in his coat pocket on that gun.

The head constable led them around a corner, past a black guard who unlocked a hallway door to let them into the cell-block. They strode past a series of insulated, locked cells, all on the left-hand side, where splicers—low enough on EVE to be containable—babbled and begged for their plasmids. A feral-looking woman, her face etched with plasmid lesions, spat at them through a barred cell-door window as they passed.

This place was grimier and crazier than Persephone. The "isolation facility" wasn't full of splicer crazies, anyhow. Just political eccentrics.

At last Harker stopped near cell 15, where a hulking constable with nervous blue eyes and a leering smile leaned on the hallway's metal wall, a tommy gun cradled in his arms. "Howdy Chief," Cavendish said.

"A little over an hour ago," Harker said, in a low voice, as Sullivan and Karlosky caught up with him at the cell door, "we bring in an unconscious splicer, right? Half-naked, lotta plasmid deformities on his face and all. Well, when we found this cocksucker he had some kind of fish-gutting hook in one hand, all covered with blood. And in the other hand he has a woman's head. Her head—cut off her body, you get me? Sliced off just under the chin! Slick as a whistle! A brunette. Mighta been a pretty woman. I think maybe I saw this chippie dancing over in that strip joint, in Fort Frolic." He licked his lips, glanced down the hall toward cell 18. "Well, this splicer, he's kinda squeezin' her head to his chest, looked like a kid hugging a baby doll. And he was sawing logs, this guy, snoring! Pat Cavendish there gets him cuffed and tries to wake him up, but the guy's too sacked out. So Patrick gets some help, brings the son of a bitch up here, puts him in cell seventeen over there. We got the broad's head in the freezer, in case you want to ID her."

"Okay," Sullivan said, shrugging. "Not the only homicidal splicer we've had. Pretty crazy, but lots of 'em are. He must've run outta EVE, got tired, plasmids needed recharging, took a snooze . . . so now you got 'im. Ryan's talking about turning guys like this over to Gil Alexander for his . . . experiments. We'll get him to a judge in the morning—"

Cavendish gave out a sniggering sound of contempt. "Boy-o have *you* got it wrong!"

Sullivan didn't like Cavendish's tone. But he didn't like Cavendish at all. One of the bad eggs. Half Irish, half Suffolk Brit. Grin like a wolf. Liked to beat up prisoners. But a good man in a fight. "He ain't run out of anything," Cavendish went on. "*Drank* himself to sleep, I figure—that's what it smelled like. Woke up still charged. He was in eighteen, last I looked."

"What do you mean, last you looked?"

"There's a new plasmid on the market," Harker put in, almost whispering, eyes darting to the door of 18. "Only—it's kind of black market. Fontaine hasn't released it publicly. It's supposed to make them extra crazy in record time, for one thing. For another—might be the most dangerous one around, if you think about it. Only, I figure these guys are probably too nuts to use it against the council. They're all about goin' with their impulses . . ."

"Use *what?*" Karlosky asked, impatiently.

"They can *disappear,*" Harker said. "And . . . go somewhere else! This guy, he comes in and out of that cell as he pleases. Pat—what do they call that plasmid?"

"*Teleport.*"

And at exactly that moment a sucking sound made them all look toward cell 18. Specks of free-floating blackness appeared in the air, sparkles of energy took on the approximate shape of a man—and the sound increased till it ended in a *shoomp!*—as a man appeared out of nowhere. He was a pale man, barefoot, naked from the waist down, wearing only a filthy, bloodstained work shirt. His hair was patchy brown; the angular face was hard to make out under all the plasmid excrescences. One of the growths had nearly blotted out his left eye. "Hey, you dog humpers is keeping me awake out here!" he snarled, spraying spittle past his snaggly yellow teeth. "I'm trying to finish my nap, for fuck's sake! Well ain't you the pips with your pretty badges! I want me one!"

Karlosky, Cavendish, Harker, and Sullivan were all bringing their guns to bear. A tommy gun, a shotgun, and two pistols—pointed at an empty space.

Empty because the splicer had teleported out of it. He still had plenty of EVE in him, and he had vanished—and reappeared behind Karlosky. He pulled Karlosky's hair, hooting gleefully, and as the Russian spun toward him with the shotgun . . . the splicer vanished again, twinkling away . . .

Only to reappear, bringing a nasty smell and posing like a

dancer, between Sullivan and the wall, yanking Sullivan's right ear and cackling, "Hiya Chief!"

Bastard acts like one of them cartoons at the movies, Sullivan thought. He made a grab for the splicer—and felt his fingers pass through air that crackled with departing energy.

He turned to see the splicer grabbing the pistol from Harker with one hand, with the other tearing the constable's badge off.

Sullivan got his pistol into play and fired at the splicer, squeezing the trigger a split second too late—the bullet passed through the place where the teleporter had been, ricocheting off the steel walls near Harker. The sucking sound came again, and then a flash of light from the cell window of 18.

Harker made a plaintive little *eep* sound, a noise you'd never expect from him—then he gasped as he slid down the wall, leaving a smear of blood. He fell on his face, squirming, groaning. The ricochet from Sullivan's gun had hit the constable, and hard.

"Dammit, Harker!" Sullivan sputtered. As if it were Harker's fault. "I'm sorry, I—"

"Just . . ." Harker gasped again. "*Get* the fucker . . ."

Tommy gun raised, Cavendish was stalking toward the window of cell 18. He peered through the small barred window in the studded-metal door . . . and his head jerked back with the bang of a gunshot from inside.

Sullivan thought at first Cavendish was dead—but then he saw the constable was just missing part of his left ear, much of it shot away. Cavendish crouched down in the corridor, put a hand over his red-streaming ear, hissing with pain. "Fuuuuuck!"

A "*tee-hee-HEEEEEE!*" came from inside the cell. "Too bad I missed, could've improved your ugly fucking face to have a bullet hole through it, dog humper! I gotta recommend that one to Steinman!"

Sullivan cocked his pistol, moving in a half crouch down the row of cells. He ignored the bearded splicer in number 16, who taunted, "You see, if you'd given us our ADAM, we'd all be happy harpies, but now, right now, you've made us into saddy soddies, and sadness hurts, it hurts, going to hurt and hurt!"

It's me that's done the hurting so far, today, Sullivan thought glumly. He'd accidentally shot Harker. This teleport thing had him shaken. He saw now why Harker'd been so unnerved.

He approached the cell door obliquely, pistol raised, trying to peer in without making himself a target. There, the semi-nude splicer was relaxing on his back in a cot against the farther wall of the padded room. His naked genitals, spattered with dried blood, all too clearly on display. He had his left arm behind his head, his right arm up, and he was spinning the pistol on his index finger and singing a Rapture advertising jingle to himself, "*Ohhh, the beer may be green, but it's mighty keen; it satisfies a man, makes him feel grand; it's Ryan's own, Ryan's own, Ryan's . . . own . . . beer!*"

On "*beer!*" the splicer stopped spinning the gun and fired it toward the barred window of the cell. The bullet struck a bar and ricocheted down the corridor. Sullivan ducked, though the bullet was already on its way by then.

He raised slowly up, only to hear that sucking sound and Cavendish yelling, "Down, Chief!"

He flattened belly-down on the floor—and saw, out of the corner of his eye, the splicer materializing over him to his right, the pistol pointed down to shoot him in the head.

A *rat-a-tat* echoed harshly in the corridor, along with the big thump of a shotgun—and the splicer was stumbling backward, stitched across the middle with blood-spouting bullet holes, right arm torn half off from a shotgun blast. Cavendish had gotten him square with the tommy gun, and Karlosky had clipped him good with the shotgun. Someone around the corner yelled in pain as part of the tommy-gun burst ricocheted down the corridor. Maybe the steel walls hadn't been such a good idea.

Sullivan got up again, coughing with the gunsmoke in the small space. Yips and jeers and shouts of derision came from the adjoining cells. But the teleport splicer was twitching, gurgling in death.

"Well, we got him, but we lost Harker," Sullivan muttered, turning to look at the dead constable.

"This is a whole new . . . how you say it? From baseball . . ." Karlosky said, looking down at the twitching splicer.

Sullivan nodded. "A whole new ballgame."

Footlight Theater
1956

Frank Fontaine took his seat near the stage in the small auditorium of the Footlight Theater. He was here to see Sander Cohen's new cabaret production, *Janus*—Cohen promoted it as "a tragic farce about identity." It was actually an oddball collaboration between Sander Cohen and the surgeon Steinman. But Fontaine's mind was elsewhere—he was remembering something Ryan had said. *Even ideas can be contraband.*

Settling into the plush seat, Fontaine smiled to himself. Ironically, Ryan had sparked an idea with that little phrase. Spread the right subversive belief, it could turn this place on its head—could dump Ryan at the bottom, lift Frank Fontaine to the top.

Feeling overfull from his dinner, a little drunk from the wine, Fontaine glanced over his shoulder at the audience crowding into the small theater. There was Steinman, the surgeon, overdressed in a tuxedo, playing "author." There was Diane McClintock, standing at the head of the aisle, in the doorway; she wore a low-cut red-beaded black frock, carried a matching beaded purse. She was frowning, looking at her diamond-crusted watch. Waiting for Ryan, no doubt—she was Ryan's fiancée as well as his receptionist.

Two seats were empty right next to Fontaine—this might be a great opportunity. He stood up and waved to Diane, though he scarcely knew the woman. He pointed to the two seats, smiling. She glanced through the door to the lobby, then nodded briskly, her lips pursed, and hurried down to him. "Mr. Fontaine . . ."

"Miss McClintock." He stepped aside so she could take a seat. "I've saved a spot for Andrew too," he said.

"If he even shows up," Diane muttered, sitting down. "He's . . . always so busy."

He sat beside her. "I understand someone might be announcing a wedding soon . . . ?"

She snorted. Then remembered herself. "Oh—yes. When he . . . decides the time is right, we'll make the announcement." She opened her purse. "You wouldn't have a cigarette . . . oh bother . . . I seem to be all out."

Fontaine noticed that most of the purse was taken up by a book. "I do have a cigarette for you," he said. "Complete with Fontaine Futuristics matchbook. Very stylish." He held the case out; she took a cigarette, and he lit it for her.

"You're a lifesaver . . ."

"Looks like you're carrying books around in that thing— does it make a better weapon that way?"

She blew smoke at the ceiling. "No need to be dismissive of a woman's desire to learn. I'm reading a Fitzgerald novel from the '20s. *The Beautiful and the Damned.*"

He thought, *What could be more fitting?* But, winking at her, he said, "One thing I'm not dismissive of is a woman's desires."

She looked at him with narrowed eyes, as if thinking of bringing him up short. Then she gave way to a titter of laughter. "Oh gosh. That kinda remark, 'a woman's desires'—makes me feel like I was back working the club where Andrew and I met . . ." She glanced over her shoulder. "You haven't seen him here, have you?"

"Afraid not." Maybe he ought to let her know, obliquely, that he might be available to squire her if Ryan gave her the brush-off. She could be useful. "If he doesn't show up, I'll heroically offer you my arm, ma'am, and escort you from here—all the way to the moon and back."

"It's even farther to the moon than it used to be, down here," she said. But she seemed pleased.

"Me, I kinda hope he doesn't show up . . ."

She glanced back at the door again and then stepped on her cigarette as the curtains parted. "Show's starting," she sighed.

It took him a moment to recognize Sander Cohen, as made up as he was—and with another face entirely slung on the back of his head. Cohen was dressed in skintight Lincoln green, had an absurd mustache and beard, and a feeble little bow and arrows slung over his shoulder. He pranced to mandolin music in front of a painted forest backdrop and broke into a song about how he "*loved to be in the Greenwood with my merry men, oh, my gay and merry men, my oh so happy men, and then came along that dreadful bitch known as Maid Marian, and OH how paradise has fallen . . . !*"

His "merry men," looking more like nearly naked Greek wrestlers, came dancing out of the wood, waving arrows and singing the chorus with him.

Oh Jesus wept, Fontaine thought.

Then the King of England came along, wearing a lion-blazoned cloak, a gold-painted crown, and a red beard that was coming loose from his chin. He brought Cohen to his castle and set him to be the new Sheriff of Nottingham; "Robin Hood" lost little time in assassinating the king—merrily stabbing him to the beat of a song—and then switching the face on the back of his head around to the front. The mask resembled the king; he dragged the body off and took the king's place.

The one-act musical mercifully ended to a smattering of applause—although Dr. Steinman stood up, clapped lustily, and shouted, "Bravo! Bravissimo!"

Fontaine helped Diane into her wrap. Maybe he could get her to a bar. After a few drinks, she might remember her cigarette-girl origins.

But suddenly Ryan was coming down the aisle, shaking hands with people, nodding—waving to Diane. "Sorry I'm late, darling . . ."

So much for that. But the evening wasn't a bust. Despite having to watch Cohen flounce about, the play had given Fontaine an idea.

On the way out of the theater, he paused to gaze at one of Ryan's earliest propaganda posters. "Rapture is the hope of the world . . ." it declared—over a picture of Andrew Ryan holding the world on his shoulders. Andrew Ryan as Atlas?

Looking to see that no one was watching, Frank Fontaine tore the poster down.

Bill McDonagh's Flat
1956

Sitting on his sofa near the big sea-view window, Bill McDonagh wondered if keeping records of his "thoughts and impressions of life in Rapture" was really a good idea. He'd tried it for a while, but it didn't come naturally. Ryan was pushing for everyone to keep recordings of their problems, their plans, for some kind of planned historical retrospective, and it was becoming something of a fad. But Bill was starting to wonder exactly how it might be used against a man . . .

The tape recorder was sitting on the coffee table by a mug of greenish beer. Neither seemed appealing. He glanced at the clock on the wall. *Seven*. Elaine would be home from Arcadia with the little one soon enough. If he was going to do this, he'd better get to it. He reached for the tape recorder, but somehow his hand found his way to the mug of beer instead.

He sighed, put down the beer, pressed the Record button on the device, and began: "Rapture's changing, but Ryan can't see the wolves in the woods. This Fontaine fellow . . . he's a crook and a proper tea leaf, but he's got the ADAM and that makes him the guv'nor. He's sinking the profits back into bigger and better plasmids and building them Fontaine poorhouses. More like Fontaine recruiting centers! 'Fore we know it, bloke's gonna have an army of splicers, and we're gonna have ourselves a whole heap of miseries."

He switched off the tape recorder. There was a lot more on his mind—but he was reluctant to make his doubts about Rapture a matter of record.

The phone on the coffee table rang. He answered the phone. "Right, Bill here."

"McDonagh? It's Sullivan. We've had another three killings in the Upper Atrium . . . and the council is calling an emergency meeting . . ."

Council Conference Room
1956

Andrew Ryan wasn't sure he wanted this special meeting of the Rapture Council. But he was reassured to see Bill McDonagh and Sullivan come in. He still felt he could trust those two.

Only six people had shown up this time, and they were gathered around the oval conference table in the ornate, gold-trimmed little room near the top of the highest "air scraper" in Rapture. Anna, Bill, Sullivan, Anton Kinkaide, Ryan, Rizzo.

Ryan missed the presence of the late Ruben Greavy. And

he could have done without Anna Culpepper, who liked to put her oar in without having anything useful to say. He should never have allowed her on the council.

Ryan toyed with an untasted cup of coffee, feeling his age. His role as Rapture's guide and mentor was becoming a weight—he could almost feel it pinching his back, making his bones creak. And some on the council were making it worse, always prodding at him with their feeble little ideas. Meanwhile, Rapture's problems had become Andrew Ryan's: crime, subversives, foolish use of plasmids, constant maintenance problems . . . these required real vision to overcome. He was seeing that more and more clearly. A man needed a willingness to institute big solutions to big problems.

"We're so close to the surface here," Anna said, sitting down with a cup of tea. "It makes me think it wouldn't be so bad to have a few . . . excursions to the surface world . . . just close by, on a boat, I mean . . ." She looked up at the glass ceiling, just a yard or two under the surface of the ocean. Moonlight penetrated the waves, came glimmering down to color the room's electric illumination with a blue-white paleness, making Anna, gazing upward, look as if she'd put on whiteface. That made Ryan think about Sander Cohen—he was glad Cohen hadn't come. The performer was getting ever more socially peculiar. He'd sent a Jet Postal note, begging off with some enigmatic excuse about being "caught up in the hunt for art, which must be captivated, bound to the stage, in preparation for the titanomachy."

Titanomachy? Whatever was he talking about?

Ryan glanced up as a shadow passed over them: the silhouette of a large, sleek shark swam overhead, circling the lighted room in curiosity.

"In time," Ryan said, "we may have an excursion, Anna. All in good time."

Anna sighed and gave him that pitying look he'd found so

infuriating lately. "Dare I point out—it has been ten years since Hiroshima; there have been no further uses of atomic weapons. The war, it appears, is a 'cold' one. That's what our radio tells us."

Rizzo sniffed disapprovingly at her skepticism. "Russkies have been stockpiling A-bombs just same as the US of A, Miss Culpepper. Why, it's a tinderbox out there! The Commies are taking over China; the Soviets got their agents every goddamn place! Only a matter of time before the atomic war comes!"

"Exactly," Ryan said. Good old Rizzo, a sensible man. "And that aside—we have to remain as hidden away here as we can. We don't want anybody taking notice of *anything* out here. The lighthouse is risky enough. If it weren't for the air draw . . ." Ryan changed the subject. "Let's get to it—we have to decide on a policy about all this violence . . ."

"It's simple, boss," Sullivan said, leaning his elbows on the table, a pinched look on his face. "We got to ban plasmids. I know how you feel about banning products. But we got no choice! You're talking about atomic power? I'm not sure these plasmids are any safer than that stuff . . ."

Sullivan's words were slurring ever so slightly. He'd been drinking before the meeting. Ryan reached for patience. "Chief—I know it was hard for you to lose Harker that way. But the market has a life of its own, and we can't choke that life off with bans or even"—he had difficulty actually saying the word—"regulations. The solution is simple. Ryan Enterprises is now in the plasmid business. A better product will draw people in—and they'll buy one that doesn't affect their minds." He glanced at Bill, thinking he looked weary and troubled. "What do you think, Bill?"

"You're seriously going into plasmids, guv?" Bill asked, seeming genuinely surprised. "It'll take more time to develop a plasmid that doesn't have side effects. Meanwhile . . ."

"Bill, it's either we go into them or ban them—and how well did Prohibition work?"

"But—they're addictive."

"So is alcohol!"

Bill shook his head. "Look what happened to Mr. Greavy! If you'd seen it . . ."

"Yes." Ruben Greavy's death was a painful subject for Ryan. "Yes, that was a great loss to me. He was an artist, an entrepreneur, a scientist, a true Renaissance man. A great loss. I feel responsible—I should have sent security along with him. But he would insist on going wherever he liked in Rapture . . ."

"I was the one with him," Bill said, looking very unhappy. "If anyone's responsible . . ."

"The only one responsible," growled Sullivan, "is that telekinetic bitch that killed him. But Mr. Ryan—if you want to continue allowing plasmid sales and get Ryan Industries into it . . ." He shook his head, wincing at the thought. "Then it's *got* to be regulated."

"We'll consider restricting *some* plasmids," Ryan said, though he had no intention of really restricting any plasmids. "This is a rough transitional period. To be expected. Part of the tumult of the market . . ."

"Do we even know for sure which plasmids are out there?" Kinkaide asked.

Sullivan shrugged. "Not for sure. I've got a partial list." He searched his pockets, looking for it. "Got it here somewhere . . . Some are kinda black market; some Fontaine sells in shops. He's selling EVE right next to it. Damned floors are littered with syringes . . . here it is . . ." He unfolded a wrinkled piece of paper.

Sullivan cleared his throat, squinted at the paper, and read out, "Electro Bolt—fires bolts of electricity. Can stun a man or kill him. Incinerate!—started with a plasmid you could use for cooking but now it's sorta like a flamethrower that comes outta your hand. I have seen Teleport—not sure how we can control that one. It's a big worry. I mean, Christ, how do you jail someone who can *teleport*? Telekinesis—that's what killed Mr. Greavy. You've all seen that. There's Winter Blast—sends out a current of supercold air. Freezes your enemy solid. And there's that Spider thing they go up the walls with. Lots of those creeps around."

"Ha, creeps," Anna said, absently glancing at the transparent ceiling. "They do creep, don't they? Good one, Chief."

He looked at her in puzzlement. He hadn't been joking.

"What about this Teleport?" Bill asked. "What do we do about the bloody Houdini Splicers? It can't be legal."

Ryan nodded. He didn't trust it either. It weakened security—it might enable people to leave Rapture. He had security cameras and turrets set up at the only egresses to Rapture, to stop anyone unauthorized from leaving; he was in the process of installing more security bots. Some plasmids could make a joke of all those wonderfully engineered devices. "We'll see what we can do to suppress that one."

Kinkaide tried to straighten his tie and only made it more crooked. "I don't understand the physics of these plasmids. Where are these new ADAM cells drawing all the energy from? If the splicer shoots out flame, does it come from his intestinal methane? Where does he get the raw materials? Does he lose a pound afterward?"

Bill looked at him. "You're the boffin—no theories, then?"

Kinkaide shrugged. "I can only speculate that all this extra energy is being drawn from the splicer's environment in some way. The air around us is charged, after all. That could account for the Electro Bolt. The mutagenic cells, once redesigned by ADAM, have a sort of secondary mitochondria that might provide specialized energy emissions. We don't know what most of our genes do—some might be designed for these powers. Which might even account for tales of supernatural beings, genies and magicians and the like—but those mutations didn't work out, you see. Perhaps because they tended to be burdened by negative side effects—like psychosis, facial excrescences, and so on . . ."

"Bit of a dodgy omen, that, innit, Kinkaide?" Bill pointed out. "I mean—if these mutations existed in the past, and they didn't make it. Didn't work out then, might not work out for Rapture, then."

"Something in that," Kinkaide allowed, nodding slightly. "But Mr. Ryan is right—if it's possible to create plasmids, then it should be possible to perfect them. We can work out the bad parts. Just imagine having rational control of telekinesis or the ability to climb walls like a fly, to hurl electricity. To become . . . superhuman. It's wonderful, in its way."

"Maybe people could just learn to use ADAM without overindulging," Anna suggested. "An education program."

Finally, Ryan thought, Anna had said something useful. "Not a bad idea. We'll look into that."

"The side effects of plasmids," Sullivan pointed out, "are the only thing keeping more people from buying ADAM. We fix the side effects, we'll have superpowered people everywhere. We'll *all* have to do it just to keep some kinda balance of power. I don't want to cough fire every time I belch."

Bill nodded eagerly. "Chief Sullivan's in the right of it—side effects or not, plasmids are just too dangerous. Rapture is made mostly of metal—but it's complex, and that makes it vulnerable, fragile in some places. Daft bastards running around shooting fire, blasting lightning about—they could bring down the whole bloody house of cards!"

Ryan made a dismissive gesture.

"We'll get the splicers under control. Meanwhile," he added musingly, "this is all part of our evolution. Just growing pains." He considered explaining fully. But they wouldn't understand if he told them what he really thought. Greavy had understood, though. He'd understood the winnowing. The subtraction of weak links from the Great Chain; what they were going through in Rapture now was the heat of a welding torch, both destructive and constructive.

"It isn't just the superpowered sons of bitches," Sullivan growled, crumpling the list of plasmids in his shaky hands. "It's the leadheads rampaging around the city, shooting guns at random. Faster reflexes from all that ADAM. We've had to kill four in the last two days. Sad thing is, they all had kids. Transferred to that new orphanage of Fontaine's . . ."

"Fontaine," Bill said, looking at Ryan significantly. "Got a finger in every bloody thing. Every kind of smuggling. He's not just bringing in cheap hooch and Bibles anymore, guv'nor."

Ryan grunted. "How's the evidence looking on Fontaine's smugglers?"

Sullivan sat up straighter, suddenly energized. "I've got enough to raid him, Mr. Ryan—then we'll have the proof! I've got a witness to the smuggling ring, up in detention, under protection."

"Then put it together," Ryan said. "We'll raid his operation and see what we get."

Kinkaide shook his head. "All that charity stuff he's behind. You've got to wonder what he's up to."

"He's up to undermining me!" Ryan said bitterly. "Charity is a form of socialism! It's too much like that Lamb woman. If they're not working together—then they will be in time. Like Lenin recruiting Stalin. Stopping Fontaine stops this propaganda tool he calls charity . . ."

"What about this plasmids business?" Rizzo asked. "We don't want to ban them or regulate them . . . so how do we control them?"

"Now that's a good question, mate," Bill said.

"I am about to announce a new Ryan Enterprises product line," Ryan said, smiling in a way he hoped was reassuring. "A new line of weapons! Chemical throwers, flamethrowers, grenade launchers, better machine guns—we can use weapons innovation to counterbalance the splicers until we get ADAM perfected."

Bill shook his head skeptically but said nothing.

"There's something else," Sullivan said, frowning. "I've got a source in Fontaine Futuristics—tells me about some kind of what they call *fairy-moan* experimentation, something like that, that can be used to get a handle on those splicers—"

"He means *pheromone,* I suspect," Kinkaide said, smirking.

"Maybe that was it," Sullivan said, unruffled. "Something about Suchong using phero . . . those things . . . to control the splicers, without the splicers even knowing it. Maybe spraying a chemical that makes them all show up in one place, so they cause problems for . . . well, anybody you wanted to cause problems for. I guess."

Ryan scowled. "Control the splicers . . . with pheromones . . ." He was intrigued. But it was troubling too. Because Suchong worked for Fontaine.

Meaning that Fontaine in turn would eventually control at least some of the splicers. And it was becoming clearer: Fontaine was a predator. If you allowed him to grab that kind of power, he would use it to take Rapture over. Probably he'd do it behind a smokescreen. As Bill had warned, Fontaine could even partner up with Lamb's followers, now that they were at loose ends.

It could mean the destruction of Rapture.

Fort Frolic, Fleet Hall, Backstage
1956

"Can anyone ever make you feel like Sander Cohen can? Rapture's most beloved musical artist returns with 'Why Even Ask?,' his greatest album yet. Songs of love. Songs of joy. Songs of passion. Buy 'Why Even Ask?' and invite Sander Cohen into your home today." Hurrying along through the empty backstage area, Martin Finnegan chuckled to himself hearing the public-service announcement playing from Cohen's dressing room. Cohen was listening to the PA announcement over and over again. *"Can anyone ever make you feel like Sander Cohen can? Rapture's most beloved musical artist returns . . ."*

Martin went down the wood-walled corridor, found Sander Cohen seated pensively in front of his gold-framed oval dressing-room mirror, putting on another layer of makeup with one hand. With the other he was shaping the needlelike points of his hooked mustache. Cohen wore a purple and blue silk smoking jacket, silk slippers, and purple silk pajamas. He looked at Martin in the mirror. "I'm running short of makeup, you know," Cohen said. He picked up the stub of an eyebrow pencil and began to darken his eyebrows. "I've asked Andrew for more, but he talks tiresomely of import priorities, the importance of creating our own goods. Does he really expect me to make my own eyebrow pencil? My, you look virile today, Martin . . ."—all said while outlining his eyebrow, looking at Martin in the mirror. That face became ever more lurid each time Martin saw it, ever more like a mad, mustachioed mime. *". . . And invite Sander Cohen into your home today . . ."* The recording ended, and Cohen restarted it. *"Can anyone ever make you feel . . ."*

"What do you think of that announcement?" Cohen asked, starting on the other eyebrow, watching him closely in the mirror. "It's going out tonight on the public address. Trying to push my new record. It seems a bit bland to me. Lacking in verve. Doesn't have that libidinous *fevre* that I so delight in . . ."

Martin sat in a wooden chair behind Cohen, wishing he'd stop playing the announcement. "I think it's good for regular folks to hear," Martin said. "Kind of family friendly, like. That's good, you need that."

"Oh God, I hope it doesn't mean they'll bring their children to my shows. I can't imagine how I was able to bear being one. Fortunately it didn't last long."

Martin shifted in the uncomfortable chair, making it squeak. "Speaking of how Sander Cohen can make me feel . . . The note you sent me mentioned trying something new . . ."

Cohen tittered, hand fluttering over his mouth. "Well . . ." He winked, and opened a dressing-table drawer and drew out two bottles, setting them down on the dressing table, one after the other. They were squat bottles filled with red fluid. Martin knew full well what they were. Cohen opened the lower drawer, took out a flat black box, and opened it. In velvet-lined compartments were two syringes filled with glowing fluid. EVE. For activating the plasmids. Staring at the bottles, Martin's mouth was dry. He and Cohen had taken cocaine together before, cut with a lot of booze. But this . . . He had seen splicers. Some of them seemed fairly together. Others, though, were like nitroglycerine, always ready to explode. And then there was the disfigurement. Those who used a great deal of ADAM ended up looking like they had a skin disease. The loony expressions glued on their faces made it all worse. On the other hand—look at that blue glow in the bottles! The implied power in it.

"Well? Shall we indulge?" Cohen asked, his mouth screwed to a cone and twisted comically to one side. "Hmm?"

"What the hell," Martin heard himself say. He knew he'd try it sooner or later. He tried everything sooner or later. As

Cohen prepared the syringes, Martin found he regretted that his first experience with ADAM was going to be with Sander Cohen. The Artiste always took everything to crazy extremes. After that last little drunken trip into Arcadia, dancing naked with the Saturnines, forcing a teenage boy to have sex with an octopus, they were all lucky not to be in the Rapture detention cells. They'd gotten out one step ahead of the constables.

But Martin did want to be a stage performer. So far, the only performance he'd done in Rapture had been at Cohen's "tableaus," where Martin and Hector Rodriguez and Silas Cobb and a couple others dressed in scanty costumes and posed heroically under the Artiste's direction, for a very small audience. Many in the audience had been touching themselves obscenely. What was it Hector had said later that night? "It could well be that all art is just grift, after all."

"Now, let us partake," said Cohen. "This bottle contains SportBoost and Winter Blast. A splicer cocktail. That's yours. Mine is something very, very hard to get—Teleport! Next I want to try those Spider Splicings . . . Well? What are you waiting for? Bottoms up! So to speak . . ."

Martin took a deep drink from the plasmids bottle. The thick fluid was surprisingly bland, though there was a chemical aftertaste, a bit of saltiness. Perhaps a suggestion of the taste of blood. And then—

A terrifying rigidity struck him. It was as if someone was running an electric current through his muscles, a charge generated from within his brain, crackling out through his nervous system—and it was making him go rigid. His arching back was threatening to snap his spine.

And then he fell to the floor, shaking with spasms, fighting for breath. Waves of dark, hissing energy unfolded in him. He felt high, but he was also terrified. He was distantly aware that Cohen was dragging down his pants—"Presto plunge-oh!"

Cohen whooped—and then came the piercing pain of the needle jabbing into Martin's gluteus maximus.

White fire exploded behind Martin's eyes, and it was all he could see for a moment—like gazing into the heart of a welding arc. Unfamiliar tastes, like random chemicals, passed in waves through his mouth. He heard his pulse hammering in his ears. And then a wave of relief came, a ripple of release, as the rigidity washed away in a rolling tide of living coolness. After a few moments he was able to move again and struggled to his knees.

"Now," Cohen said, laying the empty syringe on the makeup dresser. "I'm going to drink mine—here's the syringe for me— you do me! I mean, the syringe! And don't try to use your powers yet! You might turn me into a block of ice!"

They repeated the process for Cohen, Martin injecting him in the rump, going about it mechanically even as he struggled for some kind of inner equilibrium. He didn't feel quite *real* somehow . . .

Martin set the empty syringe aside and sat gingerly on the chair as the Artiste flopped about like a fish on the floor, the EVE merging with the ADAM, showing in alternating blue-red energies in Cohen's body.

Suddenly Cohen went limp, sighing. Then he sat up, chortled gleefully, and vanished. There was an ambient sucking sound as a thump of air rushed to fill the sparkling vacuum where he'd been.

"Sander?" Martin's tongue felt thick. It was hard to talk. His head pounded like a parade drum thumped by a cocaine fiend. But he felt good, profanely good . . .

A sucking, a sizzling, a Cohen-shaped sparkling, and there he was, materializing at the door to the corridor. "Ha ha! Look! I did it, Martin! I teleported! Ha ha ha!"

It seemed to Martin that Cohen's face was rippling within

itself, bumps rising and falling on it as if little pistons were pumping randomly under his facial skin.

Martin laughed—it didn't matter, really, what was happening to Sander Cohen. Nothing mattered! The energy roared like a tornado in the room. The sinews of visible electric power stretched and snapped in the very air.

He looked around, expecting to see these powerful forces throwing the furnishings about, whipping things through the air. But nothing was affected. He was seeing these energies in his mind.

"Come, come, follow me, I have a special delight for us in the rehearsal room!" Cohen crowed, whirling about, dancing toward the door. "Come, come and see my guests!"

"Guests? What sort, Sander? I'm not sure I can deal with guests. I feel strange . . ."

"But you must!" Cohen insisted gleefully. "This is a test! I test all my disciples! Some shine like galaxies . . . some burn like a moth at the flame! Just remember: the artist swims in a lake of pain! Perhaps he evolves into something magnificent— perhaps he drowns! Will you drown—or will you come along?"

Sander Cohen went out the door, and Martin was somehow swept along behind him, carried by some powerful inner current. He was unable to walk slowly, unable to think slowly. He was a living dynamo of energy.

No wonder people get addicted to this.

That thought came, and he pushed it rudely aside. No raining on the parade! And the parade drum thumped frantically, pacing him down the hall to the rehearsal room at the rear of the backstage area. Cohen had already teleported ahead.

Martin felt like he was waterskiing, pulled along in a bracingly cold medium by a powerful engine. He burst through the door into the rehearsal room and found Sander Cohen stalking back and forth in front of three people, their arms spread in restraints. They were bound to three interlinked metal frames bolted to the small rehearsal stage . . .

It was all seen through a glass darkly, for Martin—a filter like mental sunglasses that made some bits shine out and muted others. It seemed unreal, almost two-dimensional, like it was all happening to someone else. Like a movie . . .

"Please!" said a busty, frowzy woman with flapper-style brown hair. She was pinioned on the left side of the practice stage. "Let me go!" Her eyes kept fluttering, perhaps because one of them was losing its false eyelashes. She wore a ripped black shift and one red pump, the other foot bare.

In the center framework, a middle-aged man with a tonsure of white hair shook in his bonds in rage and fear. His suit was torn and bloody, his nose was swelling and leaking blood, his left eye swollen shut. Cohen's third "guest" was a young man in a T-shirt, with tousled blond hair and a little red-blond beard that, along with his green trousers, made Martin think of Robin Hood. He looked like he was drugged or drunk; he just sort of hung there in his restraints, murmuring inaudibly, eyes slitted, lifting his head now and then.

"We shall call these three Winken, Blinken, and Nod!" declared Cohen, parading around them, clapping his hands.

I was right; it's a movie, Martin thought. *It's not real, none of it.* He was in the audience and in the movie at the same time. It felt good to watch it and to be the hero of it.

"Please, Mr. Cohen!" the woman wailed. "I wasn't holding out on the tips! The other girls all keep the same amount!"

"The constables Hector and Cavendish caught these three for me, Martin," Cohen said, taking a cigarette lighter and a silver cigarette case from the pocket of his smoking jacket. He tapped a button on the case so that a cigarette popped out of a little hole; he lipped it up to the lighter, puffed, and blew smoke in Blinken's face.

"Cavendish!" Blinken snarled. "That crook! Supposed to be the law! You bought him off!"

"And isn't that always the case with the best policemen?" Cohen said, putting the cigarette case away. "That Sullivan is such a square. Won't take a bribe. But Cavendish likes my little gifts . . . doesn't he, Blinken?"

"That's not my goddamn name!" the older man shouted. His remaining eye blinked furiously as he struggled with the tight leather restraints around his wrists and ankles. He went angrily on, "You know damn well who I am! I worked for you a good six years, Cohen! I did a hell of a job in that crappy little casino of yours!"

"Oh, but you were skimming the winnings, old Blinken," Cohen said, his voice oily. He toyed with the cigarette lighter.

"Ask anybody in Fort Frolic; I was completely on the level!" Blinken snarled. "I was totally—"

He interrupted himself with a long, pealing scream as Sander Cohen put his cigarette out in Blinken's remaining eye.

Cohen made a face at the man's shrieking—and then came that sucking sound, the thump, the sparkling, and Cohen had vanished.

. . . Only to reappear close beside "Nod." Cohen reached out and stroked the young man's blond hair. "The problem is an artistic one, a compositional question," Cohen said, raising his voice to be heard over Blinken's cries. "Shut that one up for now, will you?"

"Sure." Martin was glad to do it. Blinken's screams were distracting him from the movie. He strode over to him, took him by the throat—but instead of squeezing, something else came from his fingers. Not quite intentionally.

Ice. It spread out from his fingers onto the man's neck, his head, and clickingly up over his chin. It covered his face like a helmet. In another second it had coated his shoulders, his torso—the man was caught in a carapace of ice.

"Stop!" Cohen barked.

Martin stepped back, unsure as to what had happened at first—then realized that he'd used the plasmid. The power of the specialized ADAM he'd been given had sent a current of entropy from his fingers, slowing molecules, drawing water vapor from the air—coating Blinken in ice.

"If I hadn't stopped you," Cohen said, playing with the lighter, flicking it on and off, "you'd have frozen him right through in another second. This way he's in a pretty cocoon of ice, for now . . ."

It was true. Blinken was wriggling in the sarcophagus of ice. A little melted water, mixed with bloody foam, slipped about his face, his cries were muffled; one wild eye was bleeding, the other rolling under its blackened, swollen lid . . .

Martin marveled that he felt so little, that he was so distanced from what was happening this close in front of him. But the rolling hotness, the transporting sweetness of the plasmid high was still upon him, dominating him, and nothing else was truly real.

"Please, Mister, don't do that!" the woman shrieked. "No no *noooo*!"

Martin turned to see Cohen flicking the lighter under her ragged clothing, her hair. Setting "Winken" on fire.

"We're almost ready, Martin!" Cohen crowed as she writhed, shrieking in a growing plume of flame. "You must capture her in ice when she's in just the right posture for the composition! We're making a glorious tableau, a lovely triptych of tragedy: the human condition! I shall entitle it, *Three Souls Revealed*! If only Steinman could see this glorious transfiguration!"

Martin could barely hear him over the woman's shrieking. Most of her hair was gone now . . .

What was this movie he was in again? What was the title? Martin couldn't remember . . .

"There!" Cohen shouted, leaping with excitement. "As she arches her back and howls and spreads her fingers! Now! *Freeze her!* Just point at her and freeze her right there!"

Martin stretched out his arm and willed the plasmid to emanate from his fingers—he felt the chill of it passing out of him, saw ice crystals shimmering in the air in front of his hand. Suddenly, the fire around the dying woman was snuffed out.

She was instantly frozen solid, her eyeless sockets—the flame had melted her eyes—filling with pockets of crushed ice. Her mouth agape around a chunk of ice, her singed-away hair replaced by icicles . . .

Martin felt a wave of nausea pass through him. He was starting to see that this was real. These people were real . . .

Cohen vanished, teleporting—then reappearing near Blinken. Who was just starting to crack out of his ice cocoon.

"As soon as he breaks out, when he opens his mouth to shout at us—freeze him!" Cohen ordered. "Freeze him solid!"

At least that would end the man's terror, Martin thought. The thought making him feel sick in itself. *This is real* . . .

He emanated the entropic power of Winter Blast—and the plasmid quickly froze the man through and through. And Martin shuddered, as if he was frozen himself.

"Ha *haaaaa!*" Cohen cackled just before he vanished—reappearing close to the groaning young man hanging slack in his bonds. "Only one panel of the triptych remains! Come, come and play with Nod, Martin!"

Martin found he was drawn to Nod, that his hands went easily to him. He was a very pretty young man, after all. Cohen took out an elegant little straight razor . . .

Medical Pavilion, Aesthetic Ideals Surgery
1956

J. S. Steinman was bemused and distracted. Admiring the eyeless, limp face he had so deftly removed from the woman's skull, holding it up to the sea light from the windows so that he could see the deep blue of the North Atlantic through her empty eye sockets, Steinman thought: *Aphrodite, your light is entering my eyes . . .*

And then the visitor buzzer razzed intrusively at him.

"Damn them, why won't they leave genius to be genius!" Steinman muttered, hanging the detached face—complete with her nose and eyebrows—over the lamp beside the operating table. The electric yellow lamplight came prettily through the sockets, but the blood emitted an awful stench in contact with the hot lamp.

The buzzer buzzed again.

"Wait here, my dear," he sighed to the faceless woman lying on the operating table. Of course, speaking to her was pure whimsy: she couldn't hear him. She was dead. She'd been a rogue splicer he had bought from a constable, who'd shot her in the head when she'd tried to decapitate someone with a fish knife. The bullet had left her alive—anyway, she'd lived until a few minutes ago—but paralyzed. So Steinman hadn't needed anesthetic or restraints to keep her quiet during the carving . . .

He left the operating theater, climbed the stairs, and went through the operating suite's door, locking it behind him. Absently toying with a scalpel, he crossed the small lobby and opened the outer door.

Steinman realized he should have cleaned up a bit before answering the door. Frank Fontaine and his bodyguards were standing outside the Medical Pavilion, staring aghast at his blood-splattered surgical coat and the bloody scalpel in his hand. The booster plasmid he'd been using was starting to make him a bit abrupt, careless perhaps. He had gone three nights without sleep.

"We didn't realize you were, um, busy, doctor," Fontaine said, rolling his eyes at his bodyguards: a thuggish sort in a tatty suit and a grubby long-haired man who looked like a dirty Jesus.

Steinman shrugged. "Just some anatomical investigation. Work on cadavers. A trifle messy. Do you wish to schedule some—"

"What I wish to *do,*" Fontaine interrupted sharply, "is to come in and talk in *private.*"

Steinman gestured with the scalpel—his movement was preternaturally brisk so that the scalpel made a whipping sound as it cut the air. The bodyguards reached for their guns.

"Take it easy," Fontaine told them, raising a calming hand. "Wait out here."

He stepped into Steinman's lobby, and closed the door behind him. But Steinman noticed that Fontaine had his left hand inside the flap of his coat. "No need to be reaching for that gun," Steinman sniffed. "I'm not some . . . lunatic. You just caught me at a bad time."

"Then maybe you could put away the scalpel?"

"Hm? Oh yes." He stuck it in his jacket pocket so it stuck up like a comb. "What can I do for you?"

Fontaine ran a hand over his bald head. "I am going to need some work done. Some on me, and some on . . . there's a guy who works for me. Kind of looks like me. I want you to make him look *a lot* like me."

"Mmm, probably," Steinman said, cleaning blood from under his fingernails. "I should have to see him to be sure. But you have a distinct face, and that helps. That chin. Yes. If you want, I might be able to do a face transplant! Yours on his, his on yours! Has never been successfully done, but I've always wanted to try it."

"Yeah well—not a chance. No, just . . . a little painless surgery so I look . . . different. And so he looks like I do now. And I want nobody to know about it but you and me . . . And I mean nobody. Not Ryan's people, not Lamb's people, not even my people."

"Lamb?"

"You haven't heard? She's got some kind of uprising cooking in Persephone. I don't trust her—don't want her knowing any of my business."

"Mum's the word!"

"So you can make me look different—in pretty short order? Painless? And not a freak like some you've been turning out. A good face. A face people'd trust . . ."

"Should be possible," Steinman allowed. "It'll cost you. I'll need a free supply of plasmids and plenty of cash."

"You'll get it—but the plasmids come *after* the operations. I don't want you crackin' up all rogue when you're working on me. You already look like you could use some sleep . . ."

Steinman waved airily. "I work long hours perfecting both my skills and my art."

"Okay. Fine. I'll get you a nice deposit so you're ready to do this at a moment's notice. It will be soon . . . Remember—not a word to anyone. Not even to Cohen—he's too close to Ryan . . ."

"Oh, I see. Fear not. I would not have mentioned it anyway. I am ever discreet. It's part of my professional code."

"Better be. Or you'll find yourself going headfirst out an air lock without a diving suit."

Now there was the real Frank Fontaine, Steinman thought. That icy voice, the even colder eyes. His true colors.

Steinman winked conspiratorially. Fontaine just looked back at him—then went out the door.

14

Chief Sullivan, Pat Cavendish, and Karlosky were waiting for Bill in Fighting McDonagh's Bar. Sullivan was wearing a trench coat; Cavendish in his usual rolled-up shirtsleeves and slacks, no matter the temperature; Karlosky in a brown leather jacket that might've come from the Soviet air force.

Bill carried a tommy gun Sullivan had issued him the night before—but he wished he didn't have to carry it. He'd gone on bombing missions, but he'd never dropped the bombs himself. Still, it was beginning to look as if guns were going to be as much a part of life in Rapture as Jet Postal and bathyspheres.

It was early morning and the bar was closed. The wooden planks of the floor creaked under his tread as he came up to the group of armed men waiting near the window. Those planks always reminded Bill reassuringly of old pubs back home. A killer whale, big as a Cadillac, cruised by the window, slick black and white, in no hurry, a large eye rolling to peer curiously in at them.

"They ready down there?" Bill asked. He was wearing a deputy constable's badge. He was even more uncomfortable with that than with the gun. Elaine had been right weepy when she'd heard he'd been deputized. It was only temporary, till they recruited more constables. Quite a number of them had been killed by splicers. It was risky—and it meant he was subject to the orders of Pat Cavendish, the new head constable, a right bastard if ever he'd met one.

Sullivan nodded. "They should be right outside the door of the wharf, keeping their goddamn mouths shut, I hope."

"Where's this hideout hiding out at?" Bill asked.

"Witness says it's in a cavern under the fisheries. We think they bring the stuff into Rapture with a sub; then they take it in an unregistered bathysphere through a tunnel to their hide-out. Right now the sub's accessible to us in bay 2—word is, they haven't moved the contraband out of the sub to the cave yet."

"We going to be able to find the contraband on the sub?" Cavendish asked. "Probably hidden good."

Sullivan scratched his unshaven chin. "We worked out that the stuff's probably being smuggled in one of the fuel tanks. They're refilling their fuel way more often than they need to. Meaning they aren't carrying as much fuel as they should. Something's taking up that fuel space."

A voice was crackling from Sullivan's handheld radio. *"Ready to go, Chief!"*

"Okay, Grogan, we're coming down," Sullivan said, speaking into the radio. "Soon as we're there—we hit 'em!" He stuck the radio in a coat pocket, hefted his shotgun, and said, "Let's go!"

Sullivan led the way; they followed him down a series of stairs, through hatches and doors, past the wharfs—and into a passage that led to the sub bay.

Six constables, heavily armed, were waiting at the rusting door to the sub bay. Sullivan trotted toward them, signaling "go ahead" with his gun hand.

Constable Grogan raised a pistol in acknowledgment. He was a stocky, freckle-faced man with sandy hair and a bushy, rust-colored mustache. A badge glinted on the lapel of his suit. He threw the latch, opened the metal door with a shove of his shoulder, and he and the others rushed in. Sullivan, Cavendish, Karlosky, and Bill were close on their heels. Cavendish was grinning like a wolf; Karlosky, smiling grimly, pistol in hand; Sullivan, pale and grave. Bill started to move past Cavendish.

"Hang back, McDonagh," Cavendish said. "Leave this to the real officers. We'll call you to the front line if we need to."

Bill had a mind to hand Cavendish his badge and tell him where to shove it, but he silently dropped back to the rear. He wasn't eager to pull the trigger on anyone.

They ran across a bank of carved-out rock into a great, echoing metal room with its own ocean-water lake. The room smelled of diesel and ocean brine. A converted 312-foot Balao-class submarine, without the deck guns, rocked in a flat calm. Lit by electric lights on steel rafters, the hangarlike room was just big enough to contain the submarine and enough water for it to submerge in. To the left, through the translucent water, Bill saw underwater steel doors that led into the air lock and the open sea. Purportedly there was another, smaller side channel, along the way, for the bathysphere to take to Smuggler's Hideout. A big yellow fishing net was folded up on the afterdeck of the floating submarine. A pontoon gangway ran from the stony verge just inside the door out to the rust-streaked vessel. On the side of the conning tower was stenciled:

R A P T U R E   5

The constables were already running along the gangway. Bill was at the rear, looking nervously around. There was no sign of life, not much noise—maybe a slight purr of an idling motor from the sub. Then Bill caught a flicker of movement up in the rafters, beyond the glare of the lights. He leaned back, craning his neck to look, shading his eyes with a hand.

He just made out a face up there, someone on a catwalk near the ceiling. Bill had seen the man with Fontaine before. Reggie, his name was, and he seemed to be speaking into a hand-held radio.

"Sullivan, Cavendish—wait!" Bill shouted, stopping on the gangway. "There's something wrong—someone's up there."

Sullivan hesitated just before the sub, looking around as if he suspected something himself. Cavendish and Karlosky stopped to look back at him in puzzlement.

Grogan was already on the submarine's top deck with two other men. Others were scrambling onto the metal grating, rushing toward the hatch.

"Get that hatch open!" Grogan yelled.

"In the rafters, up there, Sullivan!" Bill shouted. But there was a groaning, a churning at the submarine's aft. Vapor bubbled up, reeking of diesel; the water moiled and seethed . . .

The submarine began to descend. It eased forward as it sank, heading toward the underwater doors opening in the submerged wall. The unattached gangway rocked in the waves of the submarine's descent. Water surged up over the vessel's bow, rushing over the shouting men on the deck. The submarine picked up speed, suddenly spurting forward and down, as the conning tower dipped under the surface. The men on the deck were swept into the water, then sucked downward in the vessel's wake, their screams quickly drowned out. The submarine angled sharply down, completely submerged now, sailing swiftly through the opened steel doors into the shadowy undersea tunnel. Several men struggled in the sub's wake, deep underwater, silhouettes seen dimly in the water. They were like children's toys going down a drain, drawn by the suction of the closing doors.

Bill squinted up at the ceiling again, raising his tommy gun for a shot at Reggie, but he was gone.

They fished the survivors from the water. Grogan hadn't made it. He had drowned, in that tunnel somewhere.

Standing together on the stone verge just inside the door to the now strangely empty room—the sodden Sullivan, Bill, Karlosky, and Cavendish stared at the water, now calm, the gangway rocking gently on its pontoons.

"They had 'er ready to go," Bill observed. "Just threw a switch, and she's off. The bastards went out of their way to take the bloody sub down fast. They wanted to drown as many of us as they could."

"We're lucky more didn't go down with it," Sullivan said. "Goddammit . . . Grogan was a good man."

"I reckon I saw Fontaine's man Reggie, up in the rafters," Bill said. "Didn't have a chance to tell you. It was him. Whoever it was, they were using a radio."

Sullivan looked up. "Yeah? Giving the signal to submerge . . ."

"That's what I figure. They were waiting for us. Hard to keep this raid a secret—hard to keep anything a secret long in Rapture, Chief. We're too crowded and becoming too bloody incestuous."

"Of course, you know what the bastards will say," Sullivan growled. "Fontaine will say that the sub was about to depart to do a job—and we just picked a bad time to go aboard. They'll claim they had no idea we were there. But there's one thing. I've still got a witness. Herve Manuela. He can point us to more evidence."

Bill nodded. He looked toward the closed, submerged steel doors. And wondered where Grogan's body was floating now . . .

Andrew Ryan's Office
1956

"Andrew?"

Annoyed, Ryan looked up from his paperwork to see

Diane in the doorway of his office. She had a you'll-never-guess-what expression on her face. "Well?"

"Frank Fontaine is here to see you!"

Ryan sat back in his chair. He picked up a pencil and flipped it through his fingers thoughtfully. "Is he now? He has no appointment."

"So should I tell him to go away?"

"No. Is Karlosky out there?"

"He's the one who stopped Fontaine coming in. They're kind of having a big-boy pissing contest of some kind—I mean, Karlosky and that man Reggie. He's here with Fontaine."

"Tell Karlosky to come in—and then bring Fontaine and his man in. This is overdue. It may prove interesting . . ."

"Very well. Can I—"

"No. You'll wait outside."

She pouted but went out to the entry room. Ryan wished he hadn't given Elaine the day off. He was seriously tired of Diane's airs, her possessiveness. He felt less and less like spending time with Diane; he needed one of his little intervals with Jasmine Jolene. A womanly woman, that Jasmine. A childbearer, with beauty and talent.

Karlosky came in, taking a pistol from a shoulder holster. He held it down by his side and stood to Ryan's left, watching the door as Reggie came in. Reggie didn't show a gun—but Ryan knew he had one.

Reggie glanced at Karlosky. "Tell him to put that heat away, Mr. Ryan."

Ryan shrugged. "Holster the gun, if you please."

Karlosky glared at Reggie before he holstered the pistol. Reggie looked like that wasn't going to be good enough—but Frank Fontaine himself walked in then, long overcoat unbuttoned, hands in his pants pockets. He looked like a guy out for a walk on Broadway. His three-piece, light-blue suit was exquisitely tailored and pressed. Immaculate spats adorned his shoes, and a watch fob gleamed at his vest.

Fontaine looked relaxed, pleased with himself. *The arrogant rascal,* Ryan thought—almost admiringly.

"Normally," Ryan said, "I require an appointment. But I've been wanting to talk to you in person. We lost a good man trying to inspect your sub."

Fontaine grinned. "You wanted to inspect the subs, Mr. Ryan, well, *you* should have made an appointment." Fontaine spread his hands in mock regret. "If you don't tell us in advance . . . you might end up with your constables floating about facedown again."

Ryan leaned forward, letting the anger show on his face. "You knew damn well we were coming!"

"You did another inspection the very next day, and one after that. You found nothing. I'm not smuggling anything, Ryan. That's why I've come here. To set the record straight."

"I don't expect you to admit it, Fontaine. I understand that you and the truth are not on speaking terms. You were authorized to bring fish and fish only into Rapture. Unauthorized contact with the outside world is dangerous! We will put a stop to it— within the laws of Rapture . . ."

Fontaine looked at Ryan almost pityingly. "You guys are imagining things. The only outside world I'm in touch with are a lot of fish. You can't call 'em close-mouthed, but they're not telling tales about Rapture to anyone. I'm the one with a bone to pick, Ryan. I've heard rumors you're planning to ban plasmids. They're Rapture's most sought-after product. The people won't tolerate being deprived . . ."

"Deprived of their *addictions?*"

Fontaine shrugged. "Power is addictive. What do you know about that, Ryan?"

Ryan felt his hands clenching, blood rushing to his face. Then he forced himself to relax and lean back. He shook his head and chuckled. Fontaine was smart. He'd hit a nerve. "We're not going to ban all plasmids. But there are some I won't tolerate . . ."

"Such as?"

"Such as Teleport."

"Too hard to keep people in Rapture? They can't teleport that far!"

"Maybe just to a passing ship . . . and if Rapture is invaded—you'll lose all your assets. You know they'll find some excuse to seize everything."

"Now there you've got a point, Ryan." Fontaine lowered his voice and looked at Ryan earnestly. "I'm not risking Rapture— just know that much. I'm not letting anyone know we're here. I'm making a living. So I don't have to lean on plasmids too much . . ."

He said it like he was making an offer. Ryan figured Fontaine was indirectly telling him: *I'm smuggling but I'm not putting us at risk—stop worrying about my smuggling, and I'll go easy on marketing forbidden plasmids . . .*

That was a deal Ryan wasn't making. Ryan wondered if this was the moment to deal with Fontaine another way entirely—maybe it wasn't in line with Rapture philosophy to simply have Karlosky shoot him dead. But it'd save a damn lot of trouble. He was tempted. Still—there was the risk of what Reggie might do if Fontaine went down. And Fontaine's other men. He settled for an implied ultimatum. "No smuggling, Fontaine—and no Teleport."

Fontaine's smile went crooked on his face. "I'm finding Teleport problematic too. People who use it get extra crazy— they're giving me problems. I've got my own security issues . . ."

"Security issues? You act as if you have your own little fiefdom here in Rapture."

"If I do—you gave it to me, Ryan. By deceiving people

about what they'd find in your pretty undersea 'utopia.' By not providing for them once they got here."

"Everyone has a chance to earn their way," Ryan snapped back. "Only parasites and slaves remain in their little dilemmas."

"Is that right?"

Their gazes locked.

"What exactly are you up to, in that Little Sisters Orphanage, Fontaine?" Ryan asked. "You barely take care of the boys in the other wing of the orphanage. It all seems to be about the girls. If you're using them for your personal little playthings . . ."

Fontaine's eyes flashed. "What do you take me for? I'm like you. I like full-grown women. As for the orphanage," Fontaine went on blandly, "we're just trying to give back to the community."

He managed to say it with a straight face.

Ryan snorted. "I'll figure it out eventually. One thing I'm sure of—you're using that 'food for the poor' charity to recruit people into your little syndicate. I've known mobsters to do the same thing."

"Mobsters?" Fontaine took a step toward the desk. "I don't have to stand for that."

Ryan moved near the security-alert button on the edge of his desk. Maybe this was the moment after all . . .

"What I'm here for really," Fontaine said sharply, "is to tell you that if you leave me alone—I'll leave you alone. All that recruiting you're guessing about won't come and bite you in the ass. If. You back. The fuck. *Off!* You respect strength, Ryan. Well, respect mine. I've got six more armed men out in the corridor. And I'm leaving here now, so don't interfere with me. I won't distribute any new Teleport. But there just might be some other new plasmids. And you people are going to live with them. Because I'm changing everything, Ryan. I'm changing it from the inside out. And no one can stop me. We can do this easy—or the hard way . . ."

Fontaine beckoned to Reggie and they stalked out of the room.

Rapture Detention
1956

They walked under the dimming-glowing-dimming lights of the cellblock, Sullivan following Redgrave and Cavendish, their footsteps reverberating. Constable Redgrave was a medium-sized, wiry black man with a Southern accent. He was vain of his white linen suit. Cavendish spun a police truncheon on a thong as he walked along.

The overhead lights spat a few sparks and guttered again. Water dripped down. There were shallow puddles in the metal hallway.

"We're gonna get fucking electrocuted in here," Sullivan said.

"Always a possibility," Cavendish said. "Tell your friend McDonagh. Got a lot of leaks now. Can't afford to lose any more men."

Sullivan grunted to himself. "Lot of our best men transferred over to keep order in Persephone. I hear that Lamb woman is still up to some rabble-rousing . . . how she does it from jail, we don't know."

"Subversion's easier to deal with than getting electrocuted . . ."

A splicer just ahead of Cavendish reached out from the barred windows of his cell, screeching, "Electrocuted? Did I hear ya say you want to be *electrocuted*? To be *punished* for your crimes? Here you are, you bastards!"

Electricity flickered along the splicer's arm—and sputtered out.

"Don't worry about that one," Cavendish said. "He's got no EVE left in him. Can't do anything with his ADAM . . ." And Cavendish cracked the splicer's elbow hard with his truncheon. The impact made an ugly crunching sound, and the man jerked his arm back in, shrieking in pain.

"You broke it!"

"You deserved it," Cavendish said, yawning, as they passed onward. "Ah, there it is. Number twenty-nine."

As they strode up to the door, Sullivan hoped the denizen of cell number 29 was ready to talk. Herve Manuela wasn't a splicer—he was quite sane. They'd caught him carrying a large box of contraband. He'd worked closely with Fontaine's man Peach Wilkins at the fisheries. He was finally ready to make a plea deal, but he was still scared of crossing Fontaine.

"Hey, Manuela!" Sullivan called as Cavendish unlocked the door. Redgrave was standing to one side, using his white handkerchief to polish his chrome-plated revolver, whistling to himself.

As they stepped through the open door, Sullivan could smell the putrefied blood . . .

Herve Manuela was lying facedown in blood-splashed prison blues. He was missing most of his head. Strands of dark hair were glued to the wall by dried blood. It looked to Sullivan—his stomach lurching as he contemplated the mess—as if someone had grabbed Manuela and smashed his head so hard against the wall it had simply exploded. Only splicers had the strength to do that.

"Son of a bitch," Cavendish said. "Hey, Redgrave, look at this shit!"

Redgrave looked through the door and made a gagging face. "Lord, that's one bad mess, sure is! Who done that, boss?"

Sullivan turned away in disgust. "*You* didn't do this, Cavendish?"

Cavendish was capable of something like that. He was strong and brutal. He might be pretending to be surprised.

"Me? *Hell* no!"

"You definitely had the door locked?"

"Goddamn right it was locked! Hey—there's something else . . ." He pointed at the opposite wall.

Sullivan looked—and saw words written in blood:

THE BLOOD OF THE LAMB WILL CLEANSE US ALL . . . HER TIME WILL COME . . . LOVE TO ALL!

"Lamb!" Sullivan muttered. Ryan could jail the woman, but she was still a thorn in his side.

He snorted, shaking his head. "Love to all!"

Olympus Heights
1956

Jasmine Jolene had a very comfortable apartment in Olympus Heights, almost as close to the surface of the sea as the council's conference room. Sipping his martini, Ryan felt a certain pride. A chandelier gleamed; a picture window and the intricately framed skylight offered views into the sea. Turning to gaze out the broad window, Ryan could just make out the red of sunset, the setting sun adding a muted crimson to the iridescent scales of a school of big blue-fin tuna sweeping by.

He glanced at the bedroom door, wondering what was keeping Jasmine. He'd left her lolling on the enormous pink-plush bed, with its pink-satin headboard.

There was a kitchen, a Frigidaire stocked with food, and a liquor cabinet with the best brandies and wines. Andrew Ryan had given Jasmine all this. He had provided for her. The small salary Sander Cohen gave her for her rather clumsy, poorly attended performances in the Fleet Hall would not have paid for much more than Artemis Suites. But she earned her luxuries—Andrew Ryan saw to that, once or twice a month, and with some vigor for a man his age.

He tightened his red silk bathrobe and sipped his martini. Feeling the alcohol, he frowned and put the drink down on the flamboyantly carved side table. That would have been his third martini. He hadn't been much of a drinker before coming to Rapture. He'd kept it to a minimum until recently. But it seemed to be creeping up on him.

The complainers had opportunities to make a good life in Rapture. They simply did not have the *will* to make use of them. Work two jobs, three if necessary. Cut rations in half. Squandering their Rapture dollars on ADAM just to have an electrical joust with some drunk. What do you expect? But they always blamed him when they failed.

The graffiti was still out there: *Andrew Ryan doesn't own me.*

And, *Organize Artemis! The Collective Lives! Trust Lamb!* And the enigmatic: *WHO IS ATLAS?*

Slogans. It started with slogans. Then it became Communist revolution. Mass murder of real workingmen by parasites.

And indeed—who was Atlas? Sullivan's intel suggested the name was a pseudonym for some Red organizer. Some would-be Stalin . . .

Something was going out of balance. The top was spinning, left, right, left, right, wobbling, about to fall . . .

"Um, Andrew darling, there's something I need to tell you . . ."

He turned to see Jasmine, looking rather more full-figured than usual in a pink negligee. She wore pink slippers with little gold puffs on the toes. She patted her golden hair nervously, though she'd already spent some considerable time brushing and grooming after their lovemaking. "What is it, my dear?"

"I . . ." She licked her lips, and her gaze wandered restlessly to the big window. Her thick black eyelashes batted. She'd always blinked rather too much. "Um . . ."

There was something she wanted to tell him. She was afraid to, he realized. "Come, come, Jasmine, I won't bite, what is it? Out with it!"

She chewed a lip, hesitated, started to say something, then shook her head. She looked around with a quiet desperation—then pointed at the corner of a window. "Um—those. Snail things or . . . whatever they are."

He looked at the lower edge of the window. Some spiny crustacean was creeping across a corner of the glass outside. "You wish to have your window cleaned of those things? I'll try and get a crew up here when you're at work. You know how they like to stare in at you when you're home."

"You can't tell where they're looking in those big dark helmets. Scary ol' big daddies, I call 'em."

"Is there something else you wanted to tell me, Jasmine?"

She closed her eyes, pursed her lips, and shook her head. He could see she'd made up her mind not to tell him.

Ryan opened his arms to her—and she came to him. He enfolded her in a warm embrace, and they gazed out the window, where the light was fading, the shadows of the deep rising with the coming of night . . .

PART THREE

The Third Age of Rapture

But if the cause be not good, the king himself hath a heavy reckoning to make, when all those legs and arms and heads, chopped off in battle, shall join together at the latter day and cry all "We died at such a place"; some swearing, some crying for a surgeon, some upon their wives left poor behind them, some upon the debts they owe, some upon their children rawly left.

—*William Shakespeare*, Henry the Fifth

15

"So . . . if I volunteer to be a test subject for these plasmid experiments," said the man with the scars on his wrists, "I'll be let out of here . . ." Carl Wing shrugged. "Sure, I got that part—but won't I just end up locked up in some other place in Rapture?"

Sofia Lamb hesitated. She was sitting with a therapy subject in the small, overlit, metal-walled Persephone infirmary, and as the lank-haired, nervous little man in the prisoner's jumpsuit looked trustingly at her, she suddenly wanted a cigarette. She'd given up smoking, but right now she would've paid a great many Rapture dollars for a single smoke. But he was looking at her with his sad green eyes, and she had to respond. "Um—*ye-es*, in a way," she admitted, remembering to smile. "You'll be in a . . . a research facility. But you'll be able to help the cause, there, in time—it will give your life meaning. You did say, Carl, that you felt like your life was meaningless, that you had no identity here in Persephone. That . . ."

The words died on her lips. She just couldn't go on. It all sounded so hollow. She was proposing to play Sinclair's game and send this man to be an experimental subject. And she thought about Eleanor—her own child, the subject of experiments somewhere in Rapture . . .

I've lost my way, Sofia realized.

She'd been working with other prisoners in Persephone, partly to get the warden, Nigel Weir, to trust her—and partly to indoctrinate the "patients" with her philosophy. She was creating moles who would be activated when she sent them the prearranged signal, as part of her scheme to escape Persephone and overthrow Ryan . . .

The therapy sessions with Persephone prisoners under the auspices of working for the warden had seemed necessary. Part of the deal was prepping some of them for Sinclair's experiments.

But abruptly—it had become unbearable. And as she realized that, another realization swept over her like water crashing through a collapsing seawall. *The moment has come.*

She cleared her throat and said, "Carl—we're going to change course here, you and I. You won't have to volunteer for . . . experiments. If you want to help our cause, then simply go to your cell and wait till the doors unlock and you hear the signal we talked about. 'The butterfly is taking wing.' Then . . . head for the guard's tower. Overwhelm anyone who tries to stop you."

He gaped at her. "The tower? Really? When did you decide—?"

She shrugged and smiled ruefully. "Just now! I felt the movement of the body—the True Body of Rapture! Truth is in the body, Carl! The body is speaking to me—speaking *through* me!—and it is declaring that the day has come. Now go—and don't speak of this to anyone! Wait for the signal!"

He nodded eagerly, his eyes shining.

She went to the door, called for the guard, and had Carl escorted back to his cell. She didn't need an escort herself— she had a pass that allowed her to move freely from one part of Persephone to another, so long as she didn't try to leave the facility.

But today, she decided, as she strode down the corridor, she would become the one issuing passes—she would make the move for which she'd long prepared. She prepared for this day—but she hadn't felt ready, till this moment. It wasn't just Carl or the others like him. It was the thought of Eleanor—the painful fact of Sinclair and his scientists warping the girl's powerful but innocent mind. She could bear it no longer.

Sofia looked at her watch—Simon Wales, the most enthusiastic of her highly placed converts, should be coming for his visitation now. Perfect—and no coincidence. The true body of Rapture had planned it all. *The body is truth; truth is in the body.*

Would Simon have the courage to do as she asked? Many times he'd claimed he would do anything . . . *anything* . . . she asked of him. Today that claim would be tested.

She arrived at her cell, leaving the door open, in keeping with her special privileges—the same privileges that made it possible for her to receive Simon Wales here. He arrived in under a minute, looking fatigued but resolute.

"Dr. Lamb!" His eyes seemed feverish; he was dressed in a priest's garb, she noticed, complete with collar, and he'd grown out his beard. The butterfly-shaped broach he wore clipped to his shirt pocket was a bit out of place—but it signified that he had emerged from the cocoon to become one of Lamb's flock. A flock of butterflies—but butterflies with wings of razor-sharp steel.

"Have you become a priest, Simon?" Sofia asked, glancing up the corridor toward the other cells.

"I'm a priest of your church, Dr. Lamb," he said hoarsely. He ducked his head in submission to her.

"Then you are ready to do anything for the cause of the body?"

His head snapped up, his eyes glinting hotly, his hands clutching and fisting. "I am!"

"The day has come! I cannot wait any longer. Thinking about Eleanor . . . and all that I've had to do here . . . I simply can't wait another moment."

"But—Sinclair is here; I saw him go into the Persephone control tower! Shouldn't we wait till he's gone home?"

"It doesn't matter. Warden Weir will send him out at the first sign of trouble." She smiled. "The warden too awaits my signal." She lowered her voice to a whisper. "You'll take this pass from me." She took it from around her neck and hung it over his. "Go to the tower; show the camera the pass. They'll unlock the tower. You'll step inside and shoot the guards there—then throw the Emergency Cell Unlock switch . . . we've already discussed its whereabouts!"

"I remember!" he said, licking his lips.

"When the cell doors pop open—and the cellblock doors with them—you'll get on the public address system and announce, 'The butterfly is taking wing!' That'll be the signal—"

His voice quivered with hushed excitement as he said, "Yes—oh thank God—the signal to set you free!"

"I will take Persephone over—but I won't leave here immediately, till we have complete control of the area. We'll send for our followers to surround the area and protect us. When the time comes, I'll go to find Eleanor. Meanwhile—this place will change from being my jail to being my fortress."

"And the gun?"

"The gun you'll need is hidden in the utilities locker. You remember the combination?"

"I do!"

She squeezed his hand. "Then go!"

He turned and rushed from the cell, showing not a flicker of hesitation. He would either die in the control tower—or he would do the job. Simon was no gunman—but he'd been practicing, as per her orders, and with a little luck and the element of surprise . . .

Sofia waited tensely on the edge of her bunk, wringing her hands. Thinking about Eleanor.

Within ten minutes, the other cell doors suddenly clanged

open, released from within the tower. A uniformed Persephone guard looked around in confusion. "What the hell is
going on?"

Simon's voice boomed from the Persephone public address: "The butterfly takes wing! You know what to do! *The
butterfly takes wing!*"

The prisoners responded with the gleeful howls of men
suddenly set free, their long pent-up fury expanding like a
released spring.

She listened to the scuffling turmoil as the prisoners rushed
from their cells and swarmed over the guards. She winced as
shots were fired—but Sinclair's prison constables were quickly
overwhelmed. There was some shouting, hooting, two more
gunshots—screams. Inarticulate cries of triumph. An alarm
warbled—and suddenly cut off.

Sofia took a deep breath and stood up, deciding it was safe
to come out of her cell. She stepped into the corridor—was
met by Simon Wales, who was grinning with wolfish delight
as he rushed up to her. A pistol smoked in his right hand; his
left hand was red with blood.

"We have Persephone!" he crowed. "Sinclair has fled, the
guards with him—the ones we didn't kill! Weir is still here,
but he says he'll take your orders! It's all yours, Dr. Lamb!
You're in control of Persephone!"

Hephaestus
1957

Bill McDonagh hummed along to the Andrews Sisters song
playing over the PA system as he tightened the salinity sieve.
The song suddenly switched off, replaced by Andrew Ryan's
sonorous voice—one of Ryan's canned speeches.

"What is the greatest lie ever created?" said Ryan over the
public address, in his deepest intonation. There was a treacherous intimacy in that voice, like a quietly angry father. *"What*

is the most vicious obscenity ever perpetrated on mankind? Slavery? Dictatorship? No! It's the tool with which all that wickedness is built. Altruism."

Bill sighed to himself. He was no great believer in charity. But if people wanted to extend a helping hand, that was their business. Ryan's fierce rejection of altruism had been there all along. Lately, with a whole class in Rapture suffering, it was starting to grate . . .

"Whenever anyone wants others to do their work," Ryan went on, *"they call upon their altruism. 'Never mind your own needs,' they say. 'Think of the needs of . . .' of—whomever! Of the state. Of the poor. Of the army. Of the king. Of God. The list goes on and on."*

"Right," Bill muttered. "And so do you, Mr. Ryan. Go on and on, that is . . ." He glanced over at Pablo Navarro, working across the room with a clipboard. Might be a mistake, saying that kind of thing out loud. But Pablo seemed focused on writing down heat readings.

From the speakers near the ceiling, almost from the very air, Ryan went inexorably on: *"My journey to Rapture was my second exodus. In 1919 I fled a country that had traded despotism for insanity. The Marxist revolution simply traded one lie for another. And so, I came to America, where a man could own his own work—where a man could benefit from the brilliance of his own mind, the strength of his own muscles, the might of his own will."*

Now that view, Bill thought, using a tiny screwdriver to adjust the filter, was something he could appreciate. It was a view that had helped bind him to Andrew Ryan: a man being judged on what he'd achieved, what he could do—not on class, religion, race. Sure they were going through a rough time in Rapture, but he still had faith that Ryan's grand vision would see them through . . .

Quiet rage simmered in Andrew Ryan's voice as he went on, *"I thought I'd left the parasites of Moscow behind me. I had thought I had left the Marxist altruists to their collective farms and their five-year plans. But, as the German fools threw themselves on Hitler's sword for the good of the Reich, the Americans drank deeper and deeper of the Bolshevik poison, spoon-fed to them by Roosevelt and his New Dealers. And so, I asked myself, in what country was there a place for men like me? Men who refused to say yes to the parasites and the doubters. Men who believed that work was sacred and property rights inviolate. And then one day the happy answer came to me, my friends: there was NO country for people like me. And THAT was the moment I decided . . . to build one. Rapture!"* Ryan finished his speech, and the music came back on. Cheerful boogie-woogie played.

"Yeah, he decided to build Rapture," Navarro said wryly as he came over to write down readings on the meters near Bill. "He built it, and he gave us the come hither, acting like it'd belong to us too. But it's all his, really, Bill. You ever notice that?"

Bill shrugged, glancing nervously at the door. This was pretty seditious talk, the way things were lately. "Mr. Ryan did use his own money to build Rapture," he said, wiping grease from his hands with a rag. "My way of thinkin', we're all leasin' space from 'im here, Pablo. Some have *bought* space. But Mr. Ryan still owns most of Rapture, mate—he has a right to think like Rapture belongs to him . . ."

"Yipped like a true lap dog," Navarro muttered, walking away.

Bill stared after him. "Pablo," Bill called out. "Mind what you say to me. Or I'll crack you one across the beezer."

Pablo Navarro turned to him—gave a little twisted smile. And simply walked out of the room . . .

Frank Fontaine's Office, Neptune's Bounty, Rapture
1957

Late night in Rapture. Frank Fontaine sat at his desk in a cone of yellow light, writing busily, chuckling to himself now and then. A forgotten cigarette, going out, spiraled smoke from a seashell ashtray. A pint of bourbon stood beside the ashtray; he'd used it to sweeten the cup of coffee that had long ago gone cold.

Fontaine worked with pen, paper, and an open book, poring over the account by John Reed of the lives of Soviet idealists—a book he'd had to smuggle into Rapture—and he was getting lots of juicy material for his Atlas pamphlets. Just a paraphrase here, a change in terminology there, and presto: he'd soon have the Atlas manifesto.

Of course, he'd borrowed from Sofia Lamb too. She still had her followers. With luck, they'd become his followers. When the time came . . .

Hearing a soft whistling, Fontaine glanced up nervously toward the door. One of his guards was strolling by the window of his office, tommy gun in hand, whistling a tune to himself.

Getting jumpy. He poured a little more bourbon into the coffee, took in a mouthful, and grimaced.

He set to scribbling again. *"Who is Atlas? He is the people! The will of the people in the form of . . ."*

The sound of the door opening prompted him to close the notebook. He didn't want anybody to know about Atlas who didn't have to . . .

It was Reggie, closing the door behind him. "Well boss, we done it. Up in Apollo Square. Three of 'em!"

"Three! They all good and dead? Or just shot up a little?"

Reggie nodded, tapped a cigarette from a pack. "They're dead, boss. Three dead cops, laying side by side." He lit the cigarette and flicked the match so that a little trail of smoke arced to the ashtray.

"Cops?" Fontaine snorted. "Those half-assed constables aren't cops. They're bums with badges."

"Far as I'm concerned, all cops are bums with badges. Anyhow, we nailed 'em. They never knew what hit 'em. I shot two of 'em myself." He blew smoke at the lightbulb. "Boss—I don't like to question your, uh, strategy—hell, you own a big piece of this wet ol' town. But are you sure hitting these constables is going to get you what you want?"

Fontaine didn't respond immediately. He knew what Reggie was really asking: What *is* the strategy?

Fontaine reached into a drawer, found a tumbler, poured Reggie a drink. "Have a drink. Relax."

Reggie took the glass, sat in the little chair opposite the desk, raised his drink to Fontaine. "Cheers, boss." He gulped half of it. "Whew! Needed that drink. I don't like shooting guys in the back . . . Don't sit right with me . . ."

Fontaine grinned. "Just imagine how Ryan'll react to it! He'll know it was me. But he won't be able to prove it. It's just enough, though—to give him the excuse he needs. I can almost hear his speech to the council now . . ."

"You sound like you *want* Ryan to come after you, boss."

"Maybe I do. Maybe I want to go out, guns blazing. Because that'll open up a whole new playground for me. You know me, Reggie—you know I can't stay Fontaine forever."

"First time I heard you say it since you been here."

"I haven't got the muscle to take over Rapture—without Rapture's help. Without its people helping me, Reggie."

"You got some kind of revolution t'ing in mind?"

"Civil war—and revolution. I'm *pushing* Ryan with the smuggling—rubbing it in his face. I *gave* him his chance to let me have Rapture my way. He didn't go for it. Now, we bait the trap. See, people stand by him because he's the shining

example, right? But if he breaks all his own rules, does a corporate takeover . . . acts like a dictator . . . that'll turn people
against him. And they'll need someone to guide them. You
get it? I haven't got the power to hold him off for long any
other way. So I dig a hole, cover it up . . . and let him rush
into it."

"But you could end up getting killed in this little war,
boss."

"I'm counting on it. Frank Fontaine has to die. But . . . I'll
still be here, Reggie."

Reggie laughed softly and raised his glass. "Here's to you,
boss. You're the one! You sure as hell are!"

Apollo Square
1957

The lights were dimming for evening over the coliseum-sized
space of Apollo Square. The enormous four-faced clock hanging from the center of the ceiling showed eight o'clock, as
Andrew Ryan said, "This simply cannot continue." His voice
was low, and grating.

Bill nodded. "Right enough, guv," he said softly. He was
thinking of the hangings.

But Ryan probably meant the chaos that had been surging
up lately, in Apollo Square and Pauper's Drop. In other parts
of Rapture.

Pistols holstered under their coats, Andrew Ryan, Bill Mc-
Donagh, Kinkaide, and Sullivan stood together just inside the
opening of a passageway that led out into Apollo Square. Karlosky was behind them, down the corridor, watching the back
way; Head Constable Cavendish and Constable Redgrave
were standing a few paces to the right and left, both carrying
tommy guns. Rising up the brass-trimmed art-deco orna-
mented walls to either side of the doorway were the sleek

sculptures that had once reminded Bill of hood ornaments: elongated, silver figures of muscular men reaching for the sky with rocketlike verticality, and holding up the ceiling in the process. To the left yellow lettering on a scarlet banner read:

THE GREAT CHAIN IS GUIDED BY YOUR HANDS

But it was the hanged men, across from them, that captivated their attention . . .

Ryan was making his monthly inspection of Rapture. "We've had repair crews in 'ere, working on leaks," Bill said, "and the constables did a good job of protecting them. Nicking mad splicers, bunging 'em in the Dingley Dell. But it's getting right crowded in there. And in the morgue. I mean, just take a butcher's at that, hard to . . ." He chuckled to himself. He'd almost used the Cockney "rhyming slang," "hard to Adam and Eve," meaning "hard to believe," but that would be a pretty confusing expression in Rapture. "Hard to believe it's come to this."

Standing in an open space, just inside the farther doors, was a crude wooden platform and on it a T-shaped gallows made of planks pulled up from around Rapture. Bill had seen the gaping holes where the planks had been the day before. From each arm of the T, a man's body hung.

Apollo Square stank too. It stank of dead bodies. There were five of them Bill could see, four men and a woman, the corpses scattered widely about the big room, sprawled awkwardly in brown puddles of dried blood. And there were the two hanged men, slowly turning on the ropes at the far side of the big room.

The tram tracks were intact; there was no train at the moment. As far as Bill knew, the trains were still running. At Artemis Suites, faces peered out at them from the darkened recesses of the doorway. Trash lay about the square, some of it stirring in the ventilator breeze. Music played from somewhere, so distorted Bill couldn't make out what it was at first—then he recognized Bessie Smith. She seemed to be asking to be sent to the electric chair.

Laughter cackled mockingly from the ceiling. Bill looked up to see a spider splicer creeping across, upside down beside the big windows.

"Maybe you can bring him down, Cavendish," Sullivan said, glowering up at the splicer. "I don't know how good that tommy gun is at this range, but . . ."

"No!" Ryan said suddenly. "It is not against the law to use ADAM. It is not against the Rapture law to walk on walls or ceilings so long as you don't damage them. If he breaks a serious law—shoot him down. But we're not going to shoot them like rabid dogs out of hand. Some of them are employable, eh Kinkaide?"

Kinkaide sighed and shook his head doubtfully. "Employable? Only sometimes, Mr. Ryan. Offer 'em ADAM, they can be persuaded to use the Telekinesis, move the bigger Metro parts about for us. But they get distracted and fight too much. Couple of them were supposed to be moving pipes into place, ended up throwing them at each other like spears. One of them impaled, right through. Took a long time to get the pipe clean afterward."

Ryan shrugged. "ADAM will be controlled, in time." He paused thoughtfully, then went on: "As for the rogue splicers, we will only kill those we *have* to kill. We're going to control them, and we're going to have some strict rules. We will end the vigilantism; we will end the vandalistic graffiti; we will stop people from getting into lunatic fights with one another. We won't tolerate these oafs blasting out flames without thinking—disruptive fires starting. Burned up one of my splendid new curtains at the Metro station!"

"How do we get rogue splicers under control, guv?" Bill asked.

He took a deep breath, his face hardening with determination: "For starts—we are going to enforce a curfew. We'll require identification cards at checkpoints. We will increase the presence of security turrets and security bots at key points . . . Ah, speak of the mechanical devil . . . *daemon ex machina* . . ." He smiled wryly.

Two security bots whirred around the edges of the voluminous room, flying side by side, miniature self-guiding helicopters, each about the size of a fire hydrant but blockier, with built-in guns. They made Bill nervous—he never trusted the bots not to shoot him, since they were mere machines, even though he and the others here wore identification "flashers" that told the bots they were friends.

He ducked as the robots flew by, always afraid their whirring copter blades would slice into him if they came too close. The choppering security bots continued on their way, circling the big room, watching for anyone who might threaten Ryan and his entourage.

Then the full import of Ryan's words began to sink in. "'Ere, guv—did you say curfews? Checkpoints? You mean—all over Rapture?" Hadn't Ryan always claimed that that was the kind of thing the Communist dictators pulled?

"Yes," Ryan said, gazing balefully at the bodies twisting on the gallows. "Everyone will have an ID card. They must restrict themselves to authorized areas, and the ID cards will tell us where they're supposed to be. There'll be a curfew until further notice. We'll have to institute the death penalty for more crimes. We can all see for ourselves how tough the situation is. And we're losing population. We'll have to recruit new people to catch up . . . meanwhile, we've got to get things stabilized. We'll have to set up a serious large-scale raid to take Fontaine down. We're going to destroy him this time. And take over his business—for the good of Rapture. Run it responsibly . . ."

Bill was stunned. "Take over Fontaine's business? But—doesn't that kind of run against the whole spirit of Rapture?"

Ryan frowned. "Sometimes we have to fight to protect that spirit, Bill! Look what happened—right here in Apollo Square. Three constables shot dead! We're going to see to it that all enemies of Rapture are caught—and punished!"

Bill felt disoriented, almost dizzy. Ryan was sounding more like Mussolini than a man who advocated pushing out the limits of human freedom. "You plan to take over Fontaine's plasmid business—by force? That's not exactly the free market at its best, Mr. Ryan."

"No. No it isn't. But Fontaine's threatening Rapture with destruction! The whole colony will fall apart if we don't act, Bill. He *wants* chaos! He wants it because, for a demagogue of his sort, preying on the weaknesses of the masses, chaos is opportunity. Chaos is the fertile ground where the likes of Fontaine will sow the seeds of power! Lamb's followers thrive on it too!"

"I concur," said Kinkaide, nodding. "We've had enough chaos. You have to draw into some prescribed limits sometimes. Time to get tough. To take the offensive."

Bill found himself wondering if Ryan's shift into the offensive might be exactly what Fontaine wanted. Were they playing into Frank Fontaine's hands?

Atrium, near Fontaine Futuristics
1958

"Hey there, fellas," said the cheerful voice on the PA system. Frank Fontaine listened to it abstractedly as he walked across Fontaine Futuristics, to Training and Extraction. *"You know that nine out of ten ladies prefer the athletic man? Why stay on the sidelines when the new SportBoost line of plasmid tonics*

*can turn you into the jock you've always wanted to be? Come
and visit us at the Medical Plaza for a free two-hour trial. You'll
appreciate the difference; she will too . . ."*

Fontaine struggled inwardly to banish the squirming discomfort, the trapped feeling that rose up in him when he
walked up to a restricted area. No reason to feel trapped. He
had two good bodyguards with him—you needed two,
nowadays—there was Reggie, and there was Naz: the grinning, swarthy splicer looking like a mad Jesus with his long
greasy hair and curly brown beard. He wore stained fishery-
worker coveralls, his twitchy hands fiddling with that curved
fish gutter he liked to carry. Naz was proof you could train a
splicer, keep them in hand. Sort of. He was big on the Sport-
Boost plasmid. Took way too much of it—but it kept him alert.

Fontaine knew he should feel safe. Lately, though, the
closer he got to the Little Sisters, the more trapped he felt.
The public-address announcement coming on at that moment wasn't helping. The woman's soothing voice was saying:

> *"The Little Sisters Orphanage: In troubled times,
> give your little girl the life that she deserves. Boarding
> and education free of charge! After all, children ARE
> the future of Rapture."*

Orphanages. It had suited his sense of irony, and maybe
fed his bitterness, to create an orphanage.

Signaling Reggie and Naz to wait out in the hallway, he
went through the double doors, the security bots rising up in
the air at his approach. The bots scanned him and drifted
away, whirring to themselves.

A few strides more and automatic turrets, looking like
swivel chairs equipped with guns, swung to take him out,
recognized his flashers, and settled back down.

Fontaine went down the hall to the little nursery-like cells where the girls were kept awaiting implantation—and harvesting. He looked through the window in the door and saw two children playing with a wooden train set on the floor of the rose-colored room. The "Little Sisters" developed a strangely uniform look, in their little pinafores, their faces and bodies remarkably similar thanks to a side effect of the sea-slug implantation. The sea slugs were like tapeworms inside them . . .

They're not human anymore, he told himself.

After all, if you cut one of those kids, they instantly stopped bleeding. Cut off one of their little fingers, and the finger grew back, like she was some kind of lizard. The ADAM repaired them. That wasn't human—they were superhuman, almost. They didn't seem to get any older, either. They were in some weird state of growth stasis.

Brigid Tenenbaum came drifting up to him. She had that ghostly look about her again, like a stiff ventilator breeze might blow her away. Maybe he needed to resume their sexual relationship. But she was the one making excuses lately. Which was fine with him.

She looked through the window at the little girls. "They seem . . . okay," he remarked. "I always worry we're gonna get an inspection in here, people are gonna think, 'Oh, them poor little tykes.' But they don't seem unhappy."

Tenenbaum only grunted. Staring through the window, she took a cigarette from a pocket of her white lab smock and a holder from another pocket, united them, and put the holder in her mouth. Fontaine lit it for her with his platinum lighter. She blew the smoke into the air . . . but still said nothing. The hollowness in her eyes, the gauntness in her cheeks, making Fontaine think she was not so far from a "little sister" herself.

He went on, mostly to fill the silence: "But then we get people so broke in Rapture now they just turn their kids over to us."

"The children are not . . . *unhappy,* as such," Tenenbaum said, her speech carrying cigarette smoke slowly into the air. "Not in the usual sense of unhappy children. They barely remember family. Their minds—their minds are *strange.* The ADAM, the sea-slug connection—these make them strange. I find being around them very . . ." She cleared her throat. There was a wet gleaming in her eyes. ". . . very uncomfortable. Even with . . . with those things implanted in their bellies, they are still children. They play and sing. Sometimes they look at me . . ." She swallowed. ". . . And they smile."

He glanced at her. Was she cracking up? "You get paid good, Brigid. Times are hard in Rapture. You want to continue to get that research funding, just accept what you gotta do for the check."

She didn't seem to hear him. Or she didn't care. She just kept smoking, sucking through the holder, and gazing dreamily through the window at the two little girls, holding the smoke till her words carried it out. "They do not act so— unhappy. The Little Sisters. But—in their souls, they . . . Germans say 'schmerzensschrei.' They 'feel the pain.'"

"Their souls! No such thing as souls." He snorted.

"There are stories people on plasmids are seeing ghosts in Rapture . . ."

"Ghosts!" He shook his head disdainfully. "Lunatics! Where are you and Suchong in battling the side effects of the plasmids?" It was a key question for Fontaine—he figured the time would come when he'd need to use plasmids personally. Maybe a lot of them.

She didn't respond. Fontaine felt a flare of anger, took her shoulder, turned her sharply to face him. "You listening to me, Tenenbaum?"

She looked quickly away, stepping back, refusing to meet his eyes. Her voice was monotone, with perhaps a trace of amusement. "Are you trying to frighten me, Frank? I have been to hell in my time." She got all dreamy again. "I did not find tormentors there. More like kindred spirits . . . but these children—" She looked through the window again. "They awaken something in me."

"Something—like what?"

She shook her head. "I do not wish to speak of it. Ah—you wish to know about . . . side effects? Yes. ADAM acts like a benign cancer. Destroying native cells and replacing them with unstable stem versions. This instability—it transfers amazing properties, but . . ." She sighed. "It is also what causes damage. The users, they need more and more ADAM. From a medical standpoint—catastrophic. But—you are a businessman." She gave her peculiar little smile. "If you take away side effects—not addictive, perhaps. Not addictive, you don't sell so much."

"Yeah. But we need two strains of the stuff. The best stuff— for people like me, when the time comes. And the regular plasmids for everyone else. You work on that, Tenenbaum."

She shrugged. She stared at the children, becoming dreamy again. After a moment, she murmured, "One of the children—she sat on my lap. I push her off . . ." She touched the glass of the window, before going on, letting smoke drift slowly from her mouth as she looked languorously through the glass. ". . . I push her off, I shout, 'Get away from me!' I can see the ADAM oozing out of the corner of her mouth!" She closed her eyes. Remembering. "Her filthy hair hanging in her face, dirty clothes, that dead glow in her eye . . . I feel—hatred." Her voice broke. "Hatred, Frank. Like I never felt before. Bitter, burning fury. I can barely breathe. But Frank . . ." She opened her eyes and looked at him, for one surprising instant. "Then I know—*it is not this child I hate.*"

With that, Brigid Tenenbaum turned suddenly on her heel

and strolled distractedly away, back toward the lab, trailing
cigarette smoke behind her.

Fontaine stared after her. She *was* cracking up. Maybe he
should have her taken out. But she was too valuable. And
Ryan would be making his move. Everything was almost in
place . . .

"Mr. Fontaine?"

He jumped a bit, startled by Suchong's voice. Turning to
the scientist as he bustled up from the other direction.
"Christ, Suchong, you don't need to sneak up on people like
that."

"Suchong is sorry."

"The hell you are. Listen—what's going on with Tenenbaum? She losing it or what?"

"Losing . . . it?" Looking the same as ever, each hair in
place, his glasses polished, Suchong gazed placidly through
the window at the sight that had so moved Tenenbaum. It was
as if he were looking into a cage containing lab rats, which
was, of course, just what he was doing. "Ah. Perhaps so.
Suchong sometimes thinks she loses . . . objectivity."

"Speaking of nutty females—you follow up on that one I
told you about? For that special project?" This was what he'd
mainly come here for today.

Suchong glanced up and down the hall. None of the as-
sistants were in earshot. This was top secret. "Yes." His voice
was barely audible. "You were clever to put the listening device in this Jolene woman's rooms. She spoke to one of her
friends, a woman named Culpepper. This woman Culpepper,
she tries to educate Jasmine. Talks to her about Ryan. To convince her he is the great tyrant, and so on."

"Yeah, Reggie told me; he went over the transcripts. You
think he doesn't tell me everything first? Culpepper's turned
against Ryan. And Jasmine Jolene's pregnant. Or maybe I

should say Mary Catherine's pregnant—that's her real name. So—did you make her the offer?"

He bowed. "Tenenbaum made offer—she accepts! Money. So she doesn't need Ryan to live. In exchange for the fertilized egg. Ryan's baby! She came to lab, Tenenbaum extracted diploid zygote!"

"The what? Oh—basically, the kid, right? Prefetus?"

Suchong bowed. "Mr. Fontaine has it exactly."

"We got someone to bear the kid?"

Suchong blinked. "Who can bear kids? I cannot bear them. The kids, they—"

"Suchong—I mean someone to have the baby, and turn it over to us!"

"All is arranged!"

"So Ryan's bloodline, his, what do you call it—"

"His DNA. Yes. When new vita chambers work, when security is DNA specific—Ryan's DNA will protect your . . . subject."

"You think the project is doable in the short term, Suchong?" Fontaine pressed. "I mean, making it—what was it you called it?"

"Accelerated development. Child growing faster. And then—the conditioning . . ."

"That's the important part. The conditioning. Brainwashing. Kid has to respond to cues, like you said. You can do that?"

"Yes. I believe so. My experiments confirm it. Suchong use the reward system of brain, condition the organism, the human offspring—to do anything! Anything you desire of them!"

"*Anything?* On cue? I mean—even something the guy'd never ever normally do? That's what we need, see. I need to know I can use this kid against Ryan when the time comes."

"I believe so—*yes!*" Suchong's eyes were shining. Conditioning, mind control—that was his meat. It was what he gloried in. "Especially if I have him very young."

"Okay, say you've got him as a kid—and let's say he's got a puppy. Kids love dogs. You could make him *kill his own dog*? I mean, a cute little puppy, one he really loved—could you make him kill it with his bare hands? That'd be the real test . . ."

Suchong nodded, showing his teeth in a grin—very unusual for him. "Yes! Wonderful, is it not?"

"Yeah, if it works." Fontaine felt a giddiness himself. It was a real grifter's ace—a primo con. Maybe the best bunko of all. One that would take years to unfold. But that was the beauty of it. The time lag would make it something Ryan would never expect. This way, if the Atlas project didn't pan out . . . he had another way to get at Ryan.

He already had wealth and control over a great deal of Rapture. But to have a conditioned little puppet, waiting to do his bidding—it was a thrilling thought. A con carried out by *life itself* . . .

16

"What's wrong, Mary?" Jim asked, in that calm way of his. "You look like you've just heard some terrible news!"

"Capital punishment in Rapture!" Mary replied, worriedly. "This isn't what I signed up for!"

Jim's voice was almost jolly. "Now hold on there, pretty lady! The only people who face capital punishment in Rapture are smugglers, and that's because they put everything we've worked for at risk. Imagine if the Soviets found out about our wonderful city, or even the U.S. government! Our secrecy is our shield!"

"A little capital punishment is a small price to pay to protect all of our freedoms."

"Now you're talking, Mary!"

Andrew Ryan switched off the recording, leaned back in his desk chair, turned to look at Bill McDonagh, eyebrows raised. "What do you think? What's the first thought in your mind, hearing that, eh?"

"Well sir . . ."

Bill no longer felt he could say what he really thought. Especially when his first thoughts were: *I think you're looking mighty old, Mr. Ryan. Old and tired. And you smell like you've been at the martinis again . . . And that bit of propaganda is depressing . . .*

He looked around at Ryan's office—it seemed big, echoingly empty. He wished he had Wallace or Sullivan with him.

Someone to back him up. It was getting harder to show enthusiasm for Ryan's new direction.

"Go on," Ryan urged him. "Spit it out."

Bill shrugged. "We have the death penalty now, guv—I reckon people have to get used to it . . . Hard to ignore with people hanging from gallows. Council's divided . . . Maybe it's time to ease up on it . . ."

Ryan had two tape recorders on his desk—the smaller one, purchased, ironically, from Fontaine's company. He smiled coldly, reached for the small recorder, hit Record, and intoned, "The death penalty in Rapture! Council's in an uproar. Riots in the streets, they say! But this is the time for leadership. Action must be taken against the smugglers. Any contact with the surface exposes Rapture to the very world we fled from. A few stretched necks are a small price to pay for our ideals . . ." He hit the button, switching off the tape recorder, and turned to Bill with satisfaction. "There you are, Bill. I summed up my feelings about it—and recorded it for posterity. Have you been using your recorder? Rapture will define the direction of civilization for all the world, in time—and history will want to know what happened here!"

Bill nodded—without much enthusiasm. "I've been recording the odd comment, guv, like you suggested. Next one might have to be about this raid we're planning on Fontaine Futuristics. What are we going to do with the bloody thing once we have it?"

Ryan's face went blank. "That's for me to decide. In my own good time."

"I just think, 'ere—we can't just take over another man's business by force! We become bleedin' hypocrites, guv'nor! That's . . . like, what do they call it—nationalization! It'll take Rapture in another direction—opposite where we set out to go."

Ryan looked at him frostily. "Bill. It's true that I prize your . . . outspokenness. And I prize individuality. But I also prize loyalty. Whatever I decide—I hope I can count on your loyalty . . ."

Bill looked at the floor. He thought about Elaine. And their daughter. "Yes sir. Of course—you can count on that. I'm all loyalty, me. That's Bill McDonagh—straight through."

But as Ryan turned back to the tape recorder to play the service announcement once more, Bill wondered. Could he really stomach Ryan taking over Fontaine's business? There were already curfews, ID cards. How much closer to fascism could they get before they had gone into a complete, mad reversal of everything Ryan claimed to believe in?

"A little capital punishment is a small price to pay to protect all of our freedoms."

"Now you're talking, Mary!"

Ryan switched the tape recorder off and sat back, frowning thoughtfully. "I really have to make a decisive move against Fontaine. He's going to new extremes—I've reason to believe he's interfering in my private life. Jasmine! She was a real comfort to me, you know, Bill. We're both grown men here. You understand. But she's moved out of the snug little place I gave her. I know that Fontaine has his hands in this. Perhaps even putting listening devices in her apartment."

"Hmmm . . ." Bill tried to keep his face expressionless. Privately, he thought Ryan sounded like a paranoid, imagining things.

"He continues his smuggling. We have secret Christian groups forming, a result of those blasted Bibles. Letters may be going out from Rapture. He's selling weapons to Lamb's bunch too! I thought I had an understanding with Fontaine—but he's gone too far. While I was buying fish futures, he was cornering the market on genotypes and nucleotide sequences. He's become too powerful—and that makes him too dangerous. For all of us. The Great Chain is pulling away from me, Bill. It's time to give it a tug . . ."

"Right," Bill said, resigned to it. "When's this great, glorious raid coming about anyway, guv'nor?"

"Oh—two days. The twelfth, if all's well. Sullivan and I have organized a large cadre to carry it out—heavily armed. But we're not telling them where they're going till we get there."

"Well maybe I can help, guv. What's the strategy?"

"I'm telling as few people as possible about that—no need for that hurt look, Bill; it's not that I don't trust you. But if Jasmine's place was bugged—what else might be? You could be overheard talking about it to me, or Sullivan. We're going to keep this under wraps. The fewer know about it, the better. We must try to be more . . . *secure* about it this time. And hope they're not waiting for us when we get there . . ."

Fontaine Futuristics, Lab 25
1958

"Quite astonishing, the rate at which the child is growing," said Brigid Tenenbaum, staring at the toddler lying in the transparent bubbling incubator.

"Yes," muttered Dr. Suchong, as he pored over the biochemical extract results on the clipboard in his hands. "Mr. Fontaine will be quite pleased. Also—may have implications for all mankind. Children—so vile. This one . . . not child for long . . ."

They were in a cramped laboratory space lit by a yellow bulb—the door doubly locked, the air stale, smelling heavily of chemicals and hormones and electrical discharge.

The naked little boy floated on the lozenge-shaped incubator on a table between them, his sleeping face above the liquid. The child was in a kind of trance within the thick fluids.

Little "Jack" seemed older than he was—and that was as per schedule. The accelerated-growth program was really remarkable. Perhaps Suchong was right—it could lead, someday, to entirely sidestepping the need for a childhood in future children. They could be grown with fantastic acceleration and taught with conditioning—as this child was being taught. Flickering lights, recorded voices, electrodes sparking his brain imbued him with the basics of learning—the ability to walk, memories of imaginary parents—that would have taken years to accumulate normally. He was a tabula rasa—anything they wished to imprint on him could be pressed into the yielding tissues of his young brain . . . just as Frank Fontaine had requested. She had heard Fontaine refer to young Jack here as "the ultimate con." The backdoor entrance into the well-protected fortress that was Ryan. Jack had been, after all, taken from Jasmine Jolene's uterus, extracted as a tiny embryo that was just twelve days past being a mere zygote . . .

"I must complete the W-Y-K conditioning," Suchong muttered, setting the clipboard on the table. "The child must be set in bathysphere soon, sent to the surface . . . Mr. Fontaine has a boat waiting already . . ."

She frowned. "What is this W-Y-K?"

Suchong glanced over at her in rank suspicion. "You test me? You know I am not to tell you everything about conditioning!"

"Oh yes—I forgot. Scientific curiosity is strong in me, Suchong."

"Hmph, woman's curiosity, that is more to the point . . ." Suchong tinkered with a valve, increasing the flow of a hormone into the incubator. The child twitched in response . . . its legs kicked . . .

What, she wondered, were they doing to this child?

And then she wondered: *Why are such thoughts troubling me?*

But they'd troubled her increasingly. Their work with the little girls; this work with this child. It was beginning to stir memories in her. Her childhood. Her parents. Kind faces . . .

Moments of love . . .

It was as if all the exposure to children called to some child locked within her own breast. A child who wanted to be set free.

Set us all free, whispered the child.

She shook her head. No. Sympathy, caring for laboratory subjects—that was a scientific hell she would not enter.

Unless, perhaps—she was already there . . .

Neptune's Bounty
1958

"Crikey, how many men d'we have here?" Bill asked, a bit awed by the numbers of heavily armed men massing in front of the broad, steel-walled corridor outside Neptune's Bounty.

Bill was carrying a tommy gun; Sullivan had a pistol in his right hand, a hand radio in his left. Cavendish had a shotgun in one hand and the Rapture version of a search warrant in the other. "Lot of buggers for a raid, Chief, innit?" Bill asked. "We really need all these blokes?"

Sullivan muttered, "Yeah. We do. And there's a lot more moving in on Fontaine Futuristics."

"Fontaine Futuristics—what, at the same moment?"

"Same time. Boss's orders." He shook his head, his unhappiness as clear as his wide scowl. "Let's face it, these aren't exactly bloodthirsty desperadoes we're talking about. Rapture's full of poets, artists, and tennis players, not hired gorillas. But Fontaine . . . he seems to have a whole segment of Rapture in his pocket."

"So where's Fontaine? We want this raid to work, we'd better take him down personally."

"That's the plan: word is he's here today, somewhere in the fisheries—maybe on the wharf, up to something in their supply boat. Anyway, it's not just a *raid,*" Sullivan confided, in a low voice, as Cavendish opened the doors and they followed the double column of men down the wooden corridor toward the wharf. "It's an all-out *assault* . . . a military assault on Frank Fontaine and everyone around him."

"How planned is it, Chief? Remember what happened last time. Maybe we should've spent more time setting the bloody thing up?"

"It's planned, all right. We've got two waves of men going in here, two more waves ready at Fontaine Futuristics. But Ryan wanted to keep it under wraps as much as we could. Trouble is, you tell more than two people about something, maybe even just one, and ten always seem to find out about it. And Fontaine's got all kinds of splicers on his pay, cuts them free plasmids in return for info. So I'm not sure if . . ." He shook his head. "I'm—just not sure."

A crackle on the little portable shortwave Sullivan held in his left hand. "In position," came the voice over the radio.

Sullivan spoke into the radio. "Right. Move ahead when I give the designation 'Now.'" He changed frequencies and spoke to another team. "This is the chief. You ready up there?"

"Ready to hit Futuristics . . ."

"Goddamnit, don't say that name on the radio, just—never mind. Just count to thirty—and take the initiative, hit 'em. We're moving ahead, here."

Sullivan glanced at his watch, nodded to himself, looked around, made a hand signal to the others—and then they stalked up to the Securis door. He nodded to Cavendish, who swung it open, held the heavy door for the two lines of grim-faced men at ready—and shouted, "Now!"

And with a shared howl the men rushed through the door. Behind the rushing ranks—shouting in excitement, guns raised—came Sullivan, Head Constable Cavendish, Constable Redgrave, and Bill, all of them storming down onto the water-flanked wooden peninsula of the wharf toward the small tugboatlike vessel tied up there.

And suddenly the splicers were everywhere.

Some of them were literally dripping from the ceiling—spider splicers dropping down, slicing with their curved fish-gutting knives as they came, so that five men in Ryan's attack force fell within seconds, spouting scarlet blood from their slashed-through necks, headless bodies stumbling over their own heads rolling about underfoot. Bill had to step sharp to keep from stomping a man's still-twitching face. A splicer turned from its victim and slashed at Bill but he had the tommy gun ready and squeezed off a quick up-angled burst, blowing the top of the splicer's head off.

Someone nearby stopped running—and turned into a statue, coated with ice. A lobbed grenade blew up the splicer that had done the freezing—but more were coming.

Like demons out of the Bible, they are, Bill thought.

"Yippee ti-yi-yo!" howled a splicer, somewhere above. "Gene Autry's riding to the rescue!"

A prolonged rattle of machine-gun fire, and a spider splicer screamed and fell from the ceiling. A ball of fire roared from a figure dimly seen in the shadows near the far corners of the wharf, the splicer up to his waist in water. Bill winced from the heat as the ball of fire burned meteorically past, striking a man behind him in the face, scream burbling as his face boiled away. Bill fired his tommy gun at the silhouette near the wall as another fireball raced toward him, streaming black smoke. He saw the spider splicer jerk and fall with machine-gun bullets, blood splashing against the wall as a fireball went into a spiral, seeming to lose control of its direction when the spider splicer died. It veered crazily above him and then down again and hissed itself out in the water.

A thudding rattling banging booming of gunshots—shotguns thundering, machine guns clattering, pistols snapping off shots—as rising gunsmoke clouded the scene, making it all the more like hell. The blue smoke reflected red muzzle flashes and bomb blasts, explosives chucked from

ceilings, from behind pylons, from under the wharfs, blowing
Ryan's men into flinders, the splicers shrieking nonsense and
mockery—

Lots of them. And they'd been waiting, expecting them.
They'd been done over—Bill was sure of that.

A man in front of Bill went rigid and jerked about like a
marionette dangled by a palsied hand, electrocuted by a
lightning-throwing plasmid. As he fell, Bill fired a burst past
him at the splicer: a black-haired, dark-eyed woman in shorts.
She was half-hidden behind a stub of pylon, aiming her electrically sparking hand at Bill. But the tommy gun split her
chest and face asunder, and she fell backward into the water,
which was clouding up with crimson billows—the blood of
fallen men and women; human and rogue splicer.

God, Bill thought. *Ryan's got me killing women! Oh lord,
forgive me. What would Elaine think of me now?*

But a woman spider splicer on the ceiling fired a pistol at
him, the bullet grazing his ribs, and he returned fire
without hesitating—because he had to. The woman leapt
from view.

On the deck of the little boat tied up near the wharf was a
wild-eyed, patchy-haired woman pushing a baby carriage
with one hand. She reached into the carriage, snatching out a
hand grenade of some kind, tossing it in the air. Cavendish
rushed her . . .

The bomb stopped in midair, then came arcing telekinetically toward him—and he threw himself down behind a
stack of fish-reeking wooden crates. The crates caught most
of the explosion, sending splinters rocketing like javelins—
and someone behind him wailed in pain.

Bill got to his knees and peered through the smoke in time
to see the woman's head vanish in a cloud of pink and gray
in the near-point-blank double-barrel shotgun blast fired by
Cavendish. The woman sagged—

But someone else stepped from the small cabin of the little tugboatlike vessel—Frank Fontaine himself.

Fontaine had a revolver clutched in his hand, was grimacing and wild-eyed as he fired it almost randomly at them—who did he think he was, John Wayne? Didn't seem like Fontaine's style.

"I'll take you all down with me!" shouted Fontaine. "You'll never bring Frank Fontaine down without a fight!"

There was something weirdly theatrical about the way the man did it.

Fontaine reached into his coat, drew another revolver, and now he had one in each hand, was firing with both, his teeth bared, his eyes wild. A constable went down, shot through the neck by one of Fontaine's rounds.

A splicer cackled in murderous delight. "That's it, make 'em spout pretty, Frank!"

Bill took a shot at Fontaine and missed.

A constable rushed from a cloud of gunsmoke, shouting at Fontaine—and Fontaine dodged back behind the superstructure, circled it, came around behind the constable, shot the man in the back of his head. Then Fontaine dropped his pistol and scooped up the fallen constable's tommy gun—turned and fired both his guns, a pistol in his left hand, the machine gun in his right.

Bill noticed Cavendish slipping through the water, wading, head low, toward the boat. Bill fired at Fontaine to try and distract him from Cavendish, who'd slipped around to the back of the boat—then Bill had to flatten as Fontaine loosed a burst his way. Bullets strafed just over his head.

"If Frank Fontaine goes down, you're all goin' down with me!" Fontaine shouted.

Then Cavendish stepped around the superstructure of the vessel and shoved his shotgun in Fontaine's belly and—grinning—pulled the trigger, blasting Frank Fontaine off the boat, back into the water. The shotgun blast nearly cut him in half.

Cavendish turned to them and shouted in triumph, waving the shotgun over his head. "I done it! I got Frank Fontaine!" Then he ducked behind the pilothouse of the boat to avoid a bomb flying at him. Bill lost sight of him behind the smoky explosion, ducking as a blade flashed by. He turned and fired his tommy gun at the blade-flinging splicer, who ducked for cover.

Bill spotted Sullivan farther down the wharf, backing up from a leadhead. The gun-toting splicer was a barefoot man in overalls leaping about the wharf with unnatural agility, seeming to dodge Sullivan's bullets—moving so fast Sullivan couldn't get a bead. Leaping, the leadhead fired at Sullivan, who caught a round in his left shoulder and staggered with the impact.

Bill was already tracking the splicer with his weapon, and he fired the last of his rounds, shattering the splicer's head as its body twisted from the top of a pylon and fell through the thick gunsmoke to splash awkwardly into the water.

Sullivan, grimacing with pain, turned to Bill with a look of gratitude. "Come on, retreat goddammit! It's an ambush!"

Cavendish came rushing out of the smoke, coughing out, "Sullivan—I got Fontaine!"

"Just retreat, goddammit, there's too many splicers!"

A short spear of ragged wood flew by, and Sullivan turned to fire his pistol at a leering splicer. Bill jumped over the bodies of two men, stepping up beside Sullivan, and used the butt of his tommy gun to knock down a babbling splicer who was slashing a curved blade at Sullivan's face. Sullivan turned, stumbling up the wharf, and Bill followed close behind, pausing only once to duck a passing fireball.

A swag-bellied spider splicer in stained underwear, its face a welter of ADAM scars, clambered buglike on all fours along the wall above the door. Doggish yelping sounds rang in their ears as they ran toward the exit, the splicer alternating barks with phrases like, "Mommy, daddy, baby! Mommy, daddy, baby! Folks're all here! Blood in my ears!" Sullivan fired at him and missed. The spider slicer pointed a pistol down at them just as Redgrave stepped into view. From behind a pylon he fired his shotgun, blowing the splicer off the wall. The body spun heavily past them and bounced off the nearest pylon to splash into the water.

Sullivan, staggering now, led the way through the door, back into the corridor. And then they were through the door—Sullivan, Bill, Constable Redgrave, followed closely by Cavendish and several other men, one of them with his clothes on fire from a splicer fireball; another with an eye missing, the socket smoking from a lightning strike; and two others staggering with gunshot wounds . . .

Bill gave the grinning Cavendish points for nerve as he and Redgrave posted themselves at the open door, firing to cover the retreat, blasting at splicers through the doorway. Bullets pinged and Electro Bolt blasts crackled from the metal doorframe. Bill took a pistol from a collapsed constable and fired it almost point-blank into the upside-down face of a spider splicer coming across the ceiling from nowhere . . . The man dropped like a dying bat . . .

"Come on, keep moving!" Sullivan yelled. "Back!"

Then Sullivan's Special Weapons Backup Team was there, coming from the rear of the corridor, the planned second wave; they rushed between Sullivan and Bill, charging the pursuing splicers: nine constables with chemical throwers, icers, flamethrowers—clumsy weapons spewing corrosive acid, frozen entropy, and burning chaos into the onrushing splicers.

Sullivan had kept the backup team in reserve, afraid they'd hurt his own troops with their imprecise weapons. They were a bloody welcome sight to Bill now. Ryan's new weapons wreaked havoc on the splicers, making heads pop open like popcorn, faces slide off skulls in bubbling acid . . .

Stomach writhing in horror, Bill took Sullivan's good arm, helping him get back up the corridor. He called for Redgrave to give them cover. Sullivan was bleeding heavily from the shoulder wound, and they had to get him to the infirmary.

His feet slipped in Sullivan's blood; men screamed and begged not to be left behind. Guns cracked and flames roared. On and on they went . . . and somehow found that they'd made it to the Metro. They'd gotten out safely.

But as they went, Sullivan grunting with pain, Bill thought: *But maybe there is no escape for us. Not as long as we're in Rapture.*

17

"Turns out that report about the Little Sisters Orphanage was—" Sullivan paused, shaking his head sadly. "Well—it was all true."

They stood outside the "nursery," looking through the window in the door. A little bare-footed, dark-haired girl in a tattered frock was huddled on a bed, in a corner, staring into space and sucking her thumb.

Ryan let out a long, slow breath. "She's got a sea slug in her—and she's producing ADAM?"

"Yep. Apparently, the slugs didn't produce the stuff fast enough. And using the girls worked to increase the production." The disgust dripped from Sullivan's voice.

"Indeed. You've confirmed this with Suchong?"

"Yes sir. You want to ask him, we've got him under house arrest, just down the hall." He gave out a sickly grin. "Poetic justice. They're locked up together, him and Tenenbaum, in one of the rooms they had the kids in."

"I'll have a word with them." Ryan turned away from the door.

"Mr. Ryan?"

Ryan looked at him, frowning. "Yes?"

"What about the kids locked up in there? Do we let 'em out?"

"They are, I believe, actually orphans, yes?"

"Uh—yeah. One way or another."

"Orphans will need somewhere to stay. Perhaps when we find another way to . . . to produce ADAM efficiently, we'll arrange for them to be . . . adopted. Until then . . ." He shrugged. "They're better off here."

Ryan could see that Sullivan was disappointed by that response. "What do you want from me, Sullivan? These kids will be of use. In time . . . Well, we'll see. Do you think we could proceed with our inspection now—Chief?"

"Sure." Sullivan avoided his eyes. His voice was hoarse. "This way, Mr. Ryan. They're down the hall . . ."

Just two doors down, Sullivan unlocked a nearly identical cell. When Sullivan opened the door, Ryan had to step back from the reek of an overflowing chamber pot in the corner of the nursery. Toys were scattered on the floor along with tin plates of half-eaten food.

Brigid Tenenbaum was huddled on the cot in the corner, just like the little girl in the previous cell, but with a buttoned lab coat instead of a frock. She was gnawing a knuckle and the expression on her face was the same as the child's.

Suchong stood with his back to the door, writing on the wall with crayon in Korean ideograms. He had covered several square yards with the enigmatic writing.

"Suchong!" Ryan barked.

Dr. Yi Suchong turned to Ryan—and he saw that one of the lenses of Suchong's glasses had been knocked out. There was a purplish mark across that side of his face, and his lip was split.

"Doctor Suchong tried to escape when we raided the place," Sullivan explained blandly. "Had to crack him one with a truncheon."

Suchong bowed. "Suchong sorry about writing on walls. A little dissertation. No paper to write on."

"And what's the dissertation on?" Ryan asked, nostrils quivering from the stench of the chamber pot.

"Accumulation of harvestable ADAM in splicers," Suchong said. "Possible methods of extraction."

"I see. Would you two like to be released from these . . . quarters?"

Tenenbaum sat up, still gnawing her knuckle, looking at him attentively. Suchong only bowed.

"Then," Ryan went on, "I'm going to need a loyalty oath. And the understanding that breaking that oath is agreeing to execution. We are in extreme times. Extreme measures are necessary."

"And . . ." Tenenbaum's voice came in a croak. "The Little Sisters?"

Suchong frowned and shot her a warning look.

Ryan shrugged. "They will continue here—we need the . . . the commodity. In time we'll find some other way. But it seems you and Fontaine left us with this one for now . . . And, after all, the children have nowhere to go."

Sullivan muttered something inaudible. Ryan looked at him. "Something to say, Chief?"

"Oh—no, Mr. Ryan."

"Very good. Set a guard on this place—but let these two go to their previous quarters and clean up. And see that Suchong gets new glasses."

Fort Frolic, Poseidon Plaza
1958

Stepping out into Poseidon Plaza, Diane McClintock realized she felt no thrill—felt nothing at all—about winning so much money in the Sir Prize Games of Chance Casino.

She fished in her purse for cigarettes, and it took some looking because her purse was stuffed with the Rapture dollars she'd won, quite improbably, on the higher-priced slot machines. She'd had an amazing run of luck, and it meant nothing to her. It felt like mockery somehow. She couldn't spend the money on Park Avenue, in New York, where she longed to be.

She lit a cigarette, lingering outside the casino, reluctant to go home. The whirring slots and the agitated people wandering from one game to the next—they were better than no companions. She knew she could spend time with one of Andrew's friends. But they were hard to bear, after all that'd happened . . .

"Miss?" It was a woman in a blue dress, a blue velvet cap; she had mousy brown hair, large dark eyes. She clutched a handbag to her. "Miss, my name's Margie. I was wondering . . . if you could spare us a donation?"

"Who's *us*?" Diane asked, blowing smoke at the ornate ceiling. "You seem to be out here alone. Need money for kids at home?"

"No, I . . . no. I'm with Atlas's people . . ."

"Atlas! I've heard about him. Also heard about Robin Hood. I don't believe in him either."

"Oh Atlas is real, ma'am . . .

"Yeah? What's he like? A good man?"

"Oh yes. I trust him, even more than Doctor . . ." She broke off, glancing around.

Diane smiled. "More than Doctor Lamb? If that's who you were going to mention, I don't blame you for clamming up, Margie. Got traded from one radical ball team to another, huh?"

"I guess you could say that. When she got arrested, I needed someone to . . . it doesn't matter. What's important is, we're collecting money to help the poor around Rapture. Atlas, he buys canned goods and stuff with it, hands it out . . ."

Diane snorted. "All this talk of a poor underclass around Rapture. Exaggerated, from what I hear."

The girl shook her head. "I was there! I had to . . . to do some pretty awful things. You know. Just to keep going."

"Really? Is it that bad? There wasn't any other kind of, um, work?"

"No ma'am."

"Andrew says there's plenty of . . ." Diane let it trail off, seeing the fear on the girl's face. "Anyway. Donations. Sure—here." She took a wad of cash from her purse and handed it over. "More power to anyone who pisses off Andrew. But don't tell anyone it came from me."

"Oh—thank you!" Margie put the money in her handbag, took out a leaflet. "Read this—it'll tell all about him . . ." And then she hurried off into the shadows.

Diane looked at the leaflet's heading.

YES, SOMEONE CARES! ATLAS KNOWS IT FEELS AS IF NO ONE IN RAPTURE CARES! FIGHT FOR ATLAS! FIGHT FOR THE RIGHTS OF THE WORKINGMAN . . .

Diane smiled, imagining Andrew Ryan's reaction to seeing the leaflet. She crumpled it up and threw it away. But the words loitered in her mind.

Yes, someone cares . . .

Apollo Square
1958

"I wish Ryan would take down that fucking gallows," Bill McDonagh said as he and Wallace walked by, grimacing at the reek of the dangling corpses. Four bloated, purple-faced bodies, turning slowly in four nooses. Looked like new ones, since last time. It was bloody depressing.

Bill was going to be glad to get his meeting with Sullivan over and hurry home to Elaine and Sophie tonight. A man didn't feel much like taking a turn in Rapture with this kind of bleakness setting the black dog to snapping at his heels.

"What I can't figure is," said Roland Wallace, as he and Bill walked across the trash-strewn floor of Apollo Square, "how Fontaine got all those splicers there to wait for the constables? They're too loony to recruit—aren't they?"

Bill chuckled grimly. "You forget, mate, those buggers'll do anything for ADAM."

Wallace grunted. "You have a point. So Fontaine bribed them with ADAM. Show up there, take on whoever comes— and the survivors get plenty more . . ."

"That's 'ow I figure it, right enough . . . Here, what's all this then?"

A big crowd was gathered in front of Artemis Suites— where a man stood on the steps, addressing them.

"Must be that fellow calls himself Atlas," Wallace said, his voice hushed.

"Oh right—I've seen the pamphlets."

"Started with pirate-radio messages, got people all worked up. Followers leaving graffiti about . . ." Curious, Bill and Wallace paused on the outskirts of the crowd to listen to Atlas.

At least seventy-five people—most of them seeming to be still human, ostensibly, or not yet far into ADAM—were gathered around this Atlas. He wore maintenance workers' coveralls. Just one of the people. The man sounded vaguely familiar—but looking closer, Bill decided he didn't know him. Couldn't have forgotten a bloke like that, almost movie-star handsome with his lush golden-brown hair and cleft chin.

"Now back home in Dublin we had a saying," bellowed Atlas, in something like an Irish brogue. "May the cat eat you, and may the devil eat the cat! Isn't that what's happened to us, here? You bet it is, boyo! We've been eaten alive, twice! First by Rapture and then by Ryan! There's no *craik* here, no fun for the workingman, for that is reserved for the swells and their spoiled bettys up in Olympus Heights! Come and start life anew in Rapture, he said! But that was the cat talking to the mouse and the devil talking through the cat!"

Hoots of agreement from the crowd.

"Aye!" Atlas went on, his voice carrying over all Apollo Square. "We have been lied to, and lied to again! They told us it was all free market here—but what happens? Ryan takes over Fontaine Futuristics! Takes it by force, he does! He starts in with curfews and blockades—turns the place into a police state!"

An approving roar at that. Ryan's hypocrisy hadn't gone unnoticed.

"We were *lured* here!" Atlas bellowed. "Lured from a slum in Queens or Dublin or Shanghai or London—to a smaller slum under frigid water! Moving up, we are, right? Moving from living four in a room to living twenty in a room! It's theft—theft of our future, boyo! Theft of our hope! But there is another way—a way to real hope! A share-the-wealth program! Why should them hypocrites be allowed to accumulate a hundred times, two hundred times, what a workingman earns—when they get it 'cause of our hard work! We work while they sit up there in their penthouses drinking champagne and puffing cigars—imported cigars we ain't allowed to have! Why shouldn't every family be given a basic allowance—a thousand, two thousand Rapture dollars, to live on!" Roars of approval at that. His voice rose, and rose again, with every word. *"Why should the wealth of Rapture belong only to a greedy few? Now tell me THAT!"*

Fists popped up—but they were shaking in agreement. Someone started chanting. "Atlas, Atlas!"

And all the crowd took it up. *"Atlas, Atlas, Atlas!"*

Atlas had to thunder the words out to be heard over the rising chant. "And if it's got to come to a fight—armed with ADAM and armed with guns—then so be it!"

"Atlas, Atlas, Atlas, Atlas!"

"Like he's been taking notes from Sofia Lamb," Bill said in a low aside to Roland Wallace. "But he's got his own style. More the workingman's daddy . . ."

"Why—he's Huey P. Long!" Wallace said.

"What, that bloke from Louisiana?"

"No—I mean, he's borrowing from Long's playbook. The Kingfish they called him, down there in Baton Rouge, king of the southern rabble-rousers. The Kingfish talked exactly like this. Except for the Irish accent. And Atlas tossed in a little Bolshevism . . ."

Bill shook his head, puzzling over it. "Strange I 'aven't seen this bloke Atlas before. Been 'ere for years, thought I'd seen every wanker in this big leaky tank of a town."

Wallace gave him a poke in the ribs with an elbow. "Bill—look up there!"

Bill looked at the ceiling, saw spider splicers creeping across it upside down, coming from three directions—converging right above him and Wallace.

He looked around the edges of the square and saw the telekinetic splicer who'd killed Greavy. She was watching from the wall near the entrance to Artemis Suites.

"They're closing in on us, Bill."

"Right; we'll take the better part of valor and back off—fast. Come on, mate!"

They hurried back the way they'd come. They'd go the long way, through the checkpoint—they both had their ID cards—and then through the transparent passages between buildings to another bathysphere entrance to get where they were going. Or they wouldn't get there at all.

The splicers didn't seem intent on pursuing them out of Apollo Square. Which confirmed Bill's suspicion that they were somehow working for Atlas. They were remaining as his bodyguards . . .

A word popped into Bill's mind as they hurried through the passage, striding under a passing pod of dolphins. It was a simple, one-syllable word, summing up what he felt was coming from the inevitable confrontation between this new Kingfish and Andrew Ryan. *War.*

More killing. More war. More danger for Elaine and Sophie.

Something had to be done to stop it. Somehow it had to be defused . . .

A frightening notion came to him. He tried to dismiss it from his mind. But it lingered, whispering to him . . .

Ryan Industries / Fontaine Futuristics
1958

"I really must get around to taking that sign down," Ryan said as he and Karlosky walked under the words *Fontaine Futuristics.* "It's *Ryan Plasmids* now."

They passed through the double doors and walked across the polished floors, past the sculpture of Atlas holding up the world.

He glanced at his watch. He was half an hour behind time—the lights would dim for evening soon. The message from Suchong had been urgent: a crisis in ADAM production . . .

Ryan ignored the lab workers hurrying past, clipboards in hand, and hurried up the stairs, Karlosky close beside him. He rarely worried about splicers or assassins with Karlosky around—the man had eyes in the back of his head. He wondered if plasmids could make that literally possible.

They went through the sterilization air locks to find Suchong and Tenenbaum in a steamy lab, working over a sea slug in a bubbling tank. Frowning in concentration, Tenenbaum was using a pipette to draw an orange fluid from the sea slug's horny tail. Ryan noticed that her hair didn't seem to have been

washed in days and her lab coat was splashed with stains, her
nails black. There were blue circles under her eyes.

Suchong glanced up as they entered and gave them each a
short bow. Tenenbaum withdrew the pipette and released its
contents into a test tube. Ryan stepped closer to inspect the
sea slug—the creature quivered in its bath of seawater, but
otherwise seemed almost lifeless.

Ryan pointed at the sea slug. "Surely that's not the last one?"

Suchong sighed. "We have a few others in a suspension.
But they are almost gone. The fighting of the raid, all the
chaos—we lost them. Damage to the tanks. If only you'd
warned us . . ."

"Couldn't risk that. You haven't exactly earned my trust,
Suchong, working for Fontaine."

Suchong inclined his head in something that passed for
regret. "Ah. Suchong very sorry. Grave mistake to work for
Fontaine. I should have known—the intelligent man work
for men with more guns. Always the better policy. I will not
make that mistake again. You have my loyalty, Mr. Ryan."

"Do I? We'll see. Well, you sent for me and I can see the
problem for myself. No sea slugs, no ADAM. Any sugges-
tions, Doctor? What are we to do for ADAM? We have all
these lunatic ADAM addicts running about . . . a whole industry could collapse. I've taken over the plasmids business—
built the Hall of the Future to extol them. But if we run out
of them—it's all for nothing."

Tenenbaum looked up from the test tube. "There is a way,
Mr. Ryan. Until we can learn to breed more slugs . . ."

"And that is?"

"Many men are dying and dead in Rapture. But before
they die, there is a . . . how would you say it, a stage in their
metabolism of plasmids . . . in which they create a refined
ADAM inside them. It is deposited in the torso. And we believe . . ."

She looked at Suchong, who nodded at Ryan. "Yes. It can be harvested. From the dead."

Karlosky grunted and shook his head. But said nothing. Ryan glanced at him. It was hard to startle Karlosky, but it seemed they'd done it.

Ryan looked back at the sea slug. "You can get ADAM from the dead?"

Suchong removed his glasses and polished them with a silk handkerchief. "Yes. But there is a certain way to do this—the ADAM must be sensed, and drawn up into the syringe properly—and correctly transported. Little Sisters are best suited for that process . . ."

Tenenbaum shook her head. "But the girls are already . . . damaged. If we sent them to do the harvesting—who will protect them? They are . . ." She glanced at Ryan, then quickly away. "They are worth a lot of money. They will not trust ordinary guards . . . and we cannot trust ordinary men with them."

"So for that," Suchong said, "we have developed hybrids, our cyborg sea workers. Gil Alexander has made great progress with the Alpha Series—Augustus Sinclair has, ah, leased out this Johnny Topside from Persephone. Subject Delta—he is bonded with the girl we took from the Lamb woman. Eleanor Lamb."

"Bonded?" Ryan asked, not sure he liked the sound of it.

"The girls are to be bonded to the Alpha creatures. They are to be . . . surrogate fathers. Little ones call them big daddies. Most charming. The girls will be conditioned to work closely with them."

Tenenbaum made a small sound of acknowledgment. "They *do* seem to need something, some symbol of adulthood they can feel comfortable with . . ."

The conversation was getting ever more peculiar. Ryan wasn't sure he understood what they were planning.

But he knew a solution was needed. And he liked the neatness of harvesting ADAM from the dead. It closed the circle, somehow: an unexpected link in the Great Chain.

"What exactly will you need from me?" he asked, finally.

Near Fighting McDonagh's Bar
1958

This won't look too good, Sullivan thought. *Me being in charge of law enforcement in Rapture—and being the drunkest son of a bitch in Rapture tonight . . .*

He stood outside McDonagh's tavern, swaying, wondering how late it was. Long after midnight—lights had already been turned down. Couldn't even make out his watch.

How much money had he lost at the card table, in the back room? Four hundred Rapture dollars at least. Poker. His downfall. Shouldn't have drunk so much. Might've folded some of those hands before they got expensive. Maybe Shouldn't have gotten in the game . . .

But his old gambling bugaboo was back—and with a vengeance. Only way he could get his mind off the mess that Rapture was becoming—and his failure to keep the splicers at bay. He was sure Ryan was starting to look at him like he was a useless old drunk.

Maybe he needed to get married. Get married again, a nice warm wife to keep him in line.

He shuddered. *A wife.* How do guys like McDonagh do it?

He sighed and started off toward the stairs. He just had his hand on the metal door to the ramp when he heard a *boom* from behind it and a keen whistling sound.

Rogue splicers.

The corridor was twisting around from the booze and his mouth was paper dry. Too drunk to deal with this. "Gotta get backup . . ." He licked his lips and put his hand on the re-

volver in his coat pocket. But then again—he was top cop.
Had to show it. "Fuck backup."

He drew his gun, opened the door, took two steps through—
and was slammed in the chest by the force of a Sonic Boom
plasmid. The sonic shock wave made him stagger back painfully hard against the doorframe. A leering, goggle-eyed splicer
in a ragged T-shirt was crouched behind a tumble of crates.
"Gotcha big-badge! Or should I say big ass!" He pointed his
hand to fire off another Sonic Boom, but Sullivan, sobering
fast, slipped back through the door, taking cover to one side—
and a cackling made him look up, through the doorway, to see
a female splicer clinging flylike to the ceiling, wearing only
yellowed underwear and a brassiere, her long dirty hair hanging down like Spanish moss. She was pointing one grimy hand
down at the Sonic Boomer and twirling her finger—a whistling sound became a windy roaring and a small cyclone appeared, whirling bits of trash, picking up the empty crates to
smash them against the metal walls. "Ha ha haaaa!" she cackled. "Care to go for a *spin!*"

The Sonic Boomer yelled and tried to scramble clear, but
the expanding Cyclone Trap plasmid caught him, jerked him
off his feet, spun him like a ragdoll in the air—and dropped
him with a thump. He yelled in outrage as the spider splicer
giggled.

Completely out of their gourds, Sullivan thought.

"Two plasmids from one lunatic," Sullivan muttered, trying
to get a bead on her in the dim corridor with his gun. She
suddenly dropped down, landing catlike, and spun to face
him. "Puppet cop, cop it, pup! That's you!" She made a gesture, and suddenly a second splicer appeared, almost her
twin, in front of her and to one side. Sullivan fired
convulsively—and the bullet simply passed through the flickering image.

A third plasmid. "Target dummy."

She cackled again—and then looked startled, her eyes widening. She looked down to see a curved fish-gutting knife blade protruding under her breastbone, spurting blood. She toppled forward, dying, and the Sonic Boomer who'd stabbed her from behind leered . . . and gestured—*Wham*—Sullivan was flung to skid down the ramp on his back . . .

Dazed, he lay there a moment, staring at the ceiling, gasping for air—then he sat up . . . and looked through the open door, about four paces off at what he thought was the splicer, sneaking around in the shadows.

Sullivan got up, dusted himself off, put his gun in his pocket, and said, "Screw this."

He turned and walked back to the bar.

Hall of the Future
1958

Diane McClintock was on one of her long, solitary walks through Rapture. She knew it was dangerous. She had a gun in her purse.

She had four cocktails in her, too, and she didn't much care about the danger. She was heading somewhere, in a round-about way. Pauper's Drop. But she couldn't bring herself to go there directly. She was afraid Andrew might be watching her, through the cameras; through his agents. She had to take the roundabout route so he'd never guess she was hoping to get a close look at the man they called Atlas . . .

She strolled through the museum, the new Hall of the Future, with its videotaped displays glorifying plasmids—all quite ironic, considering some of the horrors plasmids had brought.

She passed onward. Footsteps echoing, she wandered through the livid colored light of Rapture; she rambled past pistons pumping mysteriously in wall niches, past the steaming pool of the baths, under iridescent panes of crystal, through high-ceilinged atriums of brass and gold and chrome, vast chambers that seemed as grandiose as any palace ballroom. A palace, that's what Rapture seemed to her, an ornate palace of Ryanium and glass, swallowed by the sea—which was ever so slowly digesting it.

And sometimes it seemed to Diane that everyone in Rapture had already died. That they were all ghosts—the ghosts of royalty and servants. She remembered Edgar Allan Poe's sunken city. She'd read all of Poe in trying to educate herself to impress Andrew and the others. Again and again she'd returned to *The City in the Sea*. She remembered Poe's lines—some seemed especially apt now . . .

> *Resignedly beneath the sky.*
> *The melancholy waters lie.*
> *No rays from holy heaven come down*
> *On the long night-time of that town;*
> *But light from out the lurid sea*
> *Streams up the turrets silently—*
> *Gleams up the pinnacles far and free*
> *Up domes—up spires—up kingly halls—*
> *Up fanes—up Babylon-like walls—*

She sighed, and she walked onward, her head throbbing. Still half-drunk.

Acting as if she went toward Pauper's Drop on a whim, she passed through the transparent corridor, and the metal door. Down a flight of steps . . .

Sullen-eyed tramps lolled against the walls of the buildings, under intricate scrawls of graffiti. They lay about smoking, drinking, talking—and looking at her with an unsettling interest.

Maybe it was time to take refuge in the Fishbowl Café. It looked civilized enough.

She hurried into the café, sat in a booth by the dusty window, and ordered coffee from the frowzy, gum-chewing waitress who already had the pot in her hand. "Sure, honey," the waitress said, giving her brown curls a toss. "You want some pie? It's seapalm pie, but they put a lotta sugar in it, not too bad . . ."

"No, thank you," Diane murmured, wondering if she could ask this woman about Atlas . . .

The waitress bustled off to deal with a thuggish-looking man at the other end of the row of booths.

Diane McClintock sipped coffee, looking out the window, hoping the caffeine would stop the thudding in her head.

Risky being here. She could easily fall into the hands of rogue splicers. But her depression had been whispering to her lately, *It might be better if they got you . . .*

Still, Rapture was in a time of relative peace, with Fontaine dead. She hoped it would last.

Atlas was said to come to Pauper's Drop pretty regularly. He moved about undercover—he was "wanted for questioning" by Sullivan's bunch. He was on the track to end up in Persephone for sure.

Why am I here? she wondered. But she knew. She wanted to see this man for herself. Her encounter with Margie outside Sir Prize, the woman's sincerity, had planted a seed.

Andrew would hate her for coming. But that was part of why she was here. Atlas was a man with something Andrew Ryan was missing—a real heart.

She was startled from her fumination by a commotion outside. Several men with shotguns were shouting at the crowd of unemployed. They seemed to be getting them organized into a line. To her surprise, the ragtag crowd passively lined up . . .

Then a man came striding onto the scene, followed by several others carrying large baskets. The man in the lead somehow drew all eyes to himself. He was a handsome figure of a man with a fine head of hair, a mustache, a cleft chin, and broad shoulders. He dressed like a workingman—with a white shirt, sleeves rolled up; suspenders; simple work trousers; boots. But he carried himself like a man in charge. Yet there was no harsh edge of authority about him. His expression was kindly, compassionate, as he took a basket from the man behind him, began quietly passing out things to the people in line. The first one, a woman with gray-streaked hair and a lined face, a tattered frock, took a package, and Diane could read the woman's trembling lips: "Thank you. Oh thank you . . ."

He spoke briefly to her, patted her arm, and then passed on to the next in line, personally handing out a pair of shoes; a sack that seemed to brim with canned goods.

Could this really be Atlas?

The waitress came to Diane's tables, asked in a bored voice, "You want some more of what passes fer coffee around here, honey, or what?"

"What I'd really like . . ." Diane took a ten-dollar bill—with Ryan's picture on it—and tucked it into the woman's apron pocket. "Is to know if that man out there is who I think it is . . ."

The waitress looked around nervously, looked into her apron pocket, then nodded. With a lowered voice she said, "Him . . . he calls himself Atlas. Only t'ing I know: the lady lives down the hall from me wouldn't have nothing to eat, weren't for him. He's helping people, that one. Gives out free stuff every week. Talks about a new order."

The waitress hurried off, and Diane turned to stare out the window at the man called Atlas. He was gentle but powerful—the kind of man she truly wanted to meet . . .

She hesitated. Did she dare go out and talk to Atlas? Suppose Andrew were having her watched?

It was too late. There was shouting, an alarm on the concourse outside the café—constables were coming. Atlas waved at his charges—and then hurried off around the corner. Her chance was gone.

But she made up her mind. One way or another, she would meet this man . . .

She would stand face-to-face with Atlas.

Fort Frolic Shooting Gallery
1958

They were alone in the long, narrow shooting gallery, firing at man-shaped targets. The air smelled of gunsmoke; brass littered the floor. Bill stood just behind his wife, looking over her shoulder. "That's it, love—take aim and shoot 'im right between the eyes."

Elaine winced and lowered the revolver. "Do you have to put it that way, Bill? Between the eyes? It's just a paper target . . ."

Bill McDonagh grinned ruefully. "Sorry, darlin', but—you said you wanted this for self-defense! And those rogue splicers don't play around—" He put his hand on her shoulder and added more gently, "If you're going to defend yourself against them, you've got to shoot to kill. I know it's bloody awful. It's been hard for me to shoot at these blokes too . . ."

Elaine took a deep breath, raised the gun at the end of her arm, clasped it with both hands, and aimed at the silhouette at the other end of the shooting gallery.

She grimaced and squeezed the trigger, blinking as the gun went *crack*.

Bill sighed. She missed the target completely. "Right. This time, let out a long breath before you fire, squeeze the trigger gently, like, and—"

"Oh Bill . . ." Elaine lowered the gun, her lips quivering, eyes welling with tears. "This is so horrible. Having to . . . Mr. Ryan never said it'd be like this . . ."

Bill glanced at the door to see if anyone was listening. They seemed to be alone. But you never knew for sure anymore . . .

"Bill . . . it's just . . . I can't raise Sophie here, in a place where I have to . . ."

He put his arm around her. "I know, love. I know."

She put her face on his shoulder and wept. *"I want to leave Rapture . . ."* she whispered.

"Elaine . . . darlin' . . . got to be careful where you talk like that . . ." He licked his lips, thinking, *Listen to me. Turning into a craven bastard.* "One thing at a time, love. Thing is— Fontaine's gone but . . . word is, Atlas is making some kind of deal with the rogue splicers. He's got a lot of ADAM stored up, somewhere. Got 'em workin' for him. And he's going to make some kind of move—he's not just handing out food and pamphlets, love. All of us on this side of the fence—we're going to have to defend ourselves. It's more dangerous out there than ever . . ."

She sniffed and wiped her nose with a kerchief she took from his coat pocket. She took a deep breath and then nodded. "Sure, okay, Bill. I just hope you're right about who we've got to shoot at." She lowered her voice to a barely audible whisper. "Far as I can tell—they might come at us from either side of the fence." She cocked the gun. "I guess I'd better . . . be ready for anything."

Elaine raised the gun and took aim at the paper outline. She let out a long, slow breath, centered the gunsights on the target's head, and squeezed the trigger.

Bill McDonagh's Flat
1958

It was Christmas Eve. Bill, Karlosky, and Redgrave sat around a card table in Bill's living room, playing poker in the light from the Christmas tree. Two bottles, one nearly empty, stood beside a plate littered with cookie crumbs. Bill was beginning to feel he'd drunk too much. Sometimes the cards in his hand seemed to recede into the distance, and the room swiveled in his peripheral vision.

"Wonder if this Atlas is going to be the problem Mr. Ryan thinks," Redgrave said, frowning over his cards. "All we got is rumors. That he's working with the splicers, givin' 'em ADAM. Where's he get all that ADAM?"

"A lot of Fontaine's supply seems to've done a vanishing act," Bill said, trying to see his own cards. Were those diamonds or hearts? "When they raided his place—most of the stuff was gone. Ryan's had Suchong hard at it making new stuff. Sometimes I wish he'd just let 'em . . ." He didn't finish saying he wished plasmids would run out completely. Karlosky might report that to Ryan. And Ryan was not in a mood to have his policies questioned.

Redgrave raised the pot, Bill folded, and Karlosky called. Redgrave showed three aces.

Karlosky scowled at Constable Redgrave and threw down his cards. "You black bastard; you cheat me again!"

The black cop chuckled and scooped up the poker chips. "I *beat* you, that's what I do, I beat you like an old rug . . ."

"Bah! Black son of a bitch!"

Shuffling the cards, Bill looked at Redgrave to see how he took Karlosky's invective.

To his relief, he saw Redgrave looking gleeful, catching the tip of his tongue between his teeth as he stacked his new chips. "Not surprised an ignorant Cossack son of a bitch like you can't play poker . . . But a Russian not being able to hold his drink? That's sad, man!"

"What!" Karlosky pretended to tremble with rage. "Not hold drink!"

He grabbed the unlabeled bottle—he had made the vodka himself from potatoes raised in Rapture hydroponics—and poured the transparent fluid into their glasses, slopping almost as much on the table. "Now! We see who can drink! A black bastard or a real man! Bill—you drink too!"

"Nah, I'm not a real man; I'm a married man! My wife'll kick me ass if I come to bed any more bladdered'n I am . . ." He'd had three shots of the crude vodka—more than enough.

"He's right about that!" Elaine said, scowling theatrically from the doorway to the bedroom. "I'll kick him right out of bed!" But she laughed.

Bill watched as Elaine went to adjust an ornament on the Christmas tree, yawning in her terrycloth robe. It was a curious thing how he could look at his wife with her hair rumpled, her face without makeup, her feet bare under a terrycloth robe that was far from enticing boudoir wear, and still feel a deep desire for her. It wasn't the vodka—he often felt that way seeing her about the flat.

"Is nice Christmas tree!" Karlosky said, toasting her.

The small Christmas tree was made out of wire and green paper, with a few colored lights—they were the only Christmas decoration Ryan allowed. No stars, no angels, no wise men, no baby Jesus. *A secular Christmas is a merry Christmas!* went the poster, put up in Apollo Square right before the holiday. The poster showed a winking dad dropping a Bible into a trashcan with one hand while handing his little girl a teddy bear with the other.

"Don't stay up too late with these drunken louts, Bill!" Elaine said, rubbing her eyes, putting on a frown again.

"Ha!" Karlosky said, punching Redgrave playfully in the shoulder. "His wife whips him like little boy, eh!"

Bill laughed, shaking his head. "Sorry, love. We're about done playing cards."

Her look of mock disapproval vanished and she winked. "No, you guys go on and play your cards! Have fun. I just came out to tell you not to be too loud so you don't wake up Sophie."

Redgrave turned her a bright smile. "Ma'am, thank you for havin' me to Christmas Eve supper. Means a lot to me!" He raised his glass to her.

"Glad you could be here, Constable Redgrave. Goodnight."

"Da!" Karlosky said. "Happy holiday, Mrs.!" He turned fiercely to Redgrave. "Now—drink up, you black bastard!"

Redgrave laughed, and they drank their vodka, clinking their glasses together when they were done.

"Okeydokey!" Karlosky said, lowering his voice as Elaine went to bed, "we will play more cards, you lose money to me—and we see if you really can drink . . . black bastard!"

"Cossack devil! Pour me another!"

Kashmir Restaurant
1958

On New Year's Eve, Bill McDonagh sat with his wife at a corner table of the luxurious restaurant, near the wall-high window looking out into the churning depths of the sea. They had taken off their silvery party masks and set them on the table next to the champagne bottle.

He glanced out the window. The illuminated skyscraper-style buildings, seen through a hundred yards of rippling seawater, seemed to shimmy to the music: a Count Basie swing number.

Bill winked at Elaine, and she returned him a strained smile. She was pretty in her pearl-trimmed, low-cut white gown, but, despite all the care she'd taken, she still looked a bit haggard. Elaine didn't sleep well anymore. None of them did. Lately, a bloke trying to sleep in Rapture was always unconsciously listening for an alarm to go off or the sounds of a security bot taking on a rogue splicer.

It was chilly near the window. The tuxedo wasn't much protection against the cold. But he didn't want to sit any closer to the entourage waiting for Ryan to show up: a group at several tables near the fountain. Sander Cohen was wearing a feathery mask and babbling madly away at a bored-looking Silas Cobb. Diane McClintock, wearing a gold party mask edged in diamonds, sat stiffly at a small table reserved for her and Ryan—she sat there alone, watching the door and muttering into her tape recorder. Ryan had gone on an errand to Hephaestus and was going to give some kind of New Year's address over the radio.

"Well, love . . ." Bill said, toasting his wife with the champagne glass. Trying to pretend he was enjoying himself. "In just a few minutes it'll be 1959 . . ."

Elaine McDonagh nodded slowly and forced another weak smile. The fear flared in her eyes, then dutifully hid itself again. She gave him the brave look that always tore at his heart. "It is! It's almost New Year's, Bill . . ." She looked at the other tables, filled with revelers in jeweled masquerade costumes and masks. They were waving noisemakers, laughing, talking loudly over the music, doing their best to celebrate. Her gaze took in the bunting, the banners, the circular hot-pink neon sign, specially made up for the party: *Happy New Year 1959.* "It's funny, Bill—all these years down here . . . Sophie growing up without seeing the sun . . . now the war . . . and it's almost 1959 . . . Time passes all funny in Rapture, doesn't it? It's slow and fast both . . ."

Bill nodded. Elaine was increasingly homesick, and scared. But he just couldn't bring himself to abandon the man who had taken him out of the loo and made him a real engineer. Sure, Ryan was giving way to hypocrisy—but he was only human. And maybe it was true that Rapture had to go through this transition period before getting back on track. They just had to clear out the Atlas types, the worst of the splicers, and Lamb's followers.

He noticed Elaine staring around at the armed men, the constables standing guard near the walls. The guards weren't wearing masquerade masks. Scores of gunmen, there to protect this exclusive gathering from rogue splicers.

Constable was the one job you could stand a good chance of getting, if you were out of work in Rapture—because the mortality rate for constables was so high.

Bill was glad to see Brenda bringing each constable a flute of champagne on a tray to get ready for midnight. Made it seem more festive.

A gun in one hand, a champagne glass in the other, he thought ruefully. *That's Rapture.*

He had a pistol under his coat; Elaine had one in her pearl-beaded white purse.

"Do you think Sophie's all right?" Elaine asked, toying with her glass, looking anxiously at the clock.

"Sure, she'll be fine."

"Bill, I want to go home as soon as we get past New Year's Eve. Like at twelve-oh-five, okay? I don't like to leave Sophie with the sitter long in this place . . . I don't know if Mariska can use a gun, really. I mean, I left her one, but . . ."

"Don't worry; we'll leave a few minutes after midnight, love."

The Count Basie song finished, and Duke Ellington started. Wearing their gawdy party masks, a half dozen couples were dancing in a cleared space between the tables, forced smiles held stiffly on their faces.

Bill wondered what music the rest of the world was listening to. Music in Rapture had to be outdated. There were rumors about something called rock 'n' roll.

Trying to change Elaine's mood, he took her hand, pulled her to her feet, got her dancing to the Duke Ellington number. They used to love going dancing together in New York . . .

Then the song stopped, simply cut off in midtune, and the countdown started, led by a giddy Sander Cohen: "Ten, nine, eight, seven, six, five, four, three, two, one, Happy New Year!"

Bill pulled Elaine close for the midnight kiss . . .

That's when the explosion came. The doors exploded inward, knocking three constables like rag dolls into the center of the room. Bill shoved their table over for partial cover, pushed Elaine to the ground behind the tabletop, and covered her with his body. Machine-gun rounds ricocheted from the bulletproof windows to slam through tuxedos, to wound squealing women in their glittering finery. Elaine was screaming something about Sophie. Another bomb flew into the room and detonated—body parts spun overhead, spraying blood. "Auld Lang Syne" was playing as machine-gun bullets raked the room—as if the gunfire were part of the New Year's Eve revelry. Screams . . . More gunshots . . .

Faces that seemed frozen, mocking: the invading splicers were wearing masquerade-party masks—domino masks, feathered masks, golden masks . . .

Andrew Ryan's voice came from the public address, at that moment, as he made his New Year's speech . . .

"Good evening, my friends. I hope you are enjoying your New Year's Eve celebration; it has been a year of trials for us all. Tonight I wish to remind each of you that Rapture is your city . . ."

Bill peered around the edge of the table, saw a splicer in a black mask yelling, "Long live Atlas!"

Another, running through the cloud of smoke at the shattered doors, bellowed: "Death to Ryan!"

". . . It was your strength of will that brought you here, and with that strength you shall rebuild. And so, Andrew Ryan offers you a toast. To Rapture, 1959. May it be our finest year."

"Diane!" Elaine shouted.

Bill turned to see Diane McClintock crawling past on her

hands and knees, dazed face bloodied, her green dress had become red-stained rags. "Diane—get down!" he called.

Beyond her, some of the constables were ducking behind the bar—and grinning. Bill realized that some of them had been in on this. A security bot went whistling by overhead, firing at a thuggish splicer cartwheeling into the room. A nitro splicer in a fur-fringed white mask was throwing another bomb, which blew up on a table under which three men in tuxes crouched—their tuxedos and their flesh mingled wetly in the blast.

Bill hoped to God the rogue splicers had the common sense not to throw too many bombs near the windows. The windows were supposed to be blast proof, but they could only take so much.

"Come on, Elaine, we're off!" he said gruffly, trying to get some steel into her spine. "And bring your purse."

He tugged out his pistol, the two of them scrambling like doughboys under barbed wire till they were under one of the few tables still standing. A bleeding thuggish splicer was crawling by like a hungry alligator, laughing insanely, his mask down around his neck. ADAM scars crisscrossed the man's face in livid pink that somehow matched the neon pink of the *Happy New Year 1959* sign. Blood was pumping from a bullet hole in the crawling splicer's neck as he sang croakily, "I'm a little hair, pulled off a chin, about to go into a spin, down the drain drain drain—!" Then he noticed Bill and Elaine—and whipped a hooked blade at Bill's face. Bill shot him in the forehead.

The blade clattered on the floor. Elaine groaned at the sight of the dead man. They crawled onward.

Bill risked a look over his shoulder and saw a group of loyal constables, including Redgrave and Karlosky, firing above an overturned table at spider splicers crawling across the ceiling near the blown-open doors. A red-masked nitro splicer made a bomb fly through the air with the power of his mind—it flew past the table, then doubled back. Karlosky and Redgrave dove to the side, and the bomb went off. Redgrave rolled, wounded. A shotgun blasted nearby—Rizzo firing over a table at the nitro splicer. The splicer's face vanished in a welter of red, and a grenade blew up in his hands, his body flying apart like a New Year's party favor.

Bill crawled onward, one arm over Elaine, who crept along beside him alternately sobbing and cursing. They'd reached the swinging doors into the back kitchen. "Okay, kid," he whispered in her ear. "On three we jump up and run through them doors. Watch out for my pistol, love, I might have to fire it. One, two—three!"

They were up and rushing through, Bill shouldering the door aside—and firing at a spider splicer hanging upside down from the low ceiling. Wounded, the splicer fell off onto the stove, clattering into pots of boiling water and lit gas burners. Shrieking in pain, the splicer flailed and tumbled off the stove and onto the floor.

Bill and Elaine rushed past into the rear hall. Bill turned left; a gun banged just beside him. He turned to see Elaine pointing her own pistol, its muzzle smoking, her face contorted with anger as a nitro splicer fell back, his head shot open. A grenade fell from his hands and bounced to the floor—

"Down!" Bill yelled, and dragged her behind a steel kitchen cart, covering her with his body—and then the bomb went off. The cart caught the blast and slammed into them with the shockwave, the steel cart cracking painfully into Bill's right arm. "Ow, buggerin' *hell* that hurts!"

"Bill—are you all right?" Elaine asked, coughing as the smoke cleared.

"I'm okay, except me bloody ears are ringing like a mad monk's church bell! Come on, we got to get up, love!"

They made their way dizzily down the smoky hallway, eyes

stinging. Gunfire rattled behind them and explosions shook the floor. Other people were running from the kitchen. He looked back and saw Redgrave stumbling along, wounded in the leg but game enough—Karlosky behind him, urging the wounded Redgrave along.

Rizzo was turning to fire behind them through the door at splicers Bill couldn't see. A swishing sound—and Rizzo shrieked, the scream becoming a gurgle as a curved blade buried itself in his throat. Rizzo fell back, blood gushing over his tuxedo . . .

Bill fired at the door—a masked splicer jerked back. Elaine kept tugging on his arm, shouting about Sophie. He let her urge him through the emergency exit to the stairs, and they saw a group of white-faced, scared-looking constables a flight below, yelling up at them: "This way! Down here!"

Hoping they weren't heading into a trap, Bill and Elaine went with the constables.

A blur of corridors, passages, a checkpoint, another, waving ID cards, an atrium, an elevator . . .

Time did indeed seem all funny, weirdly collapsed, a telescope snapped shut . . .

And then they were in their own flat, panting, Bill locking the door. Elaine with her purse in one hand and a gun in the other.

"Hello!" called Mariska Lutz, their sitter, from the next room. "Back already? Have a good time?"

Rapture Central Control, Ryan's Office
1959

"It makes me half-crazed to think of it," Ryan said, voice trembling. He balled the report in his hands and threw it into a corner. "On New Year's Eve! The cold-blooded treachery of it! They expected me to be there! It was an attack on *me*— but it was also an attack on the heart and soul of Rapture.

Our most accomplished men and women were in that room, Bill, celebrating the new year. And at least six constables betrayed us! We're lucky Pat Cavendish acted quickly—he shot most of the treasonous scum. But, by God, we must root out any other bad apples."

He sounded bitter—but rational. Lately, Bill suspected that there was something twisted growing in Andrew Ryan . . .

Bill and Ryan sat alone in his office, Bill wishing someone were here to back him up. He had to say something Ryan wasn't going to like.

Shifting in his chair, Bill rubbed his deeply bruised arm where the explosion had knocked the cart into him. His ears still rang a bit; Elaine was haunted by nightmares. "Mr. Ryan—this attack didn't come out of the blue. It's because you took out Fontaine. It's a reaction to that, really. People are saying Rapture doesn't mean what it used to—nationalizing a business . . . by force! It gave them the excuse to go a bit mad! That Atlas took the opportunity—lit the fuse of the whole bloody thing . . ."

Ryan snorted. "It's *not* nationalization. I own most of Rapture anyway. I built it! I simply—acted for the best interests of the city! Atlas is just another babbling 'Pravda,' a tissue of lies he calls truth! If we let him take hold here, he'll be another Stalin! The man wants to be dictator! If it's war—why then so be it!"

"Mr. Ryan—I don't think it's a war we can win. It's the math! Atlas just has *too many* of them rogue splicers. And too many rebels with him. We need to broker some kind of peace deal, guv—Rapture can't take a revolution! This city is *underwater,* Mr. Ryan! It's in the North Sea! It's sitting on channels of hot lava! All of that is . . . oh, crikey, it's *volatile.* We're dying the death of a thousand cuts from leaks already—but one major leak in the wrong part of Hephaestus, and we could have a hell of an explosion. Suppose some of that icy water

contacts the hot lava, in a pressurized area? The whole thing
would go up! All this fighting risks exactly that kind of damage!"

Ryan looked at him, his gaze suddenly flat. His voice was
flatter as he said, "And what do you suggest we offer them?"
He closed his eyes and visibly shuddered. *"Unions?"*

"No, guv—a lot of these blokes worked for Fontaine. The
others just want the ADAM. Crave it. Let's hand over Fontaine Futuristics to Atlas's lot. It's not right to go against our
principles—to nationalize, Mr. Ryan. We can take the high
road, show 'em we stand for something! We can go back to
the way we were and give up Fontaine Futuristics!"

"Give them . . . ?" Ryan shook his head in disbelief. "Bill—
men died to take over the plasmids industry! They will not
have died in vain."

Bill didn't believe for a moment that Ryan was concerned
about who'd died in vain. That was just an excuse. Andrew
Ryan wanted the plasmids industry. It was in his nature. He
was a tycoon. And the plasmids industry was the biggest
prize in this toy store.

"Ryan Industries owns Fontaine Futuristics now," Ryan
went on. "For the good of the city. In due time, I'll break it up.
But I'm not going to give it to that murdering parasite Atlas!"

"Mr. Ryan—we've got to stop this war. It'll destroy us
all . . . there's no place to retreat to! If we won't make peace
with them—well, if that's the case, I'll have to submit my
resignation from the council."

Ryan looked at him sadly. "So you're walking out on me
too. The one man I trusted . . . betraying me!"

"I've got to show you how strongly I feel about this—we've
got to make peace! It's not just Atlas—suppose he makes a
deal with Sofia Lamb? Her people are fanatics. Now she's
broken out, she's twice as dangerous! Her mad little cult'll
have a go at us too! We have to stop this war, Mr. Ryan!"

Ryan slammed a fist onto the desk so hard the room echoed with it. "The war can be stopped by *winning it*! It can be won with superior might, Bill! We can do more and better splicing, use pheromones, keep control of our splicers . . . and have an unstoppable army of superhuman beings! We have the labs—oh yes, we're short on ADAM now, it's true." He cracked his knuckles. "The Little Sisters we have left can't produce enough ADAM. But there's ADAM out there—in all those bodies. It lives on after the splicer dies! It can be harvested, Bill! And the Little Sisters are ideal for harvesting it. We can make this war work for us! War can be *opportunity* as well as catastrophe!"

Bill stared at him.

Ryan flapped his hand in dismissal. "It's written on your face, Bill. You've left me. You've always been loyal. But I'm afraid you will be a disappointment—like so many others. So many who've turned their backs on the grand vision. So many who've betrayed Rapture. Who've *soiled* the glorious thing I've built with my two hands." He shook his head. "The future of the world . . . betrayed!"

Bill knew he'd better turn this around, fast, if he hoped to ever see Elaine again. He could see that in Andrew Ryan's eyes. Ryan had only to call Karlosky or one of his other men and give the order, and he'd be in a cell. They might have lost control of Persephone, but there was always a lockup to be found, or an air lock to be thrown out of.

He let out a long, slow breath—and then nodded. "You're right, Mr. Ryan. I reckon I did lose faith. I'll . . ." He licked his lips. Hoped he was playing this right. "I'll give it a lot of thought. We'll find a way." He almost believed it himself.

Ryan leaned back in his chair and frowned, looking at him closely. But Bill could see Ryan wanted to believe him. He was a lonely man. He trusted few people.

"Very well, Bill. I need you. But you need to understand—

we're *here* now, in Rapture, and we're committed. And we're going to do this my way. I *built* Rapture. I'll do whatever I have to—but I will not let the parasites tear down what I have built."

Banker's Row, near Apollo Square
1959

Oh bloody hell, thought Bill McDonagh, seeing Anna Culpepper standing near the largest of Rapture's banks, up ahead. Bill was walking along beside Andrew Ryan that frightened morning—and he knew what Mr. Ryan would think when he heard her singing. He'd heard her, once, himself, warbling in her new role as protest songstress—amazed that she'd gone from taking part in the council to condemning Ryan Enterprises for the new economic depression gnawing at Rapture's soul . . .

Anna was standing on the street corner, singing to the frantic crowd, acoustic guitar in her hands. The overhead lamp flashed a golden glint from her earrings and played across her curly black hair.

"While Rome burns, she fiddles," Ryan growled, as Bill followed him down the passageway to within a few yards of the crowd surging around the First Bank of Rapture. Karlosky and two other bodyguards, big men in long coats, carrying Thompsons, were walking a couple of paces in front of Ryan. Two others followed. The memory of the New Year's Eve attack was still fresh.

Each wall along the passageway had its line of muttering, scowling customers, most of them men in work clothes or rumpled suits, clutching paperwork and shifting from foot to foot as if they were in a long line for a urinal. A wispy-haired man in frayed seersucker was peering over the shoulders of the people in front of him, trying to see into the bank, shouting past a cupped hand through the open door. "Come on, come on, we want our money; stop stalling in there!"

There were murmurs when Ryan walked up. A few glared his way and elbowed one another, but no one wanted to be the first to confront him.

"You could shut the bank down, just temporary-like, Mr. Ryan," Bill suggested in a whispered aside. "I mean—just for now, for a few days, till the hysteria's over, and we can reassure people . . ."

"No," Ryan said firmly as the bodyguards encircled him, facing outward, guns pointed at the ceiling—but ready to drop their gun muzzles on the crowd should it rush Andrew Ryan. "No, Bill—that would be interfering with the market. The fools have the right to withdraw their money."

"But a run on banks, guv—could be disastrous . . ."

"It already is. And they'll pay the price. The resulting market correction will send them scuttling for cover like rats from a hailstorm. I just wanted to know if it was true—see it with my own eyes. I can't interfere."

"We could try and talk to them right here . . ."

Ryan snorted. "Useless. I'll address them on radio, try and talk sense. But there's no use reasoning with a mob."

Karlosky turned and spoke in low tones with Ryan, out the side of his mouth. "Let's get you out of here, Mr. Ryan . . ."

"Yes, yes, we'll go . . ." But Ryan lingered, staring at the gathering crowd, people stalking from the banks counting fistfuls of Rapture dollars as they went, more men rushing up the street, eager to withdraw their money. Word had gotten out that the war with Atlas and the splicers was going to destroy the banks, somehow—that they'd be targeted by the subversives. Bill wondered if Atlas himself had spread that rumor, deliberately sparking the run on the banks. A depression gave him a propaganda victory.

Ryan's presence had quieted the crowd a little—the shouting and muttering had dropped to a droning murmur, and Bill could hear Anna Culpepper singing now. Something about Cohen—how "Ryan's songbird" was really "Ryan's stableboy."

"I've heard about this Communist versifying," Ryan said to Bill, with acid quietness, glowering at Culpepper. "Union songs, organizers singing 'folk music' about the workingman. As if a Red had even a passing acquaintance with working!"

Anna had spotted Ryan now—and Bill could see she was nervous. Her voice faltered as she looked at the armed bodyguards. But she licked her lips and resumed singing. Bill had to admire her courage.

"So Anna's turned against me," Ryan said. "I'd heard something of the sort. But to go this far . . . singing a musical score for a run on the banks! I suppose she thought she'd find sheep for Atlas's flock here. Or perhaps she's gone over to the other sheep—the Lamb cult . . ." He shook his head in disgust. "I've seen enough. Let's get out of here. I'll see to it the little Red bird stops singing . . ."

Ryan Plasmids
1959

The little girl watched, big eyed, as the enormous metal man lumbered clankingly around the room, the sensors on its round metal head glowing. It was only a remote-controlled model, really—there was no man inside it. Brigid Tenenbaum puppeted the clanking caricature of a deep-sea diver around the room from a control panel overlooking the training area. She had to be careful not to misdirect the Big Daddy model—it could run over the little girl like a freight train.

Subject 13 was a small blond child in a pink pinafore, her large azure eyes fixed on the Big Daddy. It was all part of the conditioning process—the girl had been treated with a drug that made her more susceptible to bonding with the creature that would be her guardian in the dangerous urban wilderness Rapture had become.

"He's big and strong," the little girl chirped. "He's *funny* too!"

"Yes," Brigid said. "He is your big funny friend."

"Can I play with him?" The child's voice was a little fuzzy from the drug.

"Certainly . . ." Brigid made the Big Daddy model come to a sudden stop.

Then she moved a lever, causing its right arm to lift, its hand to outstretch—reaching out to the little girl.

There was something about the sight that stabbed Brigid Tenenbaum to the core . . .

18

Hurrying out of the passage from the Metro, Diane Mc-Clintock once more felt lost—though in fact she'd come here for a reason. She was here to find Atlas. Even so, she was overcome with a sensation of insubstantiality, of being a mere ghost wandering a palace.

And then, near the blockade at the entrance into Apollo Square, something caught her eye . . . a poster plastered to the metal wall.

It asked, *Who is Atlas?*

Just those three words, under a stylized, heroic image of a stoic, confident, clean-shaven man in rolled-up shirtsleeves and suspenders, fists on his hips, gazing with visionary intensity into the workingman's future . . .

The one time she'd seen him, outside the café, he'd seemed like an ordinary man—good-looking, sturdy, but ordinary. And yet he was doing an extraordinary thing—risking Ryan's constables by engaging in flagrant altruism.

At the very least, Atlas must be a charismatic man. Someone who could inspire her—end her feeling of aimlessness . . .

She turned to the bearded sentry cradling a shotgun at the blockade—a burly, unshaven man in a work shirt and oil-spotted blue jeans. "Listen—could you tell me . . . I saw him, once—in Pauper's Drop. Atlas. He was passing out supplies. I'd . . . I'd like to talk to him. Maybe I could help. When I saw him in Pauper's Drop, I just . . ." She shook her head. "I *felt* something."

The sentry looked at her as if deciding whether or not she was sincere. Then he nodded. "I know what you mean. But I don't know as I can trust you . . ."

Diane looked around to see if anyone was watching—then she took a wad of Rapture dollars out of her purse. "Please. This is all I could get hold of today. I'll pay my way in. But I have to see him."

He looked at the money, swallowed hard—then he reached out, grabbed it, and hid it in an inside coat pocket. "Hold up right here . . ."

The bearded sentry turned and called out to another, older sentry. They spoke in low tones; the bearded sentry turned and winked at her. The older guard hurried off. The sentry went back to his post, whistling to himself. With one hand he gestured to her: *wait*. Then he pretended not to see her.

Had she thrown away her bribe? Maybe she'd thrown away her life—spider splicers watched Apollo Square from high up on the walls. It was nippy, unevenly lit in Apollo Square tonight, and there were dead men rotting not so far away. The smell made her feel sick. She was still slightly drunk, the space around her whirling ever so slowly, and she thought she might throw up if she had to smell the dead bodies much longer.

But she wasn't leaving. She was going to stick around till the splicers got her—or she got in to see Atlas.

If Ryan didn't want her, she'd decided, maybe someone else would.

A woman hurried up to the barricade. "Atlas says okay, he'll see you, McClintock," said the woman. Diane tried not to stare at the woman's scarred face—one of her eyesockets was covered over by scar tissue; her brown hair was matted. "Philo, you come on in with us."

The shotgun-toting Philo nodded and gestured at Diane with the muzzle of the gun. "You go in ahead of me."

Diane thought about backing out—but she stepped through the scrap-wood gate and followed them across Apollo Square to Artemis Suites. The one-eyed woman stepped over a low pile of trash in the doorway. Diane followed her into the reeking interior of the building.

Stomach lurching as she picked her way through moldy garbage, Diane entered a stairway that zigzagged up a graffiti-tagged concrete and steel shaft. They climbed four stories up, past drunks and groups of grubby children.

Her escorts took her through a doorway and down a carpeted, burn-scarred hall. The little bushy-haired woman never hesitated, and Philo clumped along behind Diane. The lights flickered again.

"Lights might go out," Philo remarked, his voice a slow rumble. "Ryan's turned the power off in the building. We got some jerry-rigged, but it ain't reliable."

"I got a flashlight," the woman said. They came to another stairway, and, to Diane's bafflement, this time they went down. This stairway was relatively clean, occupied only by the occasional bored sentry scratching himself and nodding as they passed.

Down and down they went, farther down than they'd gone up . . . down to a subbasement passageway.

Here, they passed under steam-shrouded pipes, their feet splashing through puddles, till they came to a small antechamber with a high, water-dripping ceiling. A Securis door was guarded by a grinning, shivering splicer in a ratty sweater and torn trousers, toes sticking out of his decaying shoes. He had the hard-core splicer's red scrofula on his face, and he juggled three scythelike fish-gutting blades from hand to hand. The curved blades hissed close to the naked lightbulb on the ceiling, missing it by no more than a quarter inch.

"Who's the extra bitch, tittle-tattle tits?" the splicer asked in a scratchy voice, never pausing in juggling the blades.

"McClintock. Atlas says she can go in."

"Says you, tittle-tattle tits—we'll fry your bits if that ain't it! Ha! Go ahead on in!"

The splicer stepped aside, still juggling, and "tittle-tattle tits" opened the Securis door for them. Diane hurried through, eager to get past the splicer.

They were in a lamplit utility area. Pipes and heating ducts came up through the floor near the walls. The room was warm and smelled of cigarette smoke and mildew and brine.

The cigarette was being smoked by a muscular man seated casually behind a battered gray-metal desk. On the desk was a tumbler and a gold cigarette box.

It was he. The man she'd seen outside the café. He wore white, rolled-up shirtsleeves, just like in the poster. A good face, she thought, that seemed to emanate trustworthiness.

Two shaggy bodyguards stood behind him, near a ganglion of valves. Both bodyguards wore coveralls and carried tommy guns. One of them had an unlit pipe dangling from the corner of his mouth.

"I'd be Atlas," said the man at the desk, with an Irish lilt, looking her over with an unsettling frankness. "And you're one of Ryan's birds?"

"I'm Diane McClintock. I work . . . I *worked* . . . for Mr. Ryan. I saw you helping people in Pauper's Drop—and it touched me. I don't feel good about the way things are going and . . . I just wanted to see if . . . to see if . . ." What was it she wanted, exactly?

He smiled impishly. "You don't seem certain of what you're wanting to see, Miss McClintock."

She sighed and unconsciously brushed her hair into place with her hand. "I'm tired. Had a few drinks. But . . . I want to know more about you—I mean, you know, in a friendly way.

I don't work with the constables. I've seen things. Heard stories . . . I don't know what to believe anymore . . . I just know—once I was passing by Apollo Square and I saw a woman come over the barricades and . . . one of the splicers working for Andrew . . ." She didn't like to remember it. The woman hurrying along, full of life, one moment. The next, a splicer had sent a ball of fire into her—and she'd sizzled away into a blackened corpse, within steps of where Diane stood. "Well the splicer burned her. And the look on her face . . . like she was trying to tell me something. So tonight . . ." She sighed. "I don't know. I'm just so tired right now . . ."

"Get the lady a chair, you great ejit," Atlas growled at Philo.

Without a word, Philo brought a metal chair from a corner, and Diane sat down. Atlas pushed the gold box across the desk toward her.

"Cigarette?"

"I'd adore one." She opened the box and took a cigarette, her hands trembling. Philo lit it for her, and she inhaled gratefully, then blew the silken smoke into the air. "This—this is a real cigarette! Virginia tobacco! And in a gold box! You do yourself well for a revolutionary . . ."

Atlas chuckled. "Oh, aye. But we took that from one of Ryan's little storerooms under Rapture. Sure, he brought it in to sell in a little shop—a shop I used to sweep out, once upon a time. I was maintenance, a janitor in Rapture—come here when they sang me a pretty lie—a promise of working in me trade. Ended up a janitor. And later—couldn't find work doing even that."

"What was your trade, before?"

"Why, I was a metal worker." He stubbed out his cigarette—his fingers looked pale and soft for a workingman. "As for what we took from that storeroom—we distributed most of it to the people. How do you think people eat round 'ere, with Ryan, the great son of Satan himself, cutting off supplies to Artemis, eh?"

She nodded. "He's talked about an amnesty for people who give up the . . . what does he call it, the Bolshevik organizing."

"Bolshevik organizing! So we're Soviets now! Asking for a fair break is hardly that!"

She tapped the cigarette over an ashtray on the desk. "Any sort of 'break' is pinko stuff to Andrew." She sniffed. "I'm fed up with him. But I've got no reason to love you people either. You can see what you did to me." She touched the scars on her cheek.

He shook his head sadly. "You were hurt in the fight, were you? A bomb? You're still a fine-looking woman, so you are. You were too strong to die there. Why, you've gotten *character* from it, that's all that's come about, Diane."

He looked at her with that disarming frankness. And she wanted to believe in him.

"Why do you call yourself Atlas? It's not your real name."

"Figure that out on your own, did you?" He grinned. "Welllll . . . Atlas takes the world on his shoulders. He's the broad back, ain't he? And who's the workingman? The workingman takes the world on his broad back too. Holds it up for the privileged—for the likes of you!"

He opened a drawer and, to her astonishment, took out a bottle of what looked like actual Irish whiskey. Jameson. "Care for hair of the dog, mebbe? Philo—find us some glasses . . ."

They drank and talked, of politics and fairness and organizing and reappropriation of goods for the working class. "And you think you're the liberator of the working class, Atlas?"

"I am not a liberator. Liberators do not exist. That's the only thing Ryan was right about. These people will liberate themselves! But they do need someone to tell them that it can be done." He toyed with his glass. Then he said, "You know about the Little Sisters, do you? What they do to them poor little orphan waifs?"

"I've heard . . . Yes, it bothers me, if that's what you're wondering."

He poured her a third drink. "Sure, and it should bother you," he said solemnly, lighting another cigarette. "It should cut you up inside! I've got a little girl meself, you know. The thought of them bastards mebbe getting hold of that child! Oh, the thought! But will it stop anyone from buying ADAM? No. Rapture can't go on like this, Diane, me dear. This cannot go on . . ."

It didn't take long for her to make up her mind. It wasn't the whiskey, or the cigarettes, or that strong chin, or those frank brown eyes, or the pungent opinions. It was thinking about going back to her place alone—and waiting to hear from Andrew Ryan.

No. Never again.

"Atlas," she said, "I'd like to help."

"And why would I believe Ryan hasn't sent you here, on the sly, like, will you tell me that now?"

"I'll show you—I'm no spy. I'll do things he would never approve of. And then . . . you'll know you can trust me."

Ryan Plasmids
1959

The odd little chamber, partly cold steel-walled lab and partly nursery, was chilly today. Drips of cold water slipped from a rusty bolt in the ceiling in a far corner. Brigid had told maintenance about the leak, but so far no one had come to fix it.

Subject 15 didn't mind—the little girl played contentedly with the drip as Brigid watched, the girl seeming to delight in this tiny little invasion of the gigantic sea into her cell. Squatting in the corner, the child tried to catch each drop as it came down. She giggled when she caught one . . .

Brigid sighed. The experiments had been going well; the attachment conditioning was working. But she felt heavier every day—as if she were carrying some hidden burden. She was beginning to feel like a Big Daddy herself, as if she too were sheathed in metal. That thought reminded Brigid—it was time.

She went to the door, opened it, took the remote control from her lab-coat pocket, and pointed the device at the hulking gray-metal figure waiting, dormant, in the corridor. Somewhere inside that metal armor was what remained of a man, who was now in a sort of comatose state, waiting for the stimuli to awaken . . . but never completely awaken. He would always be little more than a machine.

She pressed the button on the remote, and the Big Daddy responded instantly, turning with a creak, coming with clanging steps into the conditioning lab.

"Ooh!" Subject 15 chirped, clasping her wet hands together with delight when she saw the Big Daddy. "Mr. Bubbles is here!"

Brigid Tenenbaum watched as Subject 15 walked—almost like a sleepwalker—to the Big Daddy. The little girl clasped its metal hand and gazed up at it, smiling uncertainly . . .

And suddenly, for the first time in many years, Brigid Tenenbaum remembered.

She's a girl, once more, in Belorussia, watching the Nazis take her father away. It is before the war, but they are removing troublemakers. The Nazi officer in charge of the platoon turns his gray-eyed gaze on her. He is a big, craggy-faced man wearing a helmet, his hands in heavy gloves; he wears a glossy leather belt, a strap across his chest, and high, polished boots; he glints with shiny buttons and medals. He says, "Little one—you can be of use. First in the kitchens, working. In time, you go to the camps . . . Experimental subjects are needed . . ." He reaches out to her. She stares up at him, thinking he's more like a machine than a man. Her father took her to a silent movie in which she saw a man of metal, stalking about. This officer is a man of metal in a uniform, metal clothed in flesh.

She knows she'll never see her father again. She will be alone. And this man is reaching out to her. Something closes up in her heart. She thinks, *I must make friends with the metal men* . . .

She reaches out and clasps the gloved hand.

And now, in Rapture, Brigid Tenenbaum shuddered, remembering the little girl that she was . . . and the woman she became. Even before that day, she'd been distant from people; she'd always had a hard time connecting. But she'd kept a door in herself open a crack. It was at that moment, clasping that officer's hand, that she closed the door that she'd always kept open for her family. She would simply survive . . .

Now, Brigid stood there, staring at Subject 15, and the model of the Big Daddy. Subject 15—another child conditioned to attach herself to a machine. Metal men, clothed in flesh—and in Rapture, metal men, enclosing flesh. Subject 15 was a child twisted, her childlike nature distorted, for Rapture's purposes—a child so much like the little girl Brigid had been.

Brigid shuddered. "Not this one," she whispered. "No more . . ."

She felt herself turned inside out, as she said it. Feelings geysered up in her, seething in her heart. She was once more a child—and she would become a mother. She would be a mother with many adopted children. She could no longer treat these children as experimental subjects.

She went to the child and embraced her. "I am sorry," she said, tears streaming down her cheeks. "I'm so sorry."

Mercury Suites
1959

"What is the difference between a man and a parasite?" The words came over the public-address system, reverberating

from the metal walls as Bill walked down the hall to Sullivan's place. A camera swiveled to watch him as he came.

"*A man builds,*" came Andrew Ryan's recorded voice. "*A parasite asks, 'Where is my share?' A man creates. A parasite says, 'What will the neighbors think?' A man invents. A parasite says, 'Watch out or you might tread on the toes of God.'*"

Bill was beginning to think the "parasite" might be right about that last one.

He knocked on the apartment door, and Sullivan himself opened it. The security chief glanced past him to make sure he was alone, then nodded. "Come on in."

Bill could smell the booze on Sullivan's breath, and the chief of security's gait was unsteady as he walked away from the door. Bill followed him in and closed the door. Sullivan's place was laid out pretty much like his own, but it was sparer—bachelor furnishings. And there was another feature, a good many "dead soldiers," empty bottles on tables and desks, even the carpet.

Sullivan sat on the sofa, shoving an empty bottle out of the way to put a tape recorder down on the coffee table. Bill sat beside him. To their left was a big picture window into the undersea-scape. The building creaked in the current. A school of yellow-finned fish cruised by and suddenly changed direction, all of them at once darting away from the building's lights with that mysterious unanimity they had.

"Drink?" Sullivan asked, his voice lifeless. His eyes were red-rimmed. It looked like he hadn't slept in a while.

It was early for Bill, not yet five, but he didn't want to seem like he was judging Sullivan. "Just a finger or two of whatever's in that bottle there, mate."

Sullivan poured it into a glass that hadn't been clean in a long while, and Bill picked it up. "What's all the rush and worry, Chief? Urgent notes from you popping out of the pneumo and all. I had to cut work early to get here on time."

Sullivan turned to look at an unfinished red-and-black knitted blanket folded beside him on the sofa. He reached out with his free hand and caressed it, lips trembling. Then he tossed off his drink and put the glass down on the coffee table with a *clack*. "Ryan's starting his little propaganda campaign, to make the Little Sisters thing seem all hunky-dory. Using kids to farm plasmids. That going to be hunky-dory with you, Bill?"

"Christ no. I don't like plasmids—don't like 'em double when they get 'em that way. Ryan says it's only temporary, and what do you do with the orphans anyway, but . . ." He shook his head. "It can't go on forever. Things are falling apart—the city and . . . the people. The whole place will come apart at the seams if we don't . . ."

He broke off, wondering, suddenly, if he was being a fool, talking something close to sedition to Ryan's chief of security. Was all this a setup? But Sullivan had been unhappy with his job for a long time, and he'd made Bill a kind of confidante. You had to trust someone sometime. And he knew Chief Sullivan, after all these years. Sullivan wasn't much of an actor. Especially when he was drunk. This was for real.

"It's *already* come apart at the seams, Bill," Sullivan said slurringly. "I've got some recordings here—I've put them all on one tape. But they came from different times, different people . . ." He pressed the Play button on the tape recorder. "I want your opinion about this, Bill. You're the only son of a bitch I trust in this waterlogged city . . ."

The tape recorder played a guitar strumming a mocking little tune, someone whistling along in the background. A gentle drumbeat led the way to singing that Bill recognized as Anna Culpepper's voice.

"Ryan drew us in, Ryan locked us in
And Sander Cohen kept us hypnotized—

Andrew kept us thin, all for a whim,
And Sander Cohen kept us mesmerized—
With silly songs and watered drinks
And dance-dance-dancing
With silly blonds and makeup winks
All flounce-flounce-flouncing . . ."

It went on in that vein, in Culpepper's languid, teasing voice. When Sullivan hit Pause, Bill shrugged and said, "Well, what about it, Chief? I've heard this kind of daft thing before. She's swanned out of Ryan Industries and been hanging around McDonagh's, if truth be told, drinking and trying to be clever with her friends, sniping at Ryan. Songs like that are right popular with some about Rapture, but they don't sing 'em too loud."

Sullivan snorted. "You don't think it deserves . . . punishment?"

"Why? Just a song, innit?"

"'Kay, how about this?" Sullivan started the tape again. This time it was Anna Culpepper just talking. *"Cohen's not a musician, he's Ryan's stable boy. Ryan's corrupt policies crap all over the place, and Cohen flutters around, clearing it up. But instead of using a shovel, like you would with a proper mule, Cohen tidies with a catchy melody and a clever turn of phrase. But no matter how nicely it sounds, he can't really do anything about the smell."*

He paused it again, poured himself another drink, and, voice slurring even more, asked, "Whuh yuh think about that one, eh?"

"Hmm, well . . . got to admit it's pretty inflammatory, like, Chief. But them arty types will talk and talk—and talk. Don't mean much."

"You know what—listen to this . . . This is one of the guys we had to raid recently. He ducked us, and I'm glad of it, 'tween you and me, Bill . . . It's from before Fontaine went down . . ." He hit Play, and Bill heard a voice he thought was Peach Wilkins.

"We all come down here, figured we'd be part of Ryan's Great Chain. Turns out Ryan's chain is made of gold, and ours are the sort with the big iron ball around your ankle. He's up in Fort Frolic banging fashion models . . . we're down in this dump yanking guts outta fish. Fontaine's promising something better."

"Sounds like that Atlas rabble-rouser," Bill remarked. "Different voice, same ideas."

"Now, listen to this, one, Bill," Sullivan said. "This is the same guy, a bit later on."

"Fontaine's putting the screws on us and double. He's squeezing us out of eighty points of our cut with the threat of turning us in to Ryan if we don't play ball. Son of a bitch! Sammy G. comes and tells me he's thinking of going to the constable, and the next day, Sammy G. was found in a sack in the salt pond. We got no choice here."

He stopped the tape and poured himself another drink, swaying in his seat. "You see, Bill? Do you see?"

"Not exactly, Chief . . ."

"See, first they get pulled into Rapture. Like you did—like I did. Then they find out it's not all it's cracked up to be if you're not one of the big shots. Then Fontaine drags them into his *own* little 'chain.' They want out when that turns bad too—and what happens? Some of 'em start turning up dead. So what can they do? They got stuck working for Fontaine! And what happens? Ryan sends us in to catch them. Hang them for smuggling! For something they were trapped into!"

"I don't know if that was their only choice, Chief. But I see what you mean."

"And then there's that Persephone."

Bill winced. "Hate the thought of that place. Been afraid I'd end up there myself."

"Lamb's taken over that whole part of Rapture—made Persephone her base. Who gave her that base? Ryan, is who. Torturing people to find Lamb's followers . . . that just created more followers for Lamb."

"Torture? I never knew about that . . ."

"He didn't want you to know, Bill. To catch some of 'em— the Persephone Reds, the smugglers—Ryan not only used torture, he personally supervised at least one session I know of, with Pat Cavendish doing the dirty work."

"Torture!" Bill's stomach twisted at the thought. "You sure, Chief?"

"Oh yeah! I had to clean up the mesh . . . the mess. Well— maybe they had it comin'. *Maybe*. But this girl, this Culpepper, all she did was bitch 'n' moan. Or sing if you wanta call it that. Sang another funny, stupid little tune about that loony tune, Sander Cohen. You wanta know how much a loony tune he is? Listena thish . . ." He started the recorder playing once more.

Sander Cohen's distinctly demented voice minced through a recitation:

"Ahem. The Wild Bunny by Sander Cohen: I want to take the ears off, but I can't. I hop, and when I hop, I never get off the ground. It's my curse, my eternal curse! I want to take the ears off, but I can't! It's my curse, my fucking curse! I want to take the ears off! Please! Take them off! Please . . . !"

"Right," Bill said, when it ended. "We already knew the bloke was eccentric, Chief . . ."

"Eccentric? He's a *murderer*! Gone nuts on ADAM. Kills people for fun over there in the Fleet Hall. Pastes their bodies up with cement, makes them into statues for display, in his back room."

Bill stared. "You're pulling me leg."

"No. No I'm not. Like to lock him up. But Ryan insists Cohen's an ally . . ." He shook his head miserably.

"Ryan's protecting him?"

"Cohen whined about Culpepper's songs making fun of him. Said they were subjecting Ryan to ridicule too. Sent over tapes of it. Ryan went a bit mad himself . . ."

"Not taking ADAM, is he?"

"Ryan? No—he's getting into the gin. Stays cool sometimes. Paranoid other times. Two days sober, one half-drunk. Not a good pattern. I know it too well."

Bill licked his lips. His mouth was suddenly dry. "No excuse for protecting Cohen if he's really a murderer . . ." He took a long pull on the whiskey Sullivan had given him and scarcely tasted it.

"So me having to protect that little prick Cohen," Sullivan growled, "that extends to Ryan giving me orders to . . ." His voice broke. He reached over and picked up the red-and-black knit blanket. Clutched it to his chest. "Pretty, isn't it? When I was done with her, I left her as she was, in the bathroom, naked in the tub . . ."

Bill stared. "What you mean—when you were *done* with her?"

Sullivan closed his eyes, clutching the blanket to him, the sudden motion spilling his drink on his lap. "I seen she had a half-knitted blanket by her bed. It was nice. You know, black and red, real pretty. So I took it . . . Just didn't seem right to leave it lying there, all by itself . . ."

Bill finished his drink. Thought maybe he should get out of here—while Sullivan let him. But at last he asked, "Chief—are you saying that Ryan sent you to kill Anna Culpepper?"

Sullivan looked at the blanket. After a long moment, he nodded. "In her bath. Pushed her under the water . . . Her eyes, Bill—her eyes staring at me through the water . . . as I

held her under . . . when the bubbles come up, I was thinking: *there goes her life!* You know? Her life all bubblin' up from
her mouth! Just like the bubbles that come up outside that
window . . . see 'em?"

"Oh *Jay*-sus, Chief, that's . . ." Bill took a long, deep, ragged
breath. Not sure what to say. He almost felt like he ought
to comfort Sullivan. *Sorry you went through that.* But you
couldn't say that to a murderer. "Chief—I've got to get back to
my wife. This is . . . it's too late to do anything about it. We
have to . . . to let it go. And I want you to know, it's all safe
with me, mate. What you said."

"Oh—I can't let it go," Sullivan said, his eyes closed, voice
barely audible. "I'm going to Neptune's Bounty. Find a soft
spot and . . ."

Bill got up, backed away from him—then hurried to the
door. And left without another word.

Ryan Plasmids
1959

Fully dressed, Brigid Tenenbaum lay on her cot, staring at
the steel wall. She knew she would not sleep that night. She
kept seeing their faces . . . gazing up at the metal men, ador-
ingly . . .

The Little Sisters. Their large, dark, trusting eyes . . . She
could not bear it anymore. The way they would lovingly climb
into her lap—the cruelty of their innocence.

She must act—she must find relief. She could run away,
hide alone in some corner of Rapture. There was that old
maintenance dorm she'd found. But hiding there, alone,
wouldn't work—their eyes, their faces would pursue her.
There would be no hiding from them.

No. The only way was to set them free from this place.
Then she would no longer feel their pain—their release would
be hers . . .

Now was as good a time as any. The sentries had been gathering out front late at night, and it would be necessary to shut off the cameras and bots. But she knew just how to do that. She would find some way to get past the fourth man, later. Perhaps she might have to kill him.

Brigid reached under her bunk and found the bottle of vodka. She'd bought it from Karlosky, but it hadn't really helped smother the cruel feelings of caring for the children that had arisen in her. She'd given up after half a bottle.

Which left half a bottle . . .

She opened the labelless bottle, took a mouthful, swished it around, then spat it out onto her lab coat. She got her keys from the hook on the wall and then went out into the hallway. A security camera swiveled toward her and sent a bot from its cabinet to look at her. It registered her DNA-detection flasher, circled her once, and then whirred back to its container. She kept on down the hallway, made a stop in lab 16, then came back out into the corridor—and stopped dead. Two sentries were scowling at her, blocking the way with shotguns in their hands.

The tall, sallow-faced guard in the overalls was Rolf. She didn't know the squat one with the bad teeth. He had a constable badge pinned upside down on an old military coat.

"What you doing wandering 'round; this ain't your work time, lady," Rolf asked, squinting at her suspiciously.

Brigid blinked at them, swaying in what she hoped was a good simulation of drunkenness. "Could not sleep. Lonely. Thinking maybe I will make myself pretty to visit you. Maybe I will take a shower, yes? Maybe you join me in shower, eh?"

Rolf's mouth dropped open—nothing had ever surprised him more. But she could see he wanted to believe it.

The short one scratched his matted hair. "Well now . . . you mean . . . just Rolf here?"

"Oh no, plenty room for everyone; we take turns, yes?"

Pretending to swig the vodka, she turned to point at the showers, at the far end of the hall.

She turned back and grinned at them with bleary inebriation. "You take bottle and wait there, eh? I will make myself pretty . . ."

"Oh no, too many cameras . . ." Rolf began. "If someone checks . . ."

"I will turn them off!" Brigid insisted, waving the problem away. "It is nothing!"

"What's a-going on down here?" called a redheaded man, with a tommy gun in one hand, a flashlight in the other. He came stalking down the hall, lower lip thrust out disapprovingly. But his expression changed, became sheer lust, when he saw the bottle in her hand. Not lust for her . . .

"Is that . . . wine?"

Brigid shook her head at him. "No. Much stronger. You want?" She thrust the bottle into his grasp. "You take the vodka to shower; I will take care of cameras. You can share with these boys, yes? We have a small party." She wagged a finger at them. "But you must not be naughty boys in shower!" She turned away, laughing, and staggered away in the direction of the autosecurity control panels . . .

She heard them walking off, muttering, toward the showers. Rolf saying, "I dunno . . . maybe just a drink or two, but there's no way we . . ."

She used the combination lock, switched off the security cameras and bots, and then went to check the showers. It was already done. The overwhelming dose of sleeping powder she'd put in the vodka had done its work, and quickly. All three sentries were sprawled snoring on the floor. She unloaded two of the shotguns, taking the shells, and then carried the third shotgun away with her.

She got the leather tote bag she needed, with the equipment for removing the sea slugs and some canned food. She stuffed it all in the bag. The purging device would cause the sea slugs to disintegrate inside the children. They would vomit up the remains.

Brigid hurried down the dimly lit hall to the row of children's cells. She leaned the shotgun against the wall before she let the girls out, not wanting to scare them. She put a finger to her lips, to signify quiet, as she let each one out, and winked.

"Now children," she whispered, as they gathered around her, a diminutive crowd, "we will play a game of quiet—like hide-and-seek. We will get the other girls and then . . ."

"Someone's coming," said one of the moppets.

Brigid heard the heavy footsteps then. Probably the fourth sentry, who stood out in the hallway. "Hey, the system's down!" he called, from around the corner of the corridor.

"Children, we will go back into this nursery, together, all of us, and we'll wait till he goes by—we will trick him!"

The children giggled mischievously, and she hushed them, herding them into the nursery cell. One of them lay on the cot, pretending to be asleep; the others pressed into a corner near the door, squatting in excited silence with Brigid. A few moments more, and then they heard the guard striding by.

"Rolf!" the man called. "Where the hell you got to? The system's down! Christ, if the splicers've got in . . ."

Brigid and the Little Sisters waited another long, slow minute. She guessed it'd be two or three minutes before the fourth sentry found the others sleeping in the showers. There was no time to get any more children out—they were far down the hallway. She'd lose the ones she had if she tried . . .

Heart pounding, Brigid stood up, and whispered, "We must go like ghosts! Quiet as ghosts!"

"The ghosts aren't so quiet," a black-haired Little Sister remarked, twirling the ends of her hair around a finger. "I hear them talking all the time!"

"Then be *quieter* than ghosts! Come on!"

Brigid opened the door and they tiptoed through. She herded them around the hallway corner, toward the front door of the facility. They were almost running when they reached the outer corridor—the cameras out there were still angling inertly down. But that wouldn't last . . .

They got across the anteroom to the Metro just as the alarms went off behind them. But she managed to get all the Little Sisters with her into the bathysphere.

She knew an abandoned dorm that might do for a safehouse. It was a dusty place, almost forgotten now, in a basement corner of the city. There, she could clear the sea slugs from the children and give them a chance to be human beings. They would lose something, but they would gain much more.

And perhaps the cruelty of her maternal instinct would transmute—and pain would become joy.

Rapture Central Control, Ryan's Office
1959

Andrew Ryan hit the Record button on the Acu-Vox and cleared his throat: "I am told that Lamb has been seen in the streets . . . come out of her sanctum in Persephone. Rapture's split up between our territories, the Atlas turf, and Lamb's little group of psychos—my city is schismed." He sighed. "One of the Alpha Series was killed in the incident, and his bonded Sister stolen. But the counsel has no time for a manhunt; Atlas swells the ranks of his marauders by the day. Regardless, Lamb's name has already faded among the people. She is no more than a ghost who has forgotten to die . . ."

A chime came on the desk. He heard Karlosky's voice over the intercom. "Boss? Doctor Suchong is here."

Ryan switched off the tape recorder. "Very good. Send him in."

He opened a desk drawer, drew out the folder containing

Suchong's proposal, and scanned it again as the doctor came padding in. Ryan was distantly aware of Suchong bowing. "Yes . . . sit down." He heard the squeak of Suchong sitting in the chair and went on: "I've looked over this little plan of yours—frankly, Doctor Suchong—frankly, I'm shocked by your proposal." Ryan glanced up from the folder, tented his fingers, closing his eyes as if considering the idea objectively, though in fact he'd already made up his mind. "If we were to modify the structure of our commercial plasmid line as you propose, to make the user vulnerable to mental suggestion—would we not be able to effectively control the actions of citizens of Rapture? Free will is the cornerstone of this city. The thought of sacrificing it is abhorrent."

Suchong, sitting across from Ryan, nodded, somehow conveying apology, disappointing Ryan by acquiescing. He'd hoped Suchong would "talk him into it."

Ryan cleared his throat. "However, . . . we are indeed in a time of war. If Atlas and his bandits have their way, will they not turn us into slaves? And what will become of free will then? Desperate times call for desperate measures. And, after all, if you say Fontaine knew of this sort of thing—then it could be working its way to Atlas. We can't let them get the edge on us, Suchong."

Suchong looked at him attentively. "Then—you approve Suchong's plan? We can proceed with pheromone conditioning?"

"If you can guarantee the splicers respond to me. Not to anyone else."

"Suchong works for Ryan! I will see to it . . ."

"And what does Tenenbaum think? Does she think there might be a means to block this . . . this hormonal control?"

Suchong shrugged. "Suchong . . . think not. But—not sure where she is. Cannot ask."

"What? Why not?"

"You do not know? I assumed guards reported to you! She is . . . gone. Hiding somewhere in Rapture. Took Little Sisters with her."

"No one told me this." Ryan laughed softly and bitterly. "Who got to Tenenbaum? Was she paid to do this? By Atlas?"

"Something bother her for long time, Mr. Ryan."

"Had an attack of conscience, has she?"

Suchong blinked, not knowing what was meant. The English word *conscience* was one he hadn't bothered to learn. "She is . . . troubled female. She says we are harming children, even though we give them immortality! We give them power to always heal! This is harming? Suchong does not think so . . ."

"Ah." Ryan picked up a pencil and flipped it from finger to finger. He was not convinced the Little Sisters were happy little elves working away for Rapture. But—he *was* convinced that ADAM was Rapture's edge on the outside world. Suppose they were ever invaded. KGB, CIA, some other insidious "intelligence" lurkers would infiltrate. Perhaps this new pernicious influence, this Atlas, would bring them. Or some of Lamb's treacherous bunch. She could have been a KGB agent all along. And if they were invaded by the Soviets or the Brits or the USA—then what? Only the extraordinary abilities provided by plasmids could protect Rapture from outsiders. So ADAM must go on. He needed the Little Sisters more than ever.

"If she took any Little Sisters with her, plasmid production will be drastically undercut."

"Yes," Suchong smoothed his greased-back hair thoughtfully. "We will need more . . . 'Little Sisters.'"

"Well, there's no time to wait for more people to . . ." Ryan cleared his throat. "I'll tell Cavendish to see to it we have a few more until . . . something else is worked out." Ryan tossed the pencil on the desk. "As for Brigid Tenenbaum, we shall find her. If *you* betray me, Doctor—I warn you, things will not go well."

Suchong smiled sadly. "I would not respect you, if that were not the case, Mr. Ryan." Suchong bowed. Then he hurried to the door, bent on his mission.

A whisking sound—and Ryan turned to see a small package arrive for him in the pneumatic tube. The handwriting told him it was from Sullivan. He removed it from the tube and opened it. It contained a reel of recording tape and a note in Sullivan's hand:

> *Don't think you'll see me alive again, sir. I plan a quick get-together with a bullet. Can't live with what I done. She had the cutest little red and black blanket. Here's a tape, might clue you in on why Jasmine Jolene moved out. Why she's been ducking you. Owe you that, I guess, Great Man. Now I owe myself something else. A little drinky, a little bye bye.*
>
> *Bye bye, Great Man!*

Ryan stared at the note—then looked at the tape. He was strangely reluctant to listen to it. At last he put it in the tape player, and pressed Play.

19

"I just don't feel comfortable in this park anymore, Bill," Elaine said. "Bodyguards or not."

She and Bill stood on the little bridge, watching the reflected light play in the stream. The cryptic pagan graffiti of the Saturnine cult marked the wood of the little footbridge. They'd seen bullets lying about in the grass—and ADAM syringes.

Bill nodded. "Does seem daft, coming 'ere. Suppose she steps on one of those syringes? What'll that do to her?"

Elaine put her hand to her mouth. "Oh—I hadn't thought of that."

"But—she and Mascha were all atwitter about coming here, love." He slipped his arm around her shoulders. "A few minutes more, and we'll go home, eh?"

He glanced over his shoulder, saw Constable Redgrave and Karlosky, talking a few strides away, each with a shotgun and a pistol. The little girls were playing with the little wooden dolls Sam Lutz had made them over by a boulder, close to the sliding Japanese-style doors, about fifty feet away.

A drumming of propellers caught his attention, and he looked up to see a security bot fly overhead. It whined past, watching for splicers. Arcadia had been cleared of splicers and rebels—at least for the time being. Bill had requested a day with his family in the park, and Ryan had seen to it.

"I just have the worst feeling, Bill," Elaine whispered . . .

Bill sighed, wanting a cigarette. Real tobacco was in short supply. "I know. You're right. I'm going to get us out of here."

"Bill!" Redgrave called, worry in his voice.

Karlosky was already hurrying toward the boulder where the girls had been. They were gone . . .

"Sophie!" Bill shouted. He found himself running after Karlosky. "Redgrave—keep Elaine here!"

"That door—" Karlosky puffed.

Bill saw it then—the sliding door was open. And the girls were nowhere to be seen. His daughter was gone.

Then—there she was. Sophie, stepping through it, alone, tears in her eyes. "Daddy?"

Karlosky ran through the door, calling, "Mascha! Hey kid! Where you go!"

Bill ran to Sophie, swept her up in his arms. "Crikey, I was so worried, love, don't run off like that. Where's Mascha?"

"We heard someone call us—from the tea room! We went through the door, but it was someone I don't know . . . a big man . . . He said she had to go with him—for Rapture!"

"What!" Still holding her, Bill stepped through the door—and saw no one except Karlosky coming back, frowning.

Karlosky shook his head at him. "They're gone."

But there was Mascha's doll, lying on the floor. Its head was snapped off. Bill put Sophie down, placed his hands on her shoulders, and looked tenderly into her eyes. "Did he hurt you, love?" Bill asked, heart sinking as he thought about poor Mascha . . .

Her lips quivered. "I pulled at his arm, and he pushed me down! And I ran away!" And then she burst into tears.

Elaine rushed up, then, crushing Sophie to her, tears of mother and daughter running together.

Redgrave was close behind her—he'd been watching her back. "Bill—where's the other one?" Redgrave asked, looking around.

"Some bastard took her . . ."

He stepped up to Karlosky, drew him aside. "You see anything?"

"Nyet—but I think I heard Cavendish back there."

"Cavendish? I've got to get my wife and girl back to our place. You and Redgrave see if you can find Mascha, will you?"

"We try. But . . ." Karlosky shook his head. "Not much hope."

It seemed to Bill that those three words summed it all up.

Fort Frolic, Rapture
1959

"My daddy's smarter than Einstein, stronger than Hercules, and lights a fire with a snap of his finger! Are you as good as my daddy, Mister? Not if you don't visit the Gatherer's Garden, you aren't! Smart daddies get spliced at the garden!"

The automated voice at the Gatherer's Garden machine, near the entrance to the strip joint where Jasmine worked, seemed to be speaking directly to Andrew Ryan, as if teasing him, mocking him. He ignored it, as well as the startled man taking tickets at the door. He rushed into the strip club, disregarding the swaying woman on the stage.

He beelined right to that backstage door he'd been so familiar with before he'd gotten Jasmine into her luxury apartment . . .

He should have taken her in hand, forced it out of her— not gotten so caught up in other things.

But too late. He kept hearing the tape over and over in his head. *"That creepy Tenenbaum promised me it wasn't gonna be a real pregnancy; they'd just take the egg out once Mr. Ryan and I had . . . I needed the money so bad. But I know Mr. Ryan's gonna suss it out . . . gonna know I wasn't being careful . . . gonna know I sold the . . ."*

Sold his child!

He slammed into the back hallway, down the hall, into the

bedroom where strippers did their "extra" shows for special customers, and there she was, barely dressed, yawning on the wrinkled bedclothes. Jasmine Jolene, looking sleepy. Pretending all was right with them when she saw him come in. Pretending that she was glad to see him.

"I . . . I thought you'd forgotten about me . . ." she squeaked. Forgetting her elocution lessons in her fear. "But I'm so glad you didn't."

"You sold my child! To Tenenbaum! To Fontaine!"

She scrambled away from him. "I'm sorry, Mr. Ryan. I didn't know. I didn't know Fontaine had something to do with it! I . . ."

He couldn't bear to hear the lies coming out of that pretty mouth. He lunged at her, closed his hands over her soft neck.

"What are you doing?" she gasped. "No, no don't! Please! I loved you—don't, please, don't! No, *no!*"

She tried to say something else, but it was cut off, squeezed off by the inexorable pressure of his fingers tightening on her throat. Tighter, squeezing ever tighter, until her pretty eyes fairly popped out of her head . . .

Farmer's Market
1959

A security bot whirred by overhead, making that irritating whistling noise. Ryan and Bill, walking with their escort, glanced up at the bot as it whizzed by, Bill ducking.

He looked over at Elaine and Sophie, browsing together on the other side of the open-stall market. The pale, frightened little man standing behind the hydroponic vegetables rack gave them a hesitant smile. Bill glanced up at another sound—the big security camera above a fruit booth, whirring in its red pool of light to take him in. He wore his ID flasher, so it decided not to tell one of the turrets or bots to kill him.

This was no place to raise a child. Especially when they might come across a dead body at any moment. But Ryan insisted that life go on with as much normality as possible, and he'd pressured Bill to bring his family out on this walk today.

"Come along, Bill . . ." Ryan had said.

Bill had said, "Right, guv'nor, I'll get the Mrs. and the squeaker . . ." But it had taken a lot of talking to get Elaine out of the house with Sophie.

They had Redgrave and Karlosky in front of them, Linosky and Cavendish, each one of them with a machine gun in his hands. Andrew Ryan was the only one without a gun. Ryan carried that fancy walking stick now, what with him getting a bit long in the tooth. He still looked natty and confident—a bit grim, but not too worried.

A lot of men had died in the past few days. Skirmishes were popping up all over Rapture. It was a guerilla war—but it was war.

Bill had nearly left Ryan Industries after the takeover of Fontaine Futuristics—it had been a blow, Ryan nationalizing an industry. A putrid hypocrisy. And before that—Persephone. Then Sullivan telling him what Ryan had been up to, behind the scenes. Torture—and having Anna Culpepper killed. But the final, camel-busting straw was the disappearance of Mascha. He'd asked Ryan about it, and Cavendish. Ryan had said he could not be bothered with every petty crime around Rapture—and Cavendish had said, "You deal with the plumbing; we'll deal with security—now fuck off." And that was it—he'd decided right then, walking away from Cavendish's office, he was getting his family out of Rapture. It was just a question of choosing his moment.

He had a half-formed plan. Roland Wallace wanted out too. They'd talked it over: Wallace was authorized to pass through an external-access air lock. There was a minisub in bay 2. Wallace could pretend to be doing repairs on it, then slip out with it through the air lock to the open sea.

Wallace would get the little sub to one of the old sentry launches, still tied up behind the lighthouse, and bring the launch around to its entrance. Bill could get his family out through the lighthouse, which had a single cable for its cameras and turrets. He could unhook that cable. If the camera were out, the security bots wouldn't be activated when he approached the lighthouse shaft. No one but Ryan was genetically authorized to be up there—the bots would attack anyone else.

The water was rough, over Rapture. They'd have to wait on the escape; wait for better weather, in late spring. Fewer ice floes. Then they'd escape, take the launch to the sea routes, ride the currents, and flag down a passing ship.

If they could get through to the lighthouse at all—not only was Ryan's security in the way, there were rebels and rogue splicers. Atlas now controlled about forty percent of Rapture, including Apollo Square, Artemis Suites, and Neptune's Bounty, his strongholds. Lamb was mostly tied up around Persephone and Dionysus Park. They'd all have to be skirted. Bill thought about trying to make some kind of deal, on the sly, with Atlas, but he knew he couldn't be trusted . . .

As if reading his thoughts, the PA system hissed with static, whined with feedback, and then a woman's voice announced: *"Atlas is a friend of the parasite! Don't be a friend of Atlas! Ignore the lies of Atlas and his parasites! Rapture is on the rise!"*

Another hiss of static became: *"We all have bills to pay, and the temptation to break curfew to make a little extra ADAM is forgivable. Breaking the curfew is not! Stay on the level, and stay out of trouble!"* A whine of feedback, and then: *"Wanting an item from the surface is forgivable! Buying or smuggling one into Rapture is not! Attention: a new curfew will be enacted on Thursday! Citizens found in violation will be relocated!*

The parasite has his eye on Rapture—keep your eye on the parasite!"

Bill pretended an interest in the grain-based "meat" at the farmer's market "butcher's stall." But his mind was full of questions. Could he and his family really escape from Rapture? Was it possible while this war was going on? Probably too dangerous to try.

There was one other possibility. Having a couple too many glasses of Worley's brandy, he'd even recorded that possibility on an audio diary: *"I don't know if killing Mr. Ryan will stop the war, but I know it won't stop while that man breathes. I love Mr. Ryan—but I love Rapture. If I have to kill one to save the other, so be it."*

He had to erase that tape immediately. He'd be a dead man if someone found it.

"Seen Diane lately?" Ryan asked, too casually, as he picked up a rather withered apple from a stand. He smelled it, made a face, and put it back.

"Diane McClintock? No, guv, not in person, like. Last I heard she was . . . ah, that Doctor Steinman did some work on 'er."

"He was working on her in more ways than one, Bill. Your delicacy is appreciated. Yes, I was actually quite bored with her, and she became very narcissistically tiresome after the New Year's Eve attack. Whining about her scars. Went gadding about with Steinman—but he's thrown her over, I understand. Last I knew she was spending a lot of time gambling in Fort Frolic . . ."

The security bot flew past again—it was on watchful patrol status in order to protect Ryan—and Bill noticed little Sophie watching it with big eyes. Frightened of the thing that was supposed to be protecting her.

Sophie saw him looking at her and came running to him,

throwing her little arms around his waist. Elaine followed, with a strained smile, nodding to Ryan.

Ryan looked down at Sophie and smiled, patting her on the head—she shrank away from him. Ryan looked startled at that.

Then came a sad, low-pitched groaning noise and an ominous vibration of heavy footsteps—and they turned to see the hulking, plodding, clanking form of a Big Daddy. There were at present two models of Big Daddy, the Rosies and the Bouncers. This one, a Bouncer, made a drawn-out moaning sound as it came, almost as if in mourning. They all did that, of course. They all smelled rancid. Like dead things.

The Bouncer was carrying an oversized drill built into its right arm; on its back was a heavy power pack. To Bill the Big Daddies almost looked like pictures of robots he'd seen on the covers of pulp science fiction magazines. But he knew there was most of a human being inside that Big Daddy suit—some poor blighter who'd been caught breaking a rule, sometimes a criminal, sometimes a Lamb follower, sometimes just a hungry man who'd stolen an apple. The constables tranquilized "candidates" for Big Daddies and took them to Prometheus Point, where their flesh was fused with metal, their brains altered and conditioned to focus on protecting the Little Sisters and on killing anything they perceived as a threat. When the Big Daddies were damaged, repair parts were scavenged, on the sly, from the Eternal Flame Crematorium. Who was going to miss a leg or an arm when the rest had been cremated?

All over the massive Big Daddy's great round metal head were circular, glowing sensors; its huge metal-encased legs clunked along relentlessly—but careful never to injure the barefoot, grubby little tyke of a girl who scampered along beside it. Gatherers, some called the girls. This one was tiny and fragile compared with the Big Daddy, but she dominated it completely. The Little Sister wore a dirty pink smock; her face seemed faintly greenish, her eyes sunken. There was a distance in those eyes, like something Bill had seen in Brigid Tenenbaum's—as if her peculiar aloofness had been installed in her creation.

"Come on, Mr. Bubbles!" the Little Sister fluted, calling to the Big Daddy. "Come on, or we'll miss the angels!" The towering mock of a deep-sea diver lumbered after her, moaning . . .

"Oh Christ," Bill muttered.

A dark-haired Little Sister skipped past them.

"Mascha!" Sophie called out.

The Gatherer stopped, blinking, mouth open in an O, to look at Sophie for a long, puzzled moment. Then she said, "What is *that* one? That's not a Gatherer; and she's not an angel yet! We can't play with her until she's an angel!"

Then the little girl danced away. The Big Daddy gave out its long, mournful groan and clumped after her. The floor shook with the creature's going.

"Oh God, Bill," Elaine said, hugging Sophie to her. "Was that—?"

"No," he said quickly. "I'm sure it wasn't her." He doubted she believed the lie.

Bill was just grateful that Sophie hadn't seen what was left of her friend Mascha sticking a syringe in a dead body, drawing out the pulsing red effluvium of living ADAM. A sickening sight. It seemed to belong to Rapture the way giant pink elephants belonged to hallucinating drunks.

The public address chose that moment to inform them, "*The Little Sisters Orphanage: in troubled times, give your little girl the life she deserves! Boarding and education free of charge! After all, children are the future of Rapture!*"

And Bill noticed that Ryan was staring down at Sophie . . .

Olympus Heights
1959

Feeling weary, deeply weary, yet restless too, Andrew Ryan poured himself a martini from the silver shaker and settled back in his easy chair at the picture window, gazing out over the shimmering skyline of the submerged city.

I'm getting old, he thought. *The city should still be young. Yet it seems to be aging right along with me.*

A couple of squid rippled by, outlined against the glow—and then were gone. The neon signs for Rapture businesses were flickering, threatening to go out. Some of the lights supposed to shine up from the bases of the buildings were dark. But most of the lights still worked. The city of Rapture continued to glow.

The city itself was showing signs of new life. There were the new Circus of Values machines, expected to raise a great deal of revenue. There were the Gatherer's Gardens too. Scientists were working on machines that could raise man from the dead, if he hadn't been dead long, and restore him to life. Sure, the population of Rapture was depleted, but when he completed his control of ADAM and the splicers, and rid the city of the rebels, he could build Rapture up anew.

He sipped the martini, put it on the end table beside the tape recorder, and then pressed Record for his audio diary. History must have its due.

"On my walk today I had an encounter with a pair of them . . . he, a lumbering palooka in a foul-smelling diving suit, and she, an unwashed moppet in a filthy pink smock. Her pallor was off, green and morbid, and there was a rather unpleasant aspect to her demeanor, as if she were in an altogether different place than the rest of us. I understand the need for such creatures; I just wish I could make them more presentable." He chuckled to himself at that, took a sip of his martini, and made another diary entry: "Could I have made mistakes? One does not build cities if one is guided by doubt. But can one govern in absolute certainty? I know that my beliefs have elevated me, just as I know that the things I have rejected would have destroyed me." On one of the buildings outside, a light flickered and went out. He sighed. "But the city . . . it is collapsing before my . . ." He hesitated. Not able to finish the thought. It was unbearable. "Have I become so convinced by my own beliefs that I have stopped seeing the truth? But Atlas is out there, and he aims to destroy me—to question is to surrender. I will not surrender."

A letter arrived in the pneumatic tube: Ryan heard the distinctive swish of its arrival. He got wearily up, fetched the message back to his easy chair.

Grunting as he sat, he fumbled it open. He was losing some dexterity in his fingers.

He unfolded the letter—and recognized Diane Mc-Clintock's handwriting:

Dear Andrei:

Andrei Rianofski, Andrew Ryan, Mr. Ryan; the lover, the Tycoon, the Tyrant: just three of the many sides of you. I saw only the cold side recently—first you didn't show up for New Year's Eve, and I had to face rogue splicers without you. Then you didn't show up when I was recovering from the surgery. You stood me up again in Fort Frolic. You had "a meeting"! So I decided to go home. Tried to go the short route. Apollo Square was blocked off, taken over by the rebels. But I was a bit drunk, and angry, and I wanted to confront them for the damage they'd done me. Maybe I wanted them to kill me and just get it over with. A woman tried to escape—to get past Ryan's guards keeping the rebels in Apollo Square, and one of your pet splicers pointed his finger at her and she burst into flames! I

*had heard about Atlas. But it occurred to me I only had
your side of it. So I thought they were either going to kill
me—or explain themselves to me. And I bribed a guard at
the gate into letting me through.*

*Conditions are terrible in Apollo Square, and Artemis.
The crowding, the squalor. They say it was almost as bad
before the revolution. They say it was your doing—your
neglect! Graffiti is painted on the walls: "Atlas Lives!"
What do I really know about Atlas? And at last someone
took me to meet him. They know I'm your mistress, or
was, but they have learned to trust me. Atlas was surprisingly humble. I asked him if he would lead the people in
some kind of uprising against you. He said, "I am not a
liberator. Liberators do not exist. These people will liberate themselves." Isn't that strange—it's almost like something you would say! But when he said it—I understood.
It meant something. It went right to the heart of me, Andrei! I thought you were a great man. I was wrong. Atlas is
a great man. And I will serve him; I will struggle beside
him, fighting all you represent! I'm going on a raid tomorrow to get weapons and food. I will learn to fight, Andrei.
You abandoned me—now I have left you. I have left you
for Atlas—and the revolution!*

                                        Diane

Ryan folded the paper up and tore it into small bits. He let the
shreds of paper flutter to the floor, picked up his martini—and
suddenly lost control of himself, throwing the glass so that it
smashed on the big picture window, fragments of wet, broken
glass sliding down over the glowing spires of the city . . .

20

"There was meant to be a maintenance team here instead of me," Bill groused as he bent to examine the cracks in the curved metal wall of the maintenance runoff tunnel. "They had some git of a splicer, was going to creep up the walls and fix the leaks they couldn't reach. Don't know what became of the buggers . . ."

Karlosky grunted. "I think I see your maintenance team."

Bill stood up, walked over to Karlofsky—together they looked through a window into the mailroom of Jet Postal. The shadowy, indirectly lit room was scattered with undelivered mail. And with bodies—several bodies, men in maintenance coveralls lying about on the floor, motionless, pasted to the deck with their own blood. They seemed to have been hacked up by some sharp blade.

Bill sighed, stomach contracting at the sight. "Yeah. I don't see that splicer. Maybe . . ."

Karlosky nodded, musingly patting the breach of his tommy gun. "Not good workers, those splicers," he said dryly. "They go crazy; they kill. A man does not get job done when busy being crazy and killing." After a moment, he shrugged and added, "Unless killing is the job."

"Well, I'm going to make a list of cracks and leaks and get a team in here with a constable escort," Bill said. "We can't risk . . ." He broke off, staring at a small figure in a pinafore, a child, moving through the shadows of the Jet Postal sorting room. Steel boots clanked; a great metal shape loomed up behind her.

A Big Daddy and a Little Sister. She skipped along, a large syringe in one hand, singing a song they couldn't clearly hear. Something about "Mr. Bubbles" and "the angels." Her enormous chaperone stumped along close behind her.

Bill and Karlosky watched with an uneasy mix of fascination and revulsion as the little girl squatted by a man's awkwardly sprawling, facedown corpse and jammed the syringe into the back of his neck. She did something with the syringe, chirruping happily to herself, and it began to glow with extracted ADAM.

Bill stepped closer to the window and bent over to peer at the Little Sister. "Karlosky—is that Mascha?"

Karlosky groaned to himself. "Yes, maybe—maybe not. All Little Sisters look much alike to me."

"If it's her—I owe it to her folks to get her back."

"We tried, Bill! You spoke to many people—no one would help."

"That's why I've got to do this myself, right now . . ."

"Please, don't argue with Big Daddy, Bill—oh—there is splicer!"

A spider splicer was creeping upside down on the ceiling over the Little Sister. He had a hooked blade in one hand. He was chattering to himself—the intervening pane of glass muted the sound.

The Little Sister stood up, turned toward the Big Daddy—and then a blade spun past her, whipping through the air like a boomerang. The blade narrowly missed her head—so close it cut a bit of her hair, which drifted prettily away. The weapon circled the room and returned to the splicer, who caught the blade handle neatly, cackling as he did it.

The Little Sister's guardian reacted instantly. The Big Daddy stepped into a pool of light, raised a rivet gun to aim at the ceiling, and fired a long strafe of rivets at the spider splicer. The gun nailed its target at such close range it cut the splicer in half. The spider splicer's lower half and its upper half clung to the ceiling . . . separately, by feet and hands, the two halves gushing blood. Then they let go, and the halves of the splicer dropped heavily to the floor.

The little girl chirruped happily.

"You see?" Karlosky whispered. "If you interfere with her—you end up like him!"

"I've got to try," Bill said. "Maybe if you distract him, I can grab her . . ."

"Oh shit, Bill, you son of bitch bastard!" Karlosky said, and muttered another imprecation in Russian. "You get me killed!"

"I've got faith in your gift for self-preservation, mate. Come on." Bill led the way to the door of the Jet Postal sorting room. He hesitated, wondering what Elaine would want him to do. She would want Mascha rescued—if this Little Sister was in fact Mascha—but Elaine wouldn't want him to risk himself this way. Still—there probably wouldn't be another chance.

He opened the door, then stepped back, crouching down to one side, signaling to Karlosky. "Do it. Then run . . ."

Karlosky swore in Russian once more, but he raised his tommy gun and fired a short burst toward the Big Daddy—a burst from a tommy gun wasn't going to kill it, and Karlosky wouldn't risk the wrath of his employers by destroying the valuable cyborg, but it got the Big Daddy's attention. The lumbering metal golem turned and rushed like an accelerating freight train at the source of the assault. Karlosky was already running, cursing Bill as he went. The Big Daddy clanged past Bill, not seeing him crouching by the door.

Bill slipped behind the metal guardian and through the door, seeing the little girl standing up from another extraction, blood-dripping syringe in her hand. She looked at him with big eyes, mouth opened in a round O.

Was this Mascha? He wasn't sure.

"Mr. *Buuuuuuubbles!*" she called. "There is a *bad* man here waiting to be turned into an *aaaaaaangel!*"

"Mascha," Bill said. "Is that you?" He took a step toward her. "Listen . . . I'm going to pick you up, but I won't hurt you—"

Then a metallic clumping close behind Bill turned his blood cold. He spun about just in time to be struck across the chest—the Big Daddy, returned to protect its charge, swinging the weapon in its hand like a club. Bill was knocked backward, off his feet, the air smacked from his lungs, the room whirling.

Gasping, he lost consciousness for a few moments. When the spinning specks formed shapes and the room coalesced, he looked dizzily around—saw that he was sitting up on the floor, back against a bulkhead. The Big Daddy and his little charge were nowhere to be seen.

Bill got up, moaning to himself with the pain of his bruised chest, and staggered to the door. He was met by Karlosky. "You okay, Bill?"

"Yeah—good to see you alive. I thought I'd got you killed . . ."

"No, I outsmart that steel bastard. Look . . . !"

He pointed across the open space of the depot—on the far wall, the little girl was climbing into one of the key-shaped art-deco apertures that the Little Sisters used to enter hidden passageways. They scuttled through the passageways to take their scavenged ADAM back to Ryan's laboratories.

Mascha or not Mascha? He would never know. She simply vanished into the wall.

The Big Daddy waited quietly by the big art deco keyhole for his Little Sister to return.

Bill shook his head and turned away, grimacing with pain—and wanting only to get back to Elaine.

Once more, his determination to escape Rapture was un-

derscored. He had to get his family back to the surface. Back
to blue sky and sunlight and freedom . . .

Medical Pavilion, Aesthetic Ideals Surgery
1959

"Ryan and ADAM, ADAM and Ryan . . . all those years of
study, and was I ever truly a surgeon before I met them? How
we plinked away with our scalpels and toy morality! Yes, we
could lop a boil here and shave down a beak there—but
could we really change anything? No! But ADAM gives us
the means to do it, and Ryan frees us from the phony ethics
that held us back. Change your look, change your sex, change
your race. It's yours to change, nobody else's!"

Wearing a blood-soaked surgical gown and white surgeon's cap, his hands in rubber gloves, Doctor J. S. Steinman
hit Pause on the little tape recorder that he'd wedged between the blond patient's ample breasts; then he pushed the
gurney, its wheels susurrating through the shallow water
that had leaked across the floor of the surgery. He hummed
to himself, singing an Inkspots song, "If I Didn't Care," over
the muffled moaning of the patient he'd strapped to the little
wheeled bed. "Would I be sure that this is love beyond com-
pare? Would all this be true—if I didn't care . . . for . . .
you!"

He pushed the woman into place under the glaring surgical light and reached into his coat pocket for his favorite scalpel. Tiresome to do without a nurse, but he'd had to kill
Nurse Chavez when she'd started whining about his efforts
to please Aphrodite, threatening to turn him into the constables. Of course, he hadn't killed her till he'd done some fine
experimentation on her doll-like visage. He still had Chavez's
face in a refrigerator, somewhere, along with some others
he'd peeled off and saved in preservative jars, faces from patients who'd given their lives for his perfect fusion of art and

science. He really must try to organize his preserved faces with a filing system.

Steinman paused to admire this latest woman writhing in her restraints on the gurney. She'd used some low-grade plasmid to help her hack a gambling machine in Fort Frolic, and his fellow artist, Sander Cohen, who owned the casino, had caught her. It was getting hard to find voluntary patients. He did think he might get Diane McClintock to come in again. He longed to alter her in another manner entirely, according to his artistic whim—to give her a truly transcendent face. He might get hold of a telekinesis plasmid and use it to form her face from within, shape it telekinetically, into something lovely.

They were all so ugly, honestly, so plain. They didn't try hard enough to make themselves fitting vessels for Aphrodite. "But they're filthy, filthy at the core," he muttered. No knife was sharp enough to cut that filth out. He tried and tried and tried, but they were always so fat or short or . . . plain. Steinman made a *tsk* sound as the blond woman shrieked unintelligibly at him through the gag. Some insult, perhaps. "My dear, I'd love to give you some anesthetic to grace your experience, I really would, but I have quite run out of it, and anyway, there is something less aesthetically pleasing about sculpting an unconscious patient. If they are unconscious, the blood hardly spurts at all, their eyes don't have that look of possession by the god of terror, and how satisfying could *that* be, now I ask you? I may have to stop and have some more ADAM and a touch of EVE myself . . . Oh *do* try to accept this, my dear, appreciate it as a sacrificial aesthetic experience. A sacrifice to Aphrodite! Sander Cohen and I have talked about doing a performance onstage with one of my little surgeries. Can you imagine? A face sculpting set to original music? The trouble is, of course—" He bent near his wild-eyed patient to whisper confidentially. "The trouble is, my dear, Sander Cohen is *quite insane*. Mad. Out of his mind! Ha *ha-aa*! I shouldn't socialize with Cohen, that loony tune, I have my reputation to think of."

He hit Record again on the tape recorder and cleared his throat to set down another immortal memo. "With genetic modifications, beauty is no longer a goal, or even a virtue. It is a moral obligation. Still, ADAM presents new problems for the professional," he said, for the audio diary. "As your tools improve, so do your standards. There was a time I was happy enough to take off a wart or two, or turn a real circus freak into something you can show in the daylight . . ." So saying, he started carving deeply into the face of the woman on the gurney, glad he'd taken the trouble to brace her head in place because she was shaking so much with agony as he sliced away her cheeks.

He went on, ". . . But that was then, when we took what we got—but with ADAM, the flesh becomes clay. What excuse do we have not to sculpt and sculpt and sculpt until the job is done?" He hit Pause on the tape recorder, its buttons becoming slippery with the blood on his hands, and considered his work. It was hard to tell through all the blood and torn tissue. "My dear, I believe I'm going to give you some ADAM that will regrow your face into another shape entirely. Then I'll carve the new tissue some more. Then I'll regrow some *more* face on you with ADAM. Then I'll carve *that* some more. Then—"

Another muffled shriek from the woman. He sighed, shaking his head. They just would not understand. He hit Record again and accompanied his next wet, spurting spate of carving with a kind of artistic manifesto: "When Picasso became bored of painting people, he started representing them as cubes and other abstract forms. The world called him a genius! I've spent my entire surgical career creating the same tired shapes, over and over again: the upturned nose, the cleft chin, the ample bosom. Wouldn't it be wonderful if I could do with a knife what that old Spaniard did with a brush?"

Steinman hit pause again, used his left hand to wipe some blood from the recorder buttons. He returned to his patient only to find she'd died on him. "Oh dammit, not another one . . ."

Blood loss and shock, he supposed, as usual. It was really quite unfair.

They always left him too soon. It made him angry to think of their selfishness.

He slashed at her in his fury, knocking the tape recorder on the floor, cutting her throat into ribbons, long pretty ribbons . . . which he then tied into bows.

When he calmed down enough to be precise, he exposed her breasts and cut them into shapes like the sea anemones that waved in the gentle currents so restfully, so gracefully, outside the window of his office . . .

Ah, he thought: *The Rapture of the Deep* . . .

Fighting McDonagh's Bar
1959

When? It had to be soon. He was going to have to escape from Rapture, with Elaine and their daughter, and if that meant killing—

"Bill?"

Bill McDonagh nearly leapt from his barstool when Redgrave spoke at his elbow.

"Blimey, don't sneak up on a man like that!"

Redgrave smiled sadly. "Sorry. Something you ought to know, though. Your woman who cleans the rooms—she found something."

Bill sighed. He tossed down his brandy, nodded to his bartender. "Just close down when you feel like it, mate." He got off the barstool. "All right, let's have it, Redgrave . . ."

"You've been letting out some of your rooms, ain't you? Number seven—that was the Lutzes'?"

"Sure. I don't charge them for it. Christ, their little girl went missing on my watch." He couldn't resist a cold look at Redgrave. "On your watch too."

Redgrave grimaced. "We only looked away a couple of seconds. We were watching for splicers—"

"I know—forget it. What about Sam Lutz?"

"Come on."

Feeling leaden, Bill went with Redgrave to the tavern's back rooms. Number 7's combination door was open. He stepped in and immediately saw the two of them stretched out on the mattress, on their backs, side by side: two corpses holding hands, barely recognizable as Mariska and Samuel Lutz. There were a couple of empty pill bottles lying on the floor nearby.

The sunken eyes of the cadavers were closed, eyelids like wrinkled parchment, their faces yellow and emaciated. The shriveling of death had given their lips the same pinched expression of disapproval, as if they were silently judging all the living. They wore their best clothes, he noticed.

"Suicide. And there's this . . ." He pointed—beside the bodies was one of the ubiquitous tape recorders.

Bill pressed Play on the tape recorder. Mariska Lutz's voice came distant and tinny from the little recorder, as if speaking across the gulf of death: *We saw our Mascha today. We barely recognized her. 'That's her,' Sam said.* Mariska gave out a strange little sobbing laugh. *"'You're crazy,' I told him. 'That thing—that is our Mascha?' But he was right. She was drawing blood out of a corpse . . . and when she was done, she walked off hand in hand with one of those awful golems! Our Mascha!"*

Bill stopped the recording.

Redgrave cleared his throat. "Well. I expect . . . they knew they couldn't get her back. She was already . . . gone. You know, changed so much. So they . . ."

He gestured limply at the pill bottles.

Bill nodded. "Yeah. Just . . . just leave 'em here. I'll seal it up. This'll be their crypt, for now."

Redgrave stared at him as if he might object—then he shrugged. "Whatever you say." He looked back at the bodies. "We only looked away for a moment or two."

He shook his head and walked out, leaving Bill alone with the dead.

Atlas HQ, Hestia
1959

Walking up to Atlas's office, Diane was still sweaty, shaky from the raid.

She'd had some training from Atlas's guerillas, and she was almost used to slipping through the wire, waiting as the other team created the decoy, dashing past Ryan's men. More than once she'd followed the other guerillas up a side passage, up the stairs, through some old maintenance passage— all of them carrying GI backpacks, to fill with supplies stolen from one of the constabulary armories.

But this time, when the guards broke in on them, just as they finished their "harvest" of the ammo—and just as Sorenson got control of the Big Daddy—the chaos had been exhilarating and nightmarish at once. Firing her own pistols, one in each hand, her heart slamming with each shot, she'd watched a constable go down, shrieking, dying. *I've killed a man . . .*

She'd cringed from blazing return fire, seen three of her comrades falling . . .

She decided, now, to record some of her impressions on her audio diary—she had decided she was going to be the historian of the revolution. She switched the recorder on with trembling hands, as she walked along. "We went on a raid outside the wire today. We snagged thirty-one rounds of buckshot, four frag grenades, a shotgun, and thirty-four ADAM. We lost McGee, Epstein, and Vallette." She swallowed hard at that. She'd particularly liked Vallette. Too easy to reel off a list of the dead: *the butcher's bill,* the guerillas called it. She went on, "We got one of those goddamn Big Daddies in the bargain, though. It was something awful what they had to do to that little girl to get the ADAM, but we didn't start this thing. Ryan did. I can't wait to tell Atlas. He'll be so pleased . . ."

Diane stepped into Atlas's office to let him know they'd gotten a Big Daddy—and stared in surprise at the stranger sitting at Atlas's desk. He seemed to be recording an audio diary of his own. After a breathless moment, he was no longer a stranger. She hadn't recognized him at first.

Something . . . the cold, cynical expression on his face and that sneering voice talking of long cons . . . made it seem impossible he could be anyone but Frank Fontaine.

He turned a look of angry shock at her—then put on Atlas's expression. His voice became Atlas's. "Miss McClintock . . . what are you doing here? Let me just . . ." He dropped the Atlas pretense, shaking his head—seeing in her face that she *knew.* Finishing in Frank Fontaine's voice, ". . . turn this off . . ."

He switched off the tape recorder. It occurred to her that she should run. She'd found out something he would kill to keep secret.

But her feet seemed frozen to the floor; she was barely able to speak. "They trusted you! How could you let them die . . . for a lie?"

Fontaine stalked toward her, drawing a buck knife, opening it with a practiced motion, the blade making a *snick* sound as it flicked into readiness. "It don't matter, kid," he said. "Because it's *all* lies. Everything is. Except for . . ." Then she felt the cold blade slash upward, into her belly, just under her ribcage, ". . . this."

Rapture Central Control
1959

Bill McDonagh paced up and down in the passageway outside Central Control. The constables at the entrance to the hall had been friendly, glad to see him. Not knowing his mission.

He had to make his move, and soon. Then signal Wallace to take the minisub up to the boat. Conditions were as good as they were ever going to be for escape. The city's turbulence indicators showed the sea was fairly calm right now. Ryan's men were dealing with a new disruption, concentrated in sealing off Apollo Square—there weren't many of Ryan's bunch between here and the lighthouse.

Roland Wallace wouldn't take the minisub unless Bill gave him the signal. But there was something he'd have to do then. About Ryan. And Rapture. He had made up his mind that if he succeeded today, in Ryan's office, he would send his family to safety but stay in Rapture, at least for a time, and try to create a new leadership, make a peace deal with Atlas. He had helped build this place—he felt an obligation to the survivors. Eventually he could rejoin Elaine and Sophie . . .

The survivors. Quite a surprising number of people had died here or been executed. Ryan was starting to put the corpses up on stakes at the entryway to Central Control. Rapture had become a police state—it had turned into its own opposite.

Bill let out a long, slow breath, reached into his pocket for the pistol. Checked the load for the fourth time. Put it back in his blazer. Could he do this? Then he remembered Sam and Mariska Lutz.

"Got to face it, old man," he told himself. "Got to be done." He put the pistol back, took out the little radio. He clicked it and murmured into it. "Wallace?"

A crackle. Then, "Yes, Bill."

"It's time."

"Are you sure?"

"I am. Going to take care of my business and then bring the family for the . . . picnic."

"Okay. I'm ready. Meet you there."

He put the radio away. Heart pounding, he straightened his tie and opened the door. A security camera swiveled to take him in as he stepped through. He had his ID flasher on, and it let him pass without releasing the security bots. Ryan still trusted him.

He strode past the crucified corpses, smelling them but steadfastly not looking at them, and went to the door of Ryan's office. He was scanned by a turret—and it let him pass. He reached for the door just as Karlosky came out. Bill almost jumped out of his shoes.

Karlosky looked at him curiously. "Something making you nervous, Bill?"

"Me, no, it's just them bodies out there—give me the willies."

Karlosky nodded sympathetically. "Don't like that decoration either. Sometimes necessary. I'm going to get sandwich for me and Mr. Ryan. You want something?"

"Me? No, I . . ." Christ, how could he eat sandwiches with these bodies stuck up out here? However . . . "Well, yes, Ivan. Whatever . . . whatever you're having." The longer Karlosky stayed away, the better.

Karlosky nodded and strolled out. Bill went into Ryan's office.

Andrew Ryan was standing by the window, gazing out at the sea, leaning on his walking stick. He wore his tailored three-piece gray silk suit, and, in that moment, Bill felt his heart go out to him. Ryan had built this brave new world to match his dream. And it had become a nightmare.

But Bill reminded himself of those men and women crucified in the outer room. And he took a deep breath and pulled
the pistol.

Ryan didn't turn around. He seemed to know. "Go on, do
it, Bill. If you're man enough."

Bill raised the gun—and it trembled in his hand.

Ryan smiled sadly. "What was it you said, Bill? You'd stay
with me, 'from A to Zed.' Well, we're not quite at Zed yet. But
it seems you're taking your leave."

"No," Bill said, his voice breaking. "I'm staying . . . for a
while. Can't desert all these people. I helped bring 'em here."

Ryan turned toward him, hefting the gold-topped walking
stick. "Bill, you're a weak link on the Great Chain—and I
cannot leave that weak link in place . . ."

Bill aimed the gun as Ryan stalked toward him.

Bill's mouth was dry, his pulse thudding.

Ryan was almost in reach. "A man chooses, Bill—a slave
obeys. Choose. Kill me or obey your cowardice and run away!"

Andrew Ryan, the man who'd plucked him from obscurity—
who'd elevated Bill McDonagh in this great city—raised the
walking stick to strike him down. It was in Ryan's hardened
eyes, his twisted mouth: the aging tycoon had every intention
of using that gold-headed cane to crush Bill's skull.

Shoot him!

But Bill couldn't do it. This man had reached down from
Olympus and raised him up to Olympus Heights. Andrew
Ryan had trusted him. He *couldn't.*

The walking stick came whistling down—and Bill caught
it, wincing at the impact as he grabbed it with his left hand.
They struggled a moment, Ryan panting, his teeth bared—
and then Bill acted instinctively. He struck down with the
butt of the pistol like a club, cracking Andrew Ryan on the
forehead.

Ryan grunted and fell backward. He lay gasping on the

floor, eyes half-closed. Bill found that he had the walking stick in his own hand. He dropped it beside Ryan, then knelt and took Ryan's pulse. Ryan was stunned, unconscious, but his pulse was strong. Bill knew, somehow, that Ryan would survive intact.

Bill squeezed Ryan's hand. "I'm sorry, Mr. Ryan. I didn't know what else to do. I can't kill you. Best of luck, guv . . ."

He stood, pistol in hand, and started for the door, walking mechanically, feeling all lumbering and heavy like a Big Daddy. He stuck the pistol in his pocket and found his way out past the double line of dead men on stakes, out past the swiveling camera.

He stepped into the hallway, trying not to look like he was in a hurry. He and Elaine and Sophie would have to take a circuitous route. It was a long trek yet to get where they were going. He didn't have much time. Karlosky would find Ryan, and there would be an alert . . . security bots, Ryan's thugs . . .

He had to hurry or lose everything. They were waiting for him in the cemetery, a separate little park off Arcadia . . .

Cemetery near Arcadia
1959

Burials at sea were cheap. But some preferred Rapture's charming little cemetery.

Bill had liked visiting the place, and it was usually deserted, so he'd arranged to meet Elaine and Sophie here. Old-fashioned, rustic in style, the cemetery near Arcadia reminded him of the churchyard where his grandfather was buried.

But when he stepped through the archway, he found it had lost its charm.

Five paces away, a naked man, painted blue, was hunched threateningly over Elaine and Sophie, who were cowered in front of a tombstone. The man was a Saturnine, one of the "pagan" cults who'd sprung up in the vacuum of religion in

Rapture, sneaking about starkers to paint their cryptic graffiti, getting high on ADAM and coloring themselves blue. "Harness the flame, harness the mist!" the man chanted in a grating voice. The blue-painted savage gripped a large kitchen knife in his right hand. Its blade was brown with dried blood.

The man's bare foot was pressing Elaine's purse to the ground, as if crushing a small animal.

"I will give you to the flame," the Saturnine muttered. "I offer you to the mist!"

The Saturnine raised his knife high, to slash down at Elaine—

"Here's some flame, you bastard; harness this!" Bill shouted, to make him turn his way.

The Saturnine whirled to confront Bill, his face a caricature of ADAM-warped savagery, teeth bared, red foam coming from his nostrils. He threw the knife as Bill dodged to the left—the knife slashed at his right shoulder, just a razor-thin cut, and Bill shot the pagan point-blank in the chest.

The Saturnine swayed, went to his knees, and flopped facedown.

Sophie was sobbing, her hands covering her eyes. Elaine jerked her purse from under the dead man's foot, pulled out the pistol, slung the purse over her shoulder, and, with a look of steely determination in her eyes that Bill admired, pulled Sophie to her feet. "Come on, baby," Elaine told her. "We're getting the hell out of this place."

"I'm scared, Mama," Sophie said.

"I know the feeling, love," Bill said, giving the child a quick hug. "But you'll like the surface world. Don't believe what you've heard about it. Come on!"

~~~~~~~

They were surprisingly close. Bill, Elaine, and Sophie were hurrying up to the open bathysphere that would take them up the shaft of the lighthouse, to where Wallace should be waiting.

A rogue splicer slid down the cable, jumping off the bathy-sphere's top and tumbling through the air like an acrobat. He landed on his feet in front of Bill. The splicer wore a small harlequin-style New Year's Eve mask, splashed with the blood of the body he'd taken it from; he had long, dirty brown hair, a streaked red-brown beard, and glittering blue eyes. His yellow teeth were bared in a rictuslike grin. "Hee, that's me, and ooh, that's you!" he cackled. Leaping from right to left, back again, blur-fast, an elusive target. "Look at the little girly-girl! I can sell her to Ryan or keep her for play and maybe a quick bite!" He had a razor-sharp curved fish-gutting blade in each hand . . .

Sophie whimpered in fear and ducked behind her mother—Elaine and Bill fired their pistols at the splicer almost simultaneously . . . and they both missed. He'd leapt in the air, flipping over them and coming down behind: Sport-Boost, and lots of it.

The rogue splicer was spinning to slash at them—but Bill was turning at the same time, firing. The bullet cracked into one of the curved blades, knocking it away. The splicer slashed out with the other blade, which cut the air an inch from Sophie's nose.

Enraged, Bill forgot his gun and rushed at the splicer, shouting, "Bastard!" He just managed to duck under the swishing blade, to tackle the splicer around the middle, knocking him onto his back. It was like tackling a live wire—there was not a gram of fat on the splicer; he was all muscle and bone and tension—and Bill felt himself overbalanced and quickly flung off.

The splicer leapt up, stood grinning down at Bill—throwing the hooked blade before Bill could fire his pistol. Bill twisted aside, felt the curved knife shear a piece of skin from his ribs—and then there were three quick gunshots, each one making the splicer take a jerking step back. The third one went through the splicer's right eye, and the splicer went limp, falling on his back, feet twitching.

Bill turned, panting, to see his wife with the gun in her hand, a wild look in her eyes. Sophie was clinging to her mother's leg, face buried in her hip.

"You're a bloody fine shot, love," he told Elaine, "and thank God for that."

"I had a good teacher," she said numbly, staring at the splicer's body.

"Come on—into the lift . . ." Elaine nodded and took Sophie into the bathysphere. Bill climbed in after them, found the release hidden under the control panel, and activated it.

They took the bathyspheric lift up the shaft, out of the undersea—the three of them riding up into the lighthouse. Bill had cut power on the security bots and turrets guarding the way out through the lighthouse this morning, but he was afraid they'd be back on, somehow, to greet his family with a spray of bullets as soon as they stepped out of the bathysphere.

But only quiet greeted them, at first, when they stepped out. And the echo of their footsteps in the dome . . .

Sophie looked around in awe, stunned by the naked daylight coming through the entrance to the lighthouse, the unfamiliar sound of breakers outside—then, eyes wide in fear, she stared up at the enormous electroplated bust of Andrew Ryan, glaring back down at them. Ryan seemed to be holding up a banner, yellow lettering on a red field, reading:

NO GODS OR KINGS.
ONLY MAN.

"It's Mr. Ryan!" Sophie gulped, stepping back. "He's watching us!"

"It's just a statue," Elaine said.

"Oh, but she's right," said Head Constable Cavendish, coming around from the other side of the bathysphere. Bill spun, raising his gun, but then he saw that Karlosky was there too, and Redgrave; they all had tommy guns at the ready in their hands. Redgrave was pushing a despondent Roland Wallace, who had his hands bound behind him. If Bill fired, the constables would return fire, and Elaine would likely be hit. And Sophie. He couldn't get them all.

Bill lowered his pistol—and then let it slip from limp fingers to the floor.

"Drop it, lady," said Cavendish, pointing the tommy gun at her.

With a sob, she dropped her gun, and clutched Sophie to her. "Oh God, Bill, we were so close . . ."

He put his arm around her shoulders. "I'm sorry, love. I should have found a better way . . ."

Karlosky looked grim; Cavendish was grinning wolfishly— but Redgrave looked stricken, uncertain. Deeply sad.

"I tried, Bill," Wallace said. "I got the boat here. I climbed out to look for you, and there they were. Coming up in boats."

"You don't reckon Ryan has cameras none of you know about?" Cavendish sneered. "'Specially outside this place. You think you're the only ones who tried to leave? Others tried—they're Big Daddies now. The external camera caught ol' Wallace here slippin' out . . ."

"Ryan—is he dead?" Elaine asked. Her eyes showed hope; her voice was defiant.

"Nyet," Karlosky said. "A headache. But he is strong man. Not so easy to kill. Your man—he did not have nerve to finish job."

"Couldn't do it," Bill admitted miserably. "He was my friend. There was a time he was like another father to me."

Redgrave nodded. His voice was husky as he said, "I hear

that, Mr. McDonagh. I sure do. It's the same with me. I'm sorry—I'd like to help you. You were always good to me. But . . ."

"I know," Bill said. "But let me ask you one thing. Did he send you to bring my wife and child in? Or just me and Wallace?"

"I . . ." Redgrave glanced at Cavendish. "I heard him say: 'Stop Bill McDonagh. And that traitor Wallace.' That's all he said."

"He does not want *anyone* leaving," Karlosky said. "Now— all three of you, turn around. We tie your hands; you go with us. We all go back down . . ."

Bill looked at Karlosky. "I'll take what's coming to me. You can tell him anything you want about my girls. Tell Ryan that the splicers got 'em."

Cavendish snorted. "Karlosky's not doing any goddamn thing of the sort."

Bill went on, looking steadily at Karlosky. "We got drunk together, you and me, Karlosky, more than once. Christmas Eves. Holidays. Long nights with vodka. We fought side by side in battle . . ."

Karlosky licked his lips. Comradeship mattered to Karlosky.

"What's this horseshit?" Cavendish growled, seeing Karlosky hesitate. "You three turn around, like he said."

"Yes," Bill said. "Elaine, Sophie—turn around. Just do it."

Their eyes welling with tears, his wife and child turned, and Bill locked eyes with Karlosky. "What do you say, mate. One favor. I know you can't let me go . . . But you can let *them* go. With Wallace."

Redgrave looked back and forth between them, looking like he was trying to make up his own mind . . .

Cavendish frowned. "What's all this horsepucky? Come

on, let's move, stop wasting time, Karlosky, you damned Russian drunk!"

Karlosky raised his eyebrows at that, looked thoughtful. But at last he shook his head. "No, Bill—sorry. Too risky."

Redgrave sighed and pointed his gun at Karlosky. "Ivan—this man here, he and his wife had me over for dinner, more than once. Only white people in this place that done that. I can't let Bill leave Rapture. But we didn't get no orders about his family."

Cavendish snarled, twitched his gun toward Redgrave. "You black-assed son of a—"

But that's when Karlosky turned and shot Cavendish in the side of the head. Two shots. Blood and brains splashed as Cavendish jerked sideways, took a shaky step—and fell.

"Bastard," Karlosky said, spitting on the body.

Elaine and Sophie screamed, clutching at each other.

Wallace stared in dull amazement. "Christ, Karlosky!"

Elaine looked around to see what had happened—but she kept Sophie turned away.

Karlosky glared at Redgrave—then looked down at Cavendish. "I don't like to be pushed around, Redgrave," Karlosky said. "But Cavendish—he was asshole. Wanted to kill him many times! And anyway—if anyone is going to insult you . . . will be me!"

Elaine turned slowly to them, clutching Sophie to her. She winced at the sight of Cavendish's shattered head and said, "Mr. Redgrave—*can't* you let Bill go with us?" Elaine asked. "Please!"

Redgrave shook his head apologetically, swinging the gun toward Bill. "I'm sorry. Bill and Wallace got to come with me."

"I understand," Bill said, meeting Redgrave's eyes. "Ryan's the one who gave you a chance. It was the same with me."

"The launch's idling out there, Mrs. McDonagh," Wallace

said in a dead voice. "Bottom of the stairs. All you got to do is cast off, press the drive lever, head straight on the way it's pointing right now—that'll take you to the sea lanes. Someone'll see you. There's a flare gun in the launch . . ."

Elaine was turning to Bill, looking stunned. "No, Bill . . . !"

Bill took her hand and kissed it. "Elaine . . . You know what you have to do now. For Sophie."

Elaine shook her head.

Bill stepped closer, kissed her tear-stained lips. Then he pushed Sophie into her arms. "For Sophie . . ."

Her mouth buckled. But she nodded, just once. Face white, lips trembling, Elaine took Sophie by the hand and walked away from him. They walked past the bathysphere, toward the little corridor leading to the stairs . . .

"What about *Daddy*?" Sophie asked, as they went, her voice quavering.

"We'll talk about it later, hon," Elaine said. "Daddy has some business right now . . ."

Bill's daughter looked back over her shoulder at him. Bill tried to fill his mind with the last sight he would have of her. "Good-bye, love!" he called, waving once. "Your old dad loves you!" Then Elaine pulled Sophie along with her, through a doorway, and out of his sight . . .

Karlosky looked at Bill, then nodded toward a nearby window. Bill walked to the window; through it could see sun sparkling on sea. Blue sky, white clouds sailing by.

He waited. Men with guns behind him. Watching him.

After a few minutes he saw the small vessel, moving on the surface of the sea, away to the northeast, to the sea lanes.

Bill felt a hand on his shoulder. "Let's go," he said, turning away from the window.

The four of them got into the bathysphere. Karlosky and Redgrave, keeping their weapons on Bill, and Roland Wallace.

"I'm sorry, Roland," Bill said. "This is my fault, mate."

Roland shook his head. "I was going to try it anyway. Not your fault. Proud to know you."

When they got to the bottom, there were three more constables waiting. "Take this one to Suchong," Karlosky said, shoving Wallace toward them.

Wallace went meekly with them.

"What they going to do with Roland?" Bill asked softly.

"Who knows?" Redgrave said sadly.

Bill tried to think about escape. But all the fight seemed to have drained out of him. He knew he wouldn't see his baby girl or his wife again. And Karlosky was good at what he did. He'd never let Bill get by him again.

Bill walked ahead of Karlosky and Redgrave to the Metro. The journey to Central Control was like a journey back in his mind, more than ten years in Rapture. New York City. London. The war . . .

That boy being sucked out the shattered fuselage of the plane . . . He'd always felt bad, surviving when that kid had died—that young man, and other men. Friends who'd gone down in burning bombers. Well, now he had a chance to be with them . . .

They reached Central Control, and he found himself in the shadow of the dead. He looked up to see the decayed corpse of Frank Fontaine, stuck on a stake, like a Jesus who missed the resurrection boat. Ryan had the body crudely sewn up, brought here, and posted. A message to his enemies. Which is what Bill was about to be. Karlosky handed Redgrave his machine gun, then drew a pistol from under his coat, and stepped behind Bill.

Bill heard the sound of Karlosky cocking the gun. "Supposed to crucify you, before killing," Karlosky remarked. "But—I always liked you. So. Quick death."

"I guess I should've killed Ryan," Bill said. His voice sounded thick and unnatural in his own ears. "He must be gloating . . ."

"Nyet—he understands better than you think," Karlosky said. "A lot of these others out here, he watched them die. But . . . he can't be here for this. He told me. He couldn't stand to watch you die, Bill. Not good friend like you . . ."

Bill smiled. He never heard the gunshot that killed him.

Park Avenue, New York City
1959

A warm day in July . . .

"I'm too scared to go out there, Mama," Sophie said, for the tenth time in ten minutes.

Elaine sighed. "I know. But you have to."

"You have something we call agoraphobia, Sophie," the doctor said gently. He was an expensive Park Avenue psychiatrist. A kindly middle-aged man in a sweater and bowtie. He had a trim beard, a large nose, a sad smile, inquisitive eyes. But it happened he wasn't charging Elaine much. He seemed interested in Sophie's case. Perhaps even interested in Elaine herself, in another way.

"You have to do this, sweetheart," Elaine said.

"Well, no," said the doctor. "She doesn't *have* to. But—she wants to, really. She just has mixed feelings about it."

"The sky scares me," Sophie insisted.

"I know it does." The doctor smiled.

"In Rapture we don't have sky," she said. Then she told him some more about Rapture.

He listened patiently, then sent her out to wait with his receptionist, so he could talk to Elaine privately. "She has a remarkable imagination," he said, chuckling. "'Rapture'!"

Elaine didn't try to explain. She couldn't tell people about Rapture; they would never believe her. And if they did—it could lead to Ryan finding her.

So she just nodded. "Yes, Doctor . . ."

"She's been through something traumatic—perhaps in war?" he said. "Somewhere overseas?"

Elaine nodded. "Yes. In war." That was true, anyhow.

"I thought so. Well, she will heal. But we must start by dealing with her fears. I think, despite appearances, she will go outside today, for a walk in the park . . ."

To her surprise, the doctor offered to go with them. After a while, Sophie reluctantly agreed to try the park. They went down the elevator and walked slowly across the marble-floored lobby. Sophie became more frightened as they got closer to the street. Ever since they'd left the fishing boat that had picked them up off Iceland, she'd darted under cover as quickly as she could, hiding her eyes from the sky.

Then the doctor turned to Sophie and said, in a kindly voice, "May I carry you?"

Sophie looked up at him gravely. "Yes."

He nodded, equally grave, and knelt by her. She put her arms around his neck, and he lifted her up, carried her piggyback out the door, Elaine walking at his side. Elaine couldn't help making a grotesque comparison to the way Big Daddies sometimes carried Little Sisters. But she thrust it out of her mind.

"Oh!" Sophie said as they stepped out into the hot sun. But she only clung harder.

They walked over to Central Park. Sophie cried on the way, but didn't ask to hide from the sky.

They got to the park and found an open green field, with butter-colored flowers. On the edge of the field birds sang in the trees. The doctor let Sophie down, and she walked slowly out into the sunlight.

"Mama," she said, shading her eyes to look up at the blue sky. "It's nice out here. It just goes on and on. You know what?"

"What?"

"I think Daddy would have liked seeing this."

"Yes, Sophie," Elaine said, just managing not to cry. "Yes, love. Yes, he would have."

ABOUT THE AUTHOR

John Shirley won the Bram Stoker Award for his story collection *Black Butterflies* and is the author of numerous novels, including the bestseller *Demons,* the cyberpunk classics *City Come A-Walkin',* *Eclipse,* and *Black Glass,* and his latest, the urban fantasy novel *Bleak History.* He has written for television and movies and was coscreenwriter of *The Crow.*